A JEWISH MARK TWAIN?

Years ago when Sholom Aleichem came to New York, Mark Twain was among the first to visit him. "I wanted to meet you," the great American humorist said, "because I understand that I am the American Sholom Aleichem."

History is silent on what Sholom Aleichem's answer was, but it could have been: "And I wanted to meet you because I am supposed to be the Jewish Mark Twain!"

Sholom Aleichem was the pen name of Solomon Rabinowitch who was born in the Ukraine in 1859. His stories, all written in Yiddish, were an immediate success and have been translated into most of the important languages of the Western World, and are enjoyed by Jew and Gentile alike. He died in New York in 1916 and is buried in Brooklyn.

This edition is a selection of stories from TEVYE'S DAUGHTERS and THE OLD COUNTRY, translated by Julius and Frances Butwin and originally published by Crown Publishers, Inc. It includes an Introduction by Frances Butwin and a glossary of special Yiddish terms.

THE TEVYE STORIES AND OTHERS

by Sholom Aleichem

Introduction by Frances Butwin

Translated by
Julius and Frances Butwin

PUBLISHED BY POCKET BOOKS, INC. NEW YORK

THE TEVYE STORIES AND OTHERS

A *Pocket Book* edition

1st printing........January, 1965

The Tevye Stories and Others is a selection of stories from *Tevye's Daughters* and *The Old Country*, published by Crown Publishers in 1946 and 1949.

Pocket Book editions are published by Pocket Books, Inc., and are printed and distributed in the U.S.A. by Affiliated Publishers, a division of Pocket Books, Inc., 630 Fifth Avenue, New York, New York 10020. Trademark registered in the United States and other countries.

L

Printed in the U.S.A.

For My Parents

Gershon and Sonia Mazo

INTRODUCTION

I

YEARS ago when Sholom Aleichem came to New York, Mark Twain was among the first to visit him. "I wanted to meet you," he said, "because I understand that I am the American Sholom Aleichem." History does not record the answer of the man who is called variously "the Jewish Mark Twain," "the Jewish Dickens," "the modern Heine."

There should be an end to these comparisons. Sholom Aleichem was none of these things. He was like no one else. He was unique, a genius whose writings are the perfect expression of a people, their mind, their heart, their wit and above all their special idiom.

But there is no need to describe the quality of Sholom Aleichem's work. Here are the stories. Read them and see for yourself. There are sixteen stories in the book. I think you'll wish there were more.

There are more. For Jewish literature rejoices in a large body of work by Sholom Aleichem. In all, he wrote some three hundred stories, five novels, many plays, and a number of other works. And we may hope that in time all this work will be translated into English.

Sholom Aleichem is the pen name of Solomon Rabinowitch who was born in 1859 in Pereyeslav which is in the Ukraine. He died in New York in 1916 and is buried in Mt. Carmel Cemetery in Brooklyn. His grave has become a shrine and every year many Jews go there to pay homage to him.

If anyone were to ask me how my husband and I came to do this translation, I would say that it was by pure accident. Neither of us had harbored the project before, or thought of it, for that matter. Nothing led up to it. One day we were talking to so-and-so and this-and-that happened. But if you asked Tevye, whom you will meet soon, or better yet, Tevye's wife Golde, she would laugh at this glib explanation. How did we come to do it? It was *bashert* of course. It was fated. It has been inscribed in the heavenly books and so it came to pass. And who can say that Tevye's wife is completely wrong, and that accidents may not be accidents after all, but only the means by which a series of seemingly unrelated events are suddenly brought into focus?

The work of translating these stories was a delight and a challenge at the same time. Often what was entirely right and simple and flavorsome in Yiddish completely missed fire when translated literally. Some stories just could not be transplanted and had to be abandoned. Sometimes we had to use translators' license with the exact wording. This we did in *A Page from the Song of Songs* and to some extent in *The Enchanted Tailor*, stories which depend a great deal on mood and atmosphere. Others that were carried forward by action and incident like *The Miracle of Hashono Rabo* follow the original almost word for word. In a few stories we left out passages that seemed to us irrelevant or outdated. This we did in *The Fiddle* where we omitted an elaborate description of the informer, and in *The Lottery Ticket* where a whole digression occurs that has no bearing on the story. We never tampered with the main flow of the story, and we never changed the substance of a beginning or an ending. A number of words which occur over and over and which have no equivalent in English were retained in the original Yiddish. Those are words descriptive of occupations like *melamed* and *shochet* and others which are almost self-explanatory in their context. Chief among these words is *shlimazl* which means literally a person of little luck.

The choice of stories was for the main part our own. We selected those that appealed to us most and those we thought would appeal to the English reader. Some we rejected for a definite reason, because of some special problem of translation as in the monologues which depend almost entirely on the teller's idiom, or when the story turned on some phrase that was completely untranslatable. Some of the stories seemed to us to be outdated, though there were surprisingly few of those. Others centered about a complicated religious ritual which would have needed a whole essay to explain. In many cases we chose among several stories similar in type.

One of the most wonderful and at the same time the most

maddening things about these stories is the utter simplicity of their language. You ask yourself over and over, how can such a limited vocabulary be such a perfect instrument for expression? It isn't the fact that it portrays a simple people. Compared to the people of a Steinbeck or a Hemingway, these are virtuosos of the intellect. Words are their chief weapon, their joy and their ornament. But it isn't the variety of words at their command so much as the way they are put together that makes their speech distinctive—the way a phrase is chopped off or inverted or repeated with slight variations. It is like spoken Yiddish which depends for its drama on the inflection of the voice, on a pause, a raised eyebrow or a shrug of the shoulder. These things are difficult to transmit into another language, but when you feel that you've succeeded you experience the real thrill of creation.

While the language is simple, it is often violent and earthy. We had to compromise with this earthiness. Take just the small matter of the Yiddish curse. There are as many types of curses as there are people cursing, but the hardest to explain is the mother cursing her child. The child may be crying because he is hungry. The mother bursts out, "Eat, eat, eat. All you want to do is eat. May the worms eat you. May the earth open up and swallow you alive." This mother loves her child, she is only pouring out the bitterness that's in her heart in the only way she knows. But in translation she sounds like a monster.

We encountered our greatest problem in working on the Tevye stories. They are all in the first person and they all depend for their effect on Tevye's manner of expressing himself. In fact, they *are* Tevye. Tevye is the perfect *schlimazl* and also the perfect *kasril*, the man whom nothing in life can down. He considers himself a man of great learning and erudition—that is what makes his life bearable—and his speech is practically a series of Hebrew quotations from the Holy Books, most of which are, of course, misquotations, hilariously funny to the reader who could understand them, but otherwise meaningless. The problem was not only how to untangle these misquotations, but also how to render mistakes in one language within another language into a third language. We simply had to omit many passages. In others we used Biblical diction to approximate the Hebrew. Of course, some of the pungency and flavor of this most delightful and most completely realized of all of Sholom Aleichem's characters was lost in translation.

I would like to emphasize that throughout this work we made no attempt to be academic or perfectionist. These stories are not for the Hebraist or the Yiddish scholar. They are not especially for those who can read and enjoy the original. Rather, they are intended for the many Jews and non-Jews who, through a barrier of language, have had no access to the work of the most interesting and most beloved of Yiddish writers. They are intended for the general reader to whom they may open a new field of human experience.

Both of us came from The Old Country, I more recently than my husband, but it was he who had the deeper sense of identification with the past. He was brought to America at the age of one from Walkowisk in Lithuanian Russia. For forty years—that is, all of his life—he lived in a middle-sized city in Mid-America. He walked its streets as a native, he knew its buildings and people, its history and politics intimately. The tempo of this life suited him. And yet his roots were elsewhere. He used to say that he knew the geography of Walkowisk as well as that of St. Paul. Here was his grandfather's mill, there the Long Street, here the *cheder* where his father used to teach as a young man. And that mill, that street, that *cheder* could just as well have been in Kasrilevka or Verebivka, in Boiberik or Haschavata. For all of those towns, real or mythical, in White Russia or the Ukraine, in Galicia or Lithuania, belong to the same country to which our parents and grandparents referred when they spoke of *in der heim* or home.

One Sunday last November, which turned out to be the last day of his life, my husband was talking about his grandparents. He told how his grandfather used to take him walking by the river; how he loved watching his grandmother roll out the thin yellow sheets of dough for noodles. He said, "For me they were the ideal grandparents." And I think that in a restricted but no less real sense the life they represented was to him an ideal life. He was aware of its limitations, its misery and hardship, but he also understood its dignity, its warmth, and most particularly its humor. He was a product of all these things. And it gave him rare pleasure to be able through these translations to interpret that life to his contemporaries.

So that finally, these stories are intended for those to whom

The Old Country is only a name remembered from childhood and for those to whom it represents a whole complex of emotions, of words and pictures, of smells and sounds, for which they have no common frame of reference. If we have succeeded truly in bringing Sholom Aleichem to Americans, if we have succeeded in clarifying and sharpening only a few of those sounds and smells and pictures, if we have lit up only a corner of that vast and wonderful country of the heart we call The Old Country, our work has been well worth doing.

II

THE TEVYE STORIES

"The Holy One, blessed be He," quotes Tevye the Dairyman, *"wished to grant merit to Israel"*; and in his own fashion he interprets this to mean: The Lord wanted to be good to Tevye, so He blessed him with seven daughters. And what kind of daughters? Meek, ugly, sickly creatures? No! Beauties—everyone of them—fine, well-grown girls, charming and good-tempered, healthy and high-spirited—like young pine trees! But that was as far as the Lord went in His bounty. He granted to Tevye neither money nor luck. And what good are beautiful and gifted daughters if you have neither money nor luck to go along with them? "If they had been ill-tempered and ugly as scarecrows," remarks Tevye ruefully, "it would have been better for them and certainly healthier for me." But then there would have been no Tevye the Dairyman as we know him, no chronicle of Tevye's daughters, as Sholom Aleichem planned and developed it, for the honor and enrichment of Yiddish literature.

That Sholom Aleichem planned the stories of Tevye's daughters as a single chronicle, there can be no doubt. A single theme runs through them all, and the style is identical. But he wrote each one as a separate narrative, with Tevye himself doing the narrating, addressing himself to Sholom Aleichem whom he meets from time to time over a period of fifteen to twenty years—sometimes in the woods near Boiberik, sometimes in Boiberik or on a train to Yehupetz. Each story has the same form; it is enclosed in a capsule, very much like a typical Yiddish letter. Tevye usually begins by greeting his old friend Sholom Aleichem, whom he has not seen for a long time; he goes on to recapitulate something of what went on before, picks up his story from there, and ends finally with farewells and good wishes, and a promise of more to come at some future meeting. This form is peculiarly suited to Tevye's rambling and informal style of narrative, and because we wished to preserve it and also to indicate the lapse of time between the stories, or chapters, we scattered them through the book instead of presenting them in a solid block. And to make the book complete we have reprinted "Modern Children" and "Hodel" from *The Old Country*.

In spite of the fact that these stories are separated by intervals of time and that each one presents a complete incident with its own climax and denouement, taken together they have the unity of a novel. On the surface, this novel is a family chronicle whose theme is the timeless and never-resolved conflict between the younger and older generations. Examined more closely, *Tevye's Daughters* is something more than a family saga. It is a story of social conflict laid at a precise turn of history—the last days of Tsarist Russia. With the accession of Nicholas II, the government of the Tsars had reached its final peak of intrigue and corruption. This was the last stage in its battle for survival. There was wide political unrest throughout the country, culminating in the revolutionary struggle of 1905-6, whose failure was followed by counterrevolution and a general disillusionment among the masses of people.

The political events of those years are reflected both directly and indirectly in the tragedies of Tevye's daughters. And we must also remember that along with the political conflict, which made its direct impact on the Jews in the form of economic and civic oppression and bloody pogroms, went the ferment within Jewry itself—the breaking up of old paternalistic molds, the influx of new movements: Zionism, the *Haskalah*, the Bund, the spread of secular learning and the revolt against narrow religious sectarianism. In the midst of this vortex, Tevye and his wife Golde represent the comparatively peaceful, patriarchal way of life; while their daughters are acted upon by, and in turn react violently to, the sweeping new currents.

But Tevye himself is not a static figure either. He is deeply religious, but he is no fanatic. He is aware of the changes taking place about him and unconsciously absorbs the spirit of those changes. For Tevye the Dairyman, whose fame as a dealer in milk and butter and cheese has spread like the sound of the *shofar* over the world, can't avoid rubbing elbows with the world. On his rounds with his horse and wagon he has met and had dealings (much to his sorrow) with Menachem-Mendel the *luftmensch,* the entrepreneur, who "deals in things you can't put your hands on," and makes and loses fortunes in less time than it takes Tevye to recite *Shma Yisroel.* He has met and talked with the young students, the sons of shoe-makers and tailors, who have turned their backs on the study of the *Torah* and live six in a garret and feast on black bread and herring in order to attend the university. He has had dealings with the pompous *negidim* of Yehupetz who spend their summers in their *datchas* in Boiberik, and whose wives have expensive stomach ailments and travel abroad for cures. He has talked with men who understand a *medresh* and with men who don't know the difference between a *medresh* and a piece of horseflesh.

Tevye has been shaken from his moorings. He is a man in conflict with himself, he is not too sure that his way is always the best; and so we find him aiding and abetting his daughters in spite of his better, that is, more instinctive, judgment.

In "Modern Children," Tevye's oldest daughter Tzeitl defies the convention of "arranged marriages." Her mother wants her to marry the rich widower, Lazer-Wolf the Butcher. Tevye's wife Golde is, after all, nothing but a woman. Woman-like she is a realist; she sees only what's in front of her and what she sees she doesn't like. Poverty, illness, and struggle have always been her lot. She wants something better for her daughters. To her "something better" means a pantry full of good food, a fur-lined cloak for weekdays and a cloak with a ruffle for Saturdays, shoes and stockings, linen and bedding—in short, a rich husband like Lazer-Wolf the Butcher. Tevye has no objection to these things either. He doesn't hold with the new-fangled notion of romantic love; but when he is confronted with it, he weakens. We find him, against his better judgment, helping Tzeitl marry the poor tailor Motel Kamzoil from Anatevka. "That's modern children for you," says Tevye. "You sacrifice yourself for them, you slave for them day and night—and what do you get out of it?" But in his heart he is proud of his modern children, he is even proud of their defiance of him.

Hodel, the second of Tevye's daughters, has been infected with revolution. She is in love with Pertschik, the revolutionary young student, the son of the cigarette-maker. Again

Tevye helps his daughter against his better judgment. He goes so far as to fabricate a story about a rich aunt and an inheritance to explain to Golde why Pertschik has to leave right after the hasty marriage ceremony. Driving Hodel and her brand-new husband to the station in his wagon, Tevye marvels at the young couple's apparent lack of emotion. But he reserves judgment. Tevye is not an old woman, he can wait and see. He waits, and he sees Hodel follow her husband to his prison in exile. Though his heart is broken at parting from her, and though he lays no claim to understanding her motives, in a curious way he is proud of her too.

But with his third daughter, Chava, Tevye comes to real grief. Chava is in love with a gentile, the peasant Fyedka Galagan, who is "another Gorky." Now Tevye might condone modern love, he might even shrug his shoulders at revolution with its crazy nonsense of "what's yours is mine and what's mine is yours," but he will never condone apostasy. When Chava marries her Fyedka and goes over to the gentiles, she severs herself completely from her family. She forfeits all the "mercy" that Tevye might have for the weaknesses of his children. For the essence of Tevye is his religion, it is his chief *raison d'être*, the condition of his survival; and if he condoned his daughter's apostasy, he would become something very much less than Tevye. . . .

The tragedy of Schprintze is of a different sort. Schprintze has fallen in love with a rich young man, she has tried to step out of her class. Or rather she has tried to ignore the division of class. Aarontchik is a good man, she tells her father, and he is surrounded by vulgar people who know nothing but money and money and money. But Tevye is not one to scorn "vulgar money." For the first time since he lost his fortune in the deal with Menachem-Mendel he permits himself to spin a dream of wealth. . . . "Perhaps God has willed it that through this quiet little Schprintze you should be rewarded for all the pain and suffering you have undergone until now and enjoy a pleasant and restful old age? Why not? Won't the honor sit well on you?" But he knows all along that he is deceiving himself, and he tries his best to talk Schprintze out of her infatuation. For in spite of Kishinevs and Constitutions, pogroms and revolutions, in spite of all the edicts of the Tsar's ministers to whom a *Zhyd* is a *Zhyd* whether he resides in a palace in Odessa or is squeezed with a family of ten into a hut in Kasrilevka—in spite of all this, the Jews themselves are as rigidly as ever divided into the rich and poor, the haves and havenots, "those who walk on foot and those who ride on horseback." As the widow's brother, he of the barrel shape and the thick gold chain puts it, "You are an intelligent person, how could you permit this, that Tevye the Dairyman, who brings us cheese and butter, should try to marry into *our* family?"

In the story of Beilke, the youngest and most beautiful of Tevye's daughters, the circle swings around again. Here it is Beilke herself, unlike her older sisters, who insists on marrying the rich Padhatzur, who made his pile in the Russo-Japanese war. When Tevye in revulsion against the pretensions and vulgarity of his rich son-in-law tells Beilke that "your sister Hodel would have done differently," she answers him, "I've told you before not to compare me to Hodel. Hodel lived in Hodel's time and Beilke is living in Beilke's time. The distance between the two is as great as from here to Japan." Beilke is the product of disillusionment. She knows very well that Hodel's husband will die in prison unless her Padhatzur, stuffed with money he has made at the expense of the government, will bribe that same government to have Pertschik's sentence lifted. Tevye bows to the inevitable and accepts from his son-in-law a ticket to the Holy Land.

But Tevye never starts out for the Holy Land. More disasters intervene. Even the self-assured Padhatzur who "might have entertained a Rothschild in his home" meets with financial failure, and has to flee to America "where all unhappy souls go." And the wave of pogroms which has engulfed the big cities finally overtakes Tevye who was sure "they would never reach him." Tevye's family from time immemorial had lived in a village, and when the May Laws of 1882 drove the Jews out of the villages, denied them the right to own land, and herded them together in the little towns of the Jewish Pale, Tevye's family was left untouched. But now in the days of Mendel Beiliss, when the whole world "went backwards," in the days just preceding the first World War, Tevye was finally "reached." He was politely told to "Get thee out." He was ordered to leave his "fatherland," as he ironically calls it. But even in this extremity, Tevye savored a small triumph, more bitter than sweet, but still a triumph. His daughter Chava, whom he had chosen to count as dead, repents and comes back to her father and to her God. And so at the last

Tevye stands vindicated. The religion he clung to so tenaciously through all his reversals of fortune is all that is left to him. "Tell our friends not to worry," he tells Sholom Aleichem at the final parting. "Our ancient God still lives."

To understand Tevye at all we must first understand his peculiar relation to God. To Tevye, God is not a remote Deity to whom one prays on Sabbaths and High Holy Days or in times of great trouble. He is not the Lawgiver to whom Moses spoke amidst thunder and lightning on Mt. Sinai. Tevye is on much more intimate terms with God. He speaks to Him on weekdays, as well as on the Sabbath, indoors and outdoors and in all kinds of weather, just as surely as his forefathers, Abraham, Isaac and Jacob, spoke with God indoors and outdoors and in all kinds of weather. "You do not ask questions of God," says Tevye, but he persists in asking questions at all times. He never lets God alone. What are we and what is our life? What is this world and what is the next world? Why do you always pick on Tevye to do Thy will? Why don't you play with someone else for a change, a Brodsky or a Rothschild? What is the meaning of Jew and non-Jew? What and why and once more why and wherefore? If Tevye's daughters are at war with society, Tevye himself wages his own war against God and man, and since he believes men's actions to be chiefly inspired by God, God is the chief Adversary.

Tevye gives battle with the only weapon he has at his disposal—the Holy Word. He fights God with God's own weapons and on God's own ground. For Tevye considers himself a man of learning, and in his time and place learning meant one thing—the knowledge of the *Torah* and its application to daily life. He would sooner quote Scriptures than eat, and every mouthful he eats is accompanied by a quotation. As Golde says bitterly, "You drum my head full of quotations and you've done your duty by your children." Says Tevye, "I have to answer even this with a quotation." To Tevye, talk is not a substitute for action. It is the only wholly satisfying action he knows.

Though Sholom Aleichem was a humorist and Tevye is his most famous character, Tevye is not funny. Nearly everything that happens to him and his daughters is tragic. His humor lies in his evaluation of what happens to him, in what he says and the way he says it. In the fact that he misquotes more often than he quotes, and that usually his interpretation of what he is quoting is completely cockeyed, lies his all-pervading charm to the Yiddish reader. No wonder Sholom Aleichem's audiences used to roll in the aisles with laughter. The juxtaposition of a lofty phrase in Hebrew or Aramaic with a homely Yiddish phrase which is supposed to explain it but has no bearing on it whatever—that is the gist of Tevye's humor. Tevye, of course, has no idea that he is funny. He continues to quote in Hebrew, in Russian, in whatever comes in handy. It is this play on language that is so difficult to convey successfully in translation. Whenever possible I used the archaic or Biblical phraseology for the Hebrew quotations and simple idiomatic English for the Yiddish; and to indicate the former I used italics—separated by a dash from the latter.

For example: When Tevye goes to see the priest and the priest's dogs jump on him, he says, "I gave them this quotation to chew on—'*Lo yechratz kelev l'shonoh.*'" Which means literally, "Not a dog shall bark," and comes from Exodus, Chapter II, Verse 7: "But against any of the children of Israel not a dog shall bark." Tevye follows this with the Russian proverb: "*Nehai sobaka daram nie breshe,*" and interprets the whole thing to mean, "Don't let a dog bark for nothing."

Tevye likes to use the same quotation over and over, putting it to a different use each time. Speaking of the Jews who start running from town to town when there is a rumor of a pogrom, he says, "*They journeyed and they encamped, they encamped and they journeyed*" (referring of course to the Israelites wandering in the desert), and interprets this to mean, "You come to me and I will come to you." Again he assures Beilke that he will come back from Palestine. "*They journeyed and they encamped—Tuda i nazad*—I will go and I will return."

A number of times when Tevye wants to indicate that he is through and no more need be said on the subject he says impressively, "*Here ends the lesson for the Sabbath before Passover.*" He is simply repeating a phrase in the prayerbook which is the same as saying The End or Period.

Tevye is never at a loss for a quotation. When nothing apt occurs to him he reaches into his memory and snatches at the first thing that he can lay his hands on. Describing a guest of Padhatzur's who ate an enormous amount of food he says, "*Sh'loshaw she'ochlu,*" which means literally, "Three who have eaten," and comes from the passage in *Perek:* ". . . the three who have eaten and not a word of *Torah* passed between them are as those who have eaten an idolatrous sacrifice." He blithely interprets this to mean, "He ate enough for three."

Tevye is unique among Sholom Aleichem's characters. No other character displays his peculiar blend of innocence and shrewdness, kindliness and irony, weakness and toughness. He is less of a type and more of a personality than any of the others, but Tevye did not spring full-grown from a desert, he was not "God's only son." Though he lived in the country, and not in one of the little towns where the Jews were packed together "as tightly as herring in a barrel," Tevye was brother and uncle and cousin to the people of Kasrilevka and Anatevka and Mazapevka and even of Yehupetz and Odessa. He was related to Menachem-Mendel by marriage and no doubt to half of Kasrilevka as well. He knew the Benjamin Lastechkys, the Samuel Fingerhuts, the fish peddlers and tinmen, the poultrywomen and traveling salesmen, the Zaidels and the Reb Yozifels. It isn't stretching the point too far to consider them all as minor characters in the drama of Tevye and his daughters, and their stories as a background for the central action.

This background is as rich and varied as Sholom Aleichem's genius. There is the robust comedy of the Railway Stories, the puckish humor of Motel the Orphan in "What Will Become of Me," the lyric mood of "Another Page from the Song of Songs." Though they are in no sense "proletarian" stories, there is a social awareness in "The Passover Expropriation," "The Littlest of Kings," and "An Easy Fast," which illustrates and further extends the social conflict in *Tevye's Daughters.* Taken together, all of these stories are a part of the life, forever vanished, which Sholom Aleichem reproduced so faithfully, with tenderness, with humor and with sharp penetration, but never with malice or bitterness.

The nearest we come to bitterness in Tevye himself is when he reflects on the ways of the world: "I wasn't worried about God so much. I could come to terms with Him one way or another. What bothered me was people. Why should people be so cruel when they could be so kind? Why should human beings bring suffering to others and to themselves when they could all live together in peace and goodwill?" Tevye contents himself with asking questions. His daughters went a step farther. They challenged the conventions of "cruelty and suffering," they "strained after a new life" and took desperate chances to attain it. Sometimes they won, more often they lost. Their story is as pertinent today as it was when they lived it.

I wish to express thanks to Mike Baker and Dr. David Aelony who helped me over the rough spots of the translation, and especially to Rabbi Norman Frimer who so patiently traced Tevye's quotations and misquotations to their sources.

F. B.

St. Paul, August, 1948

CONTENTS

THE TEVYE STORIES AND OTHERS

The Bubble Bursts

"THERE are many thoughts in a man's heart." So I believe it is written in the Holy *Torah.* I don't have to translate the passage for you, Mr. Sholom Aleichem. But, speaking in plain Yiddish, there is a saying: "The most obedient horse needs a whip; the cleverest man can use advice." In regard to whom do I say this? I say it in regard to myself, for if I had once had the good sense to go to a friend and tell him such and such, thus and so, this calamity would never have taken place. But how is it said? *"Life and death issue from thine own lips.* —When God sees fit to punish a man he first takes away his good sense."

How many times have I thought to myself: Look, Tevye, you dolt, you are not supposed to be a complete fool. How could you have allowed yourself to be taken in so completely and in such a foolish way? Wouldn't it have been better for you if you had been content with your little dairy business whose fame has spread far and wide, everywhere from Boiberik to Yehupetz? How sweet and pleasant it would have been if your little hoard still lay in its box, buried deep where not a soul could see or know. For whose business is it whether Tevye has money or not? Was anyone concerned with Tevye when he lay buried nine feet deep, wrapped in his poverty like a dead man in his shroud? Did the world care when he starved three times a day together with his wife and children?

But lo and behold! When God turned his countenance on Tevye and caused him to prosper all at once, so that at last he was beginning to arrive somewhere, beginning to save up a *ruble* now and then, the world suddenly became aware of his presence, and overnight, mind you, plain Tevye became Reb Tevye, nothing less. Suddenly out of nowhere a multitude of friends sprang up. As it is written: *"He is beloved by everyone."* Or, as we put it: "When God gives a dot, the world adds a lot."

Everyone came to me with a different suggestion. This one

tells me to open a drygoods store, that one a grocery. Another one says to buy a building—property is a sound investment, it lasts forever. One tells me to invest in wheat, another in timber. Still another suggests auctioneering. "Friends!" I cry. "Brothers! Leave me alone. You've got the wrong man. You must think I'm Brodsky, but I am still very far from being a Brodsky. It is easy to estimate another's wealth. You see something that glitters like gold at a distance. You come close and it's only a brass button."

May no good come to them—I mean those friends of mine, those well-wishers—they cast an evil eye on me. God sent me a relative from somewhere, a distant kinsman of some kind whom I had never seen before. Menachem-Mendel is his name—a gadabout, a wastrel, a faker, a worthless vagabond, may he never stand still in one place. He got hold of me and filled my head with dreams and fantasies, things that had never been on land or sea. You will ask me: "*Wherefore did it come to pass?*" How did I ever get together with Menachem-Mendel? And I will answer in the words of the *Hagadah:* "*For we were slaves.*" It was fated, that's all. Listen to my story.

I arrived in Yehupetz in early winter, with my choicest merchandise—over twenty pounds of butter fresh from Butterland and several pails of cheese. I had salted away everything I had, you understand, didn't leave a smidgen for myself, not as much as a medicine spoon would hold. I didn't even have the time to visit all of my regular customers, the summer people of Boiberik, who await my coming as a good Jew waits for the coming of the Messiah. For say what you will, there isn't a merchant in Yehupetz who can produce a piece of goods that comes up to mine. I don't have to tell you this. As the prophet says: "*Let another praise thee.*—Good merchandise speaks for itself."

Well, I sold out everything to the last crumb, threw a bundle of hay to my horse and went for a walk around the town. "*Man is born of dust and to dust he returneth.*" After all, I am only human. I want to see something of the world, breathe some fresh air, take a look at the wonders Yehupetz displays behind glass windows, as though to say: "Use your eyes all you want, but with your hands—away!"

Standing in front of a large window filled with seven and a half *ruble* gold pieces, with piles of silver *rubles*, and stacks of paper money of all kinds, I think to myself: God in Heaven! If I had only a tenth of what all of this is worth! What more could I ask of God and who would be my equal? First of all, I would marry off my oldest daughter, give her a suitable dowry and still have enough left over for wedding expenses, gifts, and clothing for the bride. Then I would sell my horse and wagon and my cows and move into town. I would buy myself a Synagogue seat by the Eastern Wall, hang strings of pearls around my wife's neck, and hand out charity like the richest householders. I would see to it that the Synagogue got a new roof instead of standing as it does now, practically roofless, ready to cave in any minute. I would open a school for the children and build a hospital such as they have in other towns so that the town's poor and sick wouldn't have to lie underfoot in the Synagogue. And I would get rid of Yankel Sheigetz, as president of the Burial Society. There's been enough guzzling of brandy and chicken livers at public expense!

"*Sholom aleichem,* Reb Tevye," I hear a voice right in back of me. I turn around and take a look. I could swear I have seen this man somewhere before.

"*Aleichem sholom,*" I answer. "And where do you hail from?"

"Where do I hail from? From Kasrilevka," he says. "I am a relative of yours. That is, your wife Golde is my second cousin once removed."

"Hold on!" I say. "Aren't you Boruch-Hersh Leah-Dvoshe's son-in-law?"

"You've hit the nail right on the head," he says. "I am Boruch-Hersh Leah-Dvoshe's son-in-law and my wife is Sheina Sheindel Boruch-Hersh Leah-Dvoshe's daughter. Now do you know who I am?"

"Wait," I say. "Your mother-in-law's grandmother Sarah-Yenta, and my wife's aunt, Fruma-Zlata, were, I believe, first cousins, and if I am not mistaken you are the middle son-in-law of Boruch-Hersh Leah-Dvoshe's. But I forgot what they call you. Your name has flown right out of my head. Tell me, what is your name?"

"My name," he says, "is Menachem-Mendel Boruch-Hersh Leah-Dvoshe's. That's what they call me at home, in Kasrilevka."

"If that's the case," I say, "my dear Menachem-Mendel, I

really owe you a *sholom aleichem* and a hearty one! Now, tell me, my friend, what are you doing here, and how is your mother-in-law, and your father-in-law? How is your health, and how is business with you?"

"As far as my health," he says, "God be thanked. I am still alive. But business is not so gay."

"It will get better, with God's help," I tell him, stealing a look meanwhile at his shabby coat and the holes in his shoes. "Don't despair, God will come to your aid. Business will get better, no doubt. As the proverb says: '*All is vanity.*—Money is round, it is here today, gone tomorrow.' The main thing is to stay alive and keep hoping. A Jew must never stop hoping. Do we wear ourselves down to a shadow in the meanwhile? That's why we are Jews. How is it said? If you're a soldier you have to smell gunpowder. '*Man is likened to a broken pot.*—The world is nothing but a dream.' Tell me, Menachem-Mendel, how do you happen to be in Yehupetz all of a sudden?"

"What do you mean how do I happen to be in Yehupetz all of a sudden? I've been here no less than a year and a half."

"Oh," said I, "then you belong here. You are living in Yehupetz."

"Sshh," he whispers, looking all about him. "Don't talk so loud, Reb Tevye. I *am* living in Yehupetz, but that's just between you and me."

I stare at him as though he were out of his mind. "You are a fugitive," I ask, "and you hide in the middle of the public square?"

"Don't ask, Reb Tevye. You are apparently not acquainted with the laws and customs of Yehupetz. Listen and I'll explain to you how a man can live here and still not live here." And he began telling me a long tale of woe, of all the trials and tribulations of life in the city of Yehupetz.

When he finished I said to him, "Take my advice, Menachem-Mendel, come along with me to the country for a day and rest your tired bones. You will be a guest at our house, a very welcome guest. My wife will be overjoyed to have you."

Well, I talked him into it. He went with me. We arrive at home. What rejoicing! A guest! And such a guest! A second-cousin-once-removed. After all, blood is thicker than water. My wife starts right in, "What is new in Kasrilevka? How is Uncle Boruch-Hersh? And Aunt Leah-Dvoshe? And Uncle

Yossel-Menashe? And Aunt Dobrish? And how are their children? Who has died recently? Who has been married? Who is divorced? Who has given birth? And who is expecting?"

"What do you care about strange weddings and strange circumcisions?" I tell my wife. "Better see to it that we get something to eat. As it is written, '*All who are hungry enter and be fed.*—Nobody likes to dance on an empty stomach.' If you give us a *borsht*, fine. If not, I'll take *knishes* or *kreplach*, pudding or dumplings. *Blintzes* with cheese will suit me too. Make anything you like and the more the better, but do it quickly."

Well, we washed, said grace, and had our meal. "*They ate*," as Rashi says. "Eat, Menachem-Mendel, eat," I urged him. "'*Forget the world*,' as King David once said. It's a stupid world, and a deceitful one, and health and happiness, as my Grandmother Nechama of blessed memory used to say—she was a clever woman and a wise one—health and happiness are only to be found at the table."

Our guest—his hands trembled as he reached for the food, poor fellow—couldn't find enough words in praise of my wife's cooking. He swore by everything holy that he couldn't remember when he had eaten such a dairy supper, such perfect *knishes*, such delicious *vertutin*.

"Stuff and nonsense," I tell him. "You should taste her noodle pudding. Then you would know what heaven on earth can be."

After we had eaten and said our benedictions, we began talking, each one naturally talking of what concerned him most. I talk about my business, he of his. I babble of this, that, and the other, important and unimportant. He tells me stories of Yehupetz and Odessa, of how he had been ten times over, as they say, "on horseback and thrown off the horse." A rich man today, a beggar tomorrow, again a rich man, and once more a pauper. He dealt in something I had never heard of in my life—crazy-sounding things—stocks, bonds, shares-shmares, Maltzev-shmaltzev. The devil alone knew what it was. The sums that he reeled off his tongue were fantastic—ten thousand, twenty thousand, thirty thousand—he threw money around like matches.

"I'll tell you the truth, Menachem-Mendel," I say to him. "Your business sounds very involved, you need brains to understand all of that. But what puzzles me most is this: from what I know of your better half it's a wonder to me that she lets you go traipsing around the world and doesn't come riding after you on a broomstick."

"Don't remind me of that," he says with a deep sigh. "I get enough from her as it is, both hot and cold. If you could see the letters she writes me you would admit that I am a saint to put up with it. But that's a small matter. That's what a wife is for—to bury her husband alive. There are worse things than that. I have also, as you know, a mother-in-law. I don't have to go into detail. You have met her."

"It is with you as it is written: '*The flocks were speckled and streaked and spotted.*—You have a boil on top of a boil and a blister on top of that.' "

"Yes," he says. "You put it very well, Reb Tevye. The boil is bad enough in itself, but the blister—ah, that blister is worse than the boil."

Well, we kept up this palaver until late into the night. My head whirled with his tales of fantastic transactions, of thousands that rose and fell, fabulous fortunes that were won and lost and won again. I tossed all night long dreaming in snatches of Yehupetz and Brodsky, of millions of *rubles,* of Menachem-Mendel and his mother-in-law.

Early the next morning he begins hemming and hawing and finally comes out with it. Here is what he says. "Since the stock market has for a long time been in such a state that money is held in high esteem and goods are held very low, you Tevye have a chance to make yourself a pretty penny. And while you are getting rich you will at the same time be saving my life, you will actually raise me from the dead."

"You talk like a child," I say to him. "You must think I have a big sum of money to invest. Fool, may we both earn before next Passover what I lack to make me a Brodsky."

"I know," he says, "without your telling me. But what makes you think we need big money? If you give me a hundred *rubles* now, I can turn it in three or four days into two hundred or three hundred or six hundred or maybe even into a thousand *rubles.*"

"It may be as it is written: '*The profit is great, but it's far from my pocket.*' Who says I have anything to invest at all? And if there is no hundred *rubles,* it's as Rashi says: '*You came in alone and you go out by yourself.*' Or, as I put it, 'If you plant a stone, up comes a boulder.' "

"Come now," he says to me, "you know you can dig up a hundred *rubles*. With all the money you are earning and with your name . . ."

"A good name is an excellent thing," I tell him. "But what comes of it? I keep my name and Brodsky has the money. If you want to know the truth, my savings come all in all close to a hundred *rubles*. And I have two dozen uses for it. First of all, to marry off my daughter . . ."

"Just what I've been trying to tell you," he breaks in. "When will you have the opportunity to put in a hundred *rubles* and to take out, with God's help, enough to marry off your daughter and to do all the other things besides?"

And he went on with this chant for the next three hours, explaining how he could make three *rubles* out of one and ten out of three. First you bring in one hundred *rubles* somewhere, and you tell them to buy ten pieces of I-forget-what-you-call-it, then you wait a few days until they go up. You send a telegram somewhere else to sell the ten pieces and buy twice as many for the money. Then you wait and they rise again. You shoot off another telegram. You keep doing this until the hundred *rubles* become two hundred, then four hundred, then eight hundred, then sixteen hundred. It's no less than a miracle from God. There are people in Yehupetz, he tells me, who until recently went barefoot—they didn't have a pair of shoes to their names. They worked as errand boys and messengers. Now they own palatial homes, their wives have expensive stomach ailments, they go abroad for cures. They themselves fly all over Yehupetz on rubber wheels, they don't recognize old friends any more.

Well, why should I drag out the story? I caught the fever from him. Who knows, I think to myself, maybe he was sent by my good angel? He tells me that people win fortunes in Yehupetz, ordinary people with not more than five fingers to each hand. Am I any worse than they? I don't believe he is a liar, he couldn't make all these things up out of his own head. Who knows, suppose the wheel turns, and Tevye becomes a somebody in his old age? How much longer can I keep on toiling and moiling from dawn until dark? Day in and day out—the same horse and wagon, night and day the same butter and cheese? It's time, Tevye, that you took a little rest, became a man among men, went into the Synagogue once in a while, turned the pages of a holy book. Why not? And on the other hand, if I lose out, if it should fall buttered side down? But better not think of that.

"What do you say?" I ask my wife. "What do you think of his proposition?"

"What do you want me to say?" she asks. "I know that Menachem-Mendel isn't a nobody who would want to swindle you. He doesn't come from a family of nobodies. He has a very respectable father, and as for his grandfather, he was a real jewel. All his life, even after he became blind, he studied the *Torah*. And Grandmother Tzeitl, may she rest in peace, was no ordinary woman either."

"A fitting parable," I said. "It's like bringing *Hannukah* candles to a *Purim* Feast. We talk about investments and she drags in her Grandmother Tzeitl who used to bake honeycake, and her grandfather who died of drink. That's a woman for you. No wonder King Solomon traveled the world over and didn't find a female with an ounce of brains in her head."

To make a long story short, we decided to form a partnership. I put in my money and Menachem-Mendel, his wits. Whatever God gives, we will divide in half. "Believe me, Reb Tevye," he says, "you won't regret doing business with me. With God's help the money will come pouring in."

"Amen and the same to you," I say. "From your lips into God's ears. There is just one thing I want to know. How does the mountain come to the prophet? You are over there in Yehupetz and I am here in the country; and money, as you know, is a delicate substance. It isn't that I don't trust you, but as Father Abraham says, '*If you sow with tears you shall reap with joy.*—It's better to be safe than sorry.' "

"Oh," he says, "would you rather we drew up a paper? Most willingly."

"Listen," I say to him, "if you want to ruin me, what good will a piece of paper do me? '*The mouse is not the thief.*—It isn't the note that pays, but the man.' If I am hung by one foot I might as well be hung by both."

"Believe me, Reb Tevye," he says to me, "I swear to you on my word of honor, may God be my witness, that I have no tricks up my sleeve. I won't swindle you, but I will deal with you honestly. I will divide our earnings equally with you, share and share alike—a hundred to you, a hundred to me, two hundred to you, two hundred to me, four hundred to you, four hundred to me, a thousand to you, a thousand to me."

So I dug out my little hoard, counted the money over three times, my hands shaking the whole time, called over my wife as a witness, and explained to him again that this was blood-money I was giving him, and sewed it carefully inside his shirt so that no one would rob him of it on the way. He promished that he would write me not later than a week from Saturday and tell me everything in detail. Then we said goodbye with much feeling, embraced like close friends, and he went on his way.

When I was left alone there began to pass in front of my eyes all sorts of visions—visions so sweet that I wished they would never end. I saw a large house with a tin roof right in the middle of town, and inside the house were big rooms and little rooms and pantries full of good things, and around it a yard full of chickens and ducks and geese. I saw the mistress of the house walking around jingling her keys. That was my wife Golde, but what a different Golde from the one I knew. This one had the face and manner of a rich man's wife, with a double chin and a neck hung with pearls. She strutted around like a peacock giving herself airs, and yelling at the servant girls. And here were my daughters dressed in their Sabbath best, lolling around, not lifting a finger for themselves. The house was full of brightness and cheer. Supper was cooking in the oven. The samovar boiled merrily on the table. And at the head of the table sat the master of the house, Tevye himself, in a robe and skullcap, and around him sat the foremost householders of the town, fawning on him. "If you please, Reb Tevye. Pardon me, Reb Tevye."—And so on.

"What fiendish power money has!" I exclaimed.

"Whom are you cursing?" asked Golde.

"Nobody. I was just thinking," I told her. "Daydreams and moonshine . . . Tell me Golde, my love, do you know what sort of merchandise he deals in, that cousin of yours, Menachem-Mendel?"

"What's that?" she said. "Bad luck to my enemies! Here he has spent a day and a night talking with the man, and in the end he comes and asks me, 'What does he deal in?' For God's sake, you made up a contract with him. You are partners."

"Yes," I said. "We made up something, but I don't know what we made up. If my life depended on it, I wouldn't know. There is nothing, you see, that I can get hold of. But one thing has nothing to do with the other. Don't worry, my dear wife. My heart tells me that it is all for the best. We are going to make a lot of money. Say amen to that and go cook supper."

Well, a week goes by and two and three. There is no news from my partner. I am beside myself with worry. It can't be that he has just forgotten to write. He knows quite well how anxiously we are waiting to hear from him. A thought flits through my head. What shall I do if he skims off the cream for himself and tells me that there is no profit? But that, I tell myself, can't be. It just isn't possible. I treat the man like one of my own, so how can he turn around and play a trick like that on me? Then something worse occurs to me. Profit be hanged. Who cares about profit? *"Deliverance and protection will come from the Lord."* May God only keep the capital from harm. I feel a chill go up and down my back. "You old fool," I tell myself. "You idiot. You made your bed, now lie on it. For the hundred *rubles* you could have bought yourself a pair of horses such as your forefathers never had, or exchanged your old wagon for a carriage with springs."

"Tevye, why don't you think of something?" my wife pleads with me.

"What do you mean why don't I think of something? My head is splitting into little pieces from thinking and she asks why don't I think."

"Something must have happened to him on the road," says my wife. "He was attacked by robbers, or else he got sick on the way. Or he may even be dead."

"What will you dream up next, my love?" I ask. "All of a sudden she has to start pulling robbers out of thin air." But to myself I think: "No telling what can happen to a man alone on the road."

"You always imagine the worst," I tell my wife.

"He comes of such a good family," she says. "His mother, may she intercede for us in Heaven, died not long ago, she was still a young woman. He had three sisters. One died as a girl; the other one lived to get married but caught cold coming from the bath and died; and the third one lost her mind after her first child was born, ailed for a long time, and died too."

"To live until we die is our lot," I tell her. "We must all die sometime. A man is compared to a carpenter. A carpenter lives and lives until he dies, and a man lives and lives until he dies."

Well, we decided that I should go to Yehupetz. Quite a bit of merchandise had accumulated in the meanwhile—cheese and butter and cream, all of the best. My wife harnessed the horse and wagon, and *"they journeyed from Sukos"*—as Rashi says. On to Yehupetz!

Naturally my heart was heavy and my thoughts gloomy as I rode through the woods. I began to imagine the worst. Suppose, I think to myself, I arrive and begin to inquire about my man and they tell me, "Menachem-Mendel? Oh, that one? He has done well by himself. He has feathered his own nest. He owns a mansion, rides in his own carriage, you wouldn't recognize him." But just the same I gather up courage and go to his house. "Get out!" they tell me at the door, and shove me aside with their elbows. "Don't push your way, Uncle. We don't allow that."

"I am his relative," I tell them. "He is my wife's second cousin once removed."

"*Mazl-tov*," they tell me. "We are overjoyed to hear it. But just the same it won't hurt you to wait a little at the door."

It occurs to me that I should slip the doorman a bribe. As it is said: *"What goes up must come down"*; or, "If you don't grease the axle the wheels won't turn." And so I get in.

"Good morning to you, Reb Menachem-Mendel," I say.

Who? What? *"There is no speech. There are no words."* He looks at me as though he has never seen me before. "What do you want?" he says.

I am ready to faint. "What do you mean?" I say. "Don't you recognize your own cousin? My name is Tevye."

"Tevye . . ." he says slowly. "The name sounds familiar."

"So the name sounds familiar to you. Maybe my wife's *blintzes* sound familiar too? You may even remember the taste of her *knishes* and *kreplach*?"

Then I imagine exactly the opposite. I come in to see Menachem-Mendel and he meets me at the door with outstretched arms. "Welcome, Reb Tevye. Welcome. Be seated. How are you? And how is your wife? I've been waiting for you. I want to settle my account with you." And he takes my cap and pours it full of gold pieces. "This," he tells me, "is what we earned on our investment. The capital we shall leave where it is. Whatever we make we shall divide equally, share and share alike, half to me, half to you, a hundred to me, a hundred to you, two hundred to you, two hundred to me, five hundred to you, five hundred to me. . . ."

While I am lost in this dream, my horse strays from the path, the wagon gets caught against a tree, and I am jolted from behind so suddenly that sparks fly in front of my eyes. "This is all for the best," I comfort myself. "Thank God the axle didn't break."

I arrive in Yehupetz, dispose of my wares quickly and, as usual, without any trouble, and set out to look for my partner. I wander around for an hour, I wander around for two hours. It's no use. It's as Jacob said about Benjamin: "*The lad is gone.*" I can't find him anywhere. I stop people in the street and ask them, "Have you seen or have you heard of a man who goes by the elegant name of Menachem-Mendel?"

"Well, well," they tell me, "if his name is Menachem-Mendel, you can look for him with a candle. But that isn't enough. There is more than one Menachem-Mendel in the world."

"I see, you want to know his family name. At home in Kasrilevka he is known by his mother-in-law's name—Menachem-Mendel Leah-Dvoshe's. What more do you want? Even his father-in-law, who is a very old man, is known by his wife's name, Boruch-Hersh Leah-Dvoshe's. Now do you understand?"

"We understand very well," they say. "But that isn't enough. What does this Menachem-Mendel do? What is his business?"

"His business? He deals in seven and a half *ruble* gold pieces, in Putilov shares, in stocks and bonds. He shoots telegrams here, there, and everywhere—to St. Petersburg, Odessa, Warsaw."

They roll with laughter. "Oh, you mean Menachem-Mendel-who-deals-in-all-and-sundry? Turn left and follow this street and you will see many hares running around. Yours will be among them."

"Live and learn," I say to myself. "Now I am told to look for hares." I follow the street they pointed out to me. It's as crowded as our town square on market day. I can barely push my way through. People are running around like crazy—shouting, waving their hands, quarreling. It's a regular bedlam. I hear shouts of *Putilov*, "shares," "stocks . . ." "he gave me his word . . ." "here is a down payment . . ." "buy on margin . . ." "he owes me a fee . . ." "you are a sucker . . ." "spit in his face . . ." "look at that speculator." Any minute they will start fighting in earnest, dealing out blows. "*Jacob fled,*" I mutter to myself. "Get out, Tevye, before you get knocked down. God is our Father, Tevye the Dairyman is a sinner, Yehupetz is a city, and Menachem-Mendel is a breadwinner. So this is where people make fortunes? This is how they do their business? May God have mercy on you, Tevye, and on such business."

I stopped in front of a large window with a display of clothing in it and whom should I see reflected in it but my partner Menachem-Mendel. My heart was squeezed with pity at the sight. . . . *I became faint*. . . . May our worst enemies look the way Menachem-Mendel looked. You should have seen his coat. And his shoes. Or what was left of them. And his face! A corpse laid out for burial looks cheerful by comparison. "Well, Tevye," I said to myself as Esther had once said to Mordecai, " '*if I perish, I perish.*—I am done for.' You may as well kiss your savings good-bye. '*There is no bear and no woods.*—No merchandise and no money.' Nothing but a pack of troubles."

He looked pretty crestfallen on his part. We both stood there, rooted to the ground, unable to speak. There seemed to be nothing left to say, nothing left to do. We might as well pick up our sacks and go over the city begging.

"Reb Tevye," he says to me softly, barely able to utter the words, the tears are choking him so, "Reb Tevye, without luck, it's better never to have been born at all. Rather than live like this, it is better to hang from a tree or rot in the ground."

"For such a deed," I burst out, "for what you've done to me, you deserve to be stretched out right here in the middle of Yehupetz and flogged so hard that you lose consciousness. Consider for yourself what you've done. You've taken a houseful of innocent people who never did you a speck of harm, and without a knife you slit their throats clear through. How can I face my wife and children now? Tell me, you robber, you murderer, you—"

"It is all true, Reb Tevye," he says, leaning against the wall. "All true. May God have mercy on me."

"The fires of hell," I tell him, "the tortures of *Gehenna* are too good for you."

"All true," he says. "May God have pity on me. All true. Rather than to live like this, Reb Tevye, rather than to live—" And he hangs his head.

I look at him standing there, the poor *shlimazl,* leaning against the wall, his head bent, his cap awry. He sighs and he groans and my heart turns over with pity.

"And yet," I say, "if you want to look at it another way, you may not be to blame either. When I think it over, I realize that you couldn't have done it out of plain knavery. After all, you were my partner, you had a share in the business. I put in my money and you put in your brains. Woe unto us both. I am sure you meant it for the best. It must have been fate. How is it said? *'Don't rejoice today, because tomorrow—'* Or, 'Man proposes and God disposes.'

"If you want proof, just look at my business. It seems to be completely foolproof, a guaranteed thing. And yet when it came to pass last fall that one of my cows lay down and died and right after her a young calf—was there anything I could do about it? When luck turns against you, you are lost.

"I don't even want to ask you where my money is. I understand only too well. My blood money went up in smoke, it sank into the grave. . . . And whose fault is it if not mine? I let myself be talked into it. I went chasing after rainbows. If you want money, my friend, you have to work and slave for it, you have to wear your fingers to the bone. I deserve a good thrashing for it. But crying about it won't help. How is it written? *'If the maiden screamed*—You can shout until you burst a blood vessel.' Hindsight, as they say . . . It wasn't fated that Tevye should be a rich man. As Ivan says, 'Mikita never had anything and never will.' God willed it so. *'The Lord giveth and the Lord taketh away.'* Come, brother, let's go get a drink."

And that, Mr. Sholom Aleichem, is how my beautiful dream burst like a bubble and vanished into thin air. Do you think I took it to heart? Do you think I grieved over the loss of my money? Not at all. We know what the proverb says: "*The silver and the gold are mine.*—Money is worthless." Only man is important, that is, if he is really a man, a human being. For what did I grieve then? I grieved for the dream I had lost, the dream of wealth that was gone forever. For I had longed, how I had longed, to be a rich man, if only for a short while. But what did it avail me? The proverb says, "*Perforce you live and perforce you die.*—You live in spite of yourself and you wear out your shoes in spite of yourself."

"You, Tevye," says God, "stick to your cheese and butter and forget your dreams." But what about hope? Naturally, the harder life is the more you must hope. The poorer you are the more cheerful you must be.

Do you want proof? But I think I have talked too long already. I have to be on my way, I have to tend to business. As it is said: "*Every man is a liar.*—Everyone has his affliction." Farewell, be healthy and happy always. . . .

Modern Children

MODERN children, did you say? Ah, you bring them into the world, sacrifice yourself for them, you slave for them day and night—and what do you get out of it? You think that one way or another it would work out according to your ideas or station. After all, I don't expect to marry them off to millionaires, but then I don't have to be satisfied with just anyone, either. So I figured I'd have at least a little luck with my daughters. Why not? In the first place, didn't the Lord bless me with handsome girls; and a pretty face, as you yourself have said, is half a dowry. And besides, with God's help, I'm not the same Tevye I used to be. Now the best match, even in Yehupetz, is not beyond my reach. Don't you agree with me?

But there is a God in heaven who looks after everything. "*A Lord merciful and compassionate,*" who has His way with me summer and winter, in season and out. And He says to me, "Tevye, don't talk like a fool. Leave the management of the world to Me."

So listen to what can happen in this great world of ours. And to whom does it have to happen? To Tevye, *shlimazl.*

To make a long story short, I had just lost everything I had in a stockmarket investment I had gotten involved in through that relative of mine, Menachem-Mendel (may his name and memory be forever blotted out), and I was very low. It looked as if it was all over with me. No more Tevye, no more dairy business.

"Fool," my wife says to me. "You have worried enough. You'll get nowhere worrying. You'll just eat your heart out. Pretend that robbers had broken in and taken everything away. . . . I'll tell you what," she says to me. "Go out for a while. Go see Lazer-Wolf, the butcher, at Anatevka. He wants to see you about something very important."

"What's the matter?" I asked. "What is he so anxious to see

me about? If he is thinking of that milch cow of ours, let him take a stick and knock that idea out of his head."

"What are you so anxious about her for?" she says to me. "The milk that we get out of her, or the cheese or butter?"

"I'm not thinking about that," I answer. "It's just the idea. It would be a sin to give the poor thing away to be slaughtered. You can't do that to a living creature. It is written in the Bible. . . ."

"Oh, enough of that!" she comes back at me. "The whole world knows already that you're a man of learning! You do what I tell you. You go over and see Lazer-Wolf. Every Thursday when our Tzeitl goes there for meat, he won't leave her alone. 'You tell your father,' he keeps saying, 'to come and see me. It's important.' "

Well, once in a while you have to obey your wife. So I let her talk me into it, and I go over to Anatevka, about three miles away. He wasn't home. "Where can he be?" I ask a snub-nosed woman who is bustling around the place.

"They're slaughtering today," says the woman, "and he went down to bring an ox. He'll be coming back pretty soon."

So I wait. And while I'm waiting I look around the house a little. And from what I see, it looks as if Lazer-Wolf has been a good providor. There is a cupboard filled with copperware —at least a hundred and fifty *rubles'* worth; a couple of samovars, some brass trays, silver candlesticks and gilded goblets. And a fancy *Hannukah* lamp and some trinkets made of porcelain and silver and everything.

"Lord Almighty!" I think to myself. "If I can only live to see things like that at my children's homes. . . . What a lucky fellow he is—such wealth, and nobody to support! Both his children are married, and he himself is a widower. . . ."

Well, at last the door opens and in stamps Lazer-Wolf.

"Well, Reb Tevye," he says. "What's the matter? Why is it so hard to get hold of you? How goes it?"

"How should it go?" I say to him. "I go and I go, and I get nowhere. '*Neither gold nor health nor life itself*,' as the *Torah* says."

"Don't complain, Reb Tevye," he answers me. "Compared with what you were when I first knew you, you're a rich man today."

"May we both have what I still need to make me a rich

man," I say. "But I am satisfied, thank God. '*Abracadabra askakudra,*' as the *Talmud* says."

"You're always there with a line of *Talmud,*" he comes back. "What a lucky man you are, Reb Tevye, to know all these things. But what does all that wisdom and knowledge have to do with us? We have other things to talk about. Sit down, Tevye." He lets out a yell, "Let's have some tea!" And as if by magic the snub-nosed woman appears, snatches the samovar, and is off to the kitchen.

"Now that we are alone," he says to me, "we can talk business. Here is the story. I've been wanting to talk to you for a long time. I tried to reach you through your daughter. How many times have I begged you to come? You understand, I've been casting an eye . . ."

"I know," I say, "that you have been casting an eye on her, but it's no use. Your pains are wasted, Reb Lazer-Wolf. There is no use talking about it."

"Why not?" he asks, with a frightened look.

"Why yes?" says I. "I can wait. I'm in no hurry. My house isn't on fire."

"But why should you wait, if you can arrange it now?"

"Oh, that's not important," I say. "Besides, I feel sorry for the poor thing."

"Look at him," says Lazer-Wolf with a laugh. "He feels sorry for her. . . . If somebody heard you, Reb Tevye, he'd have sworn that she was the only one you had. It seems to me that you have a few more without her."

"Does it bother you if I keep them?" I say. "If anyone is jealous . . ."

"Jealous? Who is talking of jealousy?" he cries. "On the contrary, I know they're superior, and that is exactly why—you understand? And don't forget, Reb Tevye, that you can get something out of it too!"

"Of course . . . I know all a person can get from you. . . . A piece of ice—in winter. We've known that from way back."

"Forget it," he says to me, sweet as sugar. "That was a long time ago. But now—after all—you and I—we're practically in one family, aren't we?"

"Family? What kind of family? What are you talking about, Reb Lazer-Wolf?"

"You tell me, Reb Tevye. I'm beginning to wonder. . . ."

"What are you wondering about? We're talking about my milch cow. The one you want to buy from me."

Lazer-Wolf throws back his head and lets out a roar. "That's a good one!" he howls at me. "A cow! And a milch cow at that!"

"If not the cow," I say, "then what *were* we talking about? You tell me so I can laugh too."

"Why, about your daughter. We were talking about your daughter Tzeitl the whole time. You know, Reb Tevye, that I have been a widower for quite a while now. So I thought, why do I have to go looking all over the world—get mixed up with matchmakers, those sons of Satan? Here we both are. I know you, you know me. It's not like running after a stranger. I see her in my shop every Thursday. She's made a good impression on me. I've talked with her a few times. She looks like a nice, quiet girl. And as for me—as you see for yourself—I'm pretty well off. I have my own house. A couple of stores, some hides in the attic, a little money in the chest. I live pretty well. . . . Look, Tevye, why do we have to do a lot of bargaining, try to impress each other, bluff each other? Listen to me. Let's shake hands on it and call it a match."

Well, when I heard that I just sat and stared. I couldn't say a word. All I could think was: Lazer-Wolf . . . Tzeitl. . . . He had children as old as she was. But then I reminded myself: what a lucky thing for her. She'll have everything she wants. And if he is not so good looking? There were other things besides looks. There was only one thing I really had against him: he could barely read his prayers. But then, can everybody be a scholar? There are plenty of wealthy men in Anatevka, in Mazapevka, and even in Yehupetz who don't know one letter from another. Just the same, if it's their luck to have a little money they get all the respect and honor a man could want. As the saying goes, *"There's learning in a strongbox, and wisdom in a purse. . . ."*

"Well, Reb Tevye," he says. "Why don't you say something?"

"What do you want me to do? Yell out loud?" I ask mildly, as if not wanting to look anxious. "You understand, don't you, that this is something a person has to think over. It's no trifle. She's my eldest child."

"All the better," he says. "Just because she is your eldest . . . That will give you a chance to marry off your second daughter, too, and then, in time with God's help, the third. Don't you see?"

"Amen. The same to you," I tell him. "Marrying them off is no trick at all. Just let the Almighty send each one her predestined husband."

"No," he says. "That isn't what I mean. I mean something altogether different. I mean the dowry. That you won't need for her. And her clothes I'll take care of too. And maybe you'll find something in your own purse besides. . . ."

"Shame on you!" I shout at him. "You're talking just as if you were in the butcher shop. What do you mean—my purse? Shame! My Tzeitl is not the sort that I'd have to sell for money!"

"Just as you say," he answers. "I meant it all for the best. If you don't like it, let's forget it. If you're happy without that, I'm happy too. The main thing is, let's get it done with. And I mean right away. A house must have a mistress. You know what I mean. . . ."

"Just as you say," I agree. "I won't stand in your way. But I have to talk it over with my wife. In affairs like this she has her say. It's no trifle. As Rashi says: '*A mother is not a dust rag.*' Besides, there's Tzeitl herself to be asked. How does the saying go? 'All the kinsmen were brought to the wedding—and the bride was left home. . . .' "

"What foolishness!" says Lazer-Wolf. "Is this something to *ask* her about? *Tell* her, Reb Tevye! Go home. Tell her what is what, and get the wedding canopy ready."

"No, Reb Lazer-Wolf," I say. "That's not the way you treat a young girl."

"All right," he says. "Go home and talk it over. But first, Reb Tevye, let's have a little drink. How about it?"

"Just as you say," I agree. "Why not? How does the saying go? '*Man is human*—and a drink is a drink.' There is," I tell him, "a passage in the *Talmud*. . . ." And I give him a passage. I don't know myself what I said. Something from the *Song of Songs* or the *Hagadah*. . . .

Well, we took a drop or two—as it was ordained. In the meantime the woman had brought in the samovar and we made ourselves a glass or two of punch, had a very good time together, exchanged a few toasts—talked—made plans for the wedding—discussed this and that—and then back to the wedding.

"Do you realize, Reb Lazer-Wolf, what a treasure she is?"

"I know. . . . Believe me, I know. . . . If I didn't I would never have suggested anything. . . ."

And we both go on shouting. I: "A jewel! A diamond! I hope you'll know how to treat her! Not like a butcher . . ."

And he: "Don't worry, Reb Tevye. What she'll eat in my house on weekdays she never had in your house on holidays."

"Tut, tut," I said. "Feeding a woman isn't everything. The richest man in the world doesn't eat five-*ruble* gold pieces, and a pauper doesn't eat stones. You're a coarse fellow, Lazer-Wolf. You don't even know how to value her talents—her baking—her cooking! Ah, Lazer-Wolf! The fish she makes! You'll have to learn to appreciate her!"

And he: "Tevye, pardon me for saying it, but you're somewhat befuddled. You don't know your man. You don't know me at all. . . ."

And I: "Put gold on one scale and Tzeitl on the other. . . . Do you hear, Reb Lazer-Wolf, if you had a million *rubles*, you wouldn't be worth her little finger."

And he again: "'Believe me, Tevye, you're a big fool, even if you are older than I am."

We yelled away at each other that way for a long time, stopping only for a drink or two, and when I came home, it was late at night and my feet felt as if they had been shackled. And my wife, seeing right away that I was tipsy, gave me a proper welcome.

"Sh . . . Golde, control yourself," I say to her cheerfully, almost ready to start dancing. "Don't screech like that, my soul. We have congratulations coming."

"Congratulations? For what? For having sold that poor cow to Lazer-Wolf?"

"Worse than that," I say.

"Traded her for another one? And outsmarted Lazer-Wolf —poor fellow?"

"Still worse."

"Talk sense," she pleads. "Look, I have to haggle with him for every word."

"Congratulations, Golde," I say once more. "Congratulations to both of us. Our Tzeitl is engaged to be married."

"If you talk like that then I know you're drunk," she says. "And not slightly, either. You're out of your head. You must have found a real glassful somewhere."

"Yes. I had a glass of whiskey with Lazer-Wolf, and I had some punch with Lazer-Wolf, but I'm still in my right senses. Lo and behold. Golde darling, our Tzeitl has really and truly and officially become betrothed to Lazer-Wolf himself."

And I tell her the whole story from start to finish, how and what and when and why. Everything we discussed, word for word.

"Do you hear, Tevye," my wife finally says, "my heart told me all along that when Lazer-Wolf wanted to see you it was for something. Only I was afraid to think about it. Maybe nothing would come of it. Oh, dear God, I thank Thee, I thank Thee, Heavenly Father. . . . May it all be for the best. May she grow old with him in riches and honor—not like that first wife of his, Fruma-Sarah, who life with him was none too happy. She was, may she forgive me for saying it, an embittered woman. She couldn't get along with anybody. Not at all like our Tzeitl. . . . Oh, dear God, I thank Thee, dear God . . . Well, Tevye, didn't I tell you, you simpleton. . . . Did you have to worry? If a thing has to happen it will happen. . . ."

"I agree with you," said I. "There is a passage in the *Talmud* that covers that very point. . . ."

"Don't bother me with your passages," she said. "We've got to get ready for the wedding. First of all, make out a list for Lazer-Wolf of all the things Tzeitl will need. She doesn't have a stitch of underwear, not even a pair of stockings. And as for clothes, she'll need a silk dress for the wedding, and a cotton one for summer, a woolen one for winter, and petticoats, and cloaks—she should have at least two—one, a furlined cloak for weekdays and a good one with a ruffle for Saturdays. And how about a pair of button-shoes and a corset, gloves, handkerchiefs, a parasol, and all the other things that a girl nowadays has to have?"

"Where, Golde, darling, did you get acquainted with all these riggings?" I ask her.

"Why not?" says she. "Haven't I ever lived among civilized people? And didn't I see, back in Kasrilevka, how ladies dressed themselves? You let me do all the talking with him myself. Lazer-Wolf is, after all, a man of substance. He won't want everybody in the family to come bothering him. Let's do it properly. If a person has to eat pork, let him eat a bellyful. . . ."

So we talked and we talked till it was beginning to get light. "My wife," I said, "it's time to get the cheese and butter together so I can start for Boiberik. It is all very wonderful indeed, but you still have to work for a living."

And so, when it was still barely light I harnessed my little old horse and went off to Boiberik. When I got to the Boiberik market place—Oho! Can a person ever keep a secret? Everybody knew about it already, and I was congratulated from all sides. "Congratulations, congratulations! Reb Tevye, when does the wedding come off?"

"The same to you, the same to you," I tell them. "It looks as if the saying is right: 'The father isn't born yet and the son is dancing on the rooftops. . . .' "

"Forget about that!" they cry out. "You can't get away with that! What we want is treats. Why, how lucky you are, Reb Tevye! An oil well! A gold mine!"

"The well runs dry," I tell them, "and all that's left is a hole in the ground."

Still, you can't be a hog and leave your friends in the lurch. "As soon as I'm through delivering I'll be back," I tell them. "There'll be drinks and a bite to eat. Let's enjoy ourselves. As the Good Book says, *'Even a beggar can celebrate.'* "

So I got through with my work as fast as I could and joined the crowd in a drink or two. We wished each other good luck as people do, and then I got back into my cart and started for home again, happy as could be. It was a beautiful summer day, the sun was hot, but on both sides of the road there was shade, and the odor of the pines was wonderful. Like a prince I stretched myself out in the wagon and eased up on the reins. "Go along," I said to the little old horse, "go your own way. You ought to know it by now." And myself, I clear my throat and start off on some of the old tunes. I am in holiday mood, and the songs I sing are those of *Rosh Hashono* and *Yom Kippur*. As I sing I look up at the sky but my thoughts are concerned with things below. The heavens are the Lord's but the earth He gave to the Children of Adam, for them to brawl around in, to live in such luxury that they have time to tear each other apart for this little honor or that. . . . They don't even understand how one ought to praise the Lord for the good things that He gives them. . . . But we, the poor people, who do not live in idleness and luxury, give us but one good day and we thank the Lord and praise Him; we say, *"Ohavti,*

I love Him"—the Highest One—*"for He hears my voice and my prayer, He inclines His ear to me . . . For the waves of death compassed me, the floods of Belial assailed me. . . ."* Here a cow falls down and is injured, there an ill wind brings a kinsman of mine, a good-for-nothing, a Menachem-Mendel from Yehupetz who takes away my last penny; and I am sure that the world has come to an end—there is no truth or justice left anywhere on earth. . . . But what does the Lord do? He moves Lazer-Wolf with the idea of taking my daughter Tzeitl without even a dowry. . . . And therefore I give thanks to Thee, dear God, again and again, for having looked upon Tevye and come to his aid. . . . I shall yet have joy. I shall know what it is to visit my child and find her a mistress of a well-stocked home, with chests full of linens, pantries full of chicken fat and preserves, coops full of chickens, geese and ducks. . . .

Suddenly my horse dashes off downhill, and before I can lift my head to look around I find myself on the ground with all my empty pots and crocks and my cart on top of me! With the greatest difficulty I drag myself out from under and pull myself up, bruised and half dead, and I vent my wrath on the poor little horse. "Sink into the earth!" I shout. "Who asked you to show that you know how to run? You almost ruined me altogether, you devil!" And I gave him as much as he could take. You could see that he realized he had gone a little too far. He stood there with his head down, humble, ready to be milked. . . . Still cursing him, I turn the cart upright, gather up my pots, and off I go. A bad omen, I tell myself, and I wonder what new misfortunes might be awaiting me. . . .

That's just how it was. About a mile farther on, when I'm getting close to home, I see someone coming toward me. I drive up closer, look, and see that it's Tzeitl. At the sight of her my heart sinks, I don't know why. I jump down from the wagon.

"Tzeitl, is that you? What are you doing here?"

She falls on my neck with a sob. "My daughter, what are you crying about?" I ask her.

"Oh," she cries, "father, father!" And she is choked with tears.

"What is it, daughter? What's happened to you?" I say, putting my arm around her, patting and kissing her.

"Father, father, have pity on me. Help me. . . ."

"What are you crying for?" I ask, stroking her head. "Little fool, what do you have to cry for? For heaven's sake," I say, "if you say *no* it's *no*. Nobody is going to force you. We meant it for the best, we did it for your own sake. But if it doesn't appeal to you, what are we going to do? Apparently it was not ordained. . . ."

"Oh, thank you, father, thank you," she cries, and falls on my neck again and dissolves in tears.

"Look," I say, "you've cried enough for one day. . . . Even eating pastry becomes tiresome. . . . Climb into the wagon and let's go home. Lord knows what your mother will be thinking."

So we both get into the cart and I try to calm her down. I tell her that we had not meant any harm to her. God knows the truth: all we wanted was to shield our daughter from poverty. "So it was not meant," I said, "that you should have riches, all the comforts of life; or that we should have a little joy in our old age after all our hard work, harnessed, you might say, day and night to a wheelbarrow—no happiness, only poverty and misery and bad luck over and over. . . ."

"Oh, father," she cries, bursting into tears again. "I'll hire myself out as a servant. I'll carry rocks. I'll dig ditches. . . ."

"What are you crying for, silly child?" I say. "Am I forcing you? Am I complaining? It's just that I feel so wretched that I have to get it off my chest; so I talk it over with Him, with the Almighty, about the way He deals with me. He is, I say, a merciful Father, He has pity on me, but He shows me what He can do, too; and what can I say? Maybe it has to be that way. He is high in heaven, high up, and we are here below, sunk in the earth, deep in the earth. So we must say that He is right and His judgment is right; because if we want to look at it the other way round, who am I? A worm that crawls on the face of the earth, whom the slightest breeze—if God only willed it—could annihilate in the blink of an eye. So who am I to stand up against Him with my little brain and give Him advice on how to run this little world of His? Apparently if He ordains it this way, it has to be this way. What good are complaints? Forty days before you were conceived, the Holy Book tells us, an angel appeared and decreed: 'Let Tevye's daughter Tzeitl take Getzel, the son of Zorach, as her husband; and let Lazer-Wolf the Butcher go elsewhere to seek his mate.' And to you, my child, I say this: May God send you your predestined one, one worthy of you, and may he come soon, Amen. And I hope your mother doesn't yell too much. I'll get enough from her as it is."

Well, we came home at last. I unharnessed the little horse and sat down on the grass near the house to think things over, think up some fantastic tale to tell my wife. It was late, the sun was setting; in the distance frogs were croaking; the old horse, tied to a tree, was nibbling at the grass; the cows, just come from pasture, waited in the stalls to be milked. All around me was the heavenly smell of the fresh grass—like the Garden of Eden. I sat there thinking it all over. . . . How cleverly the Eternal One has created this little world of His, so that every living thing, from man to a simple cow, must earn its food. Nothing is free. If you, little cow, wish to eat—then go, let yourself be milked, be the means of livelihood for a man and his wife and children. If you, little horse, wish to chew—then run back and forth every day with the milk to Boiberik. And you, Man, if you want a piece of bread—go labor, milk the cows, carry the pitchers, churn the butter, make the cheese, harness your horse, drag yourself every dawn to the *datchas* of Boiberik, scrape and bow to the rich ones of Yehupetz, smile at them, cater to them, ingratiate yourself with them, see to it that they are satisfied, don't do anything to hurt their pride. . . . Ah, but there still remains the question: '*Mah nishtano?*' Where is it written that Tevye must labor in their behalf, must get up before daybreak when God Himself is still asleep, just so that they can have a fresh piece of cheese, and butter for their breakfast? Where is it written that I must rupture myself for a pot of thin gruel, a loaf of barley bread, while they—the rich ones of Yehupetz—loll around in their summer homes without so much as lifting a hand, and are served roast ducks and the best of *knishes, blintzes* and *vertutin?* Am I not a man as they are? Would it be a sin, for instance, if Tevye could spend one summer himself in a *datcha* somewhere? But then—where would people get cheese and butter? Who would milk the cows? The Yehupetz aristocrats, maybe? And at the very thought of it I burst out laughing. It's like the old saying: "If God listened to every fool what a different world it would be!"

And then I heard someone call out, "Good evening, Reb

Tevye." I looked up and saw a familiar face—Motel Kamzoil, a young tailor from Anatevka.

"Well, well," I say, "you speak of the Messiah and look who's here! Sit down, Motel, on God's green earth. And what brings you here all of a sudden?"

"What brings me here?" he answers. "My two feet."

And he sits down on the grass near me and looks off toward the barn where the girls are moving about with their pots and pitchers. "I have been wanting to come here for a long time, Reb Tevye," he says at last, "only I never seem to have the time. You finish one piece of work and you start the next. I work for myself now, you know, and there is plenty to do, praise the Lord. All of us tailors have as much as we can do right now. It's been a summer of weddings. Everybody is marrying off his children—everybody, even the widow Trihubecha."

"Everybody," I say. "Everybody except Tevye. Maybe I am not worthy in the eyes of the Lord."

"No," he answers quickly, still looking off where the girls are. "You're mistaken, Reb Tevye. If you only wanted to you could marry off one of your children, too. It all depends on you. . . ."

"So?" I ask. "Maybe you have a match for Tzeitl?"

"A perfect fit!" the tailor answers.

"And," I ask, "is it a good match at least?"

"Like a glove!" he cries in his tailor's language, still looking off at the girls.

I ask, "In whose behalf is it then that you come? If he smells of a butcher shop I don't want to hear another word!"

"God forbid!" he says. 'He doesn't begin to smell of a butcher shop!"

"And you really think he's a good match?"

"There never was such a match!" he answers promptly. "There are matches and matches, but this one, I want you to know, was made exactly to measure!"

"And who, may I ask, is the man? Tell me!"

"Who is it?" he says, still looking over yonder. "Who is it? Why, me—myself!"

When he said that I jumped up from the ground as if I had been scalded, and he jumped too, and there we stood facing each other like bristling roosters. "Either you're crazy," I say to him, "or you're simply out of your mind! What are you everything? The matchmaker, the bridegroom, the ushers all rolled into one? I suppose you'll play the wedding march too! I've never heard of such a thing—arranging a match for oneself!"

But he doesn't seem to listen. He goes right on talking. "Anyone who thinks I'm crazy is crazy himself! No, Reb Tevye, I have all my wits about me. A person doesn't have to be crazy in order to want to marry your Tzeitl. For example, the richest man in our town—Lazer-Wolf, the Butcher—wanted her too. Do you think it's a secret? The whole town knows it. And as for being my own matchmaker, I'm surprised at you! After all, Reb Tevye, you're a man of the world. If a person sticks his finger in your mouth you know what to do! So what are we arguing about? Here is the whole story: your daughter Tzeitl and I gave each other our pledge more than a year ago now that we would marry. . . ."

If someone had stuck a knife into my heart it would have been easier to endure than these words. In the first place, how does a stitcher like Motel fit into the picture as my son-in-law? And in the second place, what kind of words are these, "We gave each other our pledge that we would marry"? And where do I come in? . . . I ask him bluntly, "Do I still have the right to say something about my daughter, or doesn't anyone have to ask a father any more?"

"On the contrary," says Motel, "that's exactly why I came to talk with you. I heard that Lazer-Wolf has been discussing a match, and I have loved her now for over a year. More than once I have wanted to come and talk it over with you, but every time I put it off a little. First till I had saved up a few *rubles* for a sewing machine, and then till I got some decent clothes. Nowadays almost everybody has to have two suits and a few good shirts. . . ."

"You and your shirts!" I yell at him. "What childish nonsense is this? And what do you intend to do after you're married? Support your wife with shirts?"

"Why," he says, "why, I'm surprised at you, Reb Tevye! From what I hear, when you got married you didn't have your own brick mansion either, and nevertheless here you are. . . . In any case, if the whole world gets along, I'll get along, too. Besides, I have a trade, haven't I?"

To make a long story short, he talked me into it. For after all—why should we fool ourselves?—how do all Jewish children get married? If we began to be too particular, then no one in our class would ever get married at all. . . . There was only one thing still bothering me, and that I still couldn't understand. What did they mean—pledging their troth? What kind of world has this become? A boy meets a girl and says to her, "Let us pledge our troth." Why, it's just too free-and-easy, that's all!

But when I looked at this Motel standing there with his head bent like a sinner, I saw that he was not trying to get the best of anybody, and I thought: "Now, what am I becoming so alarmed about? What am I putting on such airs for? What is my own pedigree? Reb Tzotzel's grandchild! And what huge dowry can I give my daughter—and what fine clothes? So maybe Motel Kamzoil is only a tailor, but at the same time he is a good man, a worker; he'll be able to make a living. And besides, he's honest too. So what have I got against him?

"Tevye," I said to myself, "don't think up any childish arguments. Let them have their way." Yes . . . but what am I going to do about my Golde? I'll have plenty on my hands there. She'll be hard to handle. How can I make her think it's all right? . . .

"You know what, Motel," I said to the young suitor, "You go home. I'll straighten everything out here. I'll talk it over with this one and that one. Everything has to be done right. And tomorrow morning, if you haven't changed your mind by that time, maybe we'll see each other."

"Change my mind!" he yells at me. "You expect me to change my mind? If I do, I hope I never live to go away from here! May I become a stone, a bone, right here in front of you!"

"What's the use of swearing?" I ask him. "I believe you without the oath. Go along, Motel. Good night. And may you have pleasant dreams."

And I myself go to bed, too. But I can't sleep. My head is splitting. I think of one plan and then another, till at last I come upon the right one. And what is that? Listen, I'll tell you. . . .

It's past midnight. All over the house we're sound asleep. This one is snoring, that one is whistling. And suddenly I sit up and let out a horrible yell, as loud as I can: "Help! Help!

Help!" It stands to reason that when I let out this yell everybody wakes up, and first of all—Golde.

"May God be with you, Tevye," she gasps, and shakes me. "Wake up! What's the matter with you? What are you howling like this for?"

I open my eyes, look around to see where I am, and call out in terror, "Where is she? Where is she?"

"Where is who?" asks Golde. "What are you talking about?"

I can hardly answer. "Fruma-Sarah. Fruma-Sarah, Lazer-Wolf's first wife . . . She was standing here a minute ago."

"You're out of your head," my wife says to me. "May God save you, Tevye. Do you know how long Fruma-Sarah has been dead?"

"I know that she's dead," I say, "but just the same she was here just a minute ago, right here by the bed, talking to me. Then she grabbed me by the windpipe and started to choke me. . . ."

"What on earth is the matter with you, Tevye?" says my wife. "What are you babbling about? You must have been dreaming. Spit three times and tell me what you dreamt, and I'll tell you what it meant."

"Long may you live, Golde," I tell her. "It's lucky you woke me up or I'd have died of fright right on the spot. Get me a drink of water and I'll tell you my dream. Only I beg you, Golde, don't become frightened: the Holy Books tell us that sometimes only three parts of a dream come true, and the rest means nothing. Absolutely nothing. Well, here is my dream. . . .

"In the beginning I dreamt that we were having a celebration of some kind, I don't know what. Either an engagement or a wedding. The house was crowded. All the men and women we knew were there—the *rov* and the *shochet* and everybody. And musicians, too. . . . In the midst of the celebration the door opens, and in comes your grandmother Tzeitl, may her soul rest in peace. . . ."

"Grandmother Tzeitl!" my wife shouts, turning pale as a sheet. "How did she look? How was she dressed?"

"How did she look?" I say. "May our enemies look the way she looked. Yellow. A waxen yellow. And she was dressed —how do you expect?—in white. A shroud. She came up to me. 'Congratulations,' she said, 'I am so happy that you picked such a fine young man for your Tzeitl who bears my name.

He's a fine, upstanding lad—this Motel Kamzoil. . . . He was named after my uncle Mordecai, and even if he is a tailor he's still an honest boy. . . .' "

"A tailor!" gasps Golde. "Where does a tailor come into our family? In our family we have had teachers, cantors, *shamosim,* undertakers' assistants, and other kinds of poor people. But a tailor—never!"

"Don't interrupt me, Golde," I tell her. "Maybe your grandmother Tzeitl knows better. . . . When I heard her congratulate me like that, I said to her, 'What is that you said, Grandmother? About Tzeitl's betrothed being a tailor? Did you say Motel? . . . You mean a butcher, don't you? A butcher named Lazer-Wolf?'

" 'No,' says your grandmother again. 'No, Tevye. Your daughter is engaged to Motel, and he's a tailor, and she'll grow old with him—if the Lord wills—in comfort and honor.'

" 'But Grandmother,' I say again, 'what can we do about Lazer-Wolf? Just yesterday I gave him my word. . . .'

"I had barely finished saying this when I looked up, and your grandmother Tzeitl is gone. In her place is Fruma-Sarah—Lazer-Wolf's first wife—and this is what she says: 'Reb Tevye, I have always considered you an honest man, a man of learning and virtue. But how does it happen that you should do a thing like this—let your daughter take my place, live in my house, carry my keys, wear my clothes, my jewelry, my pearls?'

" 'Is it my fault,' I ask her, 'if Lazer-Wolf wanted it that way?'

" 'Lazer-Wolf!' she cries. 'Lazer-Wolf will have a terrible fate, and your Tzeitl too, if she marries him. It's a pity, Reb Tevye. I feel sorry for your daughter. She'll live with him no more than three weeks, and when the three weeks are up I'll come to her by night and I'll take her by the throat like this. . . .' And with these words Fruma-Sarah grabs me by the windpipe and begins choking me—so hard that if you hadn't waked me up, by now I'd have been—far, far away. . . ."

"Ptu, ptu, ptu," spits my wife three times. "It's an evil spirit! May it fall into the river; may it sink into the earth; may it climb into attics; may it lie in the forest—but may it never harm us or our children! May that butcher have a dream like that! A dark and horrible dream! Motel Kamzoil's smallest finger is worth more than all of him, even if Motel is only a tailor; for if he was named after my uncle Mordecai he couldn't possibly have been a tailor by birth. And if my grandmother—may she rest in peace—took the trouble to come all the way from the other world to congratulate us, why, all we can do is say that this is all for the best and it couldn't possibly be any better. Amen. Selah. . . ."

Well, why should I go on and on?

The next day they were engaged, and not long after were married. And the two of them, praise the Lord, are happy. He does his own tailoring, goes around in Boiberik from one *datcha* to another picking up work; and she is busy day and night, cooking and baking and washing and tidying and bringing water from the well. . . . They barely make enough for food. If I didn't bring her some of our cheese and butter once in a while—or a few *groschen* sometimes—they would never be able to get by. But if you ask her—my Tzeitl, I mean—she says everything is as good as it could be. Just let Motel stay in good health.

So go complain about modern children. You slave for them, do everything for them! And they tell you that they know better.

And . . . maybe they do. . . .

Another Page from the Song of Songs

"FASTER, Buzie, faster," I tell Buzie and take her hand in mine and together we race up the hill. It is the day before *Shevuos* and we are setting out to pick greens. "We haven't all day," I tell her. "We have a big mountain to climb and after the mountain there is a river. Over the river there is a trestle made of boards, that's the 'bridge.' The water runs under the bridge, the frogs croak, the boards creak and shake—and there, over there on the other side of the bridge, that's where the real Garden of Eden is, Buzie. That's where my Estates begin."

"Your Estates?"

"I mean the big meadow. It's a great field that stretches far and wide without any end. It has a green blanket over it, sprinkled with yellow dots and covered with tiny red shoots. Wait till you smell it. It has the most wonderful smells in the world. And wait till you see my trees. I have many, many trees—tall, spreading trees. And I have a little hill all my own to sit on. I can sit on top of my hill, or I can say the Magic Word and fly off like an eagle straight above the clouds. I can fly over forest and field, over sea and desert, till I come to the other side of the mountain of darkness."

"And from there," Buzie interrupts me, "you walk seven miles on foot until you come to a lake."

"No, to a deep wood. First I walk through this wood, then through another wood, then I come to the lake."

"And you swim across the lake and count seven times seven."

"And there springs up in front of me a tiny gnome with a long beard."

"And he asks you, 'What is your heart's desire?' "

"And I tell him, 'Lead me to the Queen's daughter.' "

Buzie snatches her hand out of mine and starts running

downhill. I run after her. "Buzie, why are you running away?"

Buzie does not answer. I've offended her. She doesn't like to have me talk about the Queen's daughter. She likes all my stories except the one about the Queen's daughter.

You probably remember who Buzie is. I have told you about her once before. But in case you've forgotten I shall tell you again.

I had an older brother named Benny who was drowned. He left behind him a mill, a young widow, two horses and a child. The mill was abandoned. The horses were sold. The widow remarried and moved to some distant place and the child was brought to us. That child was Buzie.

Do you want to hear something funny? Everybody thinks that Buzie and I are sister and brother. She calls my father "Father" and my mother "Mother." We live together just like sister and brother and love each other just like a sister and a brother.

Like a sister and a brother? Then why is Buzie so shy with me? Why does she act so strange sometimes?

Let me tell you something that happened once. We had been left alone, she and I, all by ourselves in the house. My father had gone to the Synagogue to say *kaddish* for my brother Benny, and my mother had gone out to buy matches. Buzie and I sat huddled together in a corner and I was telling her stories. Buzie loves to hear me tell stories, stories from *cheder* or else fairy tales I make up for her. She moved quite close to me. Her hand was clasped in mine.

"Go on, Shimek. Go on, tell me more."

Silently, night descends. Slowly the shadows cover the walls, quiver in the half-light, then creep to the ground and melt. We can barely make each other out. I can only feel her little hand trembling in mine. I can hear her heart beating and see her eyes gleaming in the dark.

Suddenly she snatches her hand away. "What is it?" I ask, surprised.

"We mustn't do it," she says.

"Mustn't do what?"

"Hold hands like this."

"Why not? Who told you we mustn't?"

"Nobody. I know it myself."

"But we aren't strangers. Aren't we brother and sister?"

"If we were only brother and sister," says Buzie softly, and it seems to me that she is speaking in the words of the *Song of Songs: "O that thou wert as my brother . . ."*

It is always like this. Whenever I speak of Buzie, I think of the *Song of Songs. . . .*

Where were we? It is the day before *Shevuos.* We are running down the hill. Buzie runs ahead and I run after her. Buzie is offended because of the Queen's daughter. She likes all my stories except the one about the Queen's daughter. But Buzie can't hold a grudge very long. She has forgotten about it in less time than it takes me to tell it. She is looking at me once more with her big lovely eyes. She tosses her hair back and calls out to me, "Shimek! Look, Shimek, can you see what I see?"

"Of course I see, silly. Why shouldn't I see? I can see the blue sky, I can feel the warm breeze. I can hear the birds chirping and see them sailing over our heads. It is our sky, our breeze, our birds. Everything is ours, ours, ours. Give me your hand, Buzie."

"No," she says. She won't give me her hand. She is suddenly shy. Why should Buzie be shy with me? Why should she blush?

"Over there," calls Buzie, running ahead. "Over there, on the other side of the bridge." And it seems to me that she speaks in the words of the Shulamite. *"Come, my beloved, let us go forth into the fields. Let us lodge in the villages. Let us get up early to the vineyards. Let us see whether the vine has budded, whether the vine blossom be opened."*

And here we are, at the bridge.

The river runs under the bridge, the frogs croak, the boards creak and shake, and Buzie trembles. "Oh, Buzie, you are . . . What are you afraid of, silly? Hold on to me or, better still, let me put my arm around you and you put your arm around me. See? Like this."

We have crossed the bridge.

And now we walk ahead, still with our arms tightly around each other, she and I, all by ourselves in the holy stillness of the first morning of Creation. Buzie holds on tightly to me, very tightly. She is silent, but it seems to me that she is speaking in the words of the *Song of Songs: "I am my beloved's and my beloved is mine."*

The meadow stretches far and wide without end. It is like a green blanket sprinkled with yellow dots, covered with red shoots. And the smells that rise from it—they are the most wonderful smells in the world. We walk along, the two of us, arm in arm, over the Garden of Eden, in the morning of the world.

"Shimek," says Buzie, looking into my eyes and moving closer to me, "when are we going to start picking greens for *Shevuos*?"

"The day is long, silly," I tell her. I am burning with excitement. I don't know where to look first, whether up at the blue cup of the sky, or down at the green blanket of the fields. Or over there, toward the end of the world, where the sky melts into the earth. Or should I look into Buzie's lovely face? Into her big thoughtful eyes, as deep as the sky, as pensive as the night? Her eyes are always pensive, always troubled. A deep sorrow lies hidden in them. I am familiar with her sorrow, I know what is troubling her. She grieves for her mother who married a stranger and went off far away, never to return.

At our house, Buzie's mother is never mentioned. It's as though Buzie never had a mother. My parents have become her parents. They love her as though she were their own child; they watch over her anxiously, let her have anything her heart desires. This morning Buzie said she wanted to go with me to pick greens for *Shevuos* (I had put her up to it). At once my father turned to my mother. "What do you think?" As he spoke, he looked at her over the tops of his silver-rimmed spectacles and with his fingers he combed the silver strands of his beard. A conversation took place between my father and mother that went something like this:

Father: What do you say?
Mother: What do *you* say?
Father: Should we let them go?
Mother: Why shouldn't we let them go?
Father: Am I saying no?
Mother: What are you saying then?
Father: I'm only saying, should they go?
Mother: Why shouldn't they go?

And so on. I know on which foot the shoe pinches. My father has told me twenty times over, and after him my mother has warned me that over there is a bridge and under the bridge there is water. A river . . . a river . . . a river . . .

Buzie and I have long ago forgotten the bridge and the river. We are wandering over the wide, open field, under the wide, open sky. We run and we fall down and roll over and over in the sweet-smelling grass. Then we get up and run, and fall down again. We haven't even started to pick greens for *Shevuos*. I lead Buzie over the broad meadow and boast to her about my possessions.

"Do you see these trees? Do you see the sand? Do you see this hill?"

"And is all of it yours?"

Buzie looks at me as she says this and her eyes laugh at me. She is always laughing at me. I can't bear to have her laughing at me. I sulk and turn away from her. Buzie sees that I am offended. She runs in front of me, looks into my eyes earnestly, takes my hand and says, "Shimek." My anger disappears and I feel good again. I take her hand and lead her to my little hill, the little hill on which I sit every year. If I want to I can sit on my hill and look over my Estates. Or else I can utter the Magic Word and be borne aloft like an eagle. I can fly above the clouds, over forest and field, over sea and desert. . . .

We sit on my hill (we still haven't picked any greens for *Shevuos)* and tell stories, that is I tell stories and Buzie listens. I tell her about how it is going to be some far-off day when we are both grown up and marry each other. We will rise up by magic and fly above the clouds, and travel over the whole world. First we will travel over the countries that Alexander of Macedonia had traveled over. Then we will take a trip to the Holy Land. There we will visit all the mountains and the vineyards, and we will fill our pockets with figs and dates and olives. Then we will get up and fly further. And everywhere we go we will play different tricks on people, because no one will be able to see us.

"No one will see us?" asks Buzie, and catches me by the hand.

"No one, no one at all. We will be able to see everybody and nobody will be able to see us."

"If so, Shimek, I want to ask a favor of you."

"A favor?"

"A tiny favor."

I know beforehand what this favor is. She wants us to fly

over there where her mother is living with her new husband. She wants me to play a trick on her stepfather.

"Why not?" I tell her. "With the greatest pleasure. You can depend on me. I will play them a trick that they will remember me by."

"Not them, just him, just him," Buzie pleads with me. But I don't consent right away. When someone has made me angry, I am terrible in my wrath. How can I forgive her so easily? The insolence of a woman—marrying a perfect stranger and going off somewhere, the devil knows where, and deserting her own child, never even writing her a letter. . . . Whoever heard of such an outrage?

I got all wrought up for nothing and now I am sorry. But it's too late. Buzie has covered her face with her hands. Is she weeping? I would gladly tear myself into little pieces for making her weep. Why did I have to wound her tenderest feelings so? In my own mind I call myself all sorts of harsh names: "You ox, you ass, you idiot, you blabber-mouth." I come close to her, take her hand in mine. "Buzie. Buzie!" I want to speak to her in the words of the *Song of Songs: "Let me see thy countenance. Let me hear thy voice."*

Suddenly I look up. Where did my father and mother come from? My father's silver-rimmed spectacles gleam at a distance. The silver strands of his beard are whipped by the breeze. My mother beckons to us from afar, waving her shawl. Buzie and I sit there as though we were turned to clay. What can our parents be doing here?

They have come to see where we are. They want to make sure that no harm has come to us. Who can tell—a bridge, a river . . . a river . . .

What queer people our parents are.

"And where are the greens?" they ask.

"The greens?"

"Yes, the greens you were going to pick for *Shevuos*."

Buzie and I look at each other. I understand the look in her eyes. It seems to me that she is saying, "*O that thou wert as my brother.*"

"Well, as for the greens, I am sure we will find some," says my father, smiling, and the silver strands of his beard shine in the rays of the noonday sun. "God be thanked that the children are well and that no harm has come to them."

"God be thanked," echoes my mother, wiping her red perspiring face with her shawl. They both look at us tenderly, beaming with unconcealed pride. . . .

What queer, queer people our parents are. . . .

Hodel

YOU LOOK, Mr. Sholom Aleichem, as though you were surprised that you hadn't seen me for such a long time. . . . You're thinking that Tevye has aged all at once, his hair has turned gray. . . .

Ah, well, if you only knew the troubles and heartaches he has endured of late! How is it written in our Holy Books? "*Man comes from dust, and to dust he returns.*—Man is weaker than a fly, and stronger than iron." Whatever plague there is, whatever trouble, whatever misfortune—it never misses me. Why does it happen that way? Maybe because I am a simple soul who believes everything that everyone says. Tevye forgets that our wise men have told us a thousand times: "Beware of dogs. . . ."

But I ask you, what can I do if that's my nature? I am, as you know, a trusting person, and I never question God's ways. Whatever He ordains is good. Besides, if you do complain, will it do you any good? That's what I always tell my wife. "Golde," I say, "you're sinning. We have a *medresh*. . . ."

"What do I care about a *medresh*?" she says. "We have a daughter to marry off. And after her are two more almost ready. And after these two—three more—may the Evil Eye spare them!"

"Tut," I say. "What's that? Don't you know, Golde, that our sages have thought of that also? There is a *medresh* for that, too. . . ."

But she doesn't let me finish. "Daughters to be married off," she says, "are a stiff *medresh* in themselves."

So try to explain something to a woman!

Where does that leave us? Oh, yes, with a houseful of daughters, bless the Lord. Each one prettier than the next. It may not be proper for me to praise my own children, but I can't help hearing what the whole world calls them, can I? Beauties, every one of them! And especially Hodel, the one that comes after Tzeitl who, you remember, fell in love with the tailor. And is this Hodel beautiful. . . . How can I describe her to you? Like Esther in the Bible, *"of beautiful form and fair to look upon."* And as if that weren't bad enough, she has to have brains, too. She can write and she can read—Yiddish and Russian both. And books—she swallows like dumplings. You may be wondering how a daughter of Tevye happens to be reading books, when her father deals in butter and cheese? That's what I'd like to know myself. . . .

But that's the way it is these days. Look at these lads who haven't got a pair of pants to their name, and still they want to study! Ask them, "What are you studying? Why are you studying?" They can't tell you. It's their nature, just as it's a goat's nature to jump into gardens. Especially since they aren't even allowed in the schools. "Keep off the grass!" read all the signs as far as they're concerned. And yet you ought to see how they go after it! And who are they? Workers' children. Tailors' and cobblers', so help me God! They go away to Yehupetz or to Odessa, sleep in garrets, eat what Pharaoh ate during the plagues—frogs and vermin—and for months on end do not see a piece of meat before their eyes. Six of them can make a banquet on a loaf of bread and a herring. Eat, drink and be merry! That's the life!

Well, so one of that band had to lose himself in our corner of the world. I used to know his father—he was a cigarette-maker, and as poor as a man could be. But that is nothing against the young fellow. For if Rabbi Jochanan wasn't too proud to mend boots, what is wrong with having a father who makes cigarettes? There is only one thing I can't understand: why should a pauper like that be so anxious to study? True, to give the devil his due, the boy has a good head on his shoulders, an excellent head. Pertschik, his name was, but we called him "Feferel"—"Peppercorn." And he looked like a peppercorn, little, dark, dried up and homely, but full of confidence and with a quick, sharp tongue.

Well, one day I was driving home from Boiberik where I had got rid of my load of milk and butter and cheese, and as usual I sat lost in thought, dreaming of many things, of this and that, and of the rich people of Yehupetz who had everything their own way while Tevye, the *shlimazl,* and his wretched little horse slaved and hungered all their days. It was summer, the sun was hot, the flies were biting, on all sides the world stretched endlessly. I felt like spreading out my arms and flying!

I lift up my eyes, and there on the road ahead of me I see a young man trudging along with a package under his arm, sweating and panting. "'*Rise, O Yokel the son of Flekel,*' as we say in the synagogue," I called out to him. "Climb into my wagon and I'll give you a ride. I have plenty of room. How is it written? '*If you see the ass of him that hateth thee lying under its burden, thou shalt forbear to pass it by.*' Then how about a human being?"

At this the *shlimazl* laughs, and climbs into the wagon.

"Where might the young gentleman be coming from?" I ask.

"From Yehupetz."

"And what might a young gentleman like you be doing in Yehupetz?" I ask.

"A young gentleman like me is getting ready for his examinations."

"And what might a young gentleman like you be studying?"

"I only wish I knew!"

"Then why does a young gentleman like you bother his head for nothing?"

"Don't worry, Reb Tevye. A young gentleman like me knows what he's doing."

"So—if you know who *I* am, tell me who *you* are!"

"Who am I? I'm a man."

"I can see that you're not a horse. I mean, as we Jews say, *whose* are you?"

"Whose should I be but God's?"

"I know that you're God's. It is written: '*All living things are His.*' I mean, whom are you descended from? Are you from around here, or from Lithuania?"

"I am *descended,*" he says, "from Adam, our father. I *come* from right around here. You know who we are."

"Well then, who is your father? Come, tell me."

"My father," he says, "was called Pertschik."

I spat with disgust. "Did you have to torture me like this all that time? Then you must be Pertschik the Cigarette-maker's son."

"Yes, that's who I am. Pertschik the Cigarette-maker's son."

"And you go to the university?"

"Yes—the university."

"Well," I said, "I'm glad to hear it. Man and fish and fowl —you're all trying to better yourselves! But tell me, my lad, what do you live on, for instance?"

"I live on what I eat."

"That's good," I say. "And what do you eat?"

"I eat anything I can get."

"I understand," I say. "You're not particular. If there is something to eat, you eat. If not, you bite your lip and go to bed hungry. But it's all worth while as long as you can attend the university. You're comparing yourself to those rich people of Yehupetz. . . ."

At these words Pertschik bursts out, "Don't you dare compare me to them! They can go to hell as far as I care!"

"You seem to be somewhat prejudiced against the rich," I say. "Did they divide your father's inheritance among themselves?"

"Let me tell you," says he, "it may well be that you and I and all the rest of us have no small share in *their* inheritance."

"Listen to me," I answer. "Let your enemies talk like that. But one thing I can see: you're not a bashful lad. You know what a tongue is for. If you have the time, stop at my house tonight and we'll talk a little more. And if you come early, you can have supper with us, too."

Our young friend didn't have to be asked twice. He arrived at the right moment—when the *borsht* was on the table and the *knishes* were baking in the oven. "Just in time!" I said. "Sit down. You can say grace or not, just as you please. I'm not God's watchman; I won't be punished for your sins." And as I talk to him I feel myself drawn to the fellow somehow; I don't know why. Maybe it's because I like a person one can talk to, a person who can understand a quotation and follow an argument about philosophy or this or that or something else. . . . That's the kind of person I am.

And from that evening on our young friend began coming to our house almost every day. He had a few private students and when he was through giving his lessons he'd come to our house to rest up and visit for a while. What the poor fellow got for his lessons you can imagine for yourself, if I tell you that the very richest people used to pay their tutors three *rubles* a month; and besides their regular duties they were expected to read telegrams for them, write out addresses, and even run errands at times. Why not? As the passage says, "*If you eat bread you have to earn it."* It was lucky for him that most of the time he used to eat with us. For this he used to give my daughters lessons, too. One good turn deserves another. And in this way he became almost a member of the family. The girls saw to it that he had enough to eat and my wife kept his shirts clean and his socks mended. And it was at this time that we changed his Russian name of Pertschik to Feferel. And it can truthfully be said that we all came to love him as though he were one of us, for by nature he was a likable young man, simple, straightforward, generous. Whatever he had he shared with us.

There was only one thing I didn't like about him, and that was the way he had of suddenly disappearing. Without warning he would get up and go off; we looked around, and there was no Feferel. When he came back I would ask, "Where were you, my fine-feathered friend?" And he wouldn't say a word. I don't know how you are, but as for me, I dislike a person with secrets. I like a person to be willing to tell what he's been up to. But you can say this for him: when he did start talking, you couldn't stop him. He poured out everything. What a tongue he had! *"Against the Lord and against His anointed; let us break their bands asunder."* And the main thing was to break the bands. . . . He had the wildest notions, the most peculiar ideas. Everything was upside down, topsy-turvy. For instance, according to his way of thinking, a poor man was far more important than a rich one, and if he happened to be a worker too, then he was really the brightest jewel in the diadem! He who toiled with his hands stood first in his estimation.

"That's good," I say, "but will that get you any money?"

At this he becomes very angry and tries to tell me that money is the root of all evil. Money, he says, is the source of all falsehood, and as long as money amounts to something, nothing will ever be done in this world in the spirit of justice. And he gives me thousands of examples and illustrations that make no sense whatever.

"According to your crazy notions," I tell him, "there is no justice in the fact that my cow gives milk and my horse draws a load." I didn't let him get away with anything. That's the kind of man Tevye is. . . .

But my Feferel can argue too. And how he can argue! If there is something on his mind, he comes right out with it.

One evening we were sitting on my stoop talking things over —discussing philosophic matters—when he suddenly said, "Do you know, Reb Tevye, you have very fine daughters."

"Is that so?" said I. "Thanks for telling me. After all, they have someone to take after."

"The oldest one especially is a very bright girl," said he. "She's all there!"

"I know without your telling me," said I. "The apple never falls very far from the tree."

And I glowed with pride. What father isn't happy when his children are praised? How should I have known that from such an innocent remark would grow such fiery love?

Well, one summer twilight I was driving through Boiberik, going from *datcha* to *datcha* with my goods, when someone stopped me. I looked up and saw that it was Ephraim the Matchmaker. And Ephraim, like all matchmakers, was concerned with only one thing—arranging marriages. So when he sees me here in Boiberik he stops me and says, "Excuse me, Reb Tevye, I'd like to tell you something."

"Go ahead," I say, stopping my horse, "as long as it's good news."

"You have," says he, "a daughter."

"I have," I answer, "seven daughters."

"I know," says he. "I have seven, too."

"Then together," I tell him, "we have fourteen."

"But joking aside," he says, "here is what I have to tell you. As you know, I am a matchmaker; and I have a young man for you to consider, the very best there is, a regular prince. There's not another like him anywhere."

"Well," I say, "that sounds good enough to me. But what do you consider a prince? If he's a tailor or a shoemaker or a teacher, you can keep him. I'll find my equal or I won't have anything. As the *medresh* says . . ."

"Ah, Reb Tevye," says he, "you're beginning with your quotations already! If a person wants to talk to you he has to study up first. . . . But better listen to the sort of match Ephraim has to offer you. Just listen and be quiet."

And then he begins to rattle off all his client's virtues. And it really sounds like something. . . . First of all, he comes from a very fine family. And that is very important to me, for I am not just a nobody either. In our family you will find all sorts of people, spotted, striped and speckled, as the Bible says.

There are plain, ordinary people, there are workers, and there are property owners. . . . Secondly, he is a learned man who can read small print as well as large; he knows all the Commentaries by heart. And that is certainly not a small thing, either, for an ignorant man I hate even worse than pork itself. To me an unlettered man is worse—a thousand times worse—than a hoodlum. You can go around bareheaded, you can even walk on your head if you like, but if you know what Rashi and the others have said, you are a man after my own heart. . . . And on top of everything, Ephraim tells me, this man of his is rich as can be. He has his own carriage drawn by two horses so spirited that you can see a vapor rising from them. And that I don't object to, either. Better a rich man than a poor one! God Himself must hate a poor man, for if He did not, would He have made him poor?

"Well," I ask, "what more do you have to say?"

"What more can I say? He wants me to arrange a match with you. He is dying, he's so eager. Not for you, naturally, but for your daughter. He wants a pretty girl."

"He is dying?" I say. "Then let him keep dying. . . . And who is this treasure of yours? What is he? A bachelor? A widower? Is he divorced? What's wrong with him?"

"He is a bachelor," says Ephraim. "Not so young any more, but he's never been married."

"And what is his name, may I ask?"

But this he wouldn't tell me. "Bring the girl to Boiberik," he says, "and then I'll tell you."

"Bring her?" says I. "That's the way one talks about a horse or a cow that's being brought to market. Not a girl!"

Well, you know what these matchmakers are. They can talk a stone wall into moving. So we agreed that early next week I would bring my daughter to Boiberik. And driving home, all sorts of wonderful thoughts came to me, and I imagined my Hodel riding in a carriage drawn by spirited horses. The whole world envied me, not so much for the carriage and horses as for the good deeds I accomplished through my wealthy daughter. I helped the needy with money—let this one have twenty-five *rubles*, that one fifty, another a hundred. How do we say it? "Other people have to live too. . . ." That's what I think to myself as I ride home in the evening, and I whip my horse and talk to him in his own language.

"Hurry, my little horse," I say, "move your legs a little faster and you'll get your oats that much sooner. As the Bible says, *'If you don't work, you don't eat. . . .'* "

Suddenly I see two people coming out of the woods—a man and a woman. Their heads are close together and they are whispering to each other. Who could they be, I wonder, and I look at them through the dazzling rays of the setting sun. I could swear the man was Feferel. But whom was he walking with so late in the day? I put my hand up and shield my eyes and look closely. Who was the damsel? Could it be Hodel? Yes, that's who it was! Hodel! So? So that's how they'd been studying their grammar and reading their books together? Oh, Tevye, what a fool you are. . . .

I stop the horse and call out: "Good evening! And what's the latest news of the war? How do you happen to be out here this time of the day? What are you looking for—the day before yesterday?"

At this the couple stops, not knowing what to do or say. They stand there, awkward and blushing, with their eyes lowered. Then they look up at me, I look at them, and they look at each other. . . .

"Well," I say, "you look as if you hadn't seen me in a long time. I am the same Tevye as ever, I haven't changed by a hair."

I speak to them half angrily, half jokingly. Then my daughter, blushing harder than ever, speaks up: "Father, you can congratulate us."

"Congratulate you?" I say. "What's happened? Did you find a treasure buried in the woods? Or were you just saved from some terrible danger?"

"Congratulate us," says Feferel this time. "We're engaged."

"What do you mean—engaged?"

"Don't you know what engaged means?" says Feferel, looking me straight in the eye. "It means that I'm going to marry her and she's going to marry me."

I look him back in the eye and say, "When was the contract signed? And why didn't you invite me to the ceremony? Don't you think I have a slight interest in the matter?" I joke with them and yet my heart is breaking. But Tevye is not a weakling. He wants to hear everything out. "Getting married," I say, "without matchmakers, without an engagement feast?"

"What do we need matchmakers for?" says Feferel. "We arranged it between ourselves."

"So?" I say. "That's one of God's wonders! But why were you so silent about it?"

"What was there to shout about?" says he. "We wouldn't have told you now, either, but since we have to part soon, we decided to have the wedding first."

This really hurt. How do they say it? It hurt to the quick. Becoming engaged without my knowledge—that was bad enough, but I could stand it. He loves her; she loves him—that I'm glad to hear. But getting married? That was too much for me. . . .

The young man seemed to realize that I wasn't too well pleased with the news. "You see, Reb Tevye," he offered, "this is the reason: I am about to go away."

"When are you going?"

"Very soon."

"And where are you going?"

"That I can't tell you. It's a secret."

What do you think of that? A secret! A young man named Feferel comes into our lives—small, dark, homely, disguises himself as a bridegroom, wants to marry my daughter and then leave her—and he won't even say where he's going! Isn't that enough to drive you crazy?

"All right," I say. "A secret is a secret. Everything you do seems to be a secret. But explain this to me, my friend. You are a man of such—what do you call it?—integrity; you wallow in justice. So tell me, how does it happen that you suddenly marry Tevye's daughter and then leave her? Is that integrity? Is that justice? It's lucky that you didn't decide to rob me or burn my house down!"

"Father," says Hodel, "you don't know how happy we are now that we've told you our secret. It's like a weight off our chests. Come, father, kiss me."

And they both grab hold of me, she on one side, he on the other, and they begin to kiss and embrace me, and I to kiss them in return. And in their great excitement they begin to kiss each other. It was like going to a play. "Well," I say at last, "maybe you've done enough kissing already? It's time to talk about practical things."

"What, for instance?" they ask.

"For instance," I say, "the dowry, clothes, wedding expenses, this, that and the other. . . ."

"We don't need a thing," they tell me. "We don't need anything. No this, no that, no other."

"Well then, what do you need?" I ask.

"Only the wedding ceremony," they tell me.

What do you think of that! . . . Well, to make a long story short, nothing I said did any good. They went ahead and had their wedding, if you want to call it a wedding. Naturally it wasn't the sort that I would have liked. A quiet little wedding—no fun at all. And besides there was a wife I had to do something about. She kept plaguing me: what were they in such a hurry about? Go try to explain their haste to a woman. But don't worry. I invented a story—"*great, powerful and marvelous,*" as the Bible says—about a rich aunt in Yehupetz, an inheritance, all sorts of foolishness.

And a couple of hours after this wonderful wedding I hitched up my horse and wagon and the three of us got in, that is, my daughter, my son-in-law and I, and off we went to the station at Boiberik. Sitting in the wagon, I steal a look at the young couple, and I think to myself: what a great and powerful Lord we have and how cleverly He rules the world. What strange and fantastic beings He has created. Here you have a new young couple, just hatched; he is going off, the Good Lord alone knows where, and is leaving her behind—and do you see either one of them shed a tear, even for appearance's sake? But never mind—Tevye is not a curious old woman. He can wait. He can watch and see. . . .

At the station I see a couple of young fellows, shabbily dressed, down-at-the-heels, coming to see my happy bridegroom off. One of them is dressed like a peasant with his blouse worn like a smock over his trousers. The two whisper together mysteriously for several minutes. "Look out, Tevye," I say to myself. "You have fallen among a band of horse thieves, pickpockets, housebreakers or counterfeiters."

Coming home from Boiberik I can't keep still any longer and tell Hodel what I suspect. She bursts out laughing and tries to assure me that they were very honest young men, honorable men, whose whole life was devoted to the welfare of humanity; their own private welfare meant nothing to them. For instance, the one with his blouse over his trousers was a rich man's son. He had left his parents in Yehupetz and wouldn't take a penny from them.

"Oh," said I, "that's just wonderful. An excellent young man! All he needs, now that he has his blouse over his trousers and wears his hair long, is a harmonica, or a dog to follow him, and then he would really be a beautiful sight!" I thought I was getting even with her for the pain she and this new husband of hers had caused me; but did she care? Not at all! She pretended not to understand what I was saying. I talked to her about Feferel and she answered me with "the cause of humanity" and "workers" and other such talk.

"What good is your humanity and your workers," I say, "if it's all a secret? There is a proverb: 'Where there are secrets, there is knavery.' But tell me the truth now. Where did he go, and why?"

"I'll tell you anything," she says, "but not that. Better don't ask. Believe me, you'll find out yourself in good time. You'll hear the news—and maybe very soon—and good news at that."

"Amen," I say. "From your mouth into God's ears! But may our enemies understand as little about it as I do."

"That," says she, "is the whole trouble. You'll never understand."

"Why not?" say I. "Is it so complicated? It seems to me that I can understand even more difficult things."

"These things you can't understand with your brain alone," she says. "You have to feel them, you have to feel them in your heart."

And when she said this to me, you should have seen how her face shone and her eyes burned. Ah, those daughters of mine! They don't do anything halfway. When they become involved in anything it's with their hearts and minds, their bodies and souls.

Well, a week passed, then two weeks—five—six—seven . . . and we heard nothing. There was no letter, no news of any kind. "Feferel is gone for good," I said, and glanced over at Hodel. There wasn't a trace of color in her face. And at the same time she didn't rest at all; she found something to do every minute of the day, as though trying to forget her troubles. And she never once mentioned his name, as if there never had been a Feferel in the world!

But one day when I came home from work I found Hodel going about with her eyes swollen from weeping. I made a few inquiries and found out that someone had been to see her, a long-haired young man who had taken her aside and talked to her for some time. Ah! That must have been the young fellow who had disowned his rich parents and pulled his blouse down over his trousers. Without further delay I called Hodel out into the yard and bluntly asked her: "Tell me, daughter, have you heard from him?"

"Yes."

"Where is he—your predestined one?"

"He is far away."

"What is he doing there?"

"He is serving time."

"Serving time?"

"Yes."

"Why? What did he do?"

She doesn't answer me. She looks me straight in the eyes and doesn't say a word.

"Tell me, my dear daughter," I say, "according to what I can understand, he is not serving for a theft. So if he is neither a thief nor a swindler, why is he serving? For what good deeds?"

She doesn't answer. So I think to myself, "If you don't want to, you don't have to. He is your headache, not mine." But my heart aches for her. No matter what you say, I'm still her father. . . .

Well, it was the evening of *Hashono Rabo*. On a holiday I'm in the habit of resting and my horse rests too. As it is written in the Bible: "*Thou shalt rest from thy labors and so shall thy wife and thine ass. . . .*" Besides, by that time of the year there is very little for me to do in Boiberik. As soon as the holidays come and the *shofar* sounds, all the summer *datchas* close down and Boiberik becomes a desert. At that season I like to sit at home on my own stoop. To me it is the finest time of the year. Each day is a gift from heaven. The sun no longer bakes like an oven, but caresses with a heavenly softness. The woods are still green, the pines give out a pungent smell. In my yard stands the *succah*—the booth I have built for the holiday, covered with branches, and around me the forest looks like a huge *succah* designed for God Himself. Here, I think, God celebrates His *Succos,* here and not in town, in the noise and tumult where people run this way and that panting for breath as they chase after a small crust of bread and all you hear is money, money, money. . . .

As I said, it is the evening of *Hashono Rabo*. The sky is a deep blue and myriads of stars twinkle and shine and blink. From time to time a star falls through the sky, leaving behind it a long green band of light. This means that someone's luck has fallen . . . I hope it isn't my star that is falling, and somehow Hodel comes to mind. She has changed in the last few days, has come to life again. Someone, it seems, has brought her a letter from him, from over there. I wish I knew what he had written, but I won't ask. If she won't speak, I won't either. Tevye is not a curious old woman. Tevye can wait.

And as I sit thinking of Hodel, she comes out of the house and sits down near me on the stoop. She looks cautiously around and then whispers, "I have something to tell you, father. I have to say good-bye to you, and I think it's for always."

She spoke so softly that I could barely hear her, and she looked at me in a way that I shall never forget.

"What do you mean—good-bye for always?" I say to her, and turn my face aside.

"I mean I am going away early tomorrow morning, and we shall possibly never see each other again."

"Where are you going, if I may be so bold as to ask?"

"I am going to him."

"To him? And where is he?"

"He is still serving, but soon they'll be sending him away."

"And you're going there to say good-bye to him?" I ask, pretending not to understand.

"No. I am going to follow him," she says. "Over there."

"There? Where is that? What do they call the place?"

"We don't know the exact name of the place, but we know that it's far—terribly, terribly far."

And she speaks, it seems to me, with great joy and pride, as though he had done something for which he deserved a medal. What can I say to her? Most fathers would scold a child for such talk, punish her, even beat her maybe. But Tevye is not a fool. To my way of thinking anger doesn't get you anywhere. So I tell her a story.

"I see, my daughter, as the Bible says, *'Therefore shalt thou leave thy father and mother'*—for a Feferel you are ready to forsake your parents and go off to a strange land, to some desert across the frozen wastes, where Alexander of Macedon, as I once read in a story book, once found himself stranded among savages. . . ."

I speak to her half in fun and half in anger, and all the time my heart weeps. But Tevye is no weakling; I control myself. And Hodel doesn't lose her dignity either; she answers me word for word, speaking quietly and thoughtfully. And Tevye's daughters can talk.

And though my head is lowered and my eyes are shut, still I seem to see her—her face is pale and lifeless like the moon, but her voice trembles. . . . Shall I fall on her neck and plead with her not to go? I know it won't help. Those daughters of mine—when they fall in love with somebody, it is with their heads and hearts, their bodies and souls.

Well, we sat on the doorstep a long time—maybe all night. Most of the time we were silent, and when we did speak it was in snatches, a word here, a word there. I said to her, "I want to ask you only one thing: did you ever hear of a girl marrying a man so that she could follow him to the ends of the earth?" And she answered, "With him I'd go anywhere." I pointed out how foolish that was. And she said, "Father, you will never understand." So I told her a little fable—about a hen that hatched some ducklings. As soon as the ducklings could move they took to the water and swam, and the poor hen stood on shore, clucking and clucking.

"What do you say to that, my daughter?"

"What can I say?" she answered. "I am sorry for the poor hen; but just because she stood there clucking, should the ducklings have stopped swimming?"

There is an answer for you. She's not stupid, that daughter of mine.

But time does not stand still. It was beginning to get light already, and from within the house my old woman was muttering. More than once she had called out that it was time to go to bed, but seeing that it didn't help she stuck her head out of the window and said to me, with her usual benediction, "Tevye, what's keeping you?"

"Be quiet, Golde," I answered. "Remember what the Psalm says, *'Why are the nations in an uproar, and why do the peo-*

ples mutter in vain?' Have you forgotten that it's *Hashono Rabo* tonight? Tonight all our fates are decided and the verdict is sealed. We stay up tonight . . . Listen to me, Golde, you light the samovar and make some tea while I go to get the horse and wagon ready. I am taking Hodel to the station in the morning." And once more I make up a story about how she has to go to Yehupetz, and from there farther on, because of that same old inheritance. It is possible, I say, that she may have to stay there through the winter and maybe the summer too, and maybe even another winter; and so we ought to give her something to take along—some linen, a dress, a couple of pillows, some pillow slips, and things like that.

And as I give these orders I tell her not to cry. "It's *Hashono Rabo* and on *Hashono Rabo* one mustn't weep. It's a law." But naturally they don't pay any attention to me, and when the time comes to say good-bye they all start weeping—their mother, the children and even Hodel herself. And when she came to say good-bye to her older sister Tzeitl (Tzeitl and her husband spend their holidays with us) they fell on each other's necks and you could hardly tear them apart.

I was the only one who did not break down. I was firm as steel—though inside I was more like a boiling samovar. All the way to Boiberik we were silent, and when we came near the station I asked her for the last time to tell me what it was that Feferel had really done. If they were sending him away, there must have been a reason. At this she became angry and swore by all that was holy that he was innocent. He was a man, she insisted, who cared nothing about himself. Everything he did was for humanity at large, especially for those who toiled with their hands—that is, the workers. That made no sense to me. "So he worries about the world," I told her. "Why doesn't the world worry a little about him? Nevertheless, give him my regards, that Alexander of Macedon of yours, and tell him I rely on his honor—for he is a man of honor, isn't he?—to treat my daughter well. And write to your old father some times."

When I finish talking she falls on my neck and begins to weep. "Good-bye, father," she cries. "Good-bye! God alone knows when we shall see each other again."

Well, that was too much for me. I remembered this Hodel when she was still a baby and I carried her in my arms, I carried her in my arms. . . . Forgive me, Mr. Sholom Aleichem, for acting like an old woman. If you only knew what a daughter she is. If you could only see the letters she writes. Oh, what a daughter. . . .

And now, let's talk about more cheerful things. Tell me, what news is there about the cholera in Odessa?

A Wedding without Musicians

THE LAST TIME I told you about our Straggler Special, I described the miracle of *Hashono Rabo*. This time I shall tell you about another miracle in which the Straggler Special figured, how thanks to the Straggler Special the town of Heissin was saved from a terrible fate.

This took place during the days of the Constitution when reprisals against the Jews were going on everywhere. Though I must tell you that we Jews of Heissin have never been afraid of pogroms. Why? Simply because there is no one in our town who can carry out a pogrom. Of course you can imagine that if we looked very hard we could find one or two volunteers who wouldn't deny themselves the pleasure of ventilating us a little, that is, breaking our bones or burning down our houses. For example, when reports of pogroms began drifting in, the few squires, who are enemies of our people, wrote confidential letters to the proper authorities, saying it might be a good idea if "something were done" in Heissin also; but since there was no one here to do it, would they be so kind as to send help, in other words, would they dispatch some "people" as quickly as possible.

And before another twenty-four hours had passed a reply came, also confidentially, that "people" were being sent. From where? From Zhmerinko, from Kazatin, Razdilno, Popelno and other such places that had distinguished themselves in beating up Jews. Do you want to know how we learned of this deep secret? We found it out through our regular source of news, Noah Tonkonoy. Noah Tonkonoy is a man whom God has endowed with a pair of extra-long legs and he uses them to good purpose. He never rests and he is seldom to be found at home. He is always busy with a thousand things and most of these things have to do with other people's business rather than his own. By trade he is a printer, and because he is the only printer in Heissin he knows all the squires and the police and has dealings with officialdom and is in on all their secrets.

Noah Tonkonoy spread the good news all over town. He told the secret to one person at a time, in strictest confidence, of course, saying, "I am telling this only to you. I wouldn't tell it to anyone else." And that was how the whole town became aware of the fact that a mob of hooligans was on the way, and that a plan for beating up Jews had been worked out. The plan told exactly when they would start, on which day, at which hour, and from which point, and by what means —everything to the last detail.

You can imagine what terror this struck in our hearts. Panic spread quickly. And among whom do you think it spread first? Among the poor, of course. It's a peculiar thing about poor people. When a rich man is afraid of a pogrom, you can understand why. He is afraid, poor fellow, that he will be turned into a pauper. But those of you who are already paupers, what are you afraid of? What have you got to lose? But you should have seen how they bundled up their children and packed up their belongings and began running hither and yon, looking for a place to hide. Where can a person hide? This one hides in a friendly peasant's cellar, another in the Notary's attic, a third in the Director's office at the factory. Everyone finds a spot for himself.

I was the only one in town who wasn't anxious to hide. I am not boasting about my bravery. But this is the way I see it: what's the sense of being afraid of a pogrom? I don't say that I am a hero. I might have been willing to hide too, when the hour of reckoning came. But I asked myself first, "How can I be sure that during the slaughter the friendly peasant in whose cellar I was hiding, or the Notary, or the Director of the factory himself, wouldn't . . ." You understand? And all that aside, how can you leave a town wide open like that? It's no trick to run away. You have to see about doing something. But, alas, what can a Jew do? He appeals to a friendly official. And that is just what we did.

In every town there is at least one friendly official you can appeal to. We had one too, the Inspector of Police, a jewel of a fellow, willing to listen to us and willing to accept a gift on occasion. We went to the Inspector with the proper gifts and asked for his protection. He reassured us at once. He told us to go home and sleep in peace. Nothing would happen. Sounds good, doesn't it? But we still had our walking newspaper, Noah, who was broadcasting another secret through the length and breadth of the town. The secret was that a telegram had just arrived. He swore by everything holy that he had seen it himself. What was in that telegram? Only one word—*Yediem*. An ugly word. It means simply, "We are coming." We ran back to the Inspector. "Your honor," we told him, "it looks bad." "What looks bad?" he asked, and we told him, "A telegram has just arrived." "From where?" We told him. "And what does it say?" We told him, "*Yediem*." At this he burst out laughing. "You are big fools," he said. "Only yesterday I ordered a regiment of Cossacks from Tolchin."

When we heard this we breathed more easily. When a Jew hears that a Cossack is coming, he takes courage, he can face the world again. The question remained: who would arrive first, the Cossacks from Tolchin, or the hooligans from Zhmerinko? Common sense told us that the hooligans would arrive first, because they were coming by train, while the Cossacks were coming on horseback. But we pinned all our hopes on the Straggler Special. God is merciful. He would surely perform a miracle and the Straggler would be at least a few hours late. This wasn't too much to hope for, since it happened nearly every day. But this one time it looked as though the miracle wouldn't take place. The Straggler kept going from station to station as regular as a clock. You can imagine how we felt when we learned, confidentially of course, through Noah Tonkonoy, that a telegram had arrived from the last station, from Krishtopovka. *Yediem* it said, and not just *yediem*—but *yediem* with a *hurrah!* in front of it.

Naturally we took this last bit of news straight to the Inspector. We begged him not to rely on the Cossacks who might or might not arrive from Tolchin sometime, but to send police to the station, at least for the sake of appearances, so that our enemies wouldn't think that we were completely at their mercy. The Inspector listened to our pleas. He did what we asked, and more. He got himself up in full uniform, with all his orders and medals, and took the whole police force, that is the gendarme and his assistant, to the station with him to meet the train.

But our enemies weren't asleep either. They also put on their full-dress uniforms, complete with ribbons and medals, took a couple of priests along, and also came to meet the train. The Inspector asked them sternly, "What are you doing here?" And they asked him the same question, "What are you doing here?" They bandied words back and forth, and the Inspector let them know in no uncertain terms that their trouble was for nothing. As long as he was in charge, there would be no pogrom in Heissin. They listened, smiled knowingly, and answered with insolence, "We shall see."

Just then a train whistle was heard from the distance. The sound struck terror to our hearts. We waited for another whistle to blow and after that for the shouts of "*Hurrah!*" What would happen after the "*Hurrah!*" we knew only too well from hearsay. We waited, but heard nothing more. What had happened? The sort of thing that could only happen to our Straggler Special.

When the Straggler Special drew into the station, the engineer stopped the locomotive, stepped out calmly and made his way toward the buffet. We met him halfway. "Well, my good fellow, and where are the cars?" "Which cars?" "Can't you see that you are here with the locomotive and without cars?"

He stared at us. "What do I care about the cars? They are the business of the crew." "Where is the crew?" "How should I know where the crew is? The conductor blows the whistle when he is ready and I whistle back to let him know that I am starting, and off we go. I don't have an extra pair of eyes in back of my head to see what's going on behind me." That was his story and according to that he was right. But right or wrong, there stood the Straggler Special without cars and without passengers. In other words, it was a wedding without musicians.

Later we learned that a band of hooligans had been on the way to Heissin, all of them handpicked youths, armed to the teeth with clubs and knives and other weapons. Their spirits were high and liquor flowed freely. At the last station, Krishtopovka, they invited the crew to join them and treated everybody to drinks—the conductor, the fireman, the gendarme. But in the midst of this revelry they forgot one little detail, to couple the cars back to the locomotive. And so the locomotive went off at the usual time to Heissin and the rest of the Straggler Special remained standing in Krishtopovka.

Neither the hooligans nor the other passengers nor the crew noticed that they were standing still. They continued to empty bottle after bottle and to make merry, until the stationmaster suddenly noticed that the locomotive had gone off and left the cars behind. He spread the alarm, the crew came tumbling out. A hue and cry was raised. The hooligans blamed the crew, the crew blamed the hooligans, but what good did it do? The cars couldn't budge without the locomotive. At last they decided that the only thing to do was to set out for Heissin on foot. They took heart and began marching toward Heissin, singing and shouting as they went.

And so they arrived in their usual good form, singing and yelling and brandishing their clubs. But it was already too late. In the streets of Heissin the Cossacks from Tolchin were riding up and down on horseback with whips in their hands. Within half an hour not one of the hooligans remained in town. They ran off like rats in a famine, they melted like ice in the summer.

Now I ask you, didn't the Straggler Special deserve to be showered with gold, or at least written up?

Chava

"*GIVE thanks unto the Lord, for He is good.*—Whatever He ordains, His way is the best." It has to be the best, for if you had the wisdom of a Solomon could you improve on it? Look at me—I wanted to be clever, I turned and twisted, this way and that, and tried everything I knew, and then when I saw it was no use, I took my hand off my chest, as the saying is, and said to myself, "Tevye, you're a fool, you won't change the world. The Lord has given us the '*pain of bringing up children,*' which means that in raising children you have to accept the bad with the good and count them as one."

Take, for instance, my oldest daughter, Tzeitl, who went and fell in love with the tailor Motel Kamzoil. Have I got anything against him? True, he is a simple, unlettered fellow, who can't read the learned footnotes at the bottom of the page, but is that anything against him? Everybody in the world can't be a scholar. At least he is an honest man and a hard-working one. She's already borne him a whole brood of young ones; they have a houseful of hungry mouths to feed, and both of them, he and she, are struggling along "*in honor and in riches,*" as the saying is. And yet if you ask her, she will tell you that she is the happiest woman in the world, no one could be happier. There is only one tiny flaw—they don't have enough to eat. "*That's the end of the first round with the Torah.*—There's Number One for you."

About my second daughter, about Hodel, I don't have to tell you. You know about her already. With her I played and I lost. I lost her forever. God knows if my eyes will ever behold her again, unless it should be in the next world. To this day I can't bring myself to talk about her calmly. I mention her name and the old pain returns. Forget her, you say? How can you forget a living human being? And especially a child like Hodel! If you could only see the letters she writes me. . . . They are doing very well, she tells me. He sits in prison and she works for a living. She washes clothes all day, reads books in between, and goes to see him once a week. She lives in the hope that very soon the pot will boil over, as they say, the sun will rise and everything become bright. He will be set free along with many others like him, and then, she says, they will all roll up their sleeves and get to work to turn the world upside down. Well, what do you think of that? Sounds promising, doesn't it?

But what does the Lord do next? He is, after all, *"a gracious and merciful Lord,"* and He says to me, "Wait, Tevye, I will bring something to pass that will make you forget all your former troubles."

And so it was. It's a story worth hearing. I would not repeat it to anyone else, for while the pain is great, the disgrace is even greater. But how is it written? *"Shall I conceal it from Abraham?*—Can I keep any secrets from you?" Whatever is on my mind I shall tell you. But one thing I want to ask of you. Let it remain between you and me. For I repeat: the pain is great, but the disgrace—the disgrace is even greater.

How is it written in *Perek? "The Holy One, blessed be He, wished to grant merit to Israel—"* The Lord wanted to be good to Tevye, so He blessed him with seven female children, that is, seven daughters, each one of them a beauty, all of them good-looking and charming, clever and healthy and sweet-tempered—like young pine trees! Alas, if only they had been ill-tempered and ugly as scarecrows, it might have been better for them, and certainly healthier for me. For what use is a fine horse, I ask you, if you have to keep it locked up in a stable? What good are beautiful daughters if you are stuck away with them in a forsaken corner of the world, where you never see a live person except for Anton Poperilo, the village mayor, or the clerk Fyedka Galagan, a young fellow with a long mane of hair and tall peasant boots, or the Russian priest, may his name be blotted out?

I can't bear to hear that priest's name mentioned, not because I am a Jew and he is a priest. On the contrary, we've been on friendly terms for a number of years. By that I don't mean that we visit at each other's homes or dance at the same weddings. I only mean that when we happen to meet we greet each other civilly. "Good morning." "Good day. What's new in the world?"

I've never liked to enter into a discussion with him, for right away the talk would turn to this business of *your God* and *my God.* Before he could get started I would recite a proverb or quote him a passage from the Bible. To which he replied that he could quote me a passage from the Bible also, and perhaps better than I, and he began to recite Scriptures to me, mimicking the sacred language like a Gentile: "*Berezhit bara alokim*—In the beginning the Lord created the Heavens. . . ." Then I told him that we had a folk tale, or a *medresh* to the effect that. . . . "A *medresh*," he interrupted me, "is the same as *Tal-mud*," and he didn't like *Talmud*, "for *Tal-mud* is nothing but sheer trickery." Then I would get good and angry and give him what he had coming. Do you think that bothered him? Not in the least. He would only look at me, and laugh, and comb his long beard with his fingers. There is nothing in the world, I tell you, so maddening as a person who doesn't answer when you abuse him. You shout and you scold, you are ready to burst a gut, and he stands there and smiles. . . . At that time I didn't understand what that smile of his meant, but now I know what was behind it. . . .

Well, to return to my story. I arrived at home one day—it was toward evening—and whom should I see but the clerk Fyedka standing outside with my Chava, that's my third daughter, the one next to Hodel. When he caught sight of me, the young fellow spun around quickly, tipped his hat to me, and was off. I asked Chava, "What was Fyedka doing here?"

"Nothing," she said.

"What do you mean nothing?"

"We were just talking."

"What business have you got talking with Fyedka?" I asked.

"We've known each other for a long time," she said.

"Congratulations!" I said. "A fine friend you've picked for yourself."

"Do you know him at all?" she asked. "Do you know who he is?"

"No," I said, "I don't know who he is. I've never seen his family tree. But I am sure he must be descended from a long and honorable line. His father," I said, "must have been either a shepherd or a janitor, or else just a plain drunkard."

To this Chava answered, "Who his father was I don't know and I don't care to know. All people are the same to me. But Fyedka himself is not an ordinary person, of that I am sure."

"Tell me," I said, "what kind of person is he? I'd like to hear."

"I would tell you," she said, "but you wouldn't understand. Fyedka is a second Gorky."

"A second Gorky? And who, may I ask, was the first Gorky?"

"Gorky," she said, "is one of the greatest men living in the world today."

"Where does he live," I asked, "this sage of yours, what is his occupation and what words of wisdom has he spoken?"

"Gorky," she said, "is a famous author. He is a writer, that is, a man who writes books. He is fine and honest and true, a person to be honored. He also comes from plain people, he was not educated anywhere, he is self-taught . . . here is his portrait." Saying this, she took a small photograph from her pocket and handed it to me.

"So this is he," I said, "this sage of yours, Reb Gorky? I can swear I have seen him somewhere before, either at the baggage depot, carrying sacks, or in the woods hauling logs."

"Is it a crime then if a man works with his hands? Don't you yourself work with your hands? Don't all of us work?"

"Yes, yes," I said, "you are right. We have a certain proverb which says, '*When thou eatest the labor of thine own hands*—If you do not work, you shall not eat.' But I still don't understand what Fyedka is doing here. I would be much happier if you were friends at a distance. You mustn't forget '*Whence thou camest and whither thou goest*—Who you are and who he is.' "

"God created all men equal," she said.

"Yes, yes," I said, "God created Adam in his own image. But we mustn't forget that each man must seek his own kind, as it is written: '*From each according to his means . . .*' "

"Marvelous!" she cried. "Unbelievable! You have a quotation for everything. Maybe you also have a quotation that explains why men have divided themselves up into Jews and Gentiles, into lords and slaves, noblemen and beggars?"

"Now, now, my daughter, it seems to me you've strayed to the '*sixth millennium.*' " And I explained to her that this had been the way of the world since the first day of Creation.

"And why," she wanted to know, "should this be the way of the world?"

"Because that's the way God created the world."

"And why did God create the world this way?"

"If we started to ask why this, and wherefore that, *'there would be no end to it*—a tale without end.' "

"But that is why God gave us intellects," she said, "that we should ask questions."

"We have an old custom," I told her, "that when a hen begins to crow like a rooster, we take her away to be slaughtered. As we say in the morning blessing, *"Who gave the rooster the ability to discern between day and night. . . .'* "

"Maybe you've done enough jabbering out there," my wife Golde called out from inside the house. "The *borsht* has been standing on the table for an hour and he is still out there singing Sabbath hymns."

"Another province heard from! No wonder our sages have said, *'The fool hath seven qualities.*—A woman talks nine times as much as a man.' We are discussing important matters and she comes barging in with her cabbage *borsht.*"

"My cabbage *borsht,*" said Golde, "may be just as important as those 'important matters' of yours."

"*Mazl-tov!* We have a new philosopher here, straight from behind the oven. It isn't enough that Tevye's daughters have become enlightened, now his wife has to start flying through the chimney right up into the sky."

"Since you mention the sky," said Golde, "I might as well tell you that I hope you rot in the earth."

Tell me, Mr. Sholom Aleichem, what do you think of such crazy goings-on on an empty stomach?

Now let us, as they say in books, leave the prince and follow the fortunes of the princess. I am speaking of the priest, may his name and memory be blotted out. Once toward nightfall I was driving home with my empty milk cans—I was nearing the village—when whom should I see but the priest in his cast-iron *britzka* or carriage, approaching from the other direction. His honor was driving the horses himself, and his long flowing beard was whipped about by the wind.

"What a happy encounter!" I thought to myself. "May the bad luck fall on his head."

"Good evening," he said to me. "Didn't you recognize me, or what?"

"It's a sign that you will get rich soon," I said, lifted my cap and was about to drive on. But he wouldn't let me pass.

"Wait a minute, Tevel, what's your hurry? I have a few words to say to you."

"Very well. If it's good news, then go ahead," I said. "But if not, leave it for some other time."

"What do you mean by some other time?" he asked.

"By some other time, I mean when the Messiah comes."

"The Messiah," said he, "has already come."

"That I have heard from you more than once," I said. "Tell me something new, little father."

"That's just what I want to tell you. I want to talk to you about yourself, that is, about your daughter."

At this my heart almost turned over. What concern could he have with my daughter? And I said to him, "My daughters are not the kind, God forbid, that need someone to do the talking for them. They can manage their own affairs."

"But this is the sort of thing she can't speak of herself. Someone else has to speak for her. It's a matter of utmost importance. Her fate is at stake."

"And who, may I ask, concerns himself with the fate of my child? It seems to me that I am still her father, am I not?"

"True," he said, "you are her father, but you are blind to her needs. Your child is reaching out for a different world, and you don't understand her, or else you don't wish to understand her."

"Whether I don't understand her, or don't wish to understand her, is beside the point. We can argue about that sometime if you like. But what has it got to do with you, little father?"

"It has quite a lot to do with me," he said, "for she is now under my protection."

"What do you mean she is under your 'protection'?"

"It means she is now in my care."

He looked me straight in the eye as he said this and stroked his long, flowing beard with his fingers.

"What!" I exclaimed. "My child is in your care? By what right?" I felt myself losing my temper.

He answered me very calmly, with a little smile, "Now don't start getting excited, Tevel. We can discuss this matter peaceably. You know that I am not, God forbid, your enemy, even though you are a Jew. As you know, I am very fond of the Jewish people, even though they are a stiff-necked race. And my heart aches for them because in their pride they refuse to admit that we mean everything for their own good."

"Don't speak to me of our own good, little father," I said, "for every word that comes from your lips is like a drop of poison to me—it's like a bullet fired straight at my heart. If you are really the friend you say you are, I ask only one thing of you—leave my daughter alone."

"You are a foolish person," he said to me. "No harm will come to your daughter. She is about to meet with a piece of great good luck. She is about to take a bridegroom—and such a bridegroom! I couldn't wish a better fate to one of my own."

"Amen," I said, forcing a laugh, though inside me burned all the fires of hell. "And who, may I ask, is this bridegroom, if I may have the honor of knowing?"

"You must be acquainted with him," he said. "He is a gallant young man, an honest fellow and quite well-educated though he is self-taught. He is very much in love with your daughter and wants to marry her, but cannot, because he is not a Jew."

"Fyedka!" I thought to myself, and the blood rushed to my head, and a cold sweat broke out all over my body, so that I could barely sit upright in my cart. But show him how I felt? Never. Without replying I picked up the reins, whipped my horse, and "*departed like Moses.*" I went off without as much as a fare-thee-well.

I arrived at home. What a scene greeted me! The children all lying with their faces buried in pillows, weeping; my Golde weaving around the house like a ghost. I looked for Chava. Where is Chava? She is nowhere to be found. I didn't ask where she was. I knew only too well. Then it was that I began to feel the tortures of a soul that is damned. I was full of rage and I didn't know against whom. I could have turned on myself with a whip. I began yelling at the children, I let out all my bitterness toward my wife. I couldn't rest in the house, so I went outside to the barn to feed my horse. I found him with one leg twisted around the block of wood. I took a stick and began laying it into him, as though I were going to strip off his skin and break his bones in half. "May you burn alive, you *shlimazl*. You can starve to death before I will give you as much as an oat. Tortures I will give you and anguish and all the ten plagues of Egypt. . . ."

But even as I shouted at him I knew that my horse did not

deserve it; poor innocent creature, what did I have against him? I poured out some chopped straw for him, went back to the house and lay down. . . . My head was ready to split in two as I lay there thinking, figuring, arguing with myself back and forth. What could it all mean? What was the significance of all this? *"What was my sin and what my transgression?"* How did Tevye sin more than all the others that he should be punished thus above all the others? " *'Oh, Lord Almighty, what are we, and what is our life?'* What sort of cursed creature am I that you should constantly bear me in mind, never let any plague that comes along, any blight or affliction pass me by?"

As I lay there torturing myself with such thoughts, I heard my wife groaning and moaning beside me. "Golde," I said, "are you sleeping?"

"No," she said. "What is it?"

"Nothing," I said. "Things are bad with us, very bad. Maybe you can think of what's to be done."

"You ask me what's to be done. Woe is me, how should I know? A child gets up in the morning, sound and fresh, gets dressed, and falls on my neck, kissing and hugging me, and weeping all the time, and she won't tell me why. I thought that, God forbid, she had lost her mind. I asked her, 'What's the matter with you, daughter?' She didn't say a word, but ran out for a while to see to the cows, and disappeared. I waited an hour, two hours, three hours. Where is Chava? There is no Chava. Then I said to the children, 'Run over and take a look at the priest's house. . . .' "

"How did you know, Golde, that she was at the priest's house?"

"How did I know? Woe is me. Don't I have eyes in my head? Am I not her mother?"

"If you do have eyes in your head, and if you are her mother, why did you keep it all to yourself? Why didn't you tell me?"

"Tell you? When are you at home that I can tell you anything? And if I do tell you something, do you listen to me? If a person says anything to you, you answer him with a quotation. You drum my head full of quotations and you've done your duty by your children."

After she finished I could hear her weeping in the dark. "She is partly right," I thought to myself, "for what can a woman understand of such matters?" My heart ached for her, I could not bear to listen to her moaning and groaning. "Look here, Golde," I said, "you are angry because I have a quotation for everything. I have to answer you even that with a quotation. It is written: *'As a father has mercy on his children.'* This means that a father loves his child. Why isn't it written: *'As a mother has mercy on her children'*? For a mother is not the same as a father. A father can speak differently with his child. You will see—tomorrow I will go and speak to her."

"I hope you will get to see her, and him also. He is not a bad man, even if he is a priest. He has compassion in his heart. You will plead with him, get down on your knees to him, maybe he will have pity on us."

"Whom are you talking about?" I said. "That priest? You want me to bow down to the priest? Are you crazy or out of your head? *'Do not give Satan an opening,'* it is said. My enemies will never live to see that day."

"What did I tell you?" she said. "There you go again."

"Did you think," I said, "that I would let a woman tell me what to do? You want me to live by your womanish brains?"

In such talk the whole night passed. At last I heard the first cock crow. I got up, said my morning prayers, took my whip with me, and went straight to the priest's house. A woman is nothing but a woman. But where else could I have gone? Into the grave?

Well, I arrived in the priest's yard and his dogs gave me a royal welcome. They leaped at me and tried to tear off my coat and sink their teeth into my calves to see if they liked the taste of a Jew's flesh. It was lucky that I had taken my whip along. I gave them this quotation to chew on—"*Not a dog shall bark.*" Or, as they say in Russian: "*Nehai sobaka daram nie breshe.*" Which means, "Don't let a dog bark for nothing."

Aroused by the barking and the commotion in the yard the priest came running out of his house and his wife after him. With some effort they drove off the happy throng that surrounded me, and invited me to come in. They received me like an honored guest and got ready to put on the samovar for me. I told the priest it wasn't necessary to put on the samovar, I had something I wanted to say to him in private. He caught on to what I meant and motioned to his spouse to please be so kind as to shut the door on the outside.

When we were alone I came straight to the point without any preambles, and asked him first of all to tell me if he believed in God. Then I asked him to tell me if he knew what it felt like to be parted from a child he loved. And then I asked him to tell me what, according to his interpretation, was right and what was wrong. And one more thing I wanted him to make clear for me. What did he think of a man who sneaked into another man's house, and began tearing it apart, turning beds, tables, and chairs—everything, upside down.

Naturally he was dumbfounded by all this, and he said to me, "Tevel, you are a clever man, it seems to me, and yet you put so many questions to me and you expect me to answer them all at one blow. Be patient and I shall answer them one at a time, the first question first and the last question last."

"No, dear little father," I said. "You will never answer my questions. Do you know why? Because I know all your answers beforehand. Just tell me this: is there any hope of my getting my child back, or not?"

He leaped up at this. "What do you mean getting her back? No harm will come to your daughter—just the opposite."

"I know," I said. "I know. You want to bring her a piece of great good luck. I am not speaking of that. I only want to know where my child is, and if I can see her."

"Everything, yes," he said, "but that, no."

"That's the way to talk," I said. "Come to the point. No mincing of words. And now good-bye. May God repay you in equal measure for everything you have done."

I came home and found Golde lying in bed all knotted up like a black ball of yarn. She had no more tears left to weep. I said to her, "Get up, my wife, take off your shoes, and let us sit down and mourn our child as God has commanded. *'The Lord hath given and the Lord hath taken away.'* We are neither the first nor the last. Let us imagine that we never had a daughter named Chava, or that like Hodel she went off to the ends of the earth. God is All-Merciful and All-Good. He knows what He does."

As I said this I felt the tears choking me, standing like a bone in my throat. But Tevye is not a woman. Tevye can restrain himself. Of course, you understand, that's only a way of speaking. First of all, think of the disgrace! And second, how can I restrain myself when I've lost my child, and especially a child like Chava. A child so precious to us, so deeply embedded in our hearts, both in her mother's and mine. I don't know why she had always seemed dearer to us than any of the other children. Maybe because as a baby she had been so sickly, and we had gone through so much with her. We used to stay up whole nights nursing her, and many a time we snatched her, literally snatched her, from the jaws of death, breathed life into her as you would into a tiny crushed chick. For if God wills it, He makes the dead come to life again, as we say in Hallel: "*I shall not die, but I will live.*—If you are not fated to die, you will not die." And maybe we loved her so because she had always been such a good child, so thoughtful and devoted, both to her mother and me. Now I ask you, how could she have done this thing to us?

Here is the answer: first of all, it is fate. I don't know about you, but as for me, I believe in Providence. Second, it was witchcraft. You may laugh at me, and I want to tell you that I am not so misguided as to believe in spirits, elves, *domovois* and such nonsense. But I do believe in witchcraft, in the evil eye. For what else could it have been? Wait, listen to the rest of the story, and you will agree with me.

Well, when the Holy Books say, "*Perforce you must live.*—Man does not take his own life—" they know what they are talking about. There is no wound so deep that it does not heal in time, there is no sorrow so great that you do not forget it eventually. That is, you do not forget, but what can you do about it? "*Man is likened to a beast.*—Man must work, man must till the earth in the sweat of his brow." And so we all went to work. My wife and children got busy with the pitchers of milk, and I took to my horse and wagon and "*the world continued in its course*—the world does not stand still." I told everyone at home to consider Chava as dead. There was no more Chava. Her name had been blotted out. Then I gathered up some dairy stuff—cheese and butter and such, all fresh merchandise—and set off for Boiberik to visit my customers in their *datchas*.

I arrived in Boiberik and I was met with great rejoicing. "How are you, Reb Tevye?" "Why don't we see you any more?" "How should I be?" I told them. '*We renew our days as of old.*—I am the same *shlimazl* as always.' One of my cows just dropped dead." They appeared surprised. "Why do so many miracles happen to you, Reb Tevye?" And they began questioning me, wanting to know what kind of cow it was that had dropped dead, how much she had cost, and if I had many cows left. They laughed and joked and made merry over me as rich people will make merry over a poor man and his troubles, when they have just eaten their fill and are in a good mood, and the weather is perfect, sunny and warm and balmy, just the weather to drowse in. But Tevye is the sort of person who can take a joke even at his own expense. I would sooner die on the spot than let them know how I felt.

When I got through with my customers, I set out for home with my empty milk cans. As I rode through the woods I slackened the horse's reins, let him nibble at will, and crop a blade of grass now and then. I let my thoughts roam at will also. I thought about life and death, this world and the next, what the world is altogether about, what man has been created for, and other such things. Anything to drive my gloom away, to keep from thinking about Chava. But just as if to spite me she kept creeping in among my thoughts.

First she appeared before me in her own image, tall, lovely, blooming, like a young tree. Then I saw her as a little baby, sick and ailing, a frail little nestling, snuggled in my arms, her head drooping over my shoulder. "What do you want, Chaveleh? Something to suck on? A piece of candy?" And for the moment I forgot what she had done to me and my heart went out to her in longing. Then I remembered and a great anger seized me. I burned with anger against her and against him and against the whole world, but mostly against myself because I wasn't able to forget her, even for a minute. Why couldn't I forget her, why couldn't I tear her out of my heart completely? Didn't she deserve to be forgotten?

For this, I thought, Tevye had to be a Jew among Jews, to suffer all his life long, to keep his nose to the grindstone, bring children into the world—in order to have them torn from him by force, to have them fall like acorns from a tree and be carried away by wind and by smoke. I thought to myself, "It's like this: a tree grows in the forest, a mighty oak with outspread branches, and an ignorant lout comes along with an axe and chops off a branch, then another and another. What is a tree without branches, alas? Go ahead, lout, chop down the whole tree and let there be an end. . . . What good is a naked oak in the forest?"

In the midst of these thoughts I suddenly became aware that my horse had stopped. What's the matter? I lift up my eyes and look. It is she, Chava. The same as before, not changed at all, she is even wearing the same dress. My first impulse was to jump off the wagon and take her in my arms. But something held me back. "What are you, Tevye? A woman? A weakling?" I pulled in my horse's reins. "Giddap, *shlimazl.*" I tried to go to the right. I look—she is also going to the right. She beckons to me with her hand as though to say, "Stop a while, I have something to tell you."

Something tears at my insides, something tugs at my heart. I feel myself going weak all over. Any moment I will jump off the wagon. But I restrain myself, pull the horse's reins in and turn left. She also turns left. She is looking at me wildly, her face is deathly pale. What shall I do? Should I stop or go on? And before I know what's happened, she's got the horse by the bridle and is saying to me, "Father, I will sooner die on the spot before I let you move another step. I beg you, father, listen to me."

"So," I think to myself, "you want to take me by force. No, my dear, if that's what you are trying to do, I see that you don't know your father very well." And I begin whipping my horse with all my might. The horse obeys me, he leaps forward. But he keeps moving his ears and turning his head back. "Giddap," I tell him. "'*Judge not the vessel but its contents.* Don't look where you aren't supposed to.'" But do you think that I myself wouldn't like to turn my head and look back at the place where I left her standing? But Tevye is not a woman. Tevye knows how to deal with Satan the Tempter.

Well, I don't want to drag my story out any longer. Your time is valuable. If I have been fated to suffer the punishments of the damned after death, I surely have expiated all my sins already. If you want to know about the tortures of hell that are described in our Holy Books, ask me. I can describe them all to you. All the rest of the way, as I drove, I thought I could hear her running after me, calling, "Listen, father, listen to me." A thought crossed my mind, "Tevye, you are taking too much upon yourself. Will it hurt you if you stop and listen to her? Maybe she has something to say that is worth hearing. Maybe—who can tell—she is regretting what she has done and wants to come back to you. Maybe she is being badly treated and wants you to save her from a living hell." Maybe and maybe and maybe . . . And I saw her as a little child once more and I was reminded of the passage: "*As a father has mercy on his children . . .*" To a father there is no such thing as a bad child. I blamed myself and I told myself, "*I do not deserve to be pitied*—I am not worthy of the earth I walk upon.

"What are you fuming and fretting for?" I asked myself. "Stubborn mule, turn your wagon around and go back and talk to her, she is your own child." And peculiar thoughts came into my mind. What is the meaning of Jew and non-Jew? Why did God create Jews and non-Jews? And since God did create Jews and non-Jews why should they be segregated from each other and hate each other, as though one were created by God and the other were not? I regretted that I wasn't as learned as some men so that I could arrive at an answer to this riddle. . . .

And in order to chase away these painful thoughts I began to chant the words of the evening prayer. "*Blessed are they who dwell in Thy house, and they shall continue to praise Thee. . . .*" But what good was this chanting when inside of me a different tune was playing? *Chava,* it went. *Cha-va.* The louder I recited the prayer, the plainer the word *Cha-va* sounded in my own ears. The harder I tried to forget her, the more vividly she appeared before me, and it seemed to me that I heard her voice calling, "Listen, father, listen to me." I covered my ears to keep from hearing her voice and I shut my eyes to keep from seeing her face, and I started saying *Shminesra,* and didn't know what I was saying. I beat my breast and cried out loud, "*For we have sinned,*" and I didn't know for what I was beating my breast.

I didn't know what I was saying or doing. My whole life was in a turmoil, and I myself was confused and unhappy. I didn't tell anyone of my meeting with Chava. I didn't speak about her to anyone and didn't ask anyone about her, though I knew quite well where they lived and what they were doing. But no one could tell from my actions. My enemies will never live to see the day when I complain to anyone. That's the kind of man Tevye is.

I wonder if all men are like me, or if I am the only crazy one. For instance, let us imagine—just suppose it should happen—if I tell you this, you won't laugh at me? I am afraid that you will laugh. But just let us suppose that one fine day I should put on my Sabbath gabardine and stroll over to the railway station as though I were going away on the train, going to see them. I walk up to the ticket window and ask for a ticket. The ticket seller asks me where I want to go. "To Yehupetz," I tell him. And he says, "There is no such place." And I say, "Well, it's not my fault then." And I turn myself around and go home again, take off my Sabbath clothes and go back to work, back to my cows and my horse and wagon. As it is written: "*Each man to his labor*—The tailor must stick to his shears and the shoemaker to his last."

I see that you are laughing at me. What did I tell you? I know what you're thinking. You're thinking that Tevye is a big imbecile. . . . That's why I say: "*Read to this part on the great Sabbath before Passover*," meaning, it's enough for one day. Be well and happy and write me often. And don't forget what I asked you. Be silent as the grave concerning this. Don't put what I told you into a book. And if you should write, write about someone else, not about me. Forget about me. As it is written: "*And he was forgotten*—" No more Tevye the Dairyman!

Schprintze

I OWE you a greeting, a hearty greeting, Mr. Sholom Aleichem. It's a score of years since we've seen each other. My, my, how much water has flown under the bridge! How much agony we have lived through, you and I, and all of Israel, in these last few years! Oh, thou Father of the Universe, our dear God in Heaven! We have lived through a Kishinev and a Constitution, through pogroms and disasters of every kind. I am only surprised, if you will forgive me for saying this, that you haven't changed by a hair. May the Evil Eye spare you! But look at me: "*Behold, I look like a man of seventy.*—I am not sixty yet, and see how white Tevye has grown." It's the same old thing: "*the pain of bringing up children.*" And who has suffered as much pain because of his children as I have? Since the last time I saw you a new misfortune happened to me, this time with my daughter Schprintze, something that put all my former troubles in the shade! And yet, as you see, I am still alive, still here. . . . As it is written: "*Perforce you must live.*" Live, though you burst asunder singing this song:

> "The world doesn't please me and life isn't funnny
> If I have no luck and I have no money."

In short what does it say in *Perek*? "*The Holy One, Blessed be He, wished to grant merit to Israel.*—God wanted to favor His chosen people." So a fresh calamity descended upon us, this time a Constitution. And such a panic overtook our rich people that they began leaving Yehupetz in droves, running off abroad, supposedly for their health, for mineral baths, salt water cures, nerves, and other such nonsense. And when Yehupetz is deserted then Boiberik with its fresh air, its pine woods, and its summer homes becomes a desert too. As we say in the morning prayer: "*Blessed be He who bestows mercy upon this earth.*"

But that isn't all. We have a great God and a mighty God

who watches over His poor and sees to it that they continue to struggle a little longer on this earth. What a summer we had! People began running to Boiberik from all over, from Odessa and Rostov, from Ekaterineslav and Mogilov, and Kishinev. There descended *"thousands upon thousands of rich men."* All the millionaires and plutocrats came to us. Apparently the Constitution was even worse for them than for us in Yehupetz, for they kept on coming, they didn't stop coming. The question is: Why should they run to us? And the answer is: Why do we run to them? It's become a custom with our people, God be praised, that as soon as there is a rumor of a pogrom we begin flying from one town to another, as it is written: *"They journeyed and they encamped, they encamped and they journeyed. . . ."* Which means, "You come to me and I will come to you."

Meanwhile you can imagine how crowded Boiberik became. It overflowed with people, it spilled over with women and children. And since children have to eat three times a day and they like to nibble besides, the demand for milk and butter and cheese kept growing. And from whom does one get milk and butter and cheese if not from Tevye? Overnight, Tevye became all the rage. From all sides you heard nothing but Tevye and Tevye and Tevye. "Reb Tevye, come to me." "Reb Tevye, you promised me." What more need I say? If God wills it, that's enough.

"And it came to pass—" Here is how it all began. Shortly before *Shevuos* I brought my wares to one of my new customers, a young widow and a rich one, from Ekaterineslav, who had just arrived with her son Aarontchik to spend the summer in Boiberik. And naturally the first person she became acquainted with in Boiberik was myself. "You've been recommended to me very highly," she says. "They tell me you have the best butter and cheese in these parts."

"How can it be otherwise?" I asked her. "Not in vain does King Solomon say that a good name can be heard like the sound of the *shofar* all over the world. And if you like," I added, "I can also tell you what a certain *medresh* has to say about that." She cut me short, however, saying that she was only a widow and inexperienced in such matters. She didn't even know what you ate it with. The important thing, she tells me, is that the butter should be fresh and the cheese taste good. There's a female for you.

Well, I began coming to the widow from Ekaterineslav twice a week, every Monday and Thursday, regularly, by the calendar. I brought her butter and cheese each time, without asking whether she needed it or not. I made myself at home in her house, took a friendly interest in the household, stuck my nose into the kitchen, told her a few times, whatever I saw fit to tell her, about the management of the house. The first time, as you might expect, I got a dressing-down from the servant who told me to mind my own business and not to stick my nose into strange pots. The second time, however, they stopped to listen, and the third time they asked my advice, because by then the widow had become aware of who Tevye was.

And so it went, until at last the widow disclosed to me her big problem, her secret sorrow, the thing that was eating away at her, and that was—Aarontchik! There he was, a young man, over twenty years old, and all he could think of was horseback riding, bicycling, fishing, and aside from that nothing! He wouldn't have anything to do with business, with the making of money. His father had left him a nice little fortune, almost a million *rubles*, but did he as much as look into it? All he cared about was spending money; his purse was wide open.

"Where is this young man?" I asked her. "Just turn him over to me. I'll have a good talk with him. I'll read him a lecture, quote him a passage or two, give him a *medresh*. . . ." She laughed at this. "A *medresh* did you say? A horse would be more like it."

Just at this moment *"the lad arrived."* Aarontchik himself walked in. He was a handsome young fellow, tall and husky, and bursting with good health. He wore a wide sash across his middle, with a watch stuck in the side, and his sleeves were rolled up above the elbows.

"Where have you been?" his mother asked him.

"I've been out in a boat," he said, "fishing."

"A fine occupation," I said, "for a young man like you. Over there in the city your inheritance is being frittered away, and you are out on the river catching fish."

I looked at the widow. She had turned as red as a beet. She must have thought her son would pick me up by the collar, *"and smite me as the Lord smote the Egyptians, with signs and symbols,"* that is, give me two slaps in the face, and throw me out of the house like a broken potsherd. Nonsense! Tevye is not afraid of such things. When I have something to say, I say it.

"*And so it was.*" When the young man heard me, he stepped back, folded his arms over his chest, looked me over from head to foot, gave a long, low whistle, and then burst out laughing. We both thought he had lost his mind. And what shall I tell you? From that moment on we became like two comrades. And I must confess that the longer I knew him the better I got to like him, even though he was a rake and a spendthrift, much too free with his money, and something of a fool besides. For instance, who else but a fool would put his hand into his pocket when he met a beggar, and give him all he had without counting it? Or take a perfectly good coat off his back and give it away? Talk about folly.

I was honestly sorry for his mother. She wept and wailed and asked me what she should do. She begged me to have a talk with him. So I did her the favor. Why should I begrudge it to her? Did it cost me anything? I sat down with him, told him stories, cited examples, plied him with quotations and drummed proverbs into his ears, as only Tevye can do. And I must say that he seemed to enjoy listening to me. He kept asking me questions about how I lived and what my home was like. "You know what, Reb Tevye," he said, "I would like to come over and see you at home some day."

"That's easy," I said. "If you want to see me at home, just pick yourself up and drive over to my farm. It seems to me you have enough horses and bicycles. And if necessary, you can even pick up your two feet and walk over. It isn't far. You just have to cut through the woods."

"And when can I find you at home?" he asked me.

"You can find me at home only on Sabbaths and holidays. But hold on!" I said. "Do you know what? A week from Friday is *Shevuos*. If you want to come over to my house for *Shevuos*, my wife will treat you to such *blintzes* as your '*blessed ancestors never ate in Egypt.*' "

"What are you referring to?" he asked me. "You know that I'm weak in Biblical quotations."

"I know you are weak," I said. "If you had studied in *cheder* the way I did, you would have known not only what the rabbi, but also what the rebbitzen, the rabbi's wife, had to say."

He laughed at this. "Good," he said, "you can expect me on the first day of *Shevuos* along with a couple of friends. But see to it that the *blintzes* are good and hot."

"*At white heat, inside and out,*" I said. "From the frying pan right into your mouth."

I came home and said to my wife, "Golde," I said, "we are going to have guests for *Shevuos.*"

"*Mazl-tov,*" she said. "And who are they?"

"That," I said, "you will find out later. Just get some eggs ready. We have plenty of butter and cheese, praise the Lord. I want you to make enough *blintzes* for three guests. And remember, they are the kind of people who believe in filling their stomachs; fine words mean nothing to them."

"I suppose you've picked up some starving wretches, some cronies of yours from Hungerland."

"You talk like a fool, Golde," I told her. "In the first place what harm would there be if we did feed some poor hungry wretch on *Shevuos?* In the second place, be thou informed, my dear spouse, my modest and pious wife, Madam Golde, that one of our guests is the widow's son, Aarontchik, the one I told you about."

"Oh," she said, "that's different."

Look at the power money has! Even my Golde, when she gets wind of money, becomes a different person. That's the way of the world. How is it written? "*Gold and silver, the work of man's hands*—Wealth is the undoing of man."

Well, *Shevuos* arrived. And how beautiful *Shevuos* in the country can be; how warm and sunny and fragrant, I don't have to tell you. The richest man in the city would envy us such a blue sky, such a green forest, such aromatic pine trees. Even the cows in the pasture keep chewing their cuds and look up at you as though to say, "Give us such grass all year round and we'll give you all the milk you want." You can tempt me all you like, you can offer me the richest livelihood in town, I wouldn't change places with you. Where can you get such a sky in town? How do we say it in Hallel: "*The heavens are the heavens of the Lord*—God's own sky." In town when you raise your head, what do you see? A brick wall, a roof, a chimney. Where will you find a tree? And if some scrubby little bush has crept in somewhere, you smother it with an overcoat.

Anyway, when my guests arrived, they couldn't find enough

words to praise the beauty of the country. They came riding, three abreast, on horseback. You should have seen those horses, especially the one Aarontchik rode. An Arab steed. I figured that you couldn't buy him for three hundred *rubles.*

"Welcome, guests," I said to them. "I see that in honor of *Shevuos* you have come riding on horseback. Never mind. Tevye is not so pious either. And if you should be whipped for your sins in the next world, my back won't be sore. Golde," I called my wife, "get the *blintzes* ready and let's bring the table outdoors. I have nothing to show off to my guests inside."

Then I called my daughters, "Schprintze, Teibel, Beilke, where are you? Get a move on you." Soon the table was brought outside, and then benches, a tablecloth, plates, forks, salt. And right after that Golde appeared with the *blintzes* piled high on a platter, plump and juicy, and as "*sweet as the life-giving manna from heaven.*" My guests ate and ate and couldn't praise them enough.

"What are you standing there for?" I said to Golde. "Repeat the same verse over again. Today is *Shevuos* and we have to say the same prayer twice." Golde didn't waste any time, but filled up the platter again, and Schprintze brought it to the table. I happened to look over at Aarontchik just then and saw him watching Schprintze. He couldn't take his eyes off her. What had he seen in her all of a sudden? "Go on and eat," I said to him. "Why aren't you eating?"

"What else am I doing if not eating?" he said. "You are looking at Schprintze," I told him. Everybody at the table burst out laughing, and Schprintze laughed too. Everybody was happy, everybody felt gay; it was a wonderful, happy *Shevuos*. How was I to know that from all this good cheer would come so much sorrow and misery? That God's punishment would descend on my head and blackest grief on my soul?

Man is a fool. If he was wise he would never let anything touch him too deeply. He would know that if things are a certain way that's the way they were intended to be. For if things were intended to be different, they wouldn't have been as they are. Don't we say in the Psalms: "*Put your trust in God?*" —Have faith in Him and He will see to it that you stagger under a load of trouble and keep on reciting: "*This too is for the best.*" Listen to what can happen in this world, but listen carefully, for this is where my story really begins.

"It was evening and it was day." Once toward evening, I came home, worn out from the day's labors, from running all over Boiberik, delivering milk and cheese from *datcha* to *datcha*. When I approached my house I saw a familiar-looking horse hitched to my front door. I could have sworn it was Aarontchik's horse, the one I had valued at three hundred *rubles*. I went up to the horse, slapped him on the rump, scratched his throat and shook him by the mane. "Here, my fine fellow," I said to him, "what are you doing here?" He turned his engaging face toward me and gave me a look, as though to say, "Why ask me? Ask my master."

I went inside and asked my wife, "Tell me, Golde my treasure, what is Aarontchik doing here?"

"How should I know?" she said. "He is a friend of yours, isn't he?"

"Where is he now?" I asked.

"He went strolling in the woods with the children."

"What's all this strolling around for all of a sudden?" I said, and told my wife to give me supper. After I had eaten, I thought to myself, "What are you getting so rattled about, Tevye? If someone comes to visit you, do you have to get so upset? You should be pleased."

As I tell myself this, I take a look outside and see my girls approaching with the young man, carrying bouquets of freshly picked flowers. The two younger girls, Teibel and Beilke, are walking together in front, and behind them are Schprintze and Aarontchik.

"Good evening."

"Good day."

Aarontchik stands at a side, stroking his horse, chewing at a blade of grass, and there is a strange look on his face. He says to me, "Reb Tevye, I want to do business with you. Let's exchange horses."

"You've found just the person to play a joke on," I said.

"No," he said, "I'm in earnest."

"So you're in earnest. And how much is your horse worth?"

"How much would you value him at?" he asks.

"I would value him at three hundred *rubles*, if not a shade more."

He burst out laughing at this and told me that the horse had cost him over three times as much. "Well, is it a deal then?"

I didn't find this kind of talk to my taste. What did he mean by wanting to change his expensive horse for my broken-down nag? I told him to put the deal off for some other time and I asked him jokingly if he had come all the way to my farm just to exchange horses. If so, I told him, he had wasted the train fare. . . .

He answered me quite seriously, "I came to see you, actually, in regard to something else. Shall we take a little stroll together, Reb Tevye?"

"What's he taken to strolling around for?" I thought to myself as I began walking with him in the direction of the wood. The sun had set some time ago and the little green wood was in darkness, the frogs were croaking in the marsh, and the grass was fragrant. Aarontchik walked and so did I. He was silent and so was I. All at once he stopped, cleared his throat and said to me, "Reb Tevye, what would you say if I told you that I am in love with your daughter Schprintze and that I want to marry her?"

"What would I say? I would say that a crazy man's name should be erased and yours put in his place."

He gave me an odd look and said, "What do you mean?"

"Just what I said."

"I don't understand you," he said.

"That shows that you are not very clever. As it is written: '*A wise man hath his eyes in his head.*' Which means that a smart man can understand a nod, but a fool needs a stick."

He said in a hurt tone of voice, "I ask you a plain question and you put me off with proverbs and quotations."

"Every cantor sings according to his ability and every orator speaks of what concerns him. If you want to know what kind of orator you are, talk it over with your mother. She will put you straight."

"I see that you take me for a child that has to run and ask his mother."

"Of course you have to ask your mother, and of course she will tell you that you are an imbecile, and what's more, she will be right."

"And she will be right?"

"Certainly she will be right. What sort of bridegroom would you make my Schprintze? And what kind of match is she for you? And most important of all, what kind of relative-by-marriage will I be to your mother?"

"If that's what's bothering you, Reb Tevye, you can rest easy. I am not a boy of eighteen and I am not looking for rich connections for my mother. I know who you are, and I know who your daughter is. She suits me and that's the way I want it, and that's the way it's going to be."

"Forgive me for interrupting you," I said to him. "I see that you are all done with one side. But have you settled it with the other side?"

"I don't know what you mean," he said.

"I mean my daughter Schprintze. Have you talked to her about all this? And what did she have to say?"

He pretended to look insulted, and then he said with a smile, "Of course I have talked with her, and more than once. I've talked to her many times. I've been coming here every day."

Did you hear that? He's been coming here every day and I knew nothing about it. "You're a donkey, not a man," I said to myself. "You should be given straw to chew on. Letting yourself be led by the nose like that. Your table and chairs could be sold out from under you and you wouldn't know it."

Thinking thus, I walked back to the house with Aarontchik. He took his leave of my family, jumped on his horse, and "*departed like Moses*—" He was off to Boiberik.

And now, it is time, as they say in books, to leave the hero, and follow the fortunes of the heroine, meaning in this case, Schprintze.

"Listen to me, my daughter," I said. "And listen well. Tell me, what did Aarontchik talk to you about behind my back?"

Does a tree answer when you speak to it? That's how she answered me. She blushed like a bride, lowered her eyes, and wouldn't utter a word.

I thought to myself, "If you won't talk now, you will later on. Tevye is not a woman. Tevye can wait." And I waited, as they say, till "*his day will come.*" I watched for the moment when we should be alone. Then I said to her, "Schprintze, answer my question. Do you at least know this Aarontchik?"

She said, "Of course I know him."

"Do you know that he is nothing but a penny-whistle?"

"What is a penny-whistle?" she asked.

"It is an empty walnut-shell that whistles when you blow into it."

"You are mistaken," she said. "Arnold is a fine person."

"So he is Arnold to you, not Aarontchik—the charlatan!"

"Arnold is not a charlatan, father," she said. "Arnold has a kind heart. He is a man with principles. He is surrounded by a house full of vulgar people who think of nothing but money, money, and more money."

"So you've become an enlightened philosopher too, Schprintze?" I said to her. "And you've learned to despise money."

I could tell from this conversation that things had gone pretty far with them and that it was too late to undo them. For I know my daughters. Tevye's daughters, as I've told you before, when they fall in love with someone, it's with their hearts and souls and bodies. And I said to myself, "Fool, why do you try to outsmart the whole world? Perhaps God has willed it that through this quiet little Schprintze you should be rewarded for all the pain and suffering you have undergone until now, and enjoy a pleasant and restful old age, and learn what life can really be like. Maybe it was fated that you should have one daughter, a millionairess. Why not? Won't the honor sit well on you? Where is it written that Tevye should be a pauper all his life, that he should always drag himself around with his horse and wagon, serving the rich people of Yehupetz who like to gorge themselves on butter and cheese? Who knows, maybe it has been inscribed above that I should become an important person in my old age, that I should dispense charity and entertain guests at my home, and sit together with the learned men and study the *Torah*?"

These and other such golden thoughts crowded through my head; as it is written in the morning prayer: "*Many thoughts are in man's heart.*" Or, as they say in Russian, "An idea enriches a fool."

I came into the house, took my wife aside and said to her, "How would you like it if your Schprintze became a millionairess?"

"What is a millionairess?" she asks me.

"A millionairess is a millionaire's wife," I tell her.

"And what is a millionaire?" she wants to know.

"A millionaire is a man who has a million."

"How much is a million?" she asks.

"If you are so simple that you don't know how much a million is, how can I talk to you?"

"Who asked you to talk to me?" she says. And she was right.

A day passed, and I came home and asked, "Has Aarontchik been here?" "No, he hasn't." Another day passed. "Was the young man here today?" "No, he wasn't." To go to the widow and ask for an explanation didn't seem proper. I didn't want her to think that Tevye was running after the match. And besides I had a feeling that this whole affair was to her like *"a rose among thorns,"* or like a fifth wheel to a wagon. Though I couldn't understand why. Because I didn't have a million? So I was getting my daughter a mother-in-law who was a millionairess. And whom would her son get for a father-in-law? A pauper, a man who had nothing, a poor wretch called Tevye the Dairyman. Of the two, who had more to boast of? I'll tell you the honest truth, I began to be a little eager for the match myself. Not so much for the sake of the money as for the honor. The devil take those rich people of Yehupetz. It was time Tevye showed them a thing or two. All you had heard in Yehupetz till now was Brodsky and Brodsky and Brodsky. Just as though the rest of us weren't human beings.

This was how I reflected one day driving home from Boiberik. When I came into the house my wife met me with glad tidings. "A messenger has just been here from Boiberik. The widow wants to see you right away. Even if you come home after dark, she wants you to turn right around and go back to Boiberik. She must see you tonight."

"What's the hurry?" I asked. "Can't she wait?" I looked over at Schprintze. She didn't say a word, but her eyes spoke for her. How they spoke! No one could understand what was in her heart as well as I. I had been afraid all along that, who knows, the whole affair might come to nothing, and I wanted to save her heartache. I had said this and that against Aarontchik, belittled him in every way I knew. I might as well have talked to a stone wall. Schprintze was wasting away like a candle.

I harnessed my horse and wagon again and toward evening I set off for Boiberik. Riding along, I thought to myself, "Why should they want to see me so urgently? To arrange a betrothal? He could have come to me for that. After all, I am the girl's father." Then I laughed at the very thought. Who had ever heard of a rich man coming to a poor man? It would mean that the world was coming to an end, and the times of the Messiah had dawned, as some of those modern young people tried to tell me. The time will come, they said, when the rich will divide up everything with the poor, share and share alike—what's yours is mine and what's mine is yours, and everybody will be equal. It seems to me that it's a clever world we live in, and yet there are such fools in it!

I arrived at Boiberik and went straight to the widow's house. I stopped my horse and got off the wagon. Where is the widow? Nowhere in sight. Where is her son? I don't see him either. Then who sent for me? "I sent for you," said a short, round barrel of a man, with a sparse little beard and a heavy gold chain around his stomach.

"And who are you?" I asked.

"I am the widow's brother, Aarontchik's uncle," he said. "I was summoned from Ekaterineslav by telegram and I have just arrived."

"If so, *sholom aleichem* to you," I said, and sat down.

When he saw me sit down, he said, "Be seated."

"Thanks, I am already sitting," I said. "How are you, and how is the Constitution in your part of the country?"

He didn't even listen to me. Instead, he spread himself out in a rocking chair, with his hands in his pockets; and with his big stomach with the gold chain around it turned toward me and said, "I understand your name is Tevye."

"That's right. When I am summoned to read the *Torah*, that's the name they call me by. 'Arise, Reb Tevye, son of Reb Shneour Zalman.' "

"Listen to me, Reb Tevye," he said. "Why should we enter into a long discussion? Let's get right down to business."

"With pleasure. King Solomon said long ago, '*There is a time for everything*.' If you have to talk business, then talk business. I am a businessman myself."

"I can see you're a businessman. That's why I'm going to talk to you like one businessman to another. I want you to tell me, but tell me frankly, how much it will cost us all told. Remember now, speak frankly."

"Since you ask me to speak frankly," I said, "I must tell you that I don't know what you are talking about."

"Reb Tevye," he said once more, without taking his hands out of his pockets, "I am asking you how much this affair will cost us?"

"It depends on what kind of affair you mean. If you want an elaborate wedding, the sort of affair you're accustomed to, I'm not in a position to do it."

He looked at me as though I were out of my mind. "Either you are playing the oaf, or you really are one. Though I don't believe you are an oaf. If you were, you wouldn't have gotten my nephew into your clutches the way you did. Pretending to invite him to your house to eat *blintzes* on *Shevuos*, then putting a pretty girl in front of him—whether she is a daughter or not a daughter I won't go so far as to say. . . . But it's plain that she turned his head, made him take a fancy to her, and she took a fancy to him, that goes without saying. She may be a good girl and mean no harm, I won't go so far as to say. But you mustn't forget who *you* are and who *we* are. It seems to me you are a man with brains, how could you permit such a thing? That Tevye the Dairyman who delivers our cheese and milk should marry into our family! You will tell me that they made promises to each other? They can take them back. It's not a great catastrophe one way or the other. If it has to cost us something, we won't argue about it either. A girl is not a young man, whether a daughter or not a daughter, I won't go so far as to say. . . ."

"God in Heaven," I thought to myself, "what does the man want from me?" But he doesn't stop ranting. I needn't think, he tells me, that it will do any good to create a scandal, to spread the news that his nephew wanted to marry my daughter. And I should get it out of my head that his sister is a person who can be milked dry. If I don't make any trouble, well and good, I can get a few *rubles* from her. She will put it down to charity. After all, they are only human, they have to help another person once in a while.

Do you want to know how I answered him? *"May my tongue cleave to the roof of my mouth."* I didn't answer him at all. I had lost my powers of speech. I got up, turned my back on him, and went. I ran as from a fire, I escaped as from a dungeon. My head was humming, everything was going around in front of my eyes, in my ears buzzed bits of his conversation—"Speak frankly now . . ." "A daughter or not a daughter . . ." ". . . milking the widow dry." "Put it down to charity." I went up to my horse, buried my face in the wagon and—you won't laugh at me?—I burst into tears. When I had cried myself out, I got up on the driver's seat, and gave my horse as much as he could hold with the whip. Then I asked God, as Job had once asked Him, "What hast Thou seen in old Job, dear Lord, that Thou never leavest him be for a moment? Are there no other people in the world but him?"

I came home and found my family sitting around the supper table very cheerful, talking and laughing. Only Schprintze was missing.

"Where is Schprintze?" I asked.

"What happened?" they all wanted to know. "What did they want you for?"

"Where is Schprintze?" I asked again.

And again they asked me, "What happened? Tell us."

"Nothing," I said. "What should happen? Everything is quiet, thank God. There is no news of pogroms."

At these words Schprintze came in, looked into my eyes, then sat down at the table, without a word, as though this had nothing to do with her. There was no expression on her face and her silence was unnatural. I didn't like the way she sat there, sunk in thought, and the way she did everything we told her to do. When we told her to sit down, she sat. When we told her to eat, she ate. When we told her to go, she went. And when we called her name, she jumped. My heart ached at the sight of her and inside me burned a fire, against whom I didn't know. "O thou Heavenly Father, God Almighty, why do you punish me so? For whose sins?"

Well, do you want to hear the end of the story? I wouldn't wish such an end to my worst enemies. It would be wrong to wish it to any human being. For the curse of the children is the worst curse in the chapter of *Admonitions*. How do I know that someone didn't visit that curse on me? You don't believe in such things? What else could it be then? Tell me if you know, but what's the good of arguing about it? Better listen to the end of the story.

One evening I was driving home from Boiberik with a heavy heart. Just imagine the grief and the feeling of shame. And then, too, my heart ached for my child. You ask what happened to the widow and her son? They had gone, vanished without a trace. They left without so much as saying good-bye. I am almost ashamed to mention this, but they left owing me a small debt for butter and cheese. But I don't hold it against them, they must have forgotten. What hurt me most was that they went without saying good-bye. What my poor child went through no living person ever knew, except me. I am her father and a father's heart understands. Do you think she uttered a word to me? Or complained, or wept, even once? Then you don't know Tevye's daughters. She kept her grief to herself, but she wasted away, she flickered like a dying candle. Only once in a while she would let out a sigh, and that sigh was enough to tear out your heart.

Well, I was driving home that evening, sunk in meditation, asking questions of the Almighty and answering them myself. I wasn't worried about God so much, I could come to terms with Him, one way or another. What bothered me was people. Why should people be so cruel to each other, when they could be so kind? Why should human beings bring suffering to one another as well as to themselves, when they could all live together in peace and good will? Could it be that God had created man on this earth just to make him suffer? What satisfaction would He get out of that?

Thinking these thoughts, I drove into my farm and saw at a distance that over by the pond a big crowd had gathered, old people, young people, men, women, children, everybody in the village. What could it be? It was not a fire. Someone must have drowned. Someone had been bathing in the pond and had met his death. No one knows where the Angel of Death lurks for him, as we say on the Day of Atonement.

Suddenly I saw Golde running, her shawl flying, her arms outstretched, and in front of her the children, Teibel and Beilke, and all three of them screaming and weeping and wailing: "Daughter!" "Sister!" "Schprintze!" I jumped off the wagon so fast that I don't know to this day how I reached the ground in one piece. But when I got to the pond it was too late. . . .

There was something I meant to ask you. What was it? Oh, yes. Have you ever seen a drowned person? When someone dies he usually dies with his eyes closed. A drowned person's eyes are wide open. Do you know the reason for this? Forgive me for taking up so much of your time. I am not a free man either. I have to get back to my horse and wagon and start delivering milk and cheese. The world is still with us. You have to think of earning a living, and forget what has been. For what the earth has covered is better forgotten. There is no help for it, and we have to return to the old saying that as long as "*my soul abides within me*"—you have to keep going, Tevye. Be well, my friend, and if you think of me sometimes, don't think ill of me.

Tevye Goes to Palestine

WELL, well, look who's here! Reb Sholom Aleichem, how are you? You're almost a stranger. I never dreamed of this pleasure. Greetings! Here I've been wondering over and over, why we haven't seen him all this time, either in Boiberik, or in Yehupetz. Who can tell? Maybe he had packed up and left us altogether—gone off yonder where people don't even know the taste of radishes and chicken fat. But then I thought: Why should *he* do such a foolish thing? A man of wisdom and learning like *him*? Well, thank God, we meet again in good health. How does the passage go? "*A wall cannot meet a wall —Man meets man. . . .*"

You are looking at me, sir, as though you didn't recognize me. It's me, your faithful old friend, Tevye. "*Look not at the pitcher but at its contents.*" Don't let my new coat fool you; it's still the same *shlimazl* who's wearing it, the same as always. It's just that when a man puts on his Sabbath clothes, right away he begins to look like somebody—as though he were trying to pass for a rich man. But when you go forth among strangers you can't do otherwise, especially if you are setting out on a long journey like this, all the way to Palestine. . . .

You look at me as if you're thinking: How does it happen that a plain little man like Tevye, who spent all his life delivering milk and butter, should suddenly get a notion like this into his head—something that only a millionaire like Brodsky could allow himself in his old age? Believe me, Mr. Sholom Aleichem, "*it is altogether questionable. . . .*" The Bible is right every time. Just move your suitcase over this way, if you will be so good, and I will sit down across from you and tell you the whole story. And then you'll know what the Lord can do. . . .

But first of all, before I go on, I must tell you that I have been a widower for some time. My Golde, may she rest in peace, is dead. She was a plain woman, without learning, without pretensions, but extremely pious. May she intercede for her children in the other world; they caused her enough suffering in this one, perhaps even brought on her untimely death. She couldn't bear it any longer, seeing them scatter and disappear the way they did, some one way, some another. "Heavens above!" she used to say. "What have I left to live for, all alone without kith or kin? Why, even a cow," she would say, "is lonesome when you wean her calf away from her."

That's the way she spoke, and she wept bitterly. I could see the poor woman wasting away, day by day, going out like a candle, right before my eyes. And I said to her with my heart full of pity, "Ah, Golde, my dear, there is a text in the Holy Book: *'Im k'vonim im k'vodim—Whether we're like children or like slaves,'* which means that you can live just as well with children as without them. We have," I told her, "a great Lord and a good Lord and a mighty Lord, but just the same I'd like to be blessed for every time He puts one of His tricks over on us."

But she was, may she forgive me for saying this, only a female. So she says to me, "It's a sin to speak this way, you mustn't sin, Tevye." "There you go," said I. "Did I speak any evil? Did I do anything contrary to the Lord's will? All I meant was that if He went ahead and did such a fine job of creating this world of His so that children are not children, and parents are no better than mud under one's feet, no doubt He knew what He was doing."

But she didn't understand me. Her mind was wandering. "I am dying, Tevye," she said. "And who will cook your supper?" She barely whispered the words and the look in her eyes was enough to melt a stone. But Tevye is not a weakling; so I answered her with a quip and a quotation and a homily. "Golde," I said to her, "you have been faithful to me these many years, you won't make a fool of me in my old age." I looked at her and became frightened. "What's the matter with you, Golde?" "Nothing," she whispered, barely able to speak. Then I saw that the game was lost. I jumped into my wagon and went off to town and came back with a doctor, the best doctor I could find. When I come home, what do I see? My Golde is laid out on the ground with a candle at her head, looking just like a little mound of earth that had been raked together and covered with a black cloth. I stand there and think to myself: "'*Is that all that man is?*—Is this the end of man?' Oh, Lord, the things you have done to your Tevye. What will I do now in my old age, forsaken and alone?" And I threw myself on the ground.

But what good is shouting and weeping? Listen to me and I will tell you something. When a person sees death in front of him he becomes a cynic. He can't help thinking, "*What are we and what is our life?*—What is this world altogether with its wheels that turn, its trains that run wildly in all directions, with all its tumult and confusion, noise and bustle?" And even the rich men with all their possessions and their wealth—in the end they come to nothing too.

Well, I hired a *kaddish* for her, for my wife Golde, and paid him for the whole year in advance. What else could I do if God had denied us sons to pray for us when we were dead, and given us only daughters, nothing but daughters one after another? I don't know if everybody else has as much trouble with his daughters, or if I'm the only *shlimazl*, but I've had no luck with any of my daughters. As far as the girls themselves are concerned, I have nothing to complain about. And as for luck—that's in God's hands. I wish I had half the happiness my girls wish me to have. If anything, they are too loyal, too faithful—and too much of even the best is superfluous. Take my youngest, for instance—Beilke we call her. Do you have any idea of the kind of girl she is? You have known me long enough to know that I am not the kind of father who will praise his children just for the sake of talking. But since I've mentioned Beilke I'll have to tell you this much: Since God first began making Beilkes, He never created another like this Beilke of mine. I won't even talk about her looks. Tevye's daughters are all famous for their great beauty, but this one, this Beilke, puts all the others in the shade. But beauty alone is nothing. When you speak of Beilke, you really have to use the words of the Proverbs regarding "*a woman of valor.*" Charms are deceitful. I am speaking of character now. She is pure goodness all the way through. She had always been devoted to me, but since Golde died I became the apple of her eye. She wouldn't let a speck of dust fall on me. I said to myself, as we say on the High Holy Days: "*The Lord precedes anger with mercy.*—God always sends a remedy for the disease." Only sometimes it's hard to tell which is worse, the remedy or the disease.

For instance, how could I have foreseen that on my account Beilke would go and sell herself for money and send her old father in his declining years to Palestine? Of course that's only a way of speaking. She is as much to blame for this as you are. It was all his fault, her chosen one. I don't want to wish him ill, may an armory collapse on him. And yet if we look at this more closely, if we dig beneath the surface, we might find out that I am to blame as much as anyone, as it says in the *Gamorah: "Man is obligated . . ."* But imagine my telling *you* what the *Gamorah* says.

But I don't want to bore you with too long a tale. One year passed, then another. My Beilke grew up and became a presentable young woman. Tevye kept on with his horse and wagon, delivering his milk and butter as usual, to Boiberik in the summer, to Yehupetz in the winter—may a deluge overtake that town, as it did Sodom. I can't bear to look at that place any more, and not so much the place as the people in it, and not so much the people as one man, Ephraim the *Shadchan*, the matchmaker, may the devil take him and his father both. Let me tell you what a man, a *shadchan*, can do.

"And it came to pass," that one time, in the middle of September, I arrived in Yehupetz with my little load. I looked up—and behold! *"Haman approacheth. . . ."* There goes Ephraim the *Shadchan*. I think I've told you about him before. He is like a burr; once he attaches himself to you, you can't get rid of him. But when you see him you have to stop—that's the power he has in him.

"Whoa, there, my sage!" I called out to my little horse. "Hold on a minute and I'll give you something to chew on." And I stop to greet the *shadchan* and start a conversation with him. "How are things going in your profession?" With a deep sigh he answers, "It's tough, very tough." "In what way?" I ask.

"There's nothing doing."

"Nothing at all?"

"Not a thing."

"What's the matter?"

"The matter is," says he, "that people don't marry off their children at home any more."

"Where do they marry them off?"

"Out of town, out of the country in fact."

"Then what can a man like me do," I say, "who has never

been away from home and whose grandmother's grandmother has never been away either?"

He offers me a pinch of snuff. "For you, Reb Tevye," he says, "I have a piece of merchandise right here on the spot."

"For instance?"

"A widow without children, and with a hundred and fifty *rubles* besides. She used to be a cook in the very best families."

I give him a look. "Reb Ephraim, for whom is this match intended?"

"For whom do you suppose? For you."

"Of all the crazy fantastic ideas anybody ever had, you've dreamed up the worst." And I whipped my horse and was ready to start off. But Ephraim stopped me. "Don't be offended, Reb Tevye, I didn't want to hurt your feelings. Tell me, whom did *you* have in mind?"

"Whom should I have in mind? My youngest daughter, of course."

At this he sprang back and slapped his forehead. "Wait!" he cried. "It's a good thing you mentioned it! God bless you and preserve you, Reb Tevye."

"The same to you," I said. "Amen. May you live until the Messiah comes. But what makes you so joyful all of a sudden?"

"It's wonderful! It's excellent! In fact, it's so good, it couldn't possibly be any better."

"What's so wonderful?" I ask him.

"I have just the thing for your daughter. A plum, a prize, the pick of the lot. He's a winner, a goldspinner, a rich man, a millionaire. He is a contractor and his name is Padhatzur."

"Hmm. Padhatzur? It sounds familiar, like a name in the Bible."

"What Bible? What's the Bible got to do with it? He is a contractor, this Padhatzur, he builds houses and factories and bridges. He was in Japan during the war and made a fortune. He rides in a carriage drawn by fiery steeds, he has a lackey at the door, a bathtub right in his own house, furniture from Paris, and a diamond ring on his finger. He's not such an old man either and he's never been married. He is a bachelor, a first-class article. And he's looking for a pretty girl; it makes no difference who she is or whether she has a stitch to her back, as long as she is good-looking."

"Whoa, there! You are going too fast. If you don't stop to

graze your horses we'll land in Hotzenplotz. Besides, if I'm not mistaken you once tried to arrange a match for this same man with my older daughter, Hodel."

When he heard this, the *shadchan* began laughing so hard I was afraid the man would get a stroke. "Oh-ho, now you're talking about something that happened when my grandmother was delivered of her firstborn. That one went bankrupt before the war and ran off to America."

" '*When you speak of a holy man, bless him. . . .*' Maybe this one will run off too."

He was outraged at this. "How can you say such a thing, Reb Tevye? The other fellow was a fraud, a charlatan, a spendthrift. This one is a contractor, with business connections, with an office, with clerks, everything."

Well, what shall I tell you—the matchmaker became so excited that he pulled me off the wagon and grabbed me by the lapels, and shook me so hard that a policeman came up and wanted to send us both to the police station. It was lucky that I remembered what the passage says: "*You may take interest from a stranger.*—You have to know how to deal with policemen."

Well, why should I drag this out? Padhatzur became engaged to my daughter Beilke. "*The days were not long.*" It was quite a while before they were married. Why do I say it was quite a while? Because Beilke was no more eager to marry him than she was to lie down and die. The more he showered her with gifts, with gold watches and rings and diamonds, the more distasteful he became to her. I am not a child when it comes to such matters. I could tell from the look on her face and from her eyes red with weeping how she felt. So one day I decided to speak to her about it. I said to her as if I had just this minute thought of it, "I am afraid, Beilke, that this groom of yours is as dear and sweet to you as he is to me."

She flared up at this. "Who told you?"

"If not," I said, "why do you cry nights?"

"Have I been crying?"

"No, you haven't been crying, you've just been bawling. Do you think if you hide your head in your pillow you can keep your tears from me? Do you think that your father is a little child, or that he is in his dotage and doesn't understand that you are doing it on his account? That you want to provide for him in his old age, so he will have a place to lay his head and won't have to go begging from house to house? If that's what you have in mind, then you are a big fool. We have an all-powerful God, and Tevye is not one of those loafers who will fold his hands and live on the bread of charity. *'Money is worthless,'* as the Bible says. If you want proof, look at your sister Hodel, who is practically a pauper; but look at what she writes from the ends of the earth, how happy she is with her Feferel." Well, do you know what she said to this? Try and make a guess.

"Don't compare me to Hodel," she said. "Hodel grew up in a time when the whole world rocked on its foundations, when it was ready at any moment to turn upside down. In those days people were concerned about the world and forgot about themselves. Now that the world is back to where it was, people think about themselves and forget about the world." That's how she answered, and how was I to know what she meant?

Well. You know what Tevye's daughters are like. But you should have seen my Beilke at her wedding. A princess, no less. All I could do was stand and gaze at her, and I thought to myself, "Is this Beilke, a daughter of Tevye? Where did she learn to stand like this, to walk like this, to hold her head like this, and to wear her clothes so that she looked as though she'd been poured into them?"

But I wasn't allowed to gaze at her very long, for that same day at about half past six in the evening the young couple arose and departed.—They went off, the Lord knows where, to Nitaly somewhere, as is the custom with the rich nowadays, and they didn't come back until around *Hannukah.* And when they came back I got a message from them *to be sure* to come to see them in Yehupetz at once, *without fail.*

What could it mean? If they just wanted me to come, they would simply have asked me to come. But why *be sure to come* and *without fail?* Something must be up. But the question was, what? All sorts of thoughts, both good and bad, crowded through my head. Could the couple have had a fight already and be ready for a divorce? I called myself a fool at once. Why did I always expect the worst? "Maybe they are lonesome for you and want to see you? Or maybe Beilke wants her father close to her? Or perhaps Padhatzur wants to give you a job, take you into the business with him, make you the manager of his enterprises?" Whatever it is, I had to go. And

I got into my wagon, and *"went forth to Heron."* On to Yehupetz!

As I rode along, my imagination carried me away. I dreamed that I had given up the farm, sold my cows, my horse and wagon and everything else, and had moved into town. I had become first a foreman for my son-in-law, then a paymaster, then a factotum, the general manager of all his enterprises, and finally a partner in his business, share and share alike, and rode along with him behind the prancing steeds, one dun-colored and the other chestnut. And I couldn't help marveling, *"What is this and what is it all for?"* How does it happen that a quiet, unassuming man like me should have suddenly become so great? And what do I need all this excitement and confusion for, all the hurry and flurry, day and night, night and day? How do you say it? *"To seat them with the mighty*—hobnobbing with all the millionaires?" Leave me be, I beg of you. All I want is peace and quiet in my old age, enough leisure so that I can look into a learned tome now and then, read a chapter of the Psalms. A person has to think once in a while of the next world too. How does King Solomon put it? Man is a fool—he forgets that no matter how long he lives he has to die sometime.

It was with thoughts like these running through my head that I arrived in Yehupetz and came to the house of Padhatzur. What's the good of boasting? Shall I describe to you his *"abundance of wealth"*? His house and grounds? I have never had the honor of visiting Brodsky's house, but I can hardly believe that it could be more splendid than my son-in-law's. You might gather what sort of place it was from the fact that the man who stood guard at the door, a fellow resplendent in a uniform with huge silver buttons, wouldn't let me in under any consideration. What kind of business was this? The door was of glass and I could see the lackey standing there brushing clothes, may his name and memory be blotted out. I wink at him, I signal to him in sign language, show him with my hands that he should let me in because the master's wife is my own flesh and blood, my daughter. But he doesn't seem to understand me at all, the pigheaded lout, and motions to me also in sign language to go to the devil, to get out of there.

What do you think of that? I have to have special influence

to get to my own daughter. "Woe unto your gray hairs," I told myself. "So this is what you have come to." I looked through the glass door again and saw a girl moving about. A chambermaid, I decided, noticing her shifty eyes. All chambermaids have shifty eyes. I am at home in rich houses and I know what the maids who work there are like.

I wink at her. "Open up, little kitty." She obeys me, opens the door and says to me in Yiddish, "Whom do you want?" And I say, "Does Padhatzur live here?" And she says, louder this time, "Whom do you want?" And I say still louder, "Answer my question first. 'Does Padhatzur live here?' " "Yes," she says. "If so," I tell her, "we can talk the same language. Tell Madame Padhatzur that she has a visitor. Her father Tevye has come to see her and has been standing outside for quite some time like a beggar at the door, for he did not have the good fortune to find favor in the eyes of this barbarian with the silver buttons whom I wouldn't exchange for your littlest finger."

After she heard me out, the girl laughed impudently, slammed the door in my face, ran into the house and up the stairs, then ran down again, opened the door and led me into a palace the like of which my father and grandfather had never seen, even in a dream. Silk and velvet and gold and crystal, and as you walked across the room you couldn't hear your own step, for your sinner's feet were sinking into the softest carpets, as soft as newly fallen snow. And clocks. Clocks everywhere. Clocks on the walls, clocks on the tables. Clocks all over the place. Dear Lord, what more can you have in store? What does a person need that many clocks for? And I keep going, with my hands clasped behind my back. I look up—several Tevyes at once are cutting across toward me from all directions. One Tevye comes this way, another Tevye that way; one is coming toward me, another away from me. How do you like that? On all sides—mirrors. Only a bird like him, that contractor of mine, could afford to surround himself with all those mirrors and clocks.

And he appeared in my mind's eyes the way he had looked the first day he came to my house—a round, fat little man with a loud voice and a sniggering laugh. He arrived in a carriage drawn by fiery steeds and proceeded to make himself at home as though he were in his own father's vineyard. He saw my Beilke, talked to her, and then called me off to one side and whispered a secret into my ear—so loud you could have heard it on the other side of Yehupetz. What was the secret? Only this—that my daughter had found favor in his eyes, and one-two-three he wanted to get married. As for my daughter's finding favor in his eyes, that was easy enough to understand, but when it came to the other part, the one-two-three—that was *"like a double edged sword to me"*—it sank like a dull knife into my heart.

What did he mean—one-two-three and get married? Where did I come into the picture? And what about Beilke? Oh, how I longed to drum some texts into his ears, and to give him a proverb or two to remember me by. But thinking it over, I decided: "Why should I come between these young people? A lot you accomplished, Tevye, when you tried to arrange the marriages of your older daughters. You talked and you talked. You poured out all your wisdom and learning. And who was made a fool of in the end? Tevye, of course."

Now let us forsake the hero, as they say in books, and follow the fortunes of the heroine. I had done what they asked me to do, I had come to Yehupetz. They greeted me effusively: *"Sholom Aleichem." "Aleichem sholom."* "How are *you?*" "And how are things with you?" "Please be seated." "Thank you, I am quite comfortable." And so on, with the usual courtesies. I was wondering whether I should speak up and ask why they had sent for me—*"Today of all days"*—but it didn't seem proper. Tevye is not a woman, he can wait.

Meanwhile, a man-servant with huge white gloves appeared and announced that supper was on the table, and the three of us got up and went into a room that was entirely furnished in oak. The table was of oak, the chairs of oak, the walls panelled in oak and the ceiling of oak, and all of it was elaborately carved and painted and curlicued and bedizened. A kingly feast was set on the table. There was coffee and tea and hot chocolate, all sorts of pastries and the best of cognacs, appetizers and other good things, as well as every kind of fruit. I am ashamed to admit it, but I am afraid that in her father's house, Beilke had never seen such delicacies.

Well, they poured me a glass, and then another glass and I drank their health. I looked over at my Beilke and thought to myself, "You have really done well by yourself, my daughter. As they say in Hallel: *'Who raiseth up the poor out of the dust . . .'* When God has been kind to a poor man, *'and lifteth up the needy out of the dunghill,'* you can't recognize him any longer." She is the same Beilke as before and yet not the same. And I thought of the Beilke that used to be and compared her to this one and my heart ached. It was as though I had made a bad bargain—let us say I had exchanged my hard-working little horse for a strange colt that might turn out to be a real horse or nothing but a dummy.

"Ah Beilke," I thought, "look at what's become of you. Remember how once you used to sit at night by a smoking lamp, sewing and singing to yourself? Or how you could milk two cows in the blink of an eye. Or roll up your sleeves and cook a good old-fashioned *borsht,* or a dish of beans or dumplings with cheese, or bake a batch of poppyseed cakes. 'Father,' you would call, 'wash up, supper is ready.' And that was the finest song of all to my ears."

And now she sits there with her Padhatzur, like a queen, and two men run back and forth waiting on the table with a great clatter of dishes. And she? Does she utter a single word? But let me tell you, her Padhatzur isn't silent. He talks enough for two. His mouth doesn't shut for a moment. In all my life I had never seen a man who could jabber so endlessly and say so little, interspersing all his talk with that sniggering laugh of his. We have a saying for this: "He makes up his own jokes and laughs at them himself."

Besides us three, there was another guest at the table—a fellow with bulging red cheeks. I don't know who or what he was, but he seemed to be a glutton of no mean proportions. All the time Padhatzur was talking and laughing, he went on stuffing himself. As it is written: "*Three who have eaten*—he ate enough for three." This one guzzled and the other one talked, such foolish empty talk—I couldn't understand a word of it. It was all about contracts, government pronouncements, banks, money, Japan.

The only thing that interested me was his mention of Japan, for I too had had dealings with that country. During the war, as you know, horses "*commanded the highest prices*—they went looking for them with a candle." Well, they finally found me too, and took my horse with them. My little horse was measured with a yardstick, put through his paces, driven back and forth, and in the end he was given a white card—an honorable discharge. I could have told them all along that their trouble was for nothing. "*The righteous man knoweth the soul of his animal."* No horse of Tevye's will ever go to war. But forgive me, Mr. Sholom Aleichem, for straying away from my subject. Let's get back to the story.

Well, we had eaten and drunk our fill, as the Lord had bade us do, and when we got up from the table, Padhatzur took my arm and led me into an office that was ornately furnished, with guns and swords hanging on the walls, and miniature cannon on the table. He sat me down on a sort of divan that was as soft as butter, and took out of a gold box two long, fat, aromatic cigars, lit one for himself and one for me. He then sat down opposite me, stretched out his legs and said, "Do you know why I have sent for you?"

"Aha," I thought, "Now he is getting down to business." But I played dumb and said, " '*Am I my brother's keeper?*'— How should I know?"

So he said, "I wanted to talk to you, and it's you yourself I want to talk about."

"If it's good news," I replied, "go ahead, let's hear it."

He took the cigar out from between his teeth, and began a long lecture. "You are a man of sense, I believe, not a fool, and you will forgive me for speaking frankly with you. You must know already that I am doing business on a very big scale, and when a man does business on such a tremendous scale . . ."

"Now he is getting there," I thought to myself, and interrupted him in the middle of his speech. "As the *Gamorah* says in the Sabbath portion: '*The more business the more worries . . .*' Do you happen to be familiar with that passage in the *Gamorah*?"

He answered me quite frankly. "I will tell you the honest truth, I have never studied the *Gamorah* and I wouldn't recognize it if I saw it." And he laughed that irritating laugh of his. What do you think of a man like that? It seems to me that if God has chastised you by making you illiterate, at least keep it under your hat instead of boasting about it. But all I said was, "I gathered that you had no knowledge of these things, but let me hear what you have to say further."

"Further I want to tell you, that it isn't fitting, considering the scale of my enterprises, and the repute in which my name is held, as well as my station in life, that you should be known as Tevye the Dairyman. I'll have you know that I am personally acquainted with the Governor, and that it is very likely that one of these days Brodsky might come to my house or Poliakov or maybe even Rothschild, whomever the devil sends."

He finished speaking, and I sat there and looked at his shiny bald spot and thought to myself, "It may be true that you are personally acquainted with the Governor, and that Rothschild might even come to your house some day, but just the same you talk like a common cur." And I said, not without a touch of resentment in my voice, "Well, and what shall we do about it, if Rothschild does happen to drop in on you?"

Do you suppose that he understood the dig? Not a bit of it. As we say: "*There was neither bear nor woods.*"

"I would like you to give up the dairy business," he said, "and go into something else."

"And what," said I, "would you suggest that I go into?"

"Anything you like. Aren't there enough different kinds of business in the world? I'll help you with money, you can have whatever you need, as long as you quit being Tevye the Dairyman. Or, look here, do you know what? Maybe you'd like to pick yourself up one-two-three and go to America?"

Having delivered himself of this, he put the cigar back between his teeth, looked me straight in the eye, and his bald head glistened.

Well, what would you say to such a vulgar person?

At first impulse I thought, "What are you sitting there for like a graven image? Get up, kiss the *mazuza*, slam the door in his face, and—'*he went to his eternal rest*'—get out without as much as a good-bye." I was as stirred up as all that. The colossal nerve of this contractor. Telling me to give up an honest, respectable livelihood and go off to America. Just because it might come to pass that on some far-off day Rothschild might condescend to enter his house, Tevye the Dairyman had to run off to the ends of the earth.

I was boiling inside and some of my anger was directed at her, at Beilke herself. How could she sit there like a queen among a hundred clocks and a thousand mirrors while her father Tevye was being tortured, was running the gauntlet? "May I have as many blessings," I thought to myself, "how much better your sister Hodel has made out than you. I grant you this, she doesn't have a house with so many fancy gew-gaws in it, but she has a husband who is a human being who can call his soul his own, even if his body is in prison.

And besides that he has a head on his shoulders, has Feferel, and not a pot with a shiny cover on it. And when he talks there is something to listen to. When you quote him a passage from the Bible he comes back at you with three more in exchange. Wait, my contractor, I will drum a quotation into your ears that will make your head swim."

And I addressed myself to him thus: "That the *Gamorah* is a closed book to you, I can easily understand. When a man lives in Yehupetz and his name is Padhatzur and his business is that of contractor, the *Gamorah* can very well hide itself in the attic as far as he is concerned. But even a peasant in wooden sandals can understand a simple text. You know what the *Targum* says about Laban the Arameian?" And I gave him a quotation in mixed Hebrew and Russian. When I finished he threw an angry look at me and said, "What does *that* mean?"

"It means this—that out of a pig's tail you cannot fashion a fur hat."

"And what, may I ask, are you referring to?"

"I am referring to the way you are packing me off to America."

At this he laughed that snickering laugh of his and said, "Well, if not America, then how would you like to go to Palestine? Old Jews are always eager to go to Palestine."

Something about his last words struck a chord in my heart. "Hold on, Tevye," I thought. "Maybe this isn't such a bad idea after all. Maybe this is the way out for you. Rather than to stay here and suffer such treatment at the hands of your children, Palestine would be better. What have you got to lose? Your Golde is dead anyway, and you are in such misery you might as well be buried six feet underground yourself. How much longer do you expect to pound this earth?" And I might as well confess, Mr. Sholom Aleichem, that I've been drawn for a long time toward the Holy Land. I would like to stand by the Wailing Wall, to see the tombs of the Patriarchs, Mother Rachel's grave, and I would like to look with my own eyes at the River Jordan, at Mt. Sinai and the Red Sea, at the great cities Pithom and Raamses. In my thoughts I am already in the Land of Canaan—*"the land flowing with milk and honey"*—when Padhatzur breaks in on me impatiently: "Why waste all this time thinking about it? Make it one-two-three and decide."

"With you, thank the Lord, a trip to Palestine is one-two-three like a simple text in the Bible. But for me it's a difficult passage to interpret. To pack up and go off to Palestine one has to have the means."

He laughs scornfully at this, gets up and goes over to a desk, opens a drawer, takes out a purse, and counts out some money—not a trifling sum, you understand—and hands it to me. I take the wad of paper he has handed to me—the power of money!—and lower it into my pocket. I would like to treat him to a few learned quotations, a *medresh* or two, that would explain everything to him, but he won't listen to me.

"This will be enough for your trip," says he, "and more than enough. And when you arrive and find that you need more money, write me a letter, and I will send it to you—one-two-three. I hope I won't have to remind you again about going, for, after all, you are a man of honor, a man with a conscience."

And he laughed again that sniggering laugh of his that penetrated to my very soul. I was tempted to fling the money into his face and to let him know that you couldn't buy Tevye for money and that you didn't speak to Tevye of "honor" and "conscience." But before I had time to open my mouth, he rang the bell, called Beilke in, and said to her, "Do you know what, my love! Your father is leaving us, he is selling everything he owns and going one-two-three to Palestine."

" '*I dreamed a dream but I do not understand it,*' as Pharaoh said to Joseph. What sort of nightmare is this?" I think to myself, and I look over at Beilke. Do you think she as much as frowned? She stood there rooted to the ground, pale and without expression on her face, looking from one to the other of us, not uttering a word. I couldn't speak either, and so we both stood there looking at each other, as the Psalm says: "*May my tongue cleave to the roof of my mouth.*" We had both lost our powers of speech.

My head was whirling and my pulse beating as though I had been breathing in charcoal fumes. I wondered why I felt so dizzy. Could it be that expensive cigar he had given me? But he was still smoking his and talking away. His mouth didn't shut for a moment, though his eyelids were drooping as though he were ready to fall asleep.

"You have to go to Odessa by train first," he said. "And

from Odessa by sea all the way to Jaffa, and the best time for a sea voyage is right now, for later on the winds and the snows and the hurricanes begin and then and then. . . ." His words were getting jumbled, he was asleep on his feet, but he didn't stop jabbering. 'And when you are ready to start let us know and we'll both come to see you off at the station, for when can we hope to see you again?" He finished at last, with a huge yawn, and said to Beilke, "Why don't you stay here awhile, my soul? I am going to lie down for a little bit."

"That's the best thing you have said so far," I thought to myself. "Now I will have a chance to pour my heart out to her." I was ready to spill out all the wrath that had been accumulating in my breast all morning. But instead Beilke fell on my neck and started weeping. You should have heard her weep! My daughters are all alike in this respect. They can be very brave and manly up to a point—then all of a sudden, when it comes to something, they break down and weep like willow trees. Take my older girl Hodel. How she carried on at the last moment when she was telling me good-bye and went to join her Feferel in his exile. But how can I compare the two? This one isn't worthy of lighting the oven for the other. . . .

I will tell you the honest truth. I myself, as you well know, am not a man who is given to tears. I wept once in my life when my Golde lay stretched out on the ground with the candles at her head, and once when Hodel went off to join her husband and I was left standing alone at the station with my horse and wagon. There may have been one or two other occasions on which I weakened, I don't remember. I am not given to weeping. But Beilke's tears wrung my heart so that I couldn't hold myself in. I didn't have the heart to scold her. You don't have to explain things to me. I am Tevye. I understood her tears. She was weeping for *"the sin I have sinned before thee"*—because she hadn't listened to her father. Instead of scolding her and voicing my anger against Padhatzur, I began to comfort her with this story and that proverb as only Tevye can do.

But she interrupted me, "No, father, that isn't why I am crying. It's only because you are leaving on my account and there is nothing I can do to stop it, that's what hurts me."

"You talk like a child," I told her. "Remember we have a merciful God and your father is still in possession of all his faculties. It's a small matter for him to take a trip to Palestine and back again. As it is written: '*They journeyed and they encamped—Tuda i nazad*—I will go and I will return.' "

As though she had guessed my thoughts, she said, "No, father, that's the way you comfort a little child, you give it a toy or a doll and tell it a story about a little white goat. If you want a story, let me tell you one instead. But the story I will tell you is more sad than beautiful."

And she began telling me a long and curious tale, a story out of the thousand and one nights, all about Padhatzur, how he came up from obscure beginnings, worked himself up by his own wits to his present station in life, rose from the lowest to the highest rank. Now that he was rich he wanted the honor of entertaining important people in his home, and to that end he was pouring out thousands of *rubles*, handing out charity in all directions. But money, it seems, isn't everything. You have to have family and background, as well. He was willing to go to any length to prove that he wasn't a nobody, he boasted that he was descended from the great Padhatzurs, that his father was a celebrated contractor too. "Though he knows," she said, "quite well, and he knows that I know, that his father was only a poor fiddler. And on top of that he keeps telling everyone that his wife's father is a millionaire."

"Whom does he mean? Me? Who knows, maybe I *was* destined at one time to be a millionaire. But I'll have to let this suffice me."

"If you only knew how I suffer when he introduces me to his friends and tells them what an important man my father is, and who my uncles were and the rest of my family. How I blush at the lies he makes up. But I have to bear it all in silence for he is very eccentric in those matters."

"You call it being an 'eccentric.' Te me he sounds like a plain liar or else a rascal."

"No, father, you don't understand him. He is not as evil as you think. He is a man whose moods change very frequently. He is really very kind-hearted and generous. If you happen to come to him when he is in one of his good moods he will give you anything you ask for. And nothing is too good for me. He would reach down and hand me the moon and the stars on a platter if I expressed a wish for them. Do you suppose I have no influence over him at all? Just recently

I persuaded him to get Hodel and her husband out of exile. He promised to spend as much money as necessary on only one condition—that they go from there straight to Japan."

"Why to Japan?" I asked. "Why not to India, or to Persia to visit the Queen of Sheba?"

"Because he has business in Japan. He has business all over the world. What he spends on telegrams alone in one day would keep us all alive for a half year." Then her voice dropped. "But what good is all this to me? I am not myself any more."

"It is said," I quoted, "'*If I am not for myself who will be for me?*—I am not I and you are not you!'"

I tried to distract her with jokes and quotations and all the time my heart was torn into pieces to see my child pining away—how do we say it—"*in riches and in honor.*"

"Your sister Hodel," I told her, "would have done differently."

"I've told you before not to compare me to Hodel. Hodel lived in Hodel's time and Beilke is living in Beilke's time. The distance between the two is as great as from here to Japan." Can you figure out the meaning of such crazy talk?

I see that you are in a hurry, but be patient for just a minute and there will be an end to all my stories. Well, after having supped well on the grief of my youngest child, I left the house "*in mourning and with bowed head,*" completely crushed and beaten. I threw the vile cigar he had given me into the street and shouted, "To the devil with you."

"Whom are you cursing, Reb Tevye?" I heard a voice behind my back. I turned around and looked. It was he, Ephraim the *Shadchan,* may no good come to him.

"God bless you, and what are you doing here?" I asked.

"What are *you* doing here?"

"I've been visiting my children."

"And how are they getting along?"

"How should they be getting along? May you and I be as lucky."

"Then I see you are satisfied with my merchandise."

"Satisfied, did you say? May God bless you doubly and trebly for what you have done."

"Thank you for the blessings. Now if you could only add to them something more substantial."

"Didn't you get your matchmaker's fee?"

"May your Padhatzur have no more than I got."

"What's the matter? Was the fee too small?"

"It isn't the size of the fee so much as the manner of giving it."

"What's the trouble then?"

"The trouble is," said he, "that there isn't a *groschen* of it left."

"Where did it disappear to?"

"I married off my daughter."

"Congratulations. Good luck to the couple and may you live to rejoice in their happiness."

"I am rejoicing in it right now. My son-in-law turned out to be a crook. He beat up my daughter, took the few *guldens* away and ran off to America."

"Why did you let him run off so far?"

"How could I stop him?"

"You could have sprinkled salt on his tail."

"I see you are feeling pretty chipper today, Reb Tevye."

"May you feel half as good as I feel."

"Is that so? And I thought you were fixed for life. If that's the case, here is a pinch of snuff."

I got rid of the matchmaker with a pinch of snuff, and went on home. I began selling out my household goods. It wasn't easy, I can tell you, to get rid of all the things that had accumulated through the years. Every old pot, every broken kettle wrenched my heart. One thing reminded me of Golde, another of the children. But nothing hurt me so much as parting with my old horse. I felt as though I owed him something. Hadn't we labored together all these years, suffered and hungered together, known good luck and bad luck together? And here I was up and selling him to a stranger. I had to dispose of him to a water-carrier, for what do you get from a teamster? Nothing but insults. Here is how the teamsters greeted me when I brought my horse to them.

"God be with you, Reb Tevye. Do you call this a horse?"

"What is it, then, a chandelier?"

"If it isn't a chandelier then it's one of the thirty-six saints who hold up the world."

"What do you mean by that?"

"We mean an old creature thirty-six years old without any teeth, with a gray lip, that shivers and shakes like an old woman saying her prayers on a frosty night."

That's teamsters' talk for you. I could swear that my little horse understood every word, as it is written: "*An ox knows his master*—An animal knows when you are offering him for sale." I was sure he understood, for when I closed the deal with the water-carrier and wished him luck, my horse turned his patient face to me and gave me a look as though to say: "*This is my portion for all my efforts.*—Is this how you reward me for my years of faithful service?"

I looked back at him for the last time as the water-carrier led him away and I was left standing all alone. I thought, "Almighty, how cleverly You have fashioned Your world. You have created Tevye and You have created his horse and to both You have given the same fate. A man can at least talk, he can complain out loud, he can unburden his soul to another, but a horse? He is nothing but a dumb beast, as it is said: '*The advantage of man over animal.*' "

You wonder at the tears in my eyes, Mr. Sholom Aleichem. You are probably thinking that I am weeping for my horse. Why only for my horse? I am weeping for everybody and everything. For I shall miss everybody and everything. I shall miss my horse and the farm, and I shall miss the mayor and the police sergeant, the summer people of Boiberik, the rich people of Yehupetz, and I shall miss Ephraim the Matchmaker, may a plague take him, for when all is said and done, if you think the whole matter over, what is he but a poor man trying to make a living?

When God brings me safely to the place where I am going, I do not know what will finally become of me, but one thing is clear in my mind—that first of all I shall visit the grave of Mother Rachel. There I will offer a prayer for my children whom I shall probably never see again and at the same time I will keep in mind Ephraim the Matchmaker, as well as yourself and all of Israel. Let us shake hands on that, and go your way in good health and give my blessings to everyone and bid everyone a kind farewell for me. And may all go well with you.

The Purim Feast

"I DON'T know what's to become of the child, what he's going to grow up into. He's like a dripping dishrag, a soggy handkerchief, like a professional mourner. . . . A child that can't stop crying."

This was my mother talking to herself as she dressed me in my holiday clothes. As she spoke she gave me now a shove, now a push, now a cuff over the head; she grabbed me by the hair or pulled my ear, pinched me, and slapped me—and with all that she expected me to be laughing instead of crying! She buttoned me up from top to toe in my best coat which was much too tight for me. I could barely breathe and my eyes almost popped out of my head. The sleeves were so short that my bluish red wrists stuck out of my cuffs as though they were swollen. This was more than my mother could bear.

"Look at that pair of hands!" And she slapped me smartly across my wrists to make me drop them. "When you sit at Uncle Hertz's table remember to keep your hands down, do you hear me? And don't let your face get as red as Yadwocha the peasant girl's. And don't roll your eyes like a tomcat. Do you hear what I'm telling you? And sit up like a human being. And the main thing—is your nose. Oh, that nose of yours. Come here, let me put your nose in order."

Alas for my poor nose when my mother decides to "put it in order." I don't know what my nose has done to deserve such a fate. It seems to me that it's a nose like all noses, short and blunt, slightly turned up at the end, pinkish in color, and usually dripping. But is that a reason for such cruel treatment? Believe me, there have been times when I have begged the Almighty to take my nose away altogether, to cause it to fall off and end my misery once for all. I used to imagine that I would wake up one fine morning without a nose. I would come up to my mother after breakfast and she would grab hold of me and cry out in a terrible voice, "Woe is me, where is your nose?"

"Which nose?" I would say innocently, passing my hand over my face. I would look at my mother's horror-stricken face and taste the joys of revenge. "Serves her right. Now she can see what her son looks like without a nose."

Childish dreams! Foolish imaginings! God didn't hear my prayer. My nose kept on growing, my mother kept on "putting it in order" and I went on suffering. My nose had to take the worst punishment when a holiday approached, for instance before *Purim* when we were getting ready to go to Uncle Hertz's for the *Purim* Feast.

Uncle Hertz was not only the rich uncle in the family, he was also the foremost citizen in our town, and in all the surrounding towns you heard nothing but Hertz and Hertz and Hertz. Of course he had a pair of high-spirited horses and a carriage of his own, and when he rode out in his carriage the wheels made such a clatter that the whole town ran outside to see Uncle Hertz riding by. There he sat, high up in his carriage, with his handsome, round, copper-colored beard and his fierce gray eyes, rocking himself back and forth and looking down at everyone through his silver-rimmed spectacles, as though to say, "How can you worms compare yourselves to me? I am Hertz the *Nogid* and I ride in a carriage, while you poor Kasriliks, you paupers, you crawl in the mud."

I don't know how the rest of the world felt about him, but I detested Uncle Hertz so that I couldn't bear to look at his fat, red face, his copper-colored beard and his silver-rimmed spectacles. I hated his big paunch and the massive gold chain that rode around his paunch, the round silk skullcap that he wore on his head, and above all I hated his little cough. He had a peculiar little cough which went along with a shrug of the shoulders, a toss of the head, and pout of the lips, as though he were saying, "Show respect. It was I, Hertz, who coughed, not because, God forbid, I have caught cold, but just because I wanted to cough."

I can't understand my family at all. What's the matter with them that they are so excited over going to Uncle Hertz's for *Purim*? It seems to me that they all love him as they love a toothache, and even my mother who is his own sister is not too crazy about him either, for when the older children are not at home (she apparently isn't embarrassed by my presence) she showers strange blessings on his head. She hopes that next year, "he will be in her circumstances." But let anyone else try to say a word against him, and she will scratch his eyes out. I happened to be by one day when my father let something fall. Do you think it was something disrespectful? Not at all. He only remarked to my mother, "Well, what's the news? Has your Hertz arrived yet, or not?" And she gave him such a fare-thee-well that my poor father didn't know whether to stand up or sit down.

"What do you mean by *my* Hertz? What kind of talk is that? What sort of expression? What do you mean he is mine?"

"Whose is he if not yours? Is he mine?" said my father trying to give battle. But he didn't advance far. My mother attacked him on all sides at once.

"Well, if he is mine, what of it? He is mine, then. You don't like it? His ancestry isn't good enough for you? You had to divide your father's inheritance with him? Is that it? You never got any favors from him? Is that it?"

"Who says I didn't?" my father offered in a milder tone, ready to surrender himself. But it didn't do any good. My mother wasn't ready to make a truce yet.

"You have better brothers than I have? Is that it? Finer men, more important, more prosperous, more respectable ones, is that it?"

"Quiet now. Let there be an end to this. Leave me alone," said my father, pulling his cap over his eyes and running out of the house. My father lost the battle and my mother remained the victor. She is always the victor. She wins every battle, not because she wears the pants in the family, but because of Uncle Hertz. Uncle Hertz is our rich uncle and we are his "poor relations."

What is Uncle Hertz to us? Do we live off him? Or have we received so many favors from him? I cannot tell you, because I don't know. I only know that everyone in our house, from the oldest to the youngest, lives in fear and trembling of Uncle Hertz. *Purim* is two weeks off and we are already getting ready for the Feast at Uncle Hertz's. My older brother, Moses Abraham, a boy with pale, sunken cheeks and sad dark eyes, strokes his earlocks when ever you mention the *Purim* Feast at Uncle Hertz's. As for my two big sisters, Miriam Reizel and Hannah Rachel, it goes without saying that they have been getting ready for a long time. They are having new dresses made in the latest fashion just for the occasion, and they have bought combs and ribbons to put in their hair. They wanted to have their shoes mended too, but my mother put that off for Passover, though it cost her plenty of heartache. She is especially concerned about Miriam Reizel, because Miriam, Reizel is engaged, and suppose her young man sees her torn shoes! She has enough trouble with that young man as it is. To begin with, he is a common fellow, a "bookkeeper" he calls himself, because he is a clerk in a store. As though that weren't bad enough, he likes to put on airs, and he expects his betrothed to go around dressed in the latest fashion, like a princess.

Every Saturday afternoon this young man comes to our house and he sits by the window with my two sisters and all they talk about is new clothes, stylish costumes, patent leather shoes, galoshes, hats with feathers, pointed parasols. They also talk about embroidered pillow cases, red pillowslips, white sheets, and fine quilts, fluffy and warm, so that it's a pleasure to get under them on a cold winter night. As he talks, I look over at my sister Miriam Reizel and see her go red as a beet. She has a habit of blushing very easily. She hides her feet under the chair, so that her young man won't see the rundown heels and shabby toes if he should look at them.

"Well, are you prepared for the Feast?" my mother asks my father the day after the reading of the *Megilah*.

"Prepared?" says my father. "With what?" And he puts on his Sabbath gabardine. "Where are the children?"

"The children are almost ready," says my mother, though she knows quite well that the children, meaning my two sisters, are far from ready. They are still washing their hair, putting almond oil on it, braiding it for each other, primping, and putting on their new dresses. They have smeared their shoes with fat to make them sparkle like new. But what good is this sparkle when the heels are almost off, and the toes show through in front? How can they keep Miriam Reizel's young man from seeing her shoes? Just then, as if some ill wind blew him in, the young man himself appears, in a new suit with a stiffly starched collar and a bright green tie. From his starched white cuffs dangle his big red hands with the black-rimmed nails. He has just had a haircut and his short hair stands on end. Out of his back pocket he pulls a huge white, starched handkerchief, redolent of spices. The strong scent of cloves and spice is wafted to my nostrils and makes me sneeze suddenly, so that I burst two buttons off my coat. My mother lets fly at me. "Look at the scamp. He can't keep a button on. May you not burst apart altogether." She picks up a needle and thread and sews the buttons back on. Now everyone is ready and we start out all together for Uncle Hertz's house.

In front of the procession walks my father, the skirts of his coat lifted high from the mud. Behind him walks my mother in high men's boots. After her come my sisters tripping daintily with parasols in their hands. (Why anyone needs a parasol at this time of year is beyond me.) After them my older brother Moses Abraham leaps through the mud, holding me by the hand and trying to find a dry spot, but landing each time in the deepest mud and jumping back as though he had been scalded. Alongside of us walks my sister's young man in his new tall galoshes. He is the only one of us who has galoshes and he calls out in a loud voice for everyone to hear, "I hope I don't get my galoshes full of mud."

Though it is still broad daylight, many candles are burning at Uncle Hertz's house. All the lamps have been lighted and sconces burn on the walls. The table has been set. A monstrous *Purim* loaf, as big as the legendary ox reserved for the pious when the Messiah comes, takes up half of the table. All around the table are gathered our relatives, all the uncles and aunts and cousins, poor people all of them, one poorer than the next. They are standing around, whispering among themselves as though they were at a circumcision ceremony waiting for the godparents to bring in the child. Uncle Hertz is nowhere to be seen, and my Aunt, a woman with a string of huge pearls around her neck and a set of false teeth, is bustling around, putting plates on the table, counting us with the left hand, apparently not afraid of the evil eye. . . .

And now the door opens and Uncle Hertz himself appears, dressed in holiday clothes, a shiny black silk coat with wide sleeves, and a fur hat on his head, which he wears only for the *Purim* Feast and the Passover *Seder*. The whole family bows to him and the men smile nervously, rubbing their hands together, and the women wish him a loud good *yom-tev*. We children stand around stiffly, not knowing what to do with our hands. Uncle Hertz gives us all a sweeping glance out of his fierce gray eyes, over the tops of his glasses, coughs and waves his hand at us. "Well, why don't you sit down? Sit down, everybody, here are the chairs."

The whole family sits down. Each one is sitting on the edge of his chair, afraid to touch anything on the table. A terrible silence reigns in the big room. You can hear the candles guttering, everything swims in front of our eyes, and our hearts are heavy. We are hungry, but nobody feels like eating. Our appetites have been taken away as if by magic.

"Why is everybody so quiet? Speak! Let's hear you tell us something," says Uncle Hertz, and he coughs his little cough, shrugs his shoulders, tosses his head and pouts with his lips.

The family is silent. No one dares to utter a word at Uncle Hertz's table. The men smile stupidly as though they would like to speak and don't know what to say. The women exchange frightened glances. We youngsters burn as if in a fever. Miriam Reizel looks over at Hannah Rachel and Hannah Rachel looks back at Miriam Reizel, as though they had never seen each other before. My brother Moses Abraham looks out at the world with a pale scared face. Nobody, nobody dares utter a word at Uncle Hertz's table. Only one person feels at home here, as he does everywhere, and at all times. That is Miriam Reizel's young man, the bookkeeper. He pulls out his huge, starched and strongly perfumed handkerchief from his back pocket, blows his nose with relish, and says, "Did anybody ever see such deep mud at this time of year? I thought sure my galoshes would be filled up."

"Who is this young man?" asks Uncle Hertz, lifting up his silver-rimmed spectacles and giving his little cough.

"He is—my Miriam Reizel's—betrothed," says my father in a low voice like a man confessing to a murder. All of us sit as though turned to stone. And Miriam Reizel, poor Miriam Reizel—her face flames like a straw roof on fire.

Uncle Hertz looks the family over once more with his fierce gray eyes, offers us another cough and a shrug, another toss of his head and pout of his lips and says, "Well, why don't you go and wash? Go on and wash your hands, the water is right here."

After we had washed our hands and said the proper prayer over the little ceremony, we sat down around the table and waited for Uncle Hertz to say grace and to cut the huge *Purim* loaf. We were getting hungry now and would have liked to start eating, but just as if to spite us Uncle Hertz took his time over the grace and the cutting up of the huge ox, prolonging the ceremony and drawing it out as though he were a rabbi in front of his congregation. At last we saw the ox slaughtered and pieces of the loaf were passed to us, but before we had swallowed the first bite Uncle Hertz looked us over with his fierce gray eyes and said, "Well, why don't you sing? Sing somebody. Let's hear a tune in honor of the Feast. The whole world is celebrating today."

The family began exchanging glances among themselves, whispering and arguing and nudging each other. "You sing." "No, you sing." "Why should I? Why not you?" This went on for some time until one of the relations, my young cousin Abraham, Uncle Itzy's son, burst into song. He was a beardless youth with a squeaky voice and blinking eyes and he fancied himself as a singer. What it was that my cousin Abraham wanted to sing, I don't know. He started in his high squeaky voice on a falsetto note that broke in the middle, and the tune was so mournful and the look on his face was so tragic and so comic at once that you had to be God himself or one of His angels to keep from laughing out loud. And especially since right opposite me sat all the boys making faces.

The first burst of laughter came from me, and it was I who caught the first slap from my mother. But the slap did not cool me off. It brought a burst of laughter from the other children, and from me as well. This burst of laughter brought another slap and the slap brought fresh laughter and the laughter another slap and this went on until I was led out of the dining room into the kitchen and from the kitchen outdoors, and then I was brought home, beaten black and blue and drowning in tears.

That night I cursed my own bones and I cursed *Purim* and the *Purim* Feast and my cousin Abraham and more than anyone else I cursed Uncle Hertz, may he forgive me, for he has long since passed on to his reward. On his grave stands a tombstone, the most imposing tombstone in the whole cemetery, and on it in gold letters are engraved the virtues in which he excelled during his life: "Here lies an honest man, kind-hearted, lovable, generous, charitable, good-tempered, devoted and faithful." And so on and so on. . . . "May he rest in peace."

The Passover Expropriation

KASRILEVKA has always been known to ape Odessa. But since the recent disturbances began, Kasrilevka hasn't deviated from Odessa by a hair's breadth. Is there a strike in Odessa? Then there is a strike in Kasrilevka. A Constitution in Odessa? Then there is a Constitution in Kasrilevka. A pogrom in Odessa? Then there is a pogrom in Kasrilevka. Once a certain wag broadcast the news that in Odessa people were beginning to cut off their noses. Right away the people of Kasrilevka began sharpening their knives. Luckily, in Kasrilevka itself, one person apes another, so that each one waited for the next person to cut off his nose first. And they are waiting to this day.

After such an introduction, you won't be surprised to hear that hardly a day passes that you don't read in the papers of some fresh catastrophe taking place in Kasrilevka. You read, for instance, of how a gang of hoodlums broke into a bakery and expropriated all the twists and *beigels.* Or of how a shoemaker who had just finished a pair of shoes—he had only to add the soles and heels—was attacked in broad daylight, told "to lift up his hands and bless the Lord" and the shoes were carried off! Or again of how a poor man was going from house to house begging—this took place on a Thursday—when he was held up in a dark side street, a pistol was stuck in front of his face, and he was cleaned out of everything he had on him. Or listen to the story a woman tells. . . . But a woman's tale is not to be trusted. Women have notoriously weak nerves, the times are unsettled, and she might have mistaken a stunted cow for a man. I don't want to be responsible for spreading idle tales.

Suffice it to say that a whole series of expropriations took place in Kasrilevka, one more terrible than the next. It got so that people trembled for their very lives. Everyone longed for the good old bygone days when a single police official, who took a bribe now and then, held the whole town in his grasp. They began to offer up prayers to God: "Have pity on us, Almighty God, permit us to go backwards, dear loving Father, renew our days as of old."

But this is still the introduction. The real story begins now.

Benjamin Lastechka is the richest man in Kasrilevka and the most important. The extent of his wealth—and of his importance—is hard to estimate. In the first place, he has rich relatives all over the world. These relatives, it is true, are not as rich as they once were. What can you expect in these times, with failures and bankruptcies taking place every day? The wonder is that people still manage to exist, and especially the people of Kasrilevka who are packed together like herring in a barrel, in one small spot, devouring each other alive. It is a lucky thing that there is an America which every year drains off almost twice as many people as are killed in pogroms or die of starvation.

And yet you see that in spite of all this, if God wills it, there is still a rich man left in Kasrilevka, a man by the name of Benjamin Lastechka, whom everyone envies because he doesn't have to ask help of anyone except his rich relatives. Asking help of rich relatives is not the easiest way in the world of earning one's bread, either, for the majority of rich relatives, if you will pardon my saying so, are notoriously hoggish by nature. And yet the fact remains that Benjamin Lastechka is still the richest man in Kasrilevka. When you need a favor, to whom do you go? To Benjamin Lastechka, of course. And Benjamin Lastechka listens to your troubles, helps out sometimes with a piece of advice, sometimes with a word of encouragement, and once in a while with a groan of sympathy. These are good too, for without them would it be any better? You'd still have the same pack of troubles.

What is the difference between a rich man of Kasrilevka and, let us say, a rich man of Yehupetz? The rich people of Yehupetz have such tender hearts that they can't bear to look on at the plight of a poor man. They keep their doors locked and a lackey stationed outside to turn away anyone who is not respectably dressed. And when summer comes, they rise up like swallows and fly off abroad. Just try and follow them. But let a Kasrilevka *nogid* attempt such a thing—he won't get far, I promise you. Whether he likes it or not, Benjamin Lastechka has the honor of being the foremost citizen in our community. In all matters of charity, he has to be the first. He has to be the first not only in giving a donation, but the first to pick up his walking stick and go from door to door collecting charity from the poor to give to the poor.

And especially when it comes to collecting "wheat tithes" or money for *matzos* for the poor before Passover. Then you should see Benjamin Lastechka. I doubt if the greatest welfare worker on earth laboring in the most important cause, has ever sweated as much as Benjamin Lastechka sweats those four weeks before Passover. He swears that between *Purim* and Passover he sleeps every night with his clothes on. We might as well take his word for it, for what does he get for his pains? You might say that he does it for glory. And why not? Everyone likes a little glory, even a king doesn't scorn it. That's only human nature.

The custom of collecting "wheat tithes" before Passover is a very old one. It is an old-fashioned form of philanthropy, and yet I don't think it's as terrible a custom as people nowadays try to make you believe. They tell you that philanthropy is the ruin of Society. I don't care to enter into a philosophical discussion on the subject. I only want to say that according to my lights there is a far worse custom than this—and that is that the rich people aren't willing to give. And a thousand times worse than that is the fact hat these noble souls who refuse to give anything try to make you believe that it's a matter of "principle" with them. I advise you to run from such people. They are as dry as a dried fish, and as lonely as a cat. . . .

Thank God that in Kasrilevka "principles" haven't become fashionable as yet. Those who don't give anything, don't give for the simple reason that they have nothing to give. But when it comes to raising "wheat tithes" for Passover, even that is no excuse. There is a common saying in Kasrilevka: "Every man must either give charity for Passover or he must receive it."

Strange people, these Kasrilevkites. Thousands of years have passed since their great-great-great-grandfathers freed themselves from their Egyptian bondage, and they still can't wean themselves away from the habit of eating *matzos* eight days in a row every year. I am afraid that this cardboard-like delicacy won't go out of fashion for a long, long time to come.

All year long a Kasrilevkite is allowed to swell up from hunger, but when Passover comes—let the world stand on its head—he must be provided with *matzos.*

And so it has never yet happened in Kasrilevka that a person has died of hunger during Passover. And if by chance such a thing did happen it should have been marked elsewhere on the calendar. For obviously he did not die because he had no *matzos* to eat during the eight days of Passover, but because he had no bread during the remaining three hundred and fifty-seven days of the year. There is, you will admit, quite a difference between the two.

However, there is no rule to which you won't find an exception. The year in which my story takes place was such an exception, something happened that had been unheard of in the annals of Kasrilevka. It turned out that there were more people asking for help than there were people giving it. If it hadn't been for a feeling of pride, almost everyone in Kasrilevka would have applied for aid. It was truly pitiful to watch our *nogid,* Benjamin Lastechka, sitting in the Committee room the day before Passover, turning away people right and left, saying over and over, "There is no more money. It's all gone. I am very sorry."

"May you live until next year," they answered, and muttered under their noses, "and come to us for charity."

One after another the people came out of the Committee room with empty hands and flushed faces, as though they were coming out of a steam bath, and cursed the rich people with every curse known to them.

The last to enter was a band of young fellows, workingmen, who had been going around all winter without a stitch of work. They were banded together like a commune. They had sold everything they had to sell, and shared the proceeds. One of them had just pawned a silver watch and bought cigarettes which they were all smoking to still their hunger pangs.

When they arrived before the Committee, the workingmen put forward as their spokesman a ladies' tailor by the name of Samuel Abba Fingerhut. But they didn't let Samuel talk alone. They all helped him present their case, talking, pleading, explaining that they were starving, that they were ready to fall down on their faces and pass out any minute. The Chairman of the Committee, Benjamin Lastechka, let them have their say, and when they were through, he spoke to them:

"I am very sorry, but you are all wasting your breath. First of all, none of you is married, and we give money only to married men. Second, you are healthy young men, well able to work and earn money for Passover. Third, we have a plentiful supply of poor people this year, a bumper crop in fact, more takers than givers. Fourth, we are ashamed to admit it, but since early morning we haven't had a crooked *kopek* in the safe. If you don't believe me, just take a look."

Saying this, the Chairman of the Committee turned all his pockets inside out for everyone to see how empty they were. The young men stood gaping, unable to speak. Only their leader Samuel Fingerhut wasn't overawed. He had a tongue in his head, that one, you didn't have to coach him. He addressed himself to the Chairman, half in Yiddish, half in Russian:

"It's a pity that you didn't start at the end, you would have saved yourself gunpowder. But I can give you an answer to all your arguments. In the first place, that we are single. That's to your advantage—you have that many less poor to provide for. In the second place, that we are able to work. *Zdelatie odolzhenie*—do us a favor: Give us work and we will turn the world upside down for you. Third, you speak of the numbers of poor people. Capitalism is to blame for that, *z'odnoi storoni*—on one side—and the exploitation of the proletariat, *z'drugoi storoni*—on the other side. Fourth, as for your turning your pockets inside out for us, that's no *dokozhatelstvo*—it doesn't prove a thing. I have no doubt, *naprimer*—for instance—that at home your cupboards are bursting with *matzos*, eggs, onions, goose fat, *i tomu podobnoie*—and other such things—as well as wine for the *Seder*. All of you on the Committee are nothing but bourgeois exploiters and men without conscience, and *bolshe nitchevo*—nothing else—*Tovarishchi*, come, let's go!"

I must report that Kasrilevka, which imitates Odessa and other big towns, has not sufficiently progressed to the extent that an exploiter like our *nogid*, Benjamin Lastechka, should throw open his cupboards, divide the *matzos*, eggs, onions, potatoes, goose fat, and wine among the poor, and leave nothing for himself and his family. But I am convinced as surely as two times two makes four that our Kasrilevka exploiters will do it only if Odessa and Yehupetz and other big cities set the example. Kasrilevka, my friends, is not obliged to be the first at the Fair.

With a clear conscience, bathed, and dressed in holiday clothes, Benjamin Lastechka sat down to the *Seder* with his wife and children the first night of Passover. He felt tranquil and at ease, like a monarch who is secure in his kingdom. On his right hand sat his Queen, his wife, Sara-Leah, also dressed in her holiday best, with a new silk kerchief on her head from the folds of which peeped two dangling earrings of genuine 84-carat silver. All around the table sat the children, the princes and princesses, a whole bouquet of newly washed heads, rosy cheeks, and sparkling eyes. Even Zlatka the servant girl, who all year long labors like a donkey harnessed to a yoke, had washed her hair, bathed with perfumed soap, and put on a new cotton dress, fancy boots, and a wide red ribbon on her black hair. They all felt happy, free and unfettered as though they themselves had just escaped from bondage. The youngest boy had just rattled off the four questions with great aplomb, and his father the King, Benjamin Lastechka, was just beginning to deliver in a slow, solemn chant, at the top of his voice, the age-old response: "Because we were slaves unto Pharaoh in Egypt and the Eternal brought us forth with a mighty hand and with many wonders. And he punished Pharaoh with ten plagues. . . ." Benjamin was just beginning to enumerate the plagues when suddenly . . .

Suddenly there was a knock on the door, then another and then two more knocks. Who could it be? To open or not to open? They decided to open, since the knocking was getting louder and more insistent. The King and Queen and the Princes and Princesses all sat very still while Zlatka the maid opened the door and the band of young fellows entered with their leader, Samuel Abba Fingerhut, in front, and greeted the assembled company with a broad, good *yom-tev*. Our *nogid*, Benjamin Lastechka, though his spirits had sunk far down into his boots at the sight, put on a cheerful face and said, "Good *yom-tev*. Good day. Look who's here! And what good news do you bring?"

Samuel Fingerhut, the spokesman, stepped out from the

rest of the group and began a speech in mingled Russian and Yiddish as was his custom:

"Here you sit, all of you, in a bright, warm room with the wine glasses in front of you, observing the holy *Seder*, while we poor proletarians are perishing of hunger outside. I consider this a great injustice. I hereby command you to have the dinner served to us instead. And if anyone of you lets out as much as a peep or opens a window, or dares call the police or—*tomu podobniu*—it will be the worse for you. *Tovarisch* Moishe—where is the bomb?"

The last words were enough to turn the family into graven images right where they sat. But when *Tovarisch* Moishe, a swarthy shoemaker with a black shock of hair falling over his eyes and grimy fingers, approached the table and placed on it a tall, rounded object, covered with a rag, the whole household became as Lot's wife when she turned to see what had become of the cities of Sodom and Gomorrah.

And then Zlatka, the servant girl, her teeth chattering with fright, brought to the table, first the hot, spicy fish, then the soup with dumplings, then the pancakes and other holiday dishes—and the guests went after the food and wine with such appetite you could see they had not eaten for many days. They pledged themselves not to leave a crumb of food or a drop of wine. They even ate up the symbolical foods—the egg and shank-bone, the parsley and the bitter herbs. When they were done, nothing remained of the *Seder* except the prayer books. And while they were eating, the tailor Samuel Fingerhut mocked his host Benjamin Lastechka in these words:

"Every year we recite the *Hagadah* and you eat the dumplings. *Wnastojatcheie wremie*—this time—you recited the *Hagadah* and for once we are eating the dumplings." He raised his wineglass. "*L'chaim*—long life to you—my bourgeois friend, may God grant that you become a proletarian like the rest of us. Next year may we celebrate the Constitution!"

It was long past midnight and the poor *nogid*, Benjamin Lastechka, and all his family still sat around the table. In front of them stood the fearful unknown—the tall, rounded object covered with a rag. The young workingmen had warned them before leaving to remain sitting in their places for two hours—or there would be trouble. That night not one of them slept. They thanked God that they had escaped alive.

Well, and what happened to the tall, rounded object that stood on the table covered with a rag, the anxious reader asks. We are happy to reassure him. A tin container, which once held shoewax, now filled with *matzo* meal is not dangerous. It can stand for a thousand years and it won't blow up anything, except, God forbid—a good *yom-tev*.

Tevye Wins a Fortune

Who raiseth up the poor out of the dust,
And lifteth up the needy out of the dunghill.
—PSALMS, 113:7.

IF YOU are destined to draw the winning ticket in the lottery, Mr. Sholom Aleichem, it will come right into your house without your asking for it. As King David says, "It never rains but it pours." You don't need wisdom or skill. And, on the contrary, if you are not inscribed as a winner in the Books of the Angels, you can talk yourself blue in the face—it won't help you. The *Talmud* is right: "You can lead a horse to water, but you cannot make him drink." A person slaves, wears himself to the bone, and gets nowhere. He might as well lie down and give up his ghost. Suddenly, no one knows how or for what reason, money rolls in from all sides. As the passage has it, "Relief and deliverance will come to the Jews." I don't have to explain that to you. It should be clear to both of us that so long as a Jew can still draw breath and feel the blood beating in his veins, he must never lose hope. I have seen it in my own experience, in the way the Lord dealt with me in providing me with my present livelihood. For how else should I happen to be selling cheese and butter all of a sudden? In my wildest dreams I had never seen myself as a dairyman.

Take my word for it, the story is worth hearing. I'll sit down for a little while here near you on the grass. Let the horse do a little nibbling meanwhile. After all, even a horse is one of God's living creatures.

Well, it was in the late spring, around *Shevuos* time. But I don't want to mislead you; it may have been a week or two before *Shevuos*, or—let's see—maybe a couple of weeks after *Shevuos*. Don't forget, this didn't happen yesterday. Wait! To be exact, it was nine or ten years ago to the day. And maybe a trifle more.

In those days I was not the man I am today. That is, I *was* the same Tevye, and yet not exactly the same. The same old woman, as they say, but in a different bonnet. How so? I was as poor as a man could be, completely penniless. If you want to know the truth I'm not a rich man now either, but compared with what I was then I can now really call myself a man of wealth. I have a horse and wagon of my own, a couple of cows that give milk, and a third that is about to calve. We can't complain. We have cheese and butter and fresh cream all the time. We make it ourselves; that is, our family does. We all work. No one is idle. My wife milks the cows; the children carry pitchers and pails, churn the butter. And I myself, as you see, drive to market every morning, go from *datcha* to *datcha* in Boiberik, visit with people, see this one and that one, all the important businessmen from Yehupetz who come there for the summer. Talking to them makes me feel that I am somebody, too; I amount to something in the world.

And when Saturday comes—then I really live like a king! I look into the Holy Books, read the weekly portion of the Bible, dip into the commentaries, Psalms, *Perek*, this, that, something else . . . Ah, you're surprised, Mr. Sholom Aleichem! No doubt you're thinking to yourself, "Ah, that Tevye—there's a man for you!"

Anyway, what did I start to tell you? That's right. Those days. Oh, was Tevye a pauper then! With God's help I starved to death—I and my wife and children—three times a day, not counting supper. I worked like a horse, pulling wagonloads of logs from the woods to the railroad station for—I am ashamed to admit it—half a *ruble* a day. And that not every day, either. And on such earnings just try to fill all those hungry mouths, not counting that boarder of mine, the poor horse, whom I can't put off with a quotation from the *Talmud*.

So what does the Lord do? He is a great, all-powerful God. He manages His little world wisely and well. Seeing how I was struggling for a hard crust of bread, He said to me: "Do you think, Tevye, that you have nothing more to live for, that the world has come to an end? If that's what you think, you're a big lummox. Soon you will see: if I will it, your luck can change in one turn of the wheel, and what was dark as the grave will be full of brightness." As we say on *Yom Kippur*, the Lord decides who will ride on horseback and who will crawl on foot. The main thing is—hope! A Jew must always hope, must never lose hope. And in the meantime, what if we waste away to a shadow? For that we are Jews—the Chosen People, the envy and admiration of the world.

Anyway, this is how it happened. As the Bible says, "And there came the day . . ." One evening in summer I was driving through the woods on my way home with an empty wagon. My head was bent, my heart was heavy. The little horse, poor thing, was barely dragging its feet. "Ah," I said to it, "crawl along, *shlimazl!* If you are Tevye's horse you too must know the pangs of hunger . . ." All around was silence, every crack of the whip echoed through the woods. As the sun set the shadows of the trees stretched out and lengthened —like our Jewish exile. Darkness was creeping in and a sadness filled my heart. Strange, faraway thoughts filled my mind, and before my eyes passed the images of people a long time dead. And in the midst of it all I thought of my home and my family. And I thought, "Woe unto us all." The wretched dark little hut that was my home, and the children barefoot and in tatters waiting for their father, the *shlimazl.* Maybe he would bring them a loaf of bread or a few stale rolls. And my wife, grumbling as a wife will: "Children I had to bear him—seven of them. I might as well take them all and throw them into the river—may God not punish me for these words!"

You can imagine how I felt. We are only human. The stomach is empty and words won't fill it. If you swallow a piece of herring you want some tea, and for tea you need sugar. And sugar, I am told, is in the grocery store. "My stomach," says my wife, "can get along without a piece of bread, but if I don't take a glass of tea in the morning, I am a dead woman. All night long the baby sucks me dry."

But in spite of everything, we are still Jews. When evening comes we have to say our prayers. You can imagine what the prayers sounded like if I tell you that just as I was about to begin *Shmin-esra* my horse suddenly broke away as if possessed by the devil and ran wildly off through the woods. Have you ever tried standing on one spot facing the east while a horse was pulling you where *it* wanted to go? I had no choice but to run after him, holding on to the reins and chanting, "*God of Abraham, God of Isaac, and God of Jacob.*" A fine way to say *Shmin-esra!* And just my luck, at a moment when I was in the mood to pray with feeling, out of the depths of my heart, hoping it would lift my spirits . . .

So there I was, running after the wagon and chanting at the top of my voice, as if I were a cantor in a synagogue: "*Thou sustainest the living with loving kindness* (and sometimes with a little food) *and keepest thy faith with them that sleep in the dust.* (The dead are not the only ones who lie in the dust; Oh, how low we the living are laid, what hells we go through, and I don't mean the rich people of Yehupetz who spend their summers at the *datchas* of Boiberik, eating and drinking and living off the fat of the land . . . Oh, Heavenly Father, why does this happen to me? Am I not as good as others? Help me, dear God!) *Look upon our afflictions.* (Look down, dear God! See how we struggle and come to the aid of the poor, because who will look out for us if you don't?) *Heal us, O Lord, and we shall be healed.* (Send us the cure, we have the ailment already.) *Bless this year for us, O Lord, our God, with every kind of produce* (corn and wheat and every other grain, and if you do, will I get anything out of it, *shlimazl* that I am? For instance, what difference does it make to my poor horse whether oats are dear or cheap?)."

But that's enough. Of God you don't ask questions. If you're one of the Chosen People you must see the good in everything and say, "This too is for the best." God must have willed it so . . .

"*And for slanderers let there be no hope,*" I chant further. The slanderers and rich scoffers who say there is no God—a fine figure they'll cut when they get *there.* They'll pay for their disbelief, and with interest too, for He is one who "breaketh his enemies and humbleth the arrogant." He pays you according to your deserts. You don't trifle with Him; you approach Him humbly, pray to Him and beg His mercy. "*O Merciful Father, hear our voice, pay heed to our lamentations. Spare us and have mercy upon us* (my wife and children too—they are hungry). *Accept, O Lord, thy people Israel and their prayer, even as you did in the days of the Holy Temple, when the priests and the Levites . . .*"

Suddenly the horse stopped. In a hurry I finish *Shmin-esra,* lift up my eyes, and behold two mysterious creatures coming toward me out of the forest, disguised or at least dressed in the strangest fashion. "Thieves," I thought, but corrected myself at once. "What is the matter with you, Tevye? You've been driving through this forest for so many years by day and by night; why should you suddenly begin to worry about thieves?"

And swinging my whip over my head, I yelled at the horse, "Giddap!"

"Mister!" one of the two creatures called out to me. "Stop! Please stop! Don't run away, Mister, we won't do you any harm!"

"An evil spirit!" I said to myself, and a second later, "You ox, Tevye, you ass! Why should evil spirits come to you all of a sudden?" And I stop the horse. I look the creatures over from head to foot: they are ordinary women. One elderly with a silk shawl on her head and the other a younger one with a *sheitel*. Both flushed and out of breath.

"Good evening," I cry out loud, trying to sound cheerful. "Look who's here! What is it you want? If you want to buy something, all I have is a gnawing stomach, a heart full of pain, a head full of worries, and all the misery and wretchedness in the world."

"Listen to him going on," they say. "That's enough. You say one word to a man and you get a lecture in return. There is nothing we want to buy. We only want to ask: do you know where the road to Boiberik is?"

"To Boiberik?" I say, and let out a laugh, still trying to sound cheerful. "You might as well ask me if I know my name is Tevye."

"Oh? So that's what they call you—Tevye? Good evening, then, Mr. Tevye. What is there to laugh at? We are strangers here. We are from Yehupetz, and we are staying at a *datcha* in Boiberik. This morning we went out for a short walk in the woods, and we've been wandering ever since, going round and round in circles. A little while ago we heard someone singing in the forest. At first we thought it was a highwayman, but when we came closer and saw it was only you, we felt relieved. Now do you understand?"

"Ha-ha!" I laughed. "A fine highwayman! Have you ever heard the story about the Jewish highwayman who waylaid a traveler in the forest and demanded—a pinch of snuff? If you'd like, I could tell it to you . . ."

"Leave that for some other time," they said. "Right now, show us how to get back to Boiberik."

"To Boiberik?" I said again. "Why, this is the way to Boiberik. Even if you don't want to, you couldn't help getting there if you followed this path."

"Oh," said they. "Is it far?"

"No, not far. Only a few *versts*. That is, five or six. Maybe seven. But certainly not more than eight."

"Eight *versts!*" they both cried out, wringing their hands and all but bursting into tears. "Do you know what you're saying? Only eight *versts!*"

"What do you want me to do about it?" I asked. "If it were up to me, I'd have made it a little shorter. But people have to have all sorts of experiences. How would you like to be in a carriage crawling up a hill through mud in a heavy rain, late Friday afternoon and almost time to light the candles for the Sabbath? Your hands are numb, you're faint with hunger . . . And crash! The axle breaks!"

"You talk like a half-wit," they said. "You must be out of your head. Why do you tell us these old-wives' tales? We're too tired to take another step. We've had nothing to eat all day except for a glass of coffee and a butter roll in the morning, and you come bothering us with foolish tales."

"Well, that's different," I told them. "You can't expect a person to dance before he's eaten. The taste of hunger is something I understand very well. You don't have to explain it to me. It's quite possible that I haven't even seen a cup of coffee or butter roll for the past year . . ." And as I utter these words a glass of steaming coffee with milk in it appears before my eyes, with rich, fresh butter rolls and other good things besides. "Oh, *shlimazl*," I say to myself, "is that what you've been raised on—coffee and butter rolls? And a plain piece of bread with herring isn't good enough for you?" But there, just to spite me, the image of hot coffee remained; just to tempt me the vision of rolls hovered before my eyes. I smelled the odor of the coffee, I savored the taste of the butter roll on my tongue—fresh and rich and sweet . . .

"Do you know what, Reb Tevye?" the women said to me. "Since we are standing right here, maybe it would be a good idea if we jumped into your wagon and you took us home to Boiberik. What do you say?"

"A fine idea," I said. "Here am I, coming *from* Boiberik, and you're going *to* Boiberik. How can I go both ways at the same time?"

"Well," they said, "don't you know what you can do? A wise and learned man can figure it out for himself. He would turn the wagon around and go back again—that's all. Don't be afraid, Reb Tevye. You can be sure that when you and the

Almighty get us back home again, we'll see to it that your kindness won't go unrewarded."

"They're talking Chaldaic," I told myself. "I don't understand them. What do they mean?" And the thought of witches and evil spirits and goblins returned to me. "Dummy, what are you standing there for?" I asked myself. "Jump into the wagon, show the horse your whip, and get away from here!" But again, as if I were under a spell, these words escaped me: "Well, get in."

The women did not wait to be asked again. Into the wagon they climbed, with me after them. I turn the wagon around, crack the whip—one, two, three, let's go . . . Who? What? When? The horse doesn't know what I'm talking about. He won't move an inch. "Ah-ha," I think to myself. "Now I can see what these women are. That's all I had to do—stop in the middle of the woods to make conversation with women!" You get the picture: on all sides the woods, silent, melancholy, with night coming on, and here behind me these two creatures in the guise of women. My imagination runs away with me. I recall a story about a teamster who once was riding through the woods by himself when he saw lying on the road a bag of oats. He jumped down, heaved the heavy sack to his back and just managed to tip it into the wagon, and went on. He rode a *verst* or two, looked around at the sack—but there was neither sack nor oats. In the wagon was a goat, a goat with a beard. The teamster tried to touch it with his hands, but the goat stuck out his tongue—a yard long—and let out a wild, piercing laugh and vanished into air . . .

"Well, what's keeping you?" ask the women.

"What's keeping me? Can't you see what's keeping me? The horse doesn't want to play. He is not in the mood."

"Well, you've got a whip, haven't you? Then use it."

"Thanks for the advice," I say. "I'm glad you reminded me. The only trouble with that is that my friend here is not afraid of such things. He is as used to the whip as I am to poverty," I add, trying to be flippant, though all the time I am shaking as if in a fever.

Well, what more can I tell you? I vented all my wrath on the poor animal. I whipped him till with God's help the horse stirred from his place, and we went on our way through the woods. And as we ride along a new thought comes to plague me. "Ah, Tevye, what a dull ox you are! You have always been good for nothing and you'll die good for nothing. Think! Here something happens to you that won't happen again in a hundred years. God Himself must have arranged it. So why didn't you make sure in advance how much it is going to be worth to you—how much you'll get for it? Even if you consider righteousness and virtue, decency and helpfulness, justice and equity and I don't know what else, there is still no harm in earning a little something for yourself out of it. Why not lick a bone for once in your life, since you have the chance? Stop your horse, you ox. Tell them what you want. Either you get so much and so much for the trip, or ask them to be so kind as to jump off the wagon at once! But then, what good would that do? What if they promised you the whole world on a platter? You have to catch a bear before you can skin it . . .

"Why don't you drive a little faster?" the women ask again, prodding me from behind.

"What's your hurry?" I say. "Nothing good can come from rushing too much." And I look around at my passengers. I'll swear they look like women, just plain ordinary women, one with a silk shawl, the other with a *sheitel.* They are looking at each other and whispering. Then one of them asks: "Are we getting closer?"

"Closer, yes. But not any closer than we really are. Pretty soon we'll go uphill and then downhill, then uphill and downhill again, and then after that we go up the steep hill and from then on it's straight ahead, right to Boiberik."

"Sounds like a *shlimazl,*" says one to the other.

"A seven-year itch," the other answers.

"As if we haven't had troubles enough already," says the first.

"A little crazy too, I'm afraid," answers the other.

"I must be crazy," I tell myself, "if I let them pull me around by the nose like that."

And to them I say, "Where do you want to be dropped off, ladies?"

"Dropped off? What do you mean—dropped off? What kind of language is that?"

"It's only an expression. You hear it among coarse and impolite drovers," I tell them. "Among genteel people like us we'd say it like this: 'Where would you wish to be transported, dear ladies, when with God's help and the blessings of Providence we arrive at Boiberik?' Excuse me if I sound inquisitive, but as the saying goes, 'It's better to ask twice than to go wrong once.' "

"Oh, so that's what you mean?" said the women. "Go straight ahead through the woods until you come to the green *datcha* by the river. Do you know where that is?"

"How could I help knowing?" I say. "I know Boiberik as well as I know my own home. I wish I had a thousand *rubles* for every log I've carried there. Last summer I brought a couple of loads of wood to that *datcha* you mention. Somebody from Yehupetz was living there then, a rich man, a millionaire. He must have been worth at least a hundred thousand *rubles.*"

"He still lives there," they tell me, looking at each other, whispering together and laughing.

"In that case," I said, "if you have some connections with the man, maybe it would be possible, if you wanted to, that is, if you could say a word or two in my behalf . . . Maybe you could get some sort of job for me, work of some kind. I know a man, a young fellow called Yisroel, who lived not far from our village—a worthless good-for-nothing. Well, he went off to the city, no one knows how it happened, and today, believe it or not, he is an important man somewhere. He makes at least twenty *rubles* a week, or maybe even forty. Who knows for sure? Some people are lucky, like our *shochet's* son-in-law. What would he ever have amounted to if he hadn't gone to Yehupetz? It is true, the first few years he starved to death. But now I wouldn't mind being in his boots. Regularly he sends money home, and he would like to bring his wife and children to Yehupetz to live with him, but he can't do it, because by law he isn't allowed to live there himself. Then how does he do it? Never mind. He has trouble aplenty, only if you live long enough . . . Oh, here we are at the river, and there is the green *datcha*!"

And I drive in smartly right up to the porch. You should have seen the excitement when they saw us. Such cheering and shouting! "Grandmother! Mother! Auntie! They've come home again! Congratulations! *Mazl-tov!* Heavens, where were you? We went crazy all day! Sent messengers in all directions. . . . We thought—who can tell? Maybe wolves, highwaymen—who knows? Tell us, what happened?"

"What happened? What should happen? We got lost in

the woods, wandered far away, till a man happened along. What kind of a man? A *shlimazl* with a horse and wagon. It took a little coaxing, but here we are."

"Of all horrible things! It's a dream, a nightmare! Just the two of you—without a guide! Thank God you're safe!"

To make a long story short, they brought lamps out on the porch, spread the table, and began bringing things out. Hot samovars, tea glasses, sugar, preserves, and fresh pastry that I could smell even from where I was standing; after that all kinds of food: rich fat soup, roast beef, goose, the best of wines and salads. I stood at the edge of the porch looking at them from a distance and thinking, "What a wonderful life these people of Yehupetz must live, praise the Lord! I wouldn't mind being one of them myself. What these people drop on the floor would be enough to feed my starving children all week long. O God, All-powerful and All-merciful, great and good, kind and just, how does it happen that to some people you give everything and to others nothing? To some people butter rolls and to others the plague?" But then I tell myself, "You big fool, Tevye! Are you trying to tell Him how to rule His world? Apparently if He wants it that way, that's the way it ought to be. Can't you see? If it should have been different it would have been? And yet, what would have been wrong to have it different? True! We were slaves in Pharaoh's day, too. That's why we are the Chosen People. That's why we must have faith and hope. Faith, first of all in a God, and hope that maybe in time, with His help, things will become a little better. . . ."

But then I hear someone say, "Wait! Where is he, this man you've mentioned? Did he drive away already—the *shlimazl*?"

"God forbid!" I call out from the edge of the porch. "What do you think? That I'd—go away like this—without saying anything? Good evening! Good evening to you all, and may the Lord bless you. Eat well, and may your food agree with you!"

"Come here!" they said to me. "What are you standing there for in the dark? Let's take a look at you, see what you are like! Maybe you'd like a little whiskey?"

"A little whiskey?" said I. "Who ever refused a drink of whiskey? How does it say in the *Talmud*? 'God is God, but whiskey is something you can drink!' To your health, ladies and gentlemen."

And I turn up the first glass. "May God provide for you," I say. "May He keep you rich and happy. Jews," I say, "must always be Jews. And may God give them the health and the strength to live through all the troubles they're born to . . ."

The *nogid* himself, a fine looking man with a skullcap, interrupts me. "What's your name?" he asks. "Where do you hail from? Where do you live now? What do you do for a living? Do you have any children? How many?"

"Children?" I say. "Do I have children? Oh . . . if it is true that each child were really worth a million, as my Golde insists, then I should be richer than the richest man in Yehupetz. The only thing wrong with this argument is that we still go to bed hungry. What does the Bible say? 'The world belongs to him who has money.' It's the millionaires who have the money; all I have is daughters. And as my grandmother used to say, 'If you have enough girls, the whole world whirls.' But I'm not complaining. God is our Father. He has His own way. He sits on high, and we struggle down below. What do I struggle with? I haul logs, lumber. What else should I do? The *Talmud* is right, 'If you can't have chicken, herring will do.' That's the whole trouble. We still have to eat. As my old grandmother—may she rest in peace—used to say, 'If we didn't have to eat, we'd all be rich.' "

I realized that my tongue was going sideways. "Excuse me, please," I said. "Beware of the wisdom of a fool and the proverbs of a drunkard."

At this the *nogid* cries out, "Why doesn't somebody bring something to eat?" And at once the table is filled with every kind of food—fish and fowl and roasts, wings and giblets and livers galore.

"Won't you take something?" they say. "Come on!"

"A sick person you ask; a healthy person you give," I say. "Thanks, anyway. A little whiskey—granted. But don't expect me to sit down and eat a meal like this while there, at home, my wife and children . . ."

Well, they caught on to what I was driving at, and you should have seen them start packing things into my wagon. This one brought rolls, that one fish, another one a roast chicken, tea, a package of sugar, a pot of chicken fat, a jar of preserves.

"This," they say, "take home for your wife and children.

And now tell us how much you'd want us to pay you for all you did for us."

"How do I know what it was worth?" I answer. "Whatever you think is right. If it's a penny more or a penny less I'll still be the same Tevye either way."

"No," they say. "We want you to tell us yourself, Reb Tevye. Don't be afraid. We won't chop your head off."

I think to myself, "What shall I do? This is bad. What if I say one *ruble* when they might be willing to give two? On the other hand, if I said two they might think I was crazy. What have I done to earn that much?" But my tongue slipped and before I knew what I was saying, I cried out, "Three *rubles*!"

At this the crowd began to laugh so hard that I wished I was dead and buried.

"Excuse me if I said the wrong thing," I stammered. "A horse, which has four feet, stumbles once in a while too, so why shouldn't a man who has but one tongue?"

The merriment increased. They held their sides laughing.

"Stop laughing, all of you!" cried the man of the house, and from his pocket he took a large purse and from the purse pulled out—how much do you think? For instance, guess! A ten *ruble* note, red as fire! As I live and breathe . . . And he says, "This is from me. And now, the rest of you, dig into your pockets and give what you think you should."

"Well, what shall I tell you? Fives and threes and ones began to fly across the table. My arms and legs trembled. I was afraid I was going to faint.

"*Nu,* what are you standing there for?" said my host. "Gather up the few *rubles* and go home to your wife and children."

"May God give you everything you desire ten times over," I babble, sweeping up the money with both hands and stuffing it into my pockets. "May you have all that is good, may you have nothing but joy. And now," I said, "good night, and good luck, and God be with you. With you and your children and grandchildren and all your relatives."

But when I turn to go back to the wagon, the mistress of the house, the woman with the silk shawl, calls to me, "Wait a minute, Reb Tevye. I want to give you something, too. Come back tomorrow morning, if all is well. I have a cow—a milch cow. It was once a wonderful cow, used to give twenty-four glasses of milk a day. But some jealous person must have cast an evil eye on it: you can't milk it any more. That is, you can milk it all right, but nothing comes."

"Long may you live!" I answer. "Don't worry. If you give us the cow we'll not only milk it—we'll get milk too! My wife, Lord bless her, is so resourceful that she makes noodles out of almost nothing, adds water and we have noodle soup. Every week she performs a miracle: we have food for the Sabbath! She has brought up seven children, though often she has nothing to give them for supper but a box on the ear! . . . Excuse me, please, if I've talked too much. Good night and good luck and God be with you," I say, and turn around to leave. I come out in the yard, reach for my horse—and stop dead! I look everywhere. Not a trace of a horse!

"Well, Tevye," I say to myself. "This time they really got you!"

And I recall a story I must have read somewhere, about a gang of thieves that once kidnapped a pious and holy man, lured him into a palace behind the town, dined him and wined him, and then suddenly vanished, leaving him all alone with a beautiful woman. But while he looked the woman changed into a tigress, and the tigress into a cat, the cat into an adder.

"Watch out, Tevye," I say to myself. "No telling what they'll do next!"

"What are you mumbling and grumbling about now?" they ask.

"What am I grumbling about? Woe is me! I'm ruined! My poor little horse!"

"Your horse," they tell me, "is in the stable."

I come into the stable, look around. As true as I'm alive, there's my bony little old nag right next to their aristocratic horses, deeply absorbed in feeding. His jaws work feverishly, as if this is the last meal he'll ever have.

"Look here, my friend," I say to him. "It's time to move along. It isn't wise to make a hog of yourself. An extra mouthful, and you may be sorry."

I finally persuaded him, coaxed him back to his harness, and in good spirits we started for home, singing one hymn after another. As for the old horse—you would never have known him! I didn't even have to whip him. He raced like the wind. We came home late, but I woke up my wife with a shout of joy.

"Good evening!" said I. "Congratulations! *Mazl-tov*, Golde!"

"A black and endless *mazl-tov* to you!" she anwers me. "What are you so happy about, my beloved bread-winner? Are you coming from a wedding or a *bris*—a circumcision feast—my goldspinner?"

"A wedding and a *bris* rolled into one," I say. "Just wait, my wife, and you'll see the treasure I've brought you! But first wake up the children. Let them have a taste of the Yehupetz delicacies, too!"

"Are you crazy?" she asks. "Are you insane, or out of your head, or just delirious? You sound unbalanced—violent!" And she lets me have it—all the curses she knows—as only a woman can.

"Once a wife always a wife," I tell her. "No wonder King Solomon said that among his thousand wives there wasn't one that amounted to anything. It's lucky that it isn't the custom to have a lot of wives any more!"

And I go out to the wagon and come back with my arms full of all the good things that they had given me. I put it all on the table, and when my crew saw the fresh white rolls and smelled the meat and fish they fell on it like hungry wolves. You should have seen them grab and stuff and chew—like the Children of Israel in the desert. The Bible says, "And they did eat," and I could say it, too. Tears came to my eyes.

"Well," says my helpmate, "tell me—who has decided to feed the countryside? What makes you so gay? Who gave you the drinks?"

"Wait, my love," I say to her. "I'll tell you everything. But first heat up the samovar. Then we'll all sit around the table, as people should now and then, and have a little tea. We live but once, my dear. Let's celebrate. We are independent now. We have a cow that used to be good for twenty-four glasses a day. Tomorrow morning, if the Lord permits, I'll bring her home. And look at this, my Golde! Look at this!" And I pull out the green and red and yellow banknotes from my pockets. "Come, my Golde, show us how smart you are! Tell me how much there is here!"

I looked across at my wife. She's dumbfounded. She can't say a word.

"God protect you, my darling!" I say to her. "What are you scared of? Do you think I stole it? I am ashamed of you, Golde! You've been Tevye's wife so many years and you think that of me! Silly, this is *kosher* money, earned honestly with my own wit and my own labor. I rescued two women from a great misfortune. If it were not for me, I don't know what would have become of them."

So I told her everything, from *a* to *z*. The whole story of my wanderings. And we counted the money over and over. There were eighteen *rubles*—for good luck, you know—and another eighteen for more good luck, and one besides. In all—thirty-seven *rubles*!

My wife began to cry.

"What are you crying for, you foolish woman?" I ask.

"How can I help crying when my tears won't stop? When your heart is full your eyes run over. May God help me, Tevye, my heart told me that you would come with good news. I can't remember when I last saw my Grandmother Tzeitl—may she rest in peace—in a dream. But just before you came home I was asleep and suddenly I dreamed I saw a milkpail full to the brim. My Grandmother Tzeitl was carrying it under her apron to shield it from an evil eye, and the children were crying, 'Mama . . .' "

"Don't eat up all the noodles before the Sabbath!" I interrupt. "May your Grandmother Tzeitl be happy in Paradise—I don't know how much she can help us right now. Let's leave that to God. He saw to it that we should have a cow of our own, so no doubt He can also make her give milk. Better give me some advice, Golde. Tell me—what shall we do with the money?"

"That's right, Tevye," says she. "What do you plan to do with so much money?"

"Well, what do you think we can do with it?" I say. "Where shall we invest it?"

And we began to think of this and that, one thing after another. We racked our brains, thought of every kind of enterprise on earth. That night we were engaged in every type of business you could imagine. We bought a pair of horses and sold them at a profit; opened a grocery store in Boiberik, sold the stock and went into the drygoods business. We bought an option on some woodland and made something on that too, then obtained the tax concession at Anatevka, and with our earnings began to loan out money on mortgages.

"Be careful! Don't be so reckless!" my wife warned me. "You'll throw it all away. Before you know it, you'll have nothing left but your whip!"

"What do you want me to do?" I ask. "Deal in grain and lose it all? Look what's happening right now in the wheat market. Go! See what's going on in Odessa!"

"What do I care about Odessa? My great-grandfather was never there, and so long as I'm alive and have my senses, my children will never be there, either!"

"Then what *do* you want?"

"What do I want? I want you to have some brains and not act like a fool."

"So you're the brainy one! You get a few *rubles* in your hand and suddenly you're wise. That's what always happens."

Well, we disagreed a few times, fell out, had some arguments, but in the end this is what we decided: to buy another cow—in addition to the one we were getting for nothing. A cow that would really give milk.

Maybe you'll say, "Why a cow?" And I'll answer, "Why not a cow?" Here we are, so close to Boiberik, where all the rich people of Yehupetz come to spend the summer at their *datchas*. They're so refined that they expect everything to be brought to them on a platter—meat and eggs, chickens, onions, pepper, parsnips—everything. Why shouldn't there be someone who would be willing to come right to their kitchen door every morning with cheese and butter and cream? Especially since the Yehupetzers believe in eating well and are ready to pay?

The main thing is that what you bring must be good—the cream must be thick, the butter golden. And where will you find cream and butter that's better than mine?

So we make a living . . . May the two of us be blessed by the Lord as often as I am stopped on the road by important people from Yehupetz—even Russians—who beg me to bring them what I can spare. "We have heard, Tevel, that you are an upright man, even if you are a Jewish dog . . ." Now, how often does a person get a compliment like that? Do our own people ever praise a man? No! All they do is envy him.

When they saw that Tevye had an extra cow, a new wagon, they began to rack their brains. "Where did he get it? How did he get it? Maybe he's a counterfeiter. Maybe he cooks alcohol in secret."

I let them worry. "Scratch your heads and rack your brains, my friends! Break your heads if you begrudge me my small living."

I don't know if you'll believe my story. You're almost the first person I've ever told it to.

But I'm afraid I've said too much already. If so, forgive me! I forgot that we all have work to do. As the Bible says, "Let the shoemaker stick to his last." You to your books, Mr. Sholom Aleichem, and I to my pots and jugs . . .

One thing I beg of you. Don't put me into one of your books, and if you do put me in, at least don't tell them my real name.

Be well and happy always.

The Enchanted Tailor

ONCE there was a man named Shimmen-Eli who lived in Zolodievka, a little town in the district of Mazapevka, not far from Haplapovitch and Kozodoievka (between Yampoli and Strishtch on the road that runs from Pischi-Yaboda through Petchi-Hvost to Tetrevitz and from there to Yehupetz). And he was known as Shimmen-Eli *Shma-Koleinu*, (the Hebrew for "Hear our voice, O Lord") because in the synagogue he shouted louder, swayed more vigorously, chanted and warbled with greater emotion than anyone else. By trade Shimmen-Eli was a tailor; not, you understand, a master tailor who sewed according to the latest fashion books, but a mender of great skill who excelled at darning holes and making patches that could never be detected, in turning a garment inside out and making the old look like new. He could take a threadbare coat and turn it into a gabardine, the gabardine into a pair of trousers, cut the trousers into a jacket, and the jacket into something else again.

This was by no means such easy work, but Shimmen-Eli *Shma-Koleinu* was an artist at it, and Zolodievka being a poor town where a new garment was a rare thing, Shimmen-Eli was held in high esteem. His only drawback was that he could never get along with the rich men of the town. He was always interfering in public affairs, defending the rights of the poor, speaking out bluntly about the town philanthropists, calling the tax-collector a blood-sucker and cannibal, and the rabbis and *shochtim* who worked together with the tax-collector a band of thieves, murderers, scoundrels and highwaymen. Let the devil take them all, together with their fathers and grandfathers and Uncle Ishmael . . .

Among his fellow workers Shimmen-Eli was considered a man of great and esoteric learning, for he was always full of quotations. He quoted passages from the Bible, which some of them knew, from *Gamorah* and *Midrash* which they had heard about, and from other commentaries whose existence they had never even suspected. No matter what the occasion, he had a Hebrew quotation at the tip of his tongue. If the quotation was usually garbled, if the beginning did not match the ending, and if none of it suited the occasion, that is not for us to judge.

In addition to his learning he had a voice that was not so bad, though possibly a little too shrill. He knew all the tunes and traditional renderings of all the prayers by heart, and he loved to lead the services in the Tailors' Chapel, where he was president—an office that brought him more grief than honor. A box in the ear, a slap in the face, was not uncommon at the Tailors' Chapel, and the president was usually at the receiving end.

Although Shimmen-Eli had been wretchedly poor all his life, a pauper actually, nevertheless he did not let his poverty get the best of him. On the contrary, he always said, "The poorer I am, the better I feel. The hungrier I am, the louder I sing. As the *Gamorah* says . . ." And here he let fly one of his famous quotations, one part Hebrew, one part Chaldaic, and the rest as often as not a knock-kneed, staggering Russian.

In appearance Shimmen-Eli was short and homely, with pins and needles sticking out all over him and bits of cotton batting clinging to his curly black hair. He had a short beard like a goat's, a flattened nose, a split lower lip and large black eyes that were always smiling. His walk was a little dance all his own and he was always humming to himself. His favorite saying was, "That's life—but don't worry."

And Shimmen-Eli was blessed with sons and daughters of all ages—mainly daughters. And he had a wife named Tsippa-Baila-Reiza who was his exact opposite; a tall, strong, red-faced, broad-shouldered woman, a regular Cossack in appearance. Ever since the day of their wedding she had taken him in hand and never loosened her hold. She was the head of the house, and her husband had the greatest respect for her. She had only to open her mouth and he trembled. In the Tailors' Chapel it was said openly that Shimmen-Eli may have patched the pants, but his wife wore them. At times, when they were alone, she was not above giving him a good slap in the face. This slap Shimmen-Eli would put into his pocket, and comfort himself with his favorite quotation: "That's life—but don't worry. The Bible says, 'And he shall rule over thee,' but it means nothing. Let all the kings of East and West do what they will, it won't help."

II

And it came to pass that one summer day Shimmen-Eli's wife, Tsippa-Baila-Reiza, came home from the market with her basket of purchases, flung down the bunch of garlic, the few parsnips and potatoes that she had bought, and cried out angrily, "The devil with it! I'm sick and tired of it all. Day after day, day after day, I break my head trying to think what to cook for dinner. You need the brains of a prime minister to think of something new. Every day it's dumplings and beans, beans and dumplings. May God forgive me for complaining but look at Nechama-Brocha, will you—a pauper like that, without a *kopek* to her name or a whole dish in her cupboard—and *she* has to have a goat! Why is it? Because her husband, though only a tailor, is still a man! So they have a goat, and if there is a goat in the house you can have a glass of milk for the children, you can cook porridge with milk, you can make a milk soup for dinner, noodles and milk for supper, and besides you can count on a pitcher of sour cream, a piece of cheese, a bit of butter. Think of it. If we only had a goat!"

"You're quite right, I'm afraid," said Shimmen-Eli mildly. "There is an ancient law that every Jew must own a goat. Let me quote you . . ."

"What good are your quotations?" cried Tsippa-Baila-Reiza. "I tell you about a goat and you give me quotations. I'll give *you* a quotation in a minute and you'll see stars! He feeds me quotations, that breadwinner of mine, the *shlimazl*. I wouldn't trade all your quotations and all your learning for one good borsht with cream! Do you hear?"

With broad hints like this Tsippa-Baila-Reiza plagued her husband constantly, until Shimmen-Eli promised her on his word of honor that from then on she could rest easily. With God's help she would get a goat.

"But how?" asked Tsippa-Baila-Reiza.

"Don't worry," answered Shimmen-Eli.

From that time on Shimmen-Eli began to save his *groschens*. He denied himself many necessary things, pawned his Sabbath gabardine, and by the greatest economy managed to save up a few *rubles*. It was decided that he should take the money and go over to Kozodoievka to buy a goat. Why to Kozodoievka? For two reasons. First of all, because Kozodoievka was famous for its goats, as the name implies—*koza* meaning *goat* in Russian. And secondly, because Tsippa-Baila-Reiza had heard from a neighbor of hers with whom she had not been on speaking terms for a number of years, and who in turn had heard it from her sister who lived in Kozodoievka and who had visited her not long before, that there was a *melamed*, a teacher, in that town, named Chaim-Chana the Wise (because he was such a fool) who had a wife named Tema-Gittel the Silent (because she was so talkative), and this Tema-Gittel owned two goats, both giving milk.

"Now, I ask you," said Tsippa-Baila-Reiza, "why should she have two goats, both of them giving milk? What harm would there be if she had only one? There are plenty of people who don't have even half a goat. And yet they live."

"You are quite right, my wife," said Shimmen-Eli. "That is an old complaint. As the saying goes . . ."

"There he goes again! Another quotation!" interrupted his wife. "You talk about a goat and he comes to you with a quotation. Take my advice. You go to that *melamed* in Kozodoievka and tell him this: 'It has come to our attention that you have two goats, both giving milk. What do you need two goats for? For pets? And since you don't need the two, why don't you sell one of them to me? Will it hurt you?' That's the only way to talk to these people, you understand?"

"Of course I understand. Why shouldn't I?" said Shimmen-Eli. "For my good money do I have to beg them? With money you can get anything in the world. 'Silver and gold,' said our wise men, 'make even pigs clean.' The only thing that's bad is not to have any money at all. As Rashi says, 'A poor man is like a dead man.' Or as it is written elsewhere, 'Without fingers you can't even thumb your nose.' Or, as another passage so appropriately puts it, '*Abracadabra* . . .' "

"Another passage! Another quotation! My head rings with his quotations! Oh, why don't you sink into the earth!" cried Tsippa-Baila-Reiza. "May you be buried nine feet deep!" And once more she instructed her husband how to approach the *melamed*, how to feel him out, and how to close the deal.

But suppose he didn't want to sell his goat? . . . Why

shouldn't he want to sell it? Why should he have two goats, both of them giving milk? There are so many people who don't have even half a goat. Well, do these people die? They manage to live.

And so on and so on, in the same vein.

III

And when it was light, our tailor arose from bed, said his prayers, took his staff and a rope, and started off on foot.

It was Sunday, a bright, warm, summer day. Shimmen-Eli could not remember when he had seen a beautiful day like this before. He could not remember the last time that he had been out in the open country. It had been a long time since his eyes had beheld such a fresh green forest, such a rich green carpet sprinkled with many-colored flowers. It had been a long time since his ears had heard the twitter of birds and the fluttering of small wings, such a long time since he had smelled the odors of the fresh countryside.

Shimmen-Eli *Shma-Koleinu* had spent his life in a different world from that. His eyes had beheld entirely different scenes: A dark cellar with an oven near the door, with pokers and shovels leaning against it, and nearby a slop-basin full to the brim. Near the oven and the basin, a bed made of three boards, with a litter of small children on it, half-naked, barefoot, unwashed, always hungry.

His ears had heard entirely different sounds: "Mother, I want some bread! Mother, I'm hungry!" And above these sounds the voice of Tsippa-Baila-Reiza herself: "You want to eat? May you eat worms! Together with that father of yours, the *shlimazl!* Oh, dear God in heaven!"

And his nose was accustomed to entirely different odors: the odor of damp walls that dripped in winter and molded in summer; the odor of sour dough and bran, of onions and cabbage, of wet plaster, of fish and entrails; the odor of old clothes steaming under the hot iron . . .

And now, having for the moment escaped from that poor, dark, unhappy world into the fragrant, unaccustomed brightness, Shimmen-Eli felt like a man who on a hot summer day dives into the ocean. The water lifts him up, the waves lap around him, he floats blissfully, deeply inhaling the fresh, salty air. He had never known anything like this before.

Shimmen-Eli walked slowly along thinking to himself, "What harm would it do if every workingman could come out here at least once a week, here in the open country, and enjoy the freedom of God's great world? Ah, what a world, what a world!" And Shimmen-Eli began to hum and then to sing under his breath. "Oh, Lord, Thou hast created Thine own world out beyond the town. Thou hast decreed that we, Thy people, should live in Zolodievka, huddled together in stifling quarters. And Thou didst give us woe and troubles, illness and poverty. These things Thou gavest us, O Lord, in Thy boundless mercy . . ."

Thus sang Shimmen-Eli under his breath, and he wanted to throw himself down on the grass, look up at the blue sky and taste just for a moment the sweetness of God's great world. But he remembered that he had work to do and he said to himself, "Enough, Shimmen-Eli, you have loitered enough. On your way, brother! It is time to go! You will rest, God willing, when you come to the Oak Tavern, where your kinsman, Dodi Rendar, will give you a drink. As the passage goes: 'A drop of whisky gladdens man's life . . .' "

And Shimmen-Eli *Shma-Koleinu* hurried on.

IV

On the road from Zolodievka, halfway to Kozodoievka, there stands a guest house called the Oak Tavern. This tavern has a power, the power of a magnet, which draws to itself all travelers who pass by. Whether they are going from Zolodievka to Kozodoievka or from Kozodoievka to Zolodievka, they all stop at the Oak Tavern, if only for a few minutes. No one has ever discovered the secret of this. Some say it is because the host, Dodi Rendar, is such a likable fellow and so hospitable. That is, for money he will give you a good glass of whisky and the best of food. Others say that it is because Dodi, although not a thief himself, has dealings with all the thieves in the vicinity, and at the same time protects all his customers from thieves. But since this is only a rumor, perhaps we had better say no more about it.

This Dodi we speak of was a coarse fellow, fat and hairy, with a large belly, a bulbous nose, and the voice of a wild boar. He had nothing to worry about. He made a good living, owned several cows, was a widower without any ties. He had no learning whatsoever; he scarcely knew the difference between a Bible and a prayer book. And for this reason Shimmen-Eli was ashamed of him. He considered it a disgrace that he, a learned man and president of his synagogue, should have such a coarse and ignorant lout for a relative. And Dodi, for his part, was ashamed to have a worthless tailor for a kinsman. Thus each one was ashamed of the other. And yet, when Dodi caught sight of Shimmen-Eli, he greeted him handsomely, not because he respected his kinsman, but because he feared his loud mouth.

"Oh," he said cheerfully, "look who's here! How are you, Shimmen-Eli? How is your Tsippa-Baila-Reiza? And how are the children?"

" 'What are we and what have we been?' " answered Shimmen-Eli, with a quotation. "How should we be? 'Who shall perish in an earthquake and who in a plague?' Sometimes better, sometimes worse . . . The important thing is, we're still alive. As it is written, '*Abracadabra* . . .'

"But how are *you*, my dear kinsman? What is new here in the country? How are your *vareniki* this year? I remember the ones you served a year ago with your drinks. *Vareniki*, that's what's important to you. The Holy Books mean nothing: you never look into them. Ah, Reb Dodi, Reb Dodi, if your father, my Uncle Gedalia-Wolf—may his soul rest in peace—were to arise now and see his son living in the country among peasants, he would die all over again. Ah, what a father you had, Reb Dodi! He was a good and pious man . . . Ah, yes, no matter what we begin with, we always arrive at death. Come, Reb Dodi, give me a drink. As Reb Pimpon says in his sixth book of commentaries, '*Kapota bimashken*,' 'Pawn your shirt, and buy yourself a drink.' "

"So!" said Dodi, bringing him a glass of whisky. "So you're throwing the Bible at me already! Leave that for later, kinsman. First tell me, Shimmen-Eli, where are you traveling to?"

"I am not traveling," said Shimmen-Eli with a shrug. "I am just taking a walk. As we say in our prayers, 'If you have legs you can walk.' "

"If that's the case," said Dodi, "then tell me, my dear friend, where are you walking to?"

"To Kozodoievka," said Shimmen-Eli, making a face. "To Kozodoievka to buy goats. As it is written, 'Thou shalt buy thyself goats.' "

"Goats?" asked Dodi in surprise. "How does a tailor come to be dealing in goats?"

"That's just a way of talking," said Shimmen-Eli. "What I meant actually was just one goat, that is, if the Lord has mercy and sends me the right kind of goat, one that won't cost too much. As far as I'm concerned, I don't want a goat, but my dear wife, Tsippa-Baila-Reiza—you know what she's like when she makes up her mind—has decided once for all that she must have a goat. And a wife, you have always maintained, must be obeyed. That's an old law. It's in the *Talmud*. You remember what the *Talmud* says . . ."

"About these things," said Dodi, "you are better informed than I am. You know well enough that I'm not even on speaking terms with the *Talmud*. But there is one thing I'd like to know, dear kinsman. How do you happen to be such an authority on goats?"

"The same way you're an authority on prayers!" said Shimmen-Eli angrily. "What does an innkeeper know about holiness? And yet when Passover comes, you recite the *Yom Kippur* prayers as well as you can, and get by with it!"

Dodi the Innkeeper understood the jibe. He bit his lip and thought to himself, "Wait, wait, you worthless tailor, you. You're a little too smart for your own good today. You're showing off your knowledge too much. You'll get a goat from me yet, and you'll be sorry!"

And Shimmen-Eli brought the conversation to an end by asking for another drink of that strong brew that is a cure for all troubles.

The truth can no longer be held back. Shimmen-Eli loved an occasional drink. But a drunkard he was not. God forbid! When was he able to buy enough whisky to become a drunkard? And yet he had this weakness: when he took one drink he had to have a second. And with the second he became quite jolly. His cheeks grew red, his eyes shone, his tongue loosened and wagged without stopping.

"Speaking of guilds," said Shimmen-Eli, "the one I belong to is the Tailors' Guild. Our emblem: Shears and Iron! Our people," he said, "have this one trait: we all like honors. At our synagogue, for instance, the least little shoemaker would like to be a chairman of something. If nothing else, then at least of the water basin. Says I, 'My friend, have it your own way. I can live without being president. Elect any shoemaker you want. I don't care for the honor and I don't want the headaches.' But they say, 'Nonsense! Once you've been elected you can't get out of it!' So I say, 'It is written in our Holy *Torah:* "Thou shalt take thy beatings and be a leader amongst men . . ."'

"But there! I've talked too much already. It's getting late. I forgot all about my goat. So good bye, Reb Dodi, be well. Say your prayers, and look after your *vareniki.*"

"Don't forget," replied Dodi. "On your way back, if God permits, you must come in again."

"If God permits and allows and wills it," said Shimmen-Eli. "After all, I am human, nothing but flesh and blood. Where else should I stop? And as for you, be sure there is whisky on hand, and a bite to eat. In the meantime, good bye. And remember our motto: Shears and Iron!"

V

And Shimmen-Eli *Shma-Koleinu* departed from the Oak Tavern in an exalted mood, cheerful as he could be. And he arrived in Kozodoievka without mishap. And as soon as he came there he began to inquire where he could find the *melamed,* Chaim-Chana the Wise, who had a wife Tema-Gittel the Silent and two goats. He did not have to search very long, since Kozodoievka is not such a large town that a person can get lost in it. The whole town lies spread out before your view. Here are the butchers' stalls with the cleavers and the dogs. Here is the marketplace where women go from one poultry-stand to another, picking up the chickens, and pinching and feeling them.

"What do you want for this hen?"

"Which hen? Oh, this one! That isn't a hen, it's a rooster."

"So let it be a rooster. But what do you want for it?"

And two steps farther along is the yard of the synagogue where old women sit over small baskets of pears, sunflower-seeds and beans; where the teachers conduct their classes and children recite their lessons out loud; and where goats—big goats, little goats, goats of all descriptions—jump about, pull straw off the roofs, or else sit on the ground warming themselves in the sun and chewing the cud. And only a few steps beyond that is the bath house, with its dark, smoke-stained walls. And beyond that, the pond covered with a green scum full of leeches and croaking frogs. The pond shines in the sun, sparkles like diamonds—and smells to high heaven. And on the other side of the pond is nothing but earth and sky. That is all there is to Kozodoievka.

When the tailor arrived at Chaim's house, he found him sitting over the *Gamorah* in his *tallis-kot'n* and skullcap, leading his pupils in a loud recitation:

"And—when—the—goat—saw—the—food—that—had—been—left—on—the—barrel—she—went—after—it—greedily . . ."

"'*Abracadabra d' barbanta,*'" said Shimmen-Eli *Shma-Koleinu* in his own Chaldaic, and quickly translated it into plain Yiddish. "Good morning to you, Rabbi, and to all your pupils. You are in the midst of the very subject about which I have come here to see your wife, Tema-Gittel, namely, a goat. True, if it depended on me, I would not be buying one, but my dear wife Tsippa-Baila-Reiza has set her heart on one once for all: she must have a goat. And a wife, you will tell me, should be obeyed. The *Gamorah* says so . . . But why are you staring at me like that? Because I am a plain workingman? 'Happy are ye who toil with your hands!'

"No doubt you have heard of me. I am Shimmen-Eli of Zolodievka, member of the Tailors' Guild and president of our synagogue, though I never asked to be chosen. 'I can get along without the honor,' I told them, 'and you keep the beatings for yourselves.' But they shouted, 'It's too late! Once we've picked you, you can't get out of it! A king and a leader you shall be to us. You'll *be* our leader, and you'll *get* the beatings!'

"But here I've been talking, and I almost forgot to greet you properly. How do you do, my Rabbi! How do you do, my boys! A fine crew of imps and mischief-makers, I see. Anxious to get on with your studies. Am I right?"

Hearing these words, the children began to pinch each other under the table and to giggle surreptitiously. They were, indeed, pleased with the interruption. They would have liked such visitors every day. But Chaim-Chana the Wise was not so pleased. He disliked to be interrupted when he was teaching. So he called in his wife Tema-Gittel and he himself returned with his pupils to the goat which had gotten hold of the food on the barrel. And again they began to chant at the tops of their voices:

"And—the—Rabbi—decreed—that—the—goat—must—pay—for—the—food—and—for—the—damage—to—the—barrel."

Shimmen-Eli, seeing that there was no use talking to the *melamed*, turned to his wife, Tema-Gittel the Silent.

"Here I am," said Shimmen-Eli. "As you see, a plain workingman. You may have heard of me, Shimmen-Eli of Zolodievka, member of the Tailors' Guild and president of our synagogue (though I didn't ask for the honor). I have come to see you about one of your goats. For my part I wouldn't be buying a goat now, but since my dear wife Tsippa-Baila-Reiza has made up her mind that she has to have a goat . . ."

Tema-Gittel, a tiny woman with a nose like a bean that she was always wiping with her two fingers, listened as long as she could, and then interrupted:

"So you want one of my goats, do you? Well, let me tell you this, my dear man. I'm not interested in selling the goat. For let's not fool ourselves: why should I sell it? For the money you offer? Money is round. It rolls away. But a goat is always a goat. Especially a goat like mine. Did I call it a goat? A sweetheart, that's what it is! How easy it is to milk her! And the amount of milk she gives! And how cheap it is to feed her! What does she eat? A measure of bran once a day, and for the rest she nibbles the straw from the roof of the synagogue. Still, if you're ready to pay what it's worth, I might think it over. Money is—how do you say it?—a temptation. If I get enough money I can buy another goat. Although a goat like mine would be hard to find. Did I call it a goat? A sweetheart, I tell you! But wait, why waste words? I'll bring the goat in and you'll see for yourself."

And Tema-Gittel ran out and came back leading a goat and carrying a pitcher full of milk that the goat had given that same day.

At the sight of the milk the tailor could not keep from licking his lips.

"Tell me, my dear woman, how much do you ask for this goat of yours? Remember, if it's too much, I'm not interested. You see, I don't even want the animal, but since my wife, Tsippa-Baila-Reiza, has set her heart . . ."

"What do you mean—how much?" burst out Tema-Gittel, wiping her tiny nose. "Let's hear first what you're willing to pay. But let me tell you, no matter how much you pay, you'll be getting a bargain. Because if you buy my goat . . ."

"Listen to that!" interrupted the tailor. "Why do you suppose I'm buying it? Because it's a goat! Naturally! I'm not looking for a snake, am I? Though to tell you the truth, I'd never have thought of buying a goat if my wife hadn't . . ."

"That's what I'm telling you," Tema-Gittel interrupted in her turn and began to recount the virtues of her goat again. But the tailor did not let her finish. They kept interrupting each other until anyone listening to them would have heard something like this:

"A goat? A sweetheart, not a goat . . . I would never be buying a goat . . . A measure of bran . . . Set her heart on it . . . Money is round . . . So easy to milk . . . Tsippa-Baila-Reiza . . . What does she eat? . . . Once for all . . . Straw from the roof of the synagogue . . . A wife must be obeyed . . . A goat? A sweetheart, not a goat!"

At this point Chaim-Chana broke in. "Maybe you've said enough about goats already? Who ever heard of such a thing? Here I am, right in the midst of a point of law, and all I hear is goat, goat, goat, goat! Heavens above! Either sell the goat, or don't sell the goat, but stop talking about it. Goats, goats, goats, goats, goats. My head is ringing with goats!"

"The Rabbi is right," said Shimmen-Eli. "Where there is learning there is wisdom. Why do we have to talk so much? I have the money and you have the goat. That should be enough. Three words can settle it. As it is written . . ."

"What do I care what's written?" said Tema-Gittel softly, arching herself like a cat and brushing her hand back and forth over her lips. "Just tell me what you want to pay."

"What should I say?" Shimmen-Eli answered as softly. "Who am I to say? Ah, well, it looks as if I've wasted a trip. Apparently I'm not buying a goat today. Forgive me for bothering you . . ."

And Shimmen-Eli turned to go.

"Now, look here, my good man," said Tema-Gittel, catching him by the sleeve. "What's your hurry? Is there a fire somewhere? It seems to me we were talking about a goat . . ."

At last the *melamed's* wife named her price, the tailor named his; they haggled back and forth, and finally agreed. Shimmen-Eli counted out the money and tied the rope around the goat's neck. Tema-Gittel took the money, spit on it to ward off the Evil Eye, wished the tailor luck, and muttering softly looked from the money to the goat, from the goat to the money. And she led the tailor out with many blessings.

"Go in good health, arrive in good health, use the goat in good health, and may God grant that she continue to be as she has been up to now. No worse. May you have her a long time, may she give milk and more milk, and never stop giving milk."

"Amen," said the tailor and started to leave. But the goat would not budge. She twisted her head, reared up her hind legs, and bleated shrilly, like a young cantor trying to impress his congregation.

But Chaim-Chana came to the rescue with the rod he used on the boys, and helped to drive the goat out of the house. And the children helped along by shouting: "*Koza! Koza!* Get out, *koza!*"

And the tailor proceeded on his way.

VI

But the goat had no desire to go to Zolodievka. She thrust herself against the wall. She twisted and turned and reared her hind legs. And Shimmen Eli pulled at the rope and gave her to understand that all her kicking and bucking was useless. He said to her:

"It is written that out of necessity must thou bear thy exile. Whether thou wilt or not; nobody asks thee. I, too, was once a free Soul, a fine young man with a starched shirt and shiny boots that croaked and clattered as I walked. What more did I need? A headache? But the Lord said unto me, 'Get thee out of thy country. Crawl, Shimmen-Eli, into thy sack. Marry Tsippa-Baila-Reiza. Beget children. Suffer all thy days and thy years. For what art thou but a tailor?' "

Thus Shimmen-Eli addressed the goat, and pulling her by the rope, he went on his way, quickly, almost at a run. A warm breeze ruffled the skirts of his patched gabardine, stole under his earlocks and stroked his little beard. It brought to his nostrils the fragrance of mint, of rosemary, and other herbs and flowers whose heavenly odors he had never smelled before. And in a spirit of ecstasy and wonder he began the afternoon prayers, very handsomely, with a noble chant like a cantor performing in the presence of an admiring congregation. Suddenly—who knows how?—an Evil Spirit came to tempt him, and whispered these words into his ear:

"Listen to me, Shimmen-Eli, you fool, you! Of all things, why burst into song? It is almost evening, you haven't had a thing in your mouth all day (except two small glasses of whisky), and you gave your kinsman your word of honor that on your way home with the goat, if all was well, you would stop to have a bite with him. It was a promise, so you'll have to keep it."

And Shimmen-Eli finished his prayers as fast as he could. Then he made his way to Dodi Rendar's tavern, entering with a joyful greeting on his lips.

"Good evening to you, dear kinsman, Reb Dodi. I have news for you. Congratulate me. 'I have dwelt with Laban . . .' I have a goat. And such a goat! Straight from goatland! A goat such as our fathers and forefathers had never known. Look her over, Reb Dodi, and give us your opinion. After all, you're a man of experience. Well, make a guess. How much should I have paid for it?"

Dodi put up his hand to shield his eyes from the setting sun, and like a true expert appraised the goat—at exactly double the figure that Shimmen-Eli had paid. At which Shimmen-Eli was so flattered that he slapped the innkeeper soundly on the back.

"Reb Dodi, dear kinsman, long life to you! This one time you didn't guess right! You were all wrong!"

Reb Dodi pursed his lips and shook his head in speechless admiration, as if to say, "What a bargain! You certainly put one over that time!"

Shimmen-Eli in his turn bent his head sideways, and with a quick gesture as if he were pulling a needle out of his vest and threading it hastily, said, "Well, Reb Dodi, what do you say now? Do I know how to look after my own affairs, or don't I? Why, if you saw how much milk she gave, you would die on the spot!"

"I'd rather see you die," said Dodi in a friendly tone.

"Amen," said Shimmen-Eli. "The same to you. And now, if I'm such a welcome guest, take my goat, Reb Dodi, and put her in the barn where no one can steal her. In the meantime I'll say my evening prayers, and then the two of us will make a toast and take a bite to eat. As the *Megila* says, 'Before eating, one is not disposed to dance.' Is that in the *Megila*, Reb Dodi, or is it somewhere else?"

"Who knows? If you say so, it must be so. After all, you're the scholar around here."

When he had finished his prayers, the tailor said to Dodi, " 'Let me swallow, I pray thee, some of this red, red pottage; for I am faint . . .' Come, my kinsman, pour out something out of that green bottle, and let us drink of it, for our health's sake. Good health, that is our first concern. As we say in our prayers every day: 'Cause us to lie down in peace and health . . .' "

Having taken a couple of drinks and a little to eat, our tailor became very talkative. He talked about his home town of Zolodievka, the community in general and his synagogue and Tailors' Guild ("Shears and Iron our emblem!") in particular. And in the process of his discourse he denounced all the leading citizens of the town, the well-to-do and influential men, and swore that as sure as his name was Shimmen-Eli, every one of them deserved to be sent to Siberia.

"You understand, Reb Dodi?" he rounded out his dissertation. "May the devil take them, these givers of charity! Is it their own money they give? All they do is suck the blood of us poor people. Out of my three *rubles* a week they make me pay twenty-five *kopeks!* But their time will come, never fear. God shall hold them to account! Although to tell you the truth, my cherished wife, Tsippa-Baila-Reiza, has long told me that I am worse than a *shlimazl,* a fool and a coward, because if I only wanted to use it, I could hold a strong whip over them! But who listens to one's wife? After all, I have something to say, too. Does not our Holy *Torah* tell us: *'V'hu yimshol b' cho?'* Shall I translate that for you, kinsman? *'V'hu*—and he, that is, the husband'—*'yimshol*—shall rule!' But instead, what happens? What should happen? Since you have started pouring, so pour a little more. Remember what the Bible says: *'Abracadabra d' barbanta!'* "

The more Shimmen-Eli talked, the more he wandered. His eyelids drooped and soon he was leaning against the wall and nodding. His head was bent sideways, his arms were crossed over his chest, and in his fingers he held his thin little beard like a man deep in thought. Had it not been for the fact that he was snoring out loud, a snore that was at once a whistling, a wheezing and a blowing, no one in the world would have dreamt that he was asleep.

But though he dozed, his brain worked busily, and he dreamed that he was home at his workbench with a strange garment spread out in front of him. Was it a pair of trousers? Then where was the crotch? There was no crotch. Was it an undershirt? Then why did it have such long sleeves? Then what could it be? It had to be something. Shimmen-Eli turned it inside out—it was a gabardine. And what a gabardine! Brand new, soft and silky to the touch, too new to be made into something else. But out of habit he took a knife out of his vest pocket and began to look for a seam. Just then Tsippa-Baila-Reiza rushed in and began to curse him:

"What are you ripping it for? May your entrails be ripped out! You green cucumber, you fine kidney bean! Can't you see it's your Sabbath gabardine that I got for you with the money I earned from the goat?"

And Shimmen-Eli remembered that he had a goat, and he rejoiced. Never in his life had he seen so many pitchers of milk, so many cheeses, and so much butter—crocks and crocks of butter! And the buttermilk, the cream, the clabber! And rolls and biscuits baked with butter, sprinkled with sugar and cinnamon! What appetizing odors! Never in his life had he smelled such odors. And then another odor crept in—a familiar one—pugh! He felt something crawl over his neck, under his collar, around his ears and over his face. It crawled right up to his nose. He reached out his fingers and caught a bedbug. He opened first one eye, then the other, stole a look toward the window . . . Good heavens, day was breaking!

"What do you think of that! I must have dozed off!" Shimmen-Eli said to himself and shrugged his shoulders. He woke up the innkeeper, ran out into the yard, opened the barn, took the goat by the rope, and started for home as quickly as he could, like a man who is afraid that he will miss—the Lord alone knows what.

VII

When Tsippa-Baila-Reiza saw that it was late and that her husband was not yet home, she began to wonder if some evil had not befallen him. Perhaps robbers had attacked him on the way, murdered him, taken his few *rubles* away and thrown him into a ditch; and here she was, a widow for the rest of her days, a widow with so many children. She might as well drown herself. All that night she did not shut her eyes, and when the first cock crowed at dawn she pulled on her dress and went outside and sat down on the doorstep to wait for her husband. Maybe God would have mercy and send him home. But what could you expect from a *shlimazl* when he goes off by himself, she thought; and she planned the welcome that he so richly deserved.

But when finally he appeared with the goat following on the rope behind him—both of them tied to the rope, the goat around the neck and Shimmen-Eli around the waist—she was so relieved that she greeted him affectionately:

"Why so late, my little canary, my almond cake! I thought you had been robbed and killed on the way, my treasure."

Shimmen-Eli loosened the rope around his waist, took the goat into the house, and breathlessly began to tell Tsippa-Baila-Reiza all that had happened to him.

"Behold, my wife, the goat which I have brought to you. A goat straight from goatland. The kind of goat that our forefathers dreamt about but never saw. She eats only once a day, a measure of bran, and otherwise she nibbles the straw from the roof of the synagogue. Milk she gives like a cow, twice a day. I saw a full pail with my eyes, I swear. Did I call it a goat? A sweetheart, not a goat. At least that's what Tema-Gittel said. And such a bargain! I practically stole it from her. Six and a half *rubles* was all I paid. But how long do you think I had to bargain with the woman? Actually she didn't want to sell the goat. All night long I had to fight with her."

And while he spoke, Tsippa-Baila-Reiza thought to herself: "So Nechama-Brocha thinks she's the only person in town who amounts to something! She can have a goat and the rest of us can't? Now watch her eyes pop out when she sees Tsippa-Baila-Reiza with a goat too! And Bluma-Zlata? And Haya-Mata? Friends they call themselves, well-wishers. May they have only half the misfortune they wish me!"

And meanwhile she made a fire in the stove and began to prepare some buckwheat noodles for breakfast. And Shimmen-Eli put on his *tallis* and *tfillin* and started the morning prayers.

It was a long time since he had prayed with such feeling. He sang like a cantor on a holiday and made so much noise that he woke the children. When they found out from their mother that their father had brought home a goat and that she was cooking noodles with milk, they screamed with joy, sprang out of their bed still in their nightgowns, and taking each other's hands, started to dance in a circle. And while they danced, they sang this song they had just made up:

"A goat, a goat, a little goat!
Papa brought a little goat!
The goat will give us mi-i-lk
And Mama will make noodles!"

Watching his children dancing and singing, Shimmen-Eli expanded with pleasure. "Poor children," he thought, "so eager for a little milk. That's all right, my children. Today you'll have as much milk as you want. And from now on you'll have a glass of milk every day, *kasha* with milk, and milk with your tea. A goat is really a blessing. Now let Fishel charge as much for his meat as he wants to. He always gave us bones instead of meat, so let him choke on his bones. What do I need his meat for if we have milk? For the Sabbath? For Sabbath we can buy fish. Where is it written that a Jew must eat meat? I have not seen a law on that anywhere. If all good Jews only listened to me, they would all buy themselves goats."

With these thoughts Shimmen-Eli *Shma-Koleinu* put away his *tallis* and *tfillin,* washed himself, made a benediction over a slice of bread, and sat down to wait for the noodles. Instead, the door flew open and in rushed Tsippa-Baila-Reiza with an empty pail, sputtering with anger, her face aflame. And a shower of curses began to descend on the head of poor Shimmen-Eli—not curses but burning stones. Fire and brimstone poured from Tsippa-Baila-Reiza's mouth.

"May your father, that drunkard, move over in his grave and make room for you!" she cried. "May you turn into a stone, a bone! May you end in hell! I could shoot you, hang you, drown you, roast you alive! I could cut you, slice you, chop you to pieces! Go, you robber, murderer, apostate! Take a look at the goat you brought me! May a scourge descend upon your head and arms and legs! God in heaven! Dear, true, loving Father!"

That was all that Shimmen-Eli heard. Pulling his cap down over his eyes, he went out of the house to see the misfortune that had befallen him.

Coming outside and seeing the goat tethered to the gatepost calmly chewing her cud, he stood fixed in his tracks, not knowing what to do or where to turn. He stood there thinking and thinking, and at last said to himself, " 'Let me die with the Philistines!' I'll get even with them yet, that *melamed* and his wife! They found the right person to play tricks on! I'll show them a few tricks they won't forget. He looked so innocent, too, that *melamed:* he didn't want anything to do with the whole transaction. And this is what he did to me . . . No wonder the children laughed when the rabbi led me out with the goat and his wife wished all that milk onto us . . . Milk I'll give them! I'll milk the blood out of those holy Kozodoievkites, those cheats, those swindlers!"

And once more he set out for Kozodoievka, with the intention of giving the teacher and his wife what they had coming . . .

A little later, passing by the Oak Tavern and seeing the innkeeper in the doorway, with his pipe between his teeth, our tailor burst out laughing.

"What are you so happy about?" asked the innkeeper. "What are you laughing for?"

"Listen to this," said the tailor, "and maybe you'll laugh, too." And he roared as though ten devils were tickling him. "Well, what do you think of my luck? Everything has to happen to me! You should have heard what I got from my wife this morning—what Pharaoh's chariots and horsemen got from the Lord. She served it up in every kind of dish, and I had to take it on an empty stomach. If I could only pass it on to the *melamed* and his wife! Believe me, I'll never let them get away with it. It will be an eye for an eye and a tooth for a tooth. I don't like to have people play tricks like this on me. But come, Dodi, put this cursed goat into the barn for a few minutes, and then pour me a drink. I'm a troubled man. I need a little strength before I face those people again.

"Ah, Reb Dodi, here's to your health. We're still men, that's the main thing. And remember what we are enjoined in the Bible: 'Do not worry . . .' You can be sure that I'll give them something to think about before this morning is over. I'll show them how to play tricks on a member of the Tailors' Guild ('Shears and Iron our emblem!')."

"Who told you it was a trick?" asked the innkeeper innocently, puffing away at his pipe. "Maybe you made a mistake in picking the goat?"

Shimmen-Eli nearly sprang at the innkeeper's throat. "Do you know what you're saying? I came and asked for a goat that would give milk, even as Jacob asked for Rachel. And I was tricked just as he was!"

Dodi puffed at his pipe, shrugged his shoulders, and threw up his hands as if to say, "Is it my fault? What can I do about it?"

And once more Shimmen-Eli took his goat and went on his way to Kozodoievka. And his anger burned within him.

VIII

And the teacher labored with his pupils, still on the same section in the *Gamorah* dealing with damages and injuries. Their voices resounded over the whole synagogue yard:

"The—cow—swung—her—tail—and—she—broke—the—pitcher!"

"Good morning to you, my Rabbi, and to you boys, and to all Israel," said Shimmen-Eli. "Give me a minute of your time, I pray you. The cow won't run away, and the broken pitcher surely will not mend itself!

"That was a fine trick you played on me, Rabbi. No doubt it was a joke, but I don't like such jokes. It's too much like that story about the two men who were taking their bath one Friday afternoon, stretched out on the top ledge at the bath house. Said one of the men to the other, 'Here is my besom. Whip me with it.' And the other, taking the besom, beat him till he was bleeding. Said the first, 'Listen, my friend! If I have wronged you and you want to pay me back now while I am naked and helpless, that is very well. But if you are doing it as a joke, I want to tell you: I don't care for such jokes!'"

"What is the point of that?" asked the *melamed*, taking off his glasses and scratching his ear with them.

"This is the point. Why did you trick me that way—giving me a goat like this? For that kind of trick," he said, showing him an open hand, "you may get something in return! You needn't think you're dealing with just anybody! I'm Shimmen-Eli of Zolodievka, member of the Tailors' Guild and president of our synagogue ('Shears and Iron' our emblem!)."

The tailor was so excited that he shook all over, and the *melamed*, putting on his glasses, stared at him in amazement. The whole room rocked with laughter.

"Why do you look at me like a crazy fool?" demanded the tailor angrily. "I come here and buy a goat from you, and you send me home with—the devil alone knows what!"

"You don't like my goat?" the teacher asked, slowly.

"The goat? If that's a goat, then you're the governor of this province."

The boys burst into laughter anew. And at this point Tema-Gittel the Silent came in and the real battle started. Shimmen-Eli yelled at Tema-Gittel and Tema-Gittel yelled back. The *Melamed* looked from one to the other, and the boys laughed louder and louder. Tema-Gittel shrieked, Shimmen-Eli roared, with neither yielding, till Tema-Gittel caught the tailor by the hand and pulled him out through the door.

"Come!" she cried. "Come to the rabbi. Let the whole world see how a Zolodievka tailor can persecute innocent people—slander them!"

"Yes, let's go," said Shimmen-Eli. "Certainly let the world see how people who are considered honest, even holy, can rob a stranger and ruin him. As we say in our prayers, 'We have become a mockery and a derision . . .' And you come too, *melamed*."

Whereupon the *melamed* put on his plush hat over his skullcap, and the four of them went to the rabbi together—the tailor, the *melamed*, his wife, and the goat.

When the delegation arrived, they found the rabbi saying his prayers. When he was through, he gathered up the skirts of his long coat and seated himself on his chair, an ancient relic that was little more than feet and armrests, shaky as the last teeth of an old man.

When he had finished hearing both parties, who had hardly let each other talk, the rabbi sent for the elders and the *shochet* and the other leading citizens of the town, and when they arrived he said to the tailor:

"Now be so kind as to repeat your story from beginning to end, and then we'll let her tell hers."

And Shimmen-Eli willingly told his story all over again. He told them who he was—Shimmen-Eli of Zolodievka, member of the Tailors' Guild and president of the synagogue (though he needed that honor like a headache). Harassed by his wife, Tsippa-Baila-Reiza, who was suddenly determined to have a goat, he had come to Kozodoievka, and there had bought from the *melamed* an animal that was supposed to be a goat. But it turned out that these people had taken away his money and passed off on him the devil alone knew what—possibly as a joke, but he, Shimmen-Eli, hated such jokes. "No doubt you have heard," he said, "the story of the two men who were taking their bath on a Friday afternoon . . ."

And the tailor, Shimmen-Eli, repeated the story of the bath, and the rabbi and the elders and the other leading citizens nodded their heads and smiled.

"Now that we have heard one side," said the rabbi, "let us hear the other."

At this Chaim-Chana the Wise arose from his seat, pulled his plush hat down over his skullcap, and began:

"Hear me, O Rabbi, this is my story, just like this. I was sitting with my pupils, sitting and studying, I was studying the Order of Injuries, that's what we were studying. *Bubi-Kama?* Yes, *Bubi-Kama.* And there walks in this man from Zolodievka, and he says he's from Zolodievka, from Zolodievka, you understand, and he greets me and tells me a long story. He tells me that he's from Zolodievka, a Zolodievkite, that is, and he has a wife whose name is Tsippa-Baila-Reiza. Yes, I'm sure it's Tsippa-Baila-Reiza. At least so it seems to me. Isn't that it?"

And he leaned over to the tailor questioningly, and the tailor, who had been standing all this time with his eyes shut, fingering his little beard, his head a little to one side, swaying back and forth, answered, "That is true. She has all three names, Tsippa and Baila and Reiza. She has been called by these names as long as I have known her, which is now—let's see—about thirty years. And now, my dear friend, let's hear what else you have to say. Don't go wandering. Get down to business. Tell them what I said and what you said. In the words of King Solomon, 'Beat not around the bush.' "

"But I don't know anything about it. I don't," said the *melamed,* frightened, and pointed to his wife. "She talked to him. She did the talking. She made the deal with him. I don't know anything."

"Then," said the rabbi, "let's hear what you have to say." And he pointed to the *melamed's* wife.

Tema-Gittel wiped her lips, leaned her chin on one hand and with the other began to tell her side of the story. She talked quickly, without stopping for breath, and her face grew redder and redder as she spoke.

"Listen to me," she said. "Here is the real story of what happened. This tailor from Zolodievka is either crazy or drunk or just doesn't know what he's talking about. Have you ever heard of such a thing? A man comes to me all the way from Zolodievka and fastens himself to us like a grease spot. He won't leave us alone. He insists: I must sell him a goat. (As you know, I had two of them.)

"The tailor makes a speech. He himself would not be buying a goat, but since his wife Tsippa-Baila-Reiza has set her heart on a goat, and a wife, he says, must be obeyed . . . Do you follow me, Rabbi? So I told him, 'What difference does that make to me? You want to buy a goat? I'll sell you a goat. That is, I wouldn't sell it for any amount, for what is money? Money is round. It rolls away, but a goat remains a goat, and especially a goat like this. It's a sweetheart, not a goat. So easy to milk! And the milk she gives! And what does she eat? Once a day a measure of oats, and for the rest some straw from the roof of the synagogue.'

"But thinking it over, I decided: after all, I have two goats, and money is a temptation. Anyway, at this point my husband told me to make up my mind, and we agreed on the price. How much do you think it was? May my enemies never have any more than we asked for that goat. And I gave him the goat, a treasure of a goat. And now he comes back, this tailor does, and tries to tell me that it's not a goat. It doesn't give milk. Do you know what? Here is the goat. Give me a milk pail, and I'll milk her right here in front of your eyes."

And she borrowed a pail from the rabbi's wife and milked the goat right there in front of their eyes, and she brought the milk to each one separately to see. First, naturally, to the rabbi, then to the elders, then to the other leading citizens, and finally to the assembled populace. And such a clamor arose! Such a tumult! This one said, "We must punish this Zolodievka tailor. Let him buy drinks for us all." Another said, "Punishing him like this is not enough. We ought to take away the goat." Still another said, "The goat is a goat. Let him keep it. Let him enjoy it to a ripe old age. What we ought to do is give him a few good kicks and send him and the goat both to the devil!"

When he saw this turn of events, Shimmen-Eli quietly slipped out of the rabbi's house, and disappeared.

IX

The tailor hastened away from the angry multitude like a man running from a fire. From time to time he looked back to see if anyone was following him, and he thanked the Lord for having escaped without a beating.

When he approached the Oak Tavern, Shimmen-Eli said to himself: "He'll never get the truth out of me."

"Well, what happened?" asked Dodi with feigned interest.

"What should happen?" said Shimmen-Eli. "People have respect for a man like me. They can't play tricks on me. After all, I'm not a schoolboy. I showed them a few things. I had a little discussion with the *melamed* too, about a few points in the *Gamorah,* and we found out that I knew more than he did. Anyway, to make a long story short, they begged my pardon and gave me the goat I had bought. Here she is. Take her for a little while, my kinsman, and then give me a drink."

"He is not only a braggart," thought Dodi to himself, "but a liar as well. I'll have to play the same game once more and see what he'll say next time."

And to the tailor he said: "I have just the thing for you—a glass of old cherry wine."

"Cherry wine!" said Shimmen-Eli and licked his lips in anticipation. "Bring it out and I'll tell you what I think of it. Not everyone knows what good wine is."

When he had drained the first glass, the tailor's tongue began wagging again. He said, "Tell me, dear kinsman, you're no fool and you have dealings with many people. Tell me, do you believe in magic, in illusions?"

"For instance?" asked Dodi, innocently.

"Why," said Shimmen-Eli, "*dybbuks,* elves, evil spirits of all sorts, wandering souls . . ."

"What makes you ask?" said Dodi, puffing at his pipe.

"Just like that," said Shimmen-Eli, and went on talking about sorcerers, witches, devils, gnomes, werewolves.

Dodi pretended to listen attentively, smoked his pipe, and then he spat and said to the tailor, "Do you know what, Shimmen-Eli? I'll be afraid to sleep tonight. I'll tell you the truth: I have always been afraid of ghosts, but from now on I'll believe in *dybbuks* and gnomes as well."

"Can you help yourself?" said the tailor. "Try not believing! Just let one good gnome come along and start playing tricks on you—upset your *borsht,* pour out your water, empty all your pitchers, break your pots, tie knots in the fringes of your *tallis knot'*, throw a cat into your bed and let it lie on your chest like a ten-pound weight . . ."

"Enough! Enough!" begged the innkeeper, spitting to ward off spirits. "Don't ever tell me stories like that so late at night!"

"Goodbye, Reb Dodi. Forgive me for teasing you. You know I'm not to blame. As the saying is, 'The old woman had no troubles . . .' You know that saying, don't you? Well, good night . . ."

X

When the tailor returned to Zolodievka he walked into the house boldly, determined to give his wife a piece of his mind; but he controlled himself. After all, what can you expect from a woman? And for the sake of harmony he told her this story:

"Believe me, Tsippa-Baila-Reiza, in spite of what you think, people have to look up to me. I wish you could have seen what I gave that *melamed* and his wife! It was as much as they could take. And then I dragged them off to the rabbi and he ruled that they must pay a fine, because when a man like Shimmen-Eli comes to buy a goat from them, he deserves the greatest consideration, for this Shimmen-Eli, says the rabbi, is a man who . . ."

But Tsippa-Baila-Reiza did not want to hear any more about the praise that had been showered on her husband. What she wanted was to see the real goat he had now brought with him, so she took her pail again and ran out of the house. But it was not long before she came running back, speechless with anger. Catching Shimmen-Eli by the collar, she gave him three good shoves, pushed him out of the house, and told him to go to the devil together with his goat.

Outside, a crowd of men, women and children quickly gathered around the tailor and his goat, and he told them the story of the goat which in Kozodoievka had given milk, but every time he brought her home was no longer a she-goat. With many oaths he swore that he himself had seen the full pail of milk that she had given in the rabbi's house. More and more people came by, examined the goat with deep interest, listened to the story, asked to have it repeated, and wondered greatly at it. Others laughed and teased him, still others shook their heads, spat on the ground, and said, "A fine goat that is. If that's a goat, then I'm the rabbi's wife!"

"What, then is it?" asked the tailor.

"A demon, can't you see? It's possessed. It's a *gilgul.*"

The crowd caught the word *gilgul,* and soon they all began to tell each other stories about spirits and ghosts, incidents that had occurred right here in Zolodievka, in Kozodoievka, in Yampoli, in Pischi-Yaboda, in Ḥaplapovitch, in Petchi-Hvost, and other places. Who had not heard the story of Lazer-Wolf's horse that had to be taken out beyond the town, killed, and buried in a shroud? Or about the fowl which had been served up for a Sabbath dinner, and when it was placed on the table began to flap its wings? Or many other such true and well-known happenings?

After several more minutes of this, Shimmen-Eli pulled once more at his rope and proceeded again on his way to Kozodoievka, followed by a band of schoolboys shouting, "Hurrah for Shimmen-Eli! Hurrah for the milking tailor!"

And everybody roared with laughter.

At this the tailor was deeply hurt. As if it were not enough to have this misfortune happen to him, they made a laughing-stock of him too. So, taking the goat, he went through the town and sounded an alarm among the members of his Guild. How could they stand by and be silent at such an outrage? And he told them the whole story of what had happened to him in Kozodoievka, showed them the goat, and at once they sent for liquor, held a meeting, and decided to go to the rabbi, the elders, and the leading citizens of the community and ask them to come to their aid. Why, who had ever heard of such an outrage? To cheat a poor tailor, take away his last few *rubles,* supposedly sell him a goat and actually palm off the devil alone knew what! And then to play the same trick on him a second time! Such an outrage had never been heard of even in Sodom!

And the delegation came to the rabbi, the elders and the leading men of the town and raised a hue and cry. Why, who had ever heard of such an outrage? To cheat a poor tailor, rob him of his last few *rubles?* And they recounted the story of the tailor and his goat in all its details.

The rabbi, the elders, and the leading men of the town listened to the complaints, and that evening held a meeting at the rabbi's house, where it was decided to write a letter then and there to the rabbi, elders and leading men of Kozodoievka. And this they did, producing a letter in classical Hebrew, written in a style as lofty as the occasion demanded.

And here is the letter, word for word, as it was written:

"To the honorable Rabbi, Elders, Sages, renowned scholars, pillars who uphold and support the entire house of Israel! Joy unto you and joy unto everyone within the sacred community of Kozodoievka! May all that is good come unto you and remain with you. Amen.

"It has come to our attention, worthy Rabbi and Elders, that a great wrong has been committed unto one of our townspeople, the tailor Shimmen-Eli, son of Bendit-Leib, known also as Shimmen-Eli *Shma-Koleinu,* as follows:

"Two of your inhabitants, the *melamed* Chaim-Chana and his spouse Tema-Gittel, did with cunning extort the following sum, six and one-half *rubles* in silver, which they took unto themselves, and wiping their lips said, 'We have done no wrong.' Now, mark you, honorable sirs, such things are not done by Jews! All of us here undersigned are witnesses that this tailor is a poor workingman and has many children whom he supports by the honest toil of his hands. As King David says in the Book of Psalms: 'When thou eatest the labor of they hands, happy shalt thou be, and it shall be well with thee.' And our sages have interpreted it thus: happy in this world, and well in the next world. Therefore do we beg you to search out and inquire as to what has been done, so that your judgment may shine forth like the sun and you may pass this proper decision: that either the tailor receive his money back entirely or that he be given the goat that he had bought, for that one which he brought home with him is not truly a goat! To this last fact our whole town can swear.

"Then let there be peace among us. As our sages have said, 'There is nothing so blessed as peace.' Peace unto you, peace unto the farthest and the nearest, peace unto all Israel. Amen.

"From us, your servants . . ."

And then they all signed their names. First the rabbi himself, then the elders, then the leading citizens, and then, one after the other, proudly if not always legibly, the entire membership of the Tailors' Guild.

XI

And it came to pass that night that the moon shone down on Zolodievka and on all its bleak tumbledown little houses huddled together without yards, without trees, without fences, like gravestones in an old cemetery. And though the air was by no means fresh and the odors of the square and the marketplace were hardly pleasant and the dust was thick everywhere, nevertheless the people all came out, like roaches from their cracks, men and women, old people and little children, for "a breath of fresh air" after the stifling hot day. They sat on their stoops, talking, gossiping, or simply looking up at the sky, watching the face of the moon and the myriads of stars that, if you had eighteen heads, you could not count.

All that night Shimmen-Eli the tailor wandered by himself through the side streets and alleys of the little town with his goat, hiding from the small mischief-makers who had followed him all through the day. He thought that when it was light enough he would start back again toward Kozodoievka. And meanwhile he slipped into Hodel's tavern to take a drink for his sorrow's sake; unburden his heart, and seek the sympathetic tavern-keeper's advice in his grievous plight.

Hodel the Tavernkeeper was a widow, a woman with brains, who knew all the public officials and was a good friend in need to all the workingmen in town. As a girl she had been known as a great beauty and had almost married a wealthy man, an excise collector. The story went that once when he was passing through Zolodievka the collector had seen her leading some geese to the *shochet*, and wanted to marry her at once. But the town gossiped so much that the match fell through. Later, against her will, she married some poor fellow, an epileptic, and again the tongues of the gossips began to wag. They said she was still in love with the exciseman, and they made up this song about her, a song which the women and maidens still sing to this day in Zolodievka.

It starts like this:

The moon was shining.
It was the middle of the night.
Hodel sat at her door.

And it ends with these words:

I love you, my soul,
Without end.
I cannot live without you.

And it was to this same Hodel that our tailor now poured out his heart. It was to her that he came for advice. "What shall I do?" he asked. "Tell me. After all, you are not only beautiful but wise. As King David—or who was it?—said in the *Song of Songs:* 'I am black but comely, O ye daughters of Jerusalem.' So tell me what to do."

"What can you do?" answered Hodel, and spat vigorously. "Can't you see it's an evil spirit? What are you keeping it for? Get rid of her. Throw her out. Or the same thing may happen to you that once happened to my Aunt Pearl, may she rest in peace."

"And what happened to her?" asked Shimmen-Eli, frightened.

"This," said Hodel, with a sigh. "My Aunt Pearl was a good honest woman (all of us have been good and honest in our family, though here in this forsaken town—may it burn to the ground—everybody always has the worst to say about everyone). Well, one day my Aunt Pearl was going to market and on the ground in front of her she saw a spool of thread. 'A spool of thread,' she thought, 'comes in handy,' so she bent down and picked it up. The spool jumped in her face and then fell to the ground. She bent down and picked it up again. Again it jumped in her face and again fell down. This happened again and again till at last she spit on it, said, 'Let the devil take it,' and started back home. Once or twice she looked back, and there was the spool of thread rolling after her. Well, she came home frightened to death, fell in a faint, and was sick for almost a whole year afterward. Now, what do you think that was? Tell me. Guess."

"Ah, they're all alike, these women!" said Shimmen-Eli. "Old wives' tales, nonsense, poppycock! If you wanted to listen to what women babbled about, you'd soon be afraid of your own shadow. It is truly written: 'And a voice was given unto them.' Geese, that's what they are! But never mind. That is life; don't worry. Good night. Good night to you."

And Shimmen-Eli went on his way.

The night was sprinkled with stars. The moon floated past clouds that were like tall dark mountains inlaid with silver. With half a face the moon looked down on the town of Zolodievka sunk in deep slumber. Some of the people of the town who were afraid of bedbugs had gone to sleep outdoors, had covered their faces with homespun sheets and were snoring lustily, dreaming sweet dreams, dreams of profitable transactions, of considerate landlords, of baskets of food brought home, dreams of wealth and honor, or of honor alone: all sorts of dreams. There was not a living creature on the streets. Not a sound was to be heard. Even the butchers' dogs who had barked and fought all day, now burrowed themselves between the logs in the back yard, hid their muzzles in their paws, and slept. From time to time a short bark escaped one of them when he dreamed of a bone that another dog was gnawing or of a fly that was buzzing in his ear. Now and then a beetle flew by, humming like the string of a bass violin, zh-zh-zh-zh, then fell to the ground and was silent. Even the town watchman who went around every night, keeping an eye on the stores and rattling his sticks over the windows, had this night become drunk, and leaning against a wall, fell fast asleep. In this silence Shimmen-Eli was the only one awake, not knowing whether to move or to stand still or to sit down.

He walked and muttered to himself, "The old woman had no troubles, so she bought herself a horse . . . Oh, this goat, this goat! May it break a leg and die! A goat? Yes, a goat. A little goat. *Chad gadyo, chad gadyo*. One little goat . . ."

He burst out laughing and was frightened by his own laughter. Passing by the old synagogue renowned for the spirits of dead men who prayed there every Saturday night in their shrouds and prayer shawls, he thought he heard a weird singing as of the wind blowing down a chimney on a winter night. And quickly turning away he found himself near the Russian church, from whose steeple a strange bird whistled shrilly. A terrible fear seized him. He tried to take heart, to steel himself with a prayer, but the words would not come.

Then looming before his eyes he saw the forms of friends long dead. And he remembered the terrifying stories he had heard in bygone days of devils, spirits, vampires, ghouls, goblins, of strange creatures that moved on tiny wheels, of some that walked on their hands, others that looked at you through a single eye, and spirits that wandered through eternity in long white shrouds. Shimmen-Eli began to think that the goat he was leading was really not a goat at all, but a sprite of some sort that at any moment would stick out its long, pointed tongue, or flap a pair of wings and utter a loud cock-a-doodle-doo. He felt his head whirling. He stopped, loosened the rope that had been tied around his waist, and urged the goat to leave him. But the goat would not budge. Shimmen-Eli took a few steps; the goat followed. He turned to the right; so did the goat. He turned left; the goat did too.

"*Shma Yisroel!*" screamed Shimmen-Eli, and started to run as fast as he could. And as he ran he imagined that someone was chasing him and mocking him in a thin, goatlike voice, but the words were the words of a human: "Blessed art thou . . . O Lord . . . who quickenest the dead . . ."

XII

When the next day dawned and the men arose to go to the synagogue, the women to market, and the young girls to lead the animals to pasture, they found Shimmen-Eli sitting on the ground and near him the goat, wagging his beard and chewing the cud. When they spoke to the tailor he did not answer. He sat like a graven image staring in front of him. Quickly a crowd gathered; people came running from all over town, and a hubbub arose: "Shimmen-Eli . . . goat . . . *Shma-Koleinu* . . . *gilgul* . . . demons . . . spirits . . . werewolves . . ." Rumors flew about, with everybody telling a different story. Someone said he had seen him riding through the night.

"Who rode whom?" asked a man, sticking his head into

the circle. "Did Shimmen-Eli ride the goat or did the goat ride Shimmen-Eli?"

The crowd burst out laughing.

"What are you laughing at?" a workingman burst out. "You ought to be ashamed of yourselves! Grown men with beards. Married men with families. Shame on you! Making fun of a poor tailor. Can't you see the man is not himself? He is a sick man. Instead of standing around sharpening your teeth, it would be better if you took him home and called the doctor!"

These words brought the people to their senses, and they stopped laughing at once. Someone ran off for water, others to get Yudel the Healer. They took Shimmen-Eli under the arms, led him home and put him to bed. Soon Yudel came running with all his paraphernalia and began to work on him. He rubbed him, blew into his face, applied leeches, tapped his vein and drew a panful of blood.

"The more blood we draw," explained Yudel, "the better it will be, for all illnesses come from within, from the blood itself." And after presenting this bit of medical theory Yudel promised to come again in the evening.

And when Tsippa-Baila-Reiza saw her husband stretched out on the broken old couch, covered with rags, his eyes rolled upward, his lips parched, raving in fever, she began to wring her hands, beat her head against the wall, wailed and wept as one weeps for the dead.

"Woe is me, wind is me! What will become of me now? What will become of me and all my children?"

And the children, naked and barefoot, gathered about their mother and joined her in her lamentations. The older ones wept silently, hiding their faces; the smaller ones who did not understand what had happened wailed out loud. And the youngest of all, a little boy of three, with a pinched yellow face, stood close to his mother with his tiny crooked legs and protruding belly and screamed loudest of all. "Ma-ma! I'm hun-gry!"

All the neighbors came to find out how Shimmen-Eli was, but the sight of the poor tailor and his family was so heart-rending that nobody could stay long. Only a few women remained, and stood with tear-stained faces near Tsippa-Baila-Reiza, their noses red from blowing, their mouths working, shaking their heads as though to say, "Poor Tsippa-Baila-Reiza. Nothing can help her now."

Wonder of wonders! For fifty years Shimmen-Eli *Shma-Koleinu* had lived in Zolodievka in poverty and oppression. For fifty years he had lain in obscurity. No one spoke of him, no one knew what sort of man he was. But now that he was so close to death, the town suddenly became aware of all his virtues. It suddenly became known that he had been a good and kind man, generous and charitable; that is to say, he had forced money out of the rich and divided it among the poor. He had fought everybody for those poor people, fought staunchly, and had shared his last bite with others. These and many other things they told about the poor tailor, as people tell about a dead man at his funeral. And they all came to see him from all directions. They did everything they could to save him, to keep him from dying before his time.

XIII

And when the sun had set and night had fallen, the members of the Tailors' Guild came together at Hodel's tavern, ordered whisky, and called a meeting. They argued, shouted, ranted, pounded on the table.

"Why isn't something done? A fine town like Zolodievka—may it burn to the ground!—with so many rich people in it, and not one of them willing to lift a finger! They all live off the sweat of us, and none of them will help us. Who puts all the money into the community fund? We do. Who is skinned alive to support the *shochet,* the bath house, the synagogue? We are! Do we have to stand for everything? Come on, let's go to the rabbi and the elders. Now it's their turn to be useful. They'll have to keep his family alive! Come, let us deal with them!"

And they went to the rabbi with their complaint. In reply, the rabbi read to them the letter that had just been brought by a teamster from Kozodoievka. And this is what it said:

"To the honorable Rabbis, elders, sages and scholars of Zolodievka! May peace reign eternally in your holy community!

"No sooner had we received your letter, which, let us assure you, was as honey in our mouths, than we congregated and carefully studied the matter you referred to. In answer we can say only this, that you have wrongfully accused a townsman of ours. This tailor of yours is a wicked man who with base slander has created a scandal between our two communities and deserves to be punished accordingly. We, the undersigned, are ready under oath to bear witness that with our own eyes we saw the goat give milk. May the goats of all our friends be as bountiful.

"Pay no heed to the accusations of the tailor. Pay no heed to the words of ignorant people who speak falsely.

"Peace be unto you and peace unto all Jews everywhere, now and forever, Amen.

"From your younger brothers who bow in the dust at your feet . . ."

When the rabbi had finished reading this letter, the delegation cried out in anger, "Aha, those Kozodoievka hooligans! They're making fun of us! Let's show them who we are and what our emblem is! Shears and Iron! Let them remember that!"

And at once they called another meeting, sent for more whisky, and it was decided to take this imitation of a goat straight to Kozodoievka, take vengeance on the teacher, wreck his *cheder* and overturn the whole town.

No sooner said than done. They mustered about sixty men for the trip, tailors, shoemakers, carpenters, blacksmiths, butchers, strong young men who enjoyed a fight, each one armed with the tools of his trade: this one with a wooden yardstick, that one with a flatiron, one with a last, another with an axe, some with hammers and cleavers, and others with ordinary household utensils, rolling pins, graters, carving knives . . . And it was decided without further delay that they should march off to Kozodoievka and make war on the town, kill and destroy and lay waste.

"Once for all!" they cried. " 'Let us die with the Philistines!' Let's kill them off and be done with it!"

"But wait," one of them called out. "You are ready for the slaughter, fully armed. But where is the goat?"

"That's right! Where did the demon go?"

"He's been swallowed up."

"Then he's not such a fool. But where could he have gone to?"

"Home to the *melamed*. Can't you understand?"

"He'd be crazy to do that!"

"Where else could he go?"

"What difference does it make? Guess what you want to. The point is, the goat has disappeared!"

XIV

Now let us leave the possessed tailor struggling with the Angel of Death and the workingmen of the town preparing for battle, and let us pass on to the demon himself, that is—the goat.

When the goat became aware of the uproar that had arisen in the town, he thought to himself: what was he going to get out of all this? What was the use of being tied to the tailor's waist and following him wherever he went and starving to death? It was better to run off into the wide world and see what freedom meant. So he made his escape, running off madly across the marketplace, his feet scarcely touching the earth, knocking over men and women, jumping over everything that stood in his way—tables of bread and rolls, baskets of grapes and currants. He leaped over crockery and glassware, scattered and shattered everything in his path. The women screamed, "Who is it? What is it? What happened? A goat, a possessed creature, a demon! Woe is me! Where is he? There, there he is! Catch him! Catch him!"

The men picked themselves up and ran after the goat as fast as they could, and the women, naturally, ran after the men. But in vain. Our goat had tasted the joys of freedom and was gone, never to be seen again.

And the unfortunate tailor? What became of him? And how did the story end? Reader, don't compel me to tell you. The end was not a happy one. The story began cheerfully enough, but it ended like most cheerful stories, very tragically. And since you know that I am not a gloomy soul who prefers tears to laughter and likes to point a moral and teach a lesson, let us part as cheerfully as we can. And I wish that all of you readers and everybody else in the world may have more opportunities to laugh than to cry.

Laughter is healthful. The doctors bid us laugh.

A Yom Kippur Scandal

"THAT'S nothing!" called out the man with round eyes, like an ox, who had been sitting all this time in a corner by the window, smoking and listening to our stories of thefts, robberies and expropriations. "I'll tell you a story of a theft that took place in our town, in the synagogue itself, and on *Yom Kippur* at that! It is worth listening to.

"Our town, Kasrilevka—that's where I'm from, you know—is a small town, and a poor one. There is no thievery there. No one steals anything for the simple reason that there is nobody to steal from and nothing worth stealing. And besides, a Jew is not a thief by nature. That is, he may be a thief, but not the sort who will climb through a window or attack you with a knife. He will divert, pervert, subvert and contravert as a matter of course; but he won't pull anything out of your pocket. He won't be caught like a common thief and led through the streets with a yellow placard on his back. Imagine, then, a theft taking place in Kasrilevka, and such a theft at that. Eighteen hundred *rubles* at one crack.

"Here is how it happened. One *Yom Yippur* eve, just before the evening services, a stranger arrived in our town, a salesman of some sort from Lithuania. He left his bag at an inn, and went forth immediately to look for a place of worship, and he came upon the old synagogue. Coming in just before the service began, he found the trustees around the collection plates. '*Sholom aleichem,*' said he. '*Aleichem sholom,*' they answered. 'Where does our guest hail from?' 'From Lithuania.' 'And your name?' 'Even your grandmother wouldn't know if I told her.' 'But you have come to our synagogue!' 'Where else should I go?' 'Then you want to pray here?' 'Can I help myself? What else can I do?' 'Then put something into the plate.' 'What did you think? That I was not going to pay?'

"To make a long story short, our guest took out three silver *rubles* and put them in the plate. Then he put a *ruble* into the cantor's plate, one into the rabbi's, gave one for the *cheder*, threw a half into the charity box, and then began to divide money among the poor who flocked to the door. And in our town we have so many poor people that if you really wanted to start giving, you could divide Rothschild's fortune among them.

"Impressed by his generosity, the men quickly found a place for him along the east wall. Where did they find room for him when all the places along the wall are occupied? Don't ask. Have you ever been at a celebration—a wedding or circumcision—when all the guests are already seated at the table, and suddenly there is a commotion outside—the rich uncle has arrived? What do you do? You push and shove and squeeze until a place is made for the rich relative. Squeezing is a Jewish custom. If no one squeezes us, we squeeze each other."

The man with the eyes that bulged like an ox's paused, looked at the crowd to see what effect his wit had on us, and went on.

"So our guest went up to his place of honor and called to the *shammes* to bring him a praying stand. He put on his *tallis* and started to pray. He prayed and he prayed, standing on his feet all the time. He never sat down or left his place all evening long or all the next day. To fast all day standing on one's feet, without ever sitting down—that only a Litvak can do!

"But when it was all over, when the final blast of the *shofar* had died down, the Day of Atonement had ended, and Chaim the *melamed*, who had led the evening prayers after *Yom Kippur* from time immemorial, had cleared his throat, and in his tremulous voice had already begun—'*Ma-a-riv a-ro-vim . . .*' suddenly screams were heard. 'Help! Help! Help!' We looked around: the stranger was stretched out on the floor in a dead faint. We poured water on him, revived him, but he fainted again. What was the trouble? Plenty! This Litvak tells us that he had brought with him to Kasrilevka eighteen hundred *rubles*. To leave that much at the inn—think of it, eighteen hundred *rubles*—he had been afraid. Whom could he trust with such a sum of money in a strange town? And yet, to keep it in his pocket on *Yom Kippur* was not exactly proper either. So at last this plan had occurred to him: he had taken the money to the synagogue and slipped it into the praying stand. Only a Litvak could do a thing like that! . . .

Now do you see why he had not stepped away from the praying stand for a single minute? And yet during one of the many prayers when we all turn our face to the wall, someone must have stolen the money . . .

"Well, the poor man wept, tore his hair, wrung his hands. What would he do with the money gone? It was not his own money, he said. He was only a clerk. The money was his employer's. He himself was a poor man, with a houseful of children. There was nothing for him to do now but go out and drown himself, or hang himself right here in front of everybody.

"Hearing these words, the crowd stood petrified, forgetting that they had all been fasting since the night before and it was time to go home and eat. It was a disgrace before a stranger, a shame and a scandal in our own eyes. A theft like that—eighteen hundred *rubles!* And where? In the Holy of Holies, in the old synagogue of Kasrilevka. And on what day? On the holiest day of the year, on *Yom Kippur!* Such a thing had never been heard of before.

" '*Shammes,* lock the door!' ordered our Rabbi. We have our own Rabbi in Kasrilevka, Reb Yozifel, a true man of God, a holy man. Not too sharp witted, perhaps, but a good man, a man with no bitterness in him. Sometimes he gets ideas that you would not hit upon if you had eighteen heads on your shoulders . . . When the door was locked, Reb Yozifel turned to the congregation, his face pale as death and his hands trembling, his eyes burning with a strange fire.

"He said, 'Listen to me, my friends, this is an ugly thing, a thing unheard of since the world was created—that here in Kasrilevka there should be a sinner, a renegade to his people, who would have the audacity to take from a stranger, a poor man with a family, a fortune like this. And on what day? On the holiest day of the year, on *Yom Kippur,* and perhaps at the last, most solemn moment—just before the *shofar* was blown! Such a thing has never happened anywhere. I cannot believe it is possible. It simply cannot be. But perhaps—who knows? Man is greedy, and the temptation—especially with a sum like this, eighteen hundred *rubles,* God forbid—is great enough. So if one of us was tempted, if he were fated to commit this evil on a day like this, we must probe the matter thoroughly, strike at the root of this whole affair. Heaven and earth have sworn that the truth must always rise as oil upon the waters. Therefore, my friends, let us search each other now, go through each other's garments, shake out our pockets —all of us from the oldest householder to the *shammes*, not leaving anyone out. Start with me. Seach my pockets first.'

"Thus spoke Reb Yozifel, and he was the first to unbind his gabardine and turn his pockets inside out. And following his example all the men loosened their girdles and showed the linings of their pockets, too. They searched each other, they felt and shook one another, until they came to Lazer Yossel, who turned all colors and began to argue that, in the first place, the stranger was a swindler; that his story was the pure fabrication of a Litvak. No one had stolen any money from him. Couldn't they see that it was all a falsehood and a lie?

"The congregation began to clamor and shout. What did he mean by this? All the important men had allowed themselves to be searched, so why should Lazer Yossel escape? There are no privileged characters here. 'Search him! Search him!' the crowd roared.

"Lazer Yossel saw that it was hopeless, and began to plead for mercy with tears in his eyes. He begged them not to search him. He swore by all that was holy that he was as innocent in this as he would want to be of any wrongdoing as long as he lived. Then why didn't he want to be searched? It was a disgrace to him, he said. He begged them to have pity on his youth, not to bring this disgrace down on him. 'Do anything you wish with me,' he said, 'but don't touch my pockets.' How do you like that? Do you suppose we listened to him?

"But wait . . . I forgot to tell you who this Lazer Yossel was. He was not a Kasrilevkite himself. He came from the Devil knows where, at the time of his marriage, to live with his wife's parents. The rich man of our town had dug him up somewhere for his daughter, boasted that he had found a rare nugget, a fitting match for a daughter like his. He knew a thousand pages of *Talmud* by heart, and all of the Bible. He was a master of Hebrew, arithmetic, bookkeeping, algebra, penmanship—in short, everything you could think of. When he arrived in Kasrilevka—this jewel of a young man—everyone came out to gaze at him. What sort of bargain had the rich man picked out? Well, to look at him you could tell nothing. He was a young man, something in trousers. Not bad looking, but with a nose a trifle too long, eyes that burned like two coals, and a sharp tongue. Our leading citizens began to work on him: tried him out on a page of *Gamorah*, a chapter from the Scriptures, a bit of *Rambam*, this, that and the other. He was perfect in everything, the dog! Whenever you went after him, he was at home. Reb Yozifel himself said that he could have been a rabbi in any Jewish congregation. As for world affairs, there is nothing to talk about. We have an authority on such things in our town, Zaidel Reb Shaye's, but he could not hold a candle to Lazer Yossel. And when it came to chess—there was no one like him in all the world! Talk about versatile people . . . Naturally the whole town envied the rich man his find, but some of them felt he was a little too good to be true. He was too clever (and too much of anything is bad!). For a man of his station he was too free and easy, a hail-fellow-well-met, too familiar with all the young folk—boys, girls, and maybe even loose women. There were rumors . . . At the same time he went around alone too much, deep in thought. At the synagogue he came in last, put on his *tallis*, and with his skullcap on askew, thumbed aimlessly through his prayerbook without ever following the services. No one ever saw him doing anything exactly wrong, and yet people murmured that he was not a God-fearing man. Apparently a man cannot be perfect . . .

"And so, when his turn came to be searched and he refused to let them do it, that was all the proof most of the men needed that he was the one who had taken the money. He begged them to let him swear any oath they wished, begged them to chop him, roast him, cut him up—do anything but shake his pockets out. At this point even our Rabbi, Reb Yozifel, although he was a man we had never seen angry, lost his temper and started to shout.

" 'You!' he cried. 'You thus and thus! Do you know what you deserve? You see what all these men have endured. They were able to forget the disgrace and allowed themselves to be searched; but you want to be the only exception! God in heaven! Either confess and hand over the money, or let us see for ourselves what is in your pockets. You are trifling now with the entire Jewish community. Do you know what they can do to you?'

"To make a long story short, the men took hold of this young upstart, threw him down on the floor with force, and began to search him all over, shake out every one of his pockets. And finally they shook out . . . Well, guess what! A couple of well-gnawed chicken bones and a few dozen plum pits still moist from chewing. You can imagine what an impression this made—to discover food in the pockets of our prodigy on this holiest of fast days. Can you imagine the look on the young man's face, and on his father-in-law's? And on that of our poor Rabbi?

"Poor Reb Yozifel! He turned away in shame. He could look no one in the face. On *Yom Kippur,* and in his synagogue . . . As for the rest of us, hungry as we were, we could not stop talking about it all the way home. We rolled with laughter in the streets. Only Reb Yozifel walked home alone, his head bowed, full of grief, unable to look anyone in the eyes, as though the bones had been shaken out of his own pockets."

The story was apparently over. Unconcerned, the man with the round eyes of an ox turned back to the window and resumed smoking.

"Well," we all asked in one voice, "and what about the money?"

"What money?" asked the man innocently, watching the smoke he had exhaled.

"What do you mean—what money? The eighteen hundred *rubles!*"

"Oh," he drawled. "The eighteen hundred. They were gone."

"Gone?"

"Gone forever."

The Fiddle

TODAY I'll play you something on the fiddle.

I don't know how you feel, but as for me, there is nothing more wonderful than to be able to play a fiddle. As far back as I can remember my heart has gone out to the fiddle. In fact, I loved everything about music. Whenever there was a wedding in our town I was the first one on hand to greet the musicians. I would steal up behind the bass violin, pluck a string—boom!—and run off. Boom—and run off again. For doing this I once caught the devil from Berel Bass. Berel Bass, a fierce-looking man with a flat nose and a sharp eye, pretended not to see me as I stole up behind his bass violin. But just as I was stretching my hand out to pull at the string he caught me by the ear and led me to the door with a great show of courtesy.

"Don't forget to kiss the *mazuza* on your way out," he said.

But that experience taught me nothing. I couldn't stay away from musicians. I was in love with every one of them, from Shaike Fiddele, with his fine black beard and slim white fingers to round-shouldered Getzie Peikler with the big bald spot that reached down to his ears. Many a time when they chased me away, I hid myself under a bench and listened to them playing. From under the bench I watched Shaike's nimble fingers dancing over the strings and listened to the sweet tones that he so skillfully drew out of his little fiddle.

After that I would go around for days in a trance with Shaike and his fiddle constantly before my eyes and moving through my dreams at night. Pretending that I was Shaike, I would crook my left arm, move my fingers, and draw the right arm across as though I held a bow. All this while I threw my head to one side and dreamily shut my eyes. Just like Shaike. Exactly like him.

When the rabbi caught me—this was in *cheder*—drumming my fingers in the air, throwing my head back and rolling my eyes, he gave me a loud smack. "You rascal, you are supposed to be learning something, and here you are—fooling around—catching flies!"

I vowed to myself, "Let the world come to an end, I must have a fiddle. No matter what it cost, I must have one." But how do you make a fiddle? Naturally, of cedarwood. It is easy to say—cedarwood. But where do you get this wood that is supposed to grow only in the Holy Land? So what does God do? He gives me this idea: we had an old sofa at our house, an inheritance from my grandfather, Reb Anshel, over which my two uncles and my father had quarreled for a long time. My uncle Ben argued that he was the oldest son, therefore the sofa was his. Uncle Sender argued that he was the youngest, therefore the sofa belonged to him. My father admitted that he, being only a son-in-law, had no claim to the sofa, but since his wife, my mother, was my grandfather's only daughter, the sofa rightfully belonged to her. All this time the sofa remained at our house. But my two aunts, Aunt Itke and Aunt Zlatke, entered the feud. They carried their bickerings back and forth between them. The sofa this, the sofa that. Your sofa, my sofa. The whole town rocked with it. Meanwhile, the sofa remained our sofa.

This sofa of which I speak had a wooden frame with a thin veneer which was loose and puffed out in several places. Now this veneer, which was loose in spots, was the real cedarwood that fiddles are made of. That was what I had heard in *cheder*. The sofa had one drawback which was really a virtue. When you sat down on it you couldn't get up, because it sloped—there was a bulge on one end and a depression in the middle. This meant that no one wanted to sit on it. So it was put away in a corner and was pensioned off.

But now I began to cast an eye at this sofa. I had already arranged for a bow a long time ago. I had a friend, Yudel the Teamster's Shimeleh, and he promised me as many hairs as I would need from the tail of his father's horse. And a piece of resin, to rub the bow with, I had all my own. I hated to rely on miracles. I got it in a trade with another friend of mine—Maier, Lippe-Sarah's boy—for a small piece of steel from my mother's old crinoline that had been lying up in the attic. Later, out of this piece of steel, Maier made himself a knife sharpened at both ends, and I was even ready to trade back with him, but he wouldn't think of it. He shouted at me:

"You think you're smart! You and your father, too! Here I go and work for three nights, sharpening and sharpening, and cut all my fingers, and you come around and want it back again!"

Well, I had everything. There was only one thing to do—to pick off enough of the cedar veneer from the sofa. And for that I chose a very good time—when my mother was out shopping and my father lay down for his afternoon nap. I crept into the corner with a big nail and began clawing away with real energy. In his sleep my father heard someone burrowing, and apparently thought it was a mouse. He began to hiss: "Shhh, shhhhh." I didn't move, I didn't breathe.

My father turned over on his other side and when I heard that he was snoring again I went back to my work. Suddenly I looked up—there stood my father, watching me with a puzzled look. At first he didn't seem to know what was going on, but when he saw the gouged-out sofa he dragged me out by the ear and shook me till I rattled. I thought I was going to faint.

"God help you—what are you doing to the child?" my mother screamed from the threshold.

"Your pride and joy! He's driving me into my grave!" gasped my father, pale as the white-washed wall, as he clasped at his heart and went into a coughing spell.

"Why do you eat yourself up like that?" asked my mother. "You're sick enough without that. Just take a look at yourself, just look!"

The desire to play the fiddle grew as I grew. The older I grew, the more anxious I was to be able to play, and as if in spite I had to listen to music every day. Just about halfway between home and *cheder* there was a small sod-covered shack, and whenever you passed that shack you heard all sorts of sounds, the strains of all kinds of instruments, and especially the sound of a fiddle. It was the home of a musician, Naftaltzi Bezborodka, a Jew with a shortened coat, with clipped earlocks and with a starched collar. His nose was large and looked almost as if it were pasted on, his lips were thick, his teeth black, his face was pockmarked and without the trace of a beard. And that was why they called him Bezborodka, the beardless one. His wife was a crone who was known as Mother Eve, and they had at least a dozen and a half children—

tattered, half-naked, barefoot, and every one of them, from the oldest to the youngest, played on some instrument—this one the fiddle, that one the cello, the other the bass, one the trumpet, another the flute, the bassoon, the harp, the cymbal, the balalaika, the drum. Some of them could whistle the most complicated melody with their lips, or through their teeth, on glass tumblers or pots, or on pieces of wood. They were magicians—or devils of some sort!

With this family I became acquainted in a most unexpected way. I was standing under their window one day, drinking in the music, when one of the boys caught sight of me and came out. He was Pinny, the flutist, a boy about fifteen, but barefoot like the rest.

"What do you think of the music?" he asked.

"I wish I could play that well in ten years," I told him.

"You can," he said, and explained that for two *rubles* a month his father would teach me to play. Or, if I wanted, he himself would teach me.

"What instrument would you like to play?" he asked. "The fiddle?"

"The fiddle," I said.

"The fiddle," he repeated. "Could you pay a *ruble* and a half a month—or are you as penniless as I am?"

"I can pay," I told him. "But there is one thing. Neither my father nor my mother nor my rabbi must know a thing about it."

"God forbid!" he exclaimed. "Why should anyone find out?" He moved up closer to me and whispered, "Have you got a cigar butt—or a cigarette?" I shook my head. "No? You don't smoke? Well, then, lend me a few *groschen* so I can buy some cigarettes. But don't tell anybody. My father doesn't know that I smoke, and if my mother found out she'd take the money away and buy some bread."

He took the money and said in a friendly voice, "Come on in. You'll get nothing done standing out here."

With great fear, my heart pounding and my legs trembling, I crossed the threshold of this small paradise.

My new friend Pinny introduced me to his father. "This is Sholom—Nochem-Vevik's. A rich man's son . . . He wants to learn to play the fiddle."

Naftaltzi Bezborodka pulled at his earlock, straightened his collar, and buttoned up his coat. Then he began a long and detailed lecture on the subject of music in general and fiddle-playing in particular. He gave me to understand that the fiddle was the best and finest of all instruments—there was no instrument that ranked higher. Else why is the fiddle the chief instrument in an orchestra, and not the trombone or the flute? Because the fiddle is the mother of all instruments . . .

Thus Naftaltzi spoke, accompanying his words with motions of his hands and large nose. I stood gaping at him, swallowing every word that came out.

"The fiddle," Naftaltzi continued, apparently pleased with his lecture, "the fiddle, you understand, is an instrument that is older than all other instruments. The first fiddler in the world was Tubal Cain or Methuselah, I am not sure which. You may know, you study such things in *cheder*. The second fiddler was King David. The third, a man named Paganini, also a Jew. The best fiddlers have always been Jews. I can name you a dozen. Not to mention myself . . . They say I don't play badly, but how can I compare myself to Paganini? Paganini, we are told, sold his soul to the devil for a fiddle. He never would play for the great of the world—the kings and the princes—no matter how much they gave him. He preferred to play for the common people in the taverns and the villages, or even in the woods for the beasts and birds. Ah, what a fiddler Paganini was!"

Suddenly he turned around: "Fellow artists—to your instruments!"

Thus Naftaltzi called out to his band of children, who gathered about him immediately, each with his own instrument. Naftaltzi himself struck the table with his bow, threw a sharp look at each child separately and at all of them at once, and the concert began. They went at it with such fury that I was almost knocked off my feet. Each one tried to outdo the other, but loudest of all played a little boy named Chemeleh, a thin child with a running nose and bare spindly legs. Chemeleh played a strange instrument—some sort of a sack—and when he blew, it gave out an unearthly shriek, like a cat when its tail is stepped on. With his bare foot Chemeleh marked time and all the while watched me out of his small impish eyes and winked at me as if to say, "I am doing well, ain't I?" . . . But hardest of all worked Naftaltzi himself. He both played and conducted, working with his hands, his feet, his nose, his eyes, his whole body; and if anyone made a mistake, he gritted his teeth and yelled out:

"*Forte*, you fool! *Forte, fortissimo!* Count, stupid—count! One, two, three! One, two, three!"

I arranged with Naftaltzi Bezborodka to take three lessons a week, an hour and a half each time, for two *rubles* a month. I begged him over and over to keep this a secret, or I would get into trouble. He gave me his word of honor that he would breathe it to no one.

"We are people," he said gravely, adjusting his collar, "of small means, but when it comes to honor and integrity, we have more than the richest of the rich. By the way—can you spare me a few *groschen*?"

I pulled a *ruble* out of my pocket. Naftaltzi took it from me like a professor—very refined—with the tips of his fingers. Then he called Mother Eve, and hardly looking at her, said, "Here, get something for dinner."

Mother Eve took the money from him with both hands and every one of her fingers, inspected it carefully, and said, "What shall I buy?"

"Anything you want," he said with a show of indifference. "Get a few rolls—two or three herring—a sausage. And don't forget—an onion, some vinegar and oil—and, maybe, a bottle of brandy . . ."

When the food was laid out on the table the crowd fell on it with such gusto as after a fast. Watching them made me so ravenous that when they asked me to join them I couldn't refuse. And I don't know when I enjoyed any food as much as I did that meal.

When we were through, Bezborodka winked at the crowd, signaled for them to reach for their instruments, and I was treated to another concert, this time an "original composition." This they played with such verve and spirit that my ears rang and my head swam and I left the house drunk with Naftaltzi Bezborodka's "composition."

All that day in *cheder* the rabbi, the boys and the books all danced before my eyes and the music rang incessantly in my ears. At night I dreamed of Paganini riding the devil. He hit me over the head with his fiddle. I woke screaming, my head splitting, and I began to babble—I don't know what. Later my older sister Pessel told me that I was out of my head.

What I said made no sense—crazy words like "composition," "Paganini," "the devil" . . . Another thing my sister told me was that while I was sick someone came to ask about me—somebody from Naftaltzi the musician—a barefoot boy. He was chased away and told never to come back.

"What did that fiddler's boy want from you?" my sister nagged, but I held my tongue.

"I don't know. I don't know a thing. What are you talking about?"

"How does it look?" my mother said. "You are a grown boy already—we are trying to arrange a match for you—and you pick yourself friends like these. Barefoot fiddlers! What have you got to do with musicians anyway? What did Naftaltzi's boy want of you?"

"Which Naftaltzi?" I asked innocently. "What musicians?"

"Look at him!" my father broke in. "He doesn't know a thing. Poor little fellow! At your age I was engaged a long time already, and you are still playing games with children. Get dressed and go to *cheder*. And if you meet Hershel Beltax on the way and he asks what was the matter with you, tell him you had a fever. Do you hear what I said? A fever."

I didn't begin to understand. What did I have to do with Hershel Beltax? And why did I have to tell him about a fever? In a few weeks my question was answered.

Hershel Beltax (he was called that because he and his father and his grandfather had all worked for the tax collector) was a man with a round little belly, a short red beard, small moist eyes and a broad white forehead—the mark of a wise man. He had the reputation in town of being an intelligent man, accomplished and learned—up to a certain point—in the *Torah*. He was a fine writer—that is, he had a clear handwriting. It was said that at one time his writings were known all over the countryside. And besides that he had money and a daughter, an only daughter, with red hair and moist eyes—the exact image of him. Her name was Esther, she was called by a nickname—Flesterl. She was timid and delicate, and terribly afraid of us schoolboys because we teased her all the time. When we met her we sang this song:

Esther, Flester,
Where is your sister?

What was so terrible about that? Nothing, it seemed to me, and yet when Esther heard it she covered her ears and ran off crying. She would hide in her room and not go out on the street for days.

But that was a long time ago when she was a child. Now she was a grown girl with long red braids and went about dressed in the latest fashion. My mother was very fond of her. "Gentle as a dove," she used to say. Sometimes on Saturday Esther used to come to visit my sister and when she saw me she would turn even redder than she was and drop her eyes. And my sister would call me over and start asking me questions—and watch us both to see how we acted.

One day—into the *cheder* walked my father with Hershel Beltax, and behind them trailed Reb Sholom-Shachne, the matchmaker, a man with a curly black beard, a man with six fingers, as people used to say. Seeing such guests, the rabbi, Reb Zorach, grabbed his coat and put on his hat in such a hurry that one of his earlocks was caught behind his ear, and his skullcap stuck out from under his hat, and his cheeks began to flame. We could see that something unusual was about to happen. Lately Reb Sholom-Shachne the Matchmaker had been coming to the *cheder* frequently and each time he came he called the rabbi out of the room and there through the doorway we could see them whispering together, shrugging their shoulders, gesturing with their hands—ending up with a sigh.

"Well, it's the same old story. If it's to be, it will be. Regardless."

Now when these guests came in, the rabbi, Reb Zorach, was so confused he didn't know what to do or where to seat them. He grabbed hold of a low bench on which his wife used to salt the meat, and carried it around the room with him, till he finally put it down and sat on it himself. But he quickly jumped up and said to his guests, "Here is a bench. Won't you sit down?"

"That's all right, Reb Zorach," said my father. "We just came in for a minute. We'd like to hear my son recite something—out of the Bible." And he inclined his head toward Hershel Beltax.

"Surely, why not?" said the rabbi, and picking up the Bible he handed it to Hershel Beltax, with a look that said, "Here—do what you can with it."

Hershel Beltax took the Bible like a man who knew what he was doing, bent his head sideways, shut one eye, shuffled the pages and handed it to me open at the first paragraph of the *Song of Songs.*

"The *Song of Songs?*" said Reb Zorach with a smile, as though to say, "You couldn't find something harder?" "The *Song of Songs,*" says Hershel Beltax, "is not as easy as you think. One has to understand it."

"That's not a lie," said Reb Sholom-Shachne, the matchmaker, with a laugh.

The rabbi beckons to me. I walk up to the table, and begin to chant in a loud voice, with a fine rhythm:

"The *Song of Songs!* A song above all other songs. Other songs have been sung by a prophet, but this song was sung by a prophet who was the son of a prophet. Other songs have been sung by a sage, but this was sung by a sage who was the son of a sage. Other songs have been sung by a king. This was sung by a king who was the son of a king."

While I sang I watched my examiners and saw on the face of each of them a different expression. On my father's face I saw great pride and joy. On the rabbi's face was fear lest I make a mistake. His lips silently repeated each word. Hershel Beltax sat with his head bent sideways, his beard between his lips, one eye shut, and the other raised aloft, listening with a very knowing look. Reb Sholom-Shachne the matchmaker did not take his eyes off Hershel Beltax the whole time. He sat with his body bent forward, swaying back and forth along with me, interrupting me with a sound that was part exclamation, part laugh, part a cough, pointing his fingers at me:

"When I said he knew it I really meant he knew it."

A few weeks later plates were broken, and I became engaged to Hershel Beltax's daughter, Flesterl.

Sometimes it happens that a person ages more in one day than in ten years. When I became engaged I suddenly felt grown up—seemingly the same boy and yet not the same. From the smallest boy to the rabbi himself they all treated me with respect. After all, I was a young man engaged to be married—and I had a watch! No longer did my father scold me—and as for whippings—that was out of the question. How could you whip a young man who wore a gold watch? It would be a shame and a disgrace. Once a boy named Eli who, like me, was engaged to be married, received a whipping in *cheder* because he was caught skating on the ice with some peasant boys. The whole town talked about it, and when his fiancée learned of the scandal she cried so long that her parents broke the engagement. And the young man, Eli, was so heartbroken and so ashamed that he wanted to throw himself into the river. Fortunately, the water was frozen over . . .

Such a calamity befell me, too, but not over a whipping, and not over skating on ice, but over a fiddle. And here is the story:

In our tavern we had a frequent guest, Tchetchek, the bandleader, whom we called Colonel. He was a strapping fellow, tall, with a large, round beard and sinister eyebrows. His speech was a mixture of several languages, and when he spoke he moved his eyebrows up and down. When he lowered his eyebrows his face became black as night, and when he raised them, his face glowed like the sun, because under those thick eyebrows were a pair of eyes that were bright blue and full of laughter. He wore a uniform with gold buttons and that was why we called him Colonel. He came to our tavern frequently—not because he was a heavy drinker, but because my father used to make a raisin wine—"the best—and rarest—Hungarian wine" that Tchetchek could hardly praise enough. He would put his enormous hand on my father's thin shoulder and roar in his queer mixed language:

"Herr Kellermeister, you have the best Hungarian wine in the world. There is no such wine even in Budapest, *predbozhe*."

Tchetchek was very friendly with me. He praised me for my stories and liked to ask questions like: "Who was Adam? Who was Isaac? Who was Joseph?"

"You mean—*Yosef*?" I would say.

"I mean Joseph."

"*Yosef*," I corrected him again.

"To us he is Joseph, to you he is *Yosef*," he would say and pinch my cheek. "Joseph or *Yosef*, *Yosef* or Joseph, it's all the same, all equal—*wszystko yedno*."

But when I became engaged Tchetchek's attitude also changed. Instead of treating me like a child he began to talk to me as to an equal, to tell me stories of the army and of musicians. (The Colonel had wonderful stories to tell but no one had time to listen except me.) Once, when he was talking about music, I questioned him, "What instrument does the Colonel play?"

"All instruments," he said, and raised his eyebrows.

"The fiddle too?" I asked, and his face became in my eyes the face of an angel.

"Come to my house some day," he said, "and I will play for you."

"I can only come on the Sabbath. But please, Colonel, no one must know." "*Przed bohem,*" he said fervently and raised his eyebrows.

Tchetchek lived far off beyond the town in a small white cottage with small windows and brightly painted shutters, surrounded by a garden full of bright, yellow sunflowers that carried themselves as proudly as lilies or roses. They bent their heads a little, swayed in the breeze and beckoned to me, "Come to us, young man, come to us. Here is space, here is freedom, here it is bright and fresh, warm and cheerful." And after the stench and heat and dust of the town, the noise and turmoil of the crowded *cheder,* I was glad to come, for here was space and freedom, here it was bright and fresh, warm and cheerful. I felt like running, leaping, yelling, singing, or like throwing myself on the ground with my face deep in the fragrant grass. But that is not for you, Jewish children. Yellow sunflowers, green grass, fresh air, the clean earth, the clear sky, these are not for you . . .

When I came to the gate the first time, I was met by a shaggy, black dog with fiery, red eyes, who jumped at me with such force that I was almost knocked over. Luckily he was tied to a rope. When Tchetchek heard me yell he came running out of the house, without his uniform on, and told the dog to be quiet. Then he took me by the hand and led me up to the black dog. He told me not to be afraid. "Here, pat him—he won't hurt you." And taking my hand he passed it over the dog's fur, calling him odd names in a kindly voice. The dog dropped his tail, licked himself all over and gave me a look that said, "Lucky for you my master is standing here, or you would be leaving without a hand."

Having recovered from my fright, I entered the house with the Colonel and there I was struck dumb: all the walls were covered with guns, and on the floor lay a skin with the head of a lion—or maybe a leopard—with fierce teeth. The lion didn't bother me so much—he was dead. But those guns—all those guns! I didn't enjoy the fresh plums and juicy apples with which my host treated me. I couldn't keep my eyes away from the walls. But later, when Tchetchek took out of its red case a small round fiddle with an odd belly, spread over it his large round beard and placed on it his huge powerful hand and passed the bow over it a few times, and the first melody poured out, I forgot in one instant the black dog, the fierce lion and the loaded guns. I saw only Tchetchek's spreading beard, his overhanging eyebrows, I saw only a round fiddle with an odd belly, and fingers which danced over the strings with such speed that it was hard to imagine where so many fingers came from.

Then Tchetchek himself disappeared—with his spreading beard, his thick eyebrows, and his wonderful fingers—and I saw nothing in front of me. I only heard a singing, a sighing, a weeping, a sobbing, a talking, a roaring—all sorts of strange sounds that I had never heard in my life before. Sounds sweet as honey, smooth as oil, kept pouring without end straight into my heart, and my soul soared far far away into another world, into a paradise of pure sound.

"Would you like some tea?" calls out Tchetchek, putting down the fiddle and slapping me on the back.

I felt as though I had fallen from the seventh heaven down to earth again.

After that I visited Tchetchek every Saturday to listen to his playing. I went straight to the house, not afraid of anyone, and I even became so familiar with the black dog that he would wag his tail when he saw me, and try to lick my hand. But I wouldn't allow that. "Let's be friends at a distance," I said.

At home no one knew where I spent my Saturdays. No one stopped me. After all, I was not a child any more.

And they wouldn't have known until now if a fresh calamity had not occurred—a great calamity which I shall now describe.

Who should care if a young fellow takes a Sabbath walk by himself a short distance out of town? Whose business is it? Apparently there are people who care, and one such person was Ephraim Klotz, a busybody who knew what was cooking in every pot. He made it his business to know. This man watched me closely, followed me, found out where I was going, and later swore with many pious oaths that he had seen me at the Colonel's house eating pork and smoking cigarettes on the Sabbath.

Every Saturday when I was on my way to Tchetchek's I would meet him on the bridge, walking along in a sleeveless, patched, summer coat that reached to his ankles. He walked with his arms folded behind him, his overcoat flapping, humming to himself in a thin voice.

"A good Sabbath," I would say to him.

"Good Sabbath," he would reply. "Where is the young man going?"

"Just for a walk," I said.

"For a walk? Alone?" he repeated, with a meaningful smile . . .

One afternoon when I was sitting with Tchetchek and drinking tea, we heard the dog barking and tearing at his rope. Looking out of the window, I thought I saw someone small and dark with short legs running out of sight. From his way of running I could swear it was Ephraim Klotz.

That night, when I got home, I saw Ephraim Klotz sitting at the table. He was talking with great animation and laughing his odd little laugh that sounded like dried peas pouring out of a dish. Seeing me, he fell silent and began to drum with his short fingers on the table. Opposite him sat my father, his face pale, twisting his beard and tearing hairs out one by one—a sign that he was angry.

"Where are you coming from?" asked my father, with a glance at Ephraim Klotz.

"Where should I be coming from?" I said.

"Where have you been all day?" said my father.

"Where should I be all day? In *shul.*"

"What did you do there all day?"

"What should I be doing there? Studying . . ."

"What were you studying?" said my father.

"What should I be studying? The *Gamorah* . . ."

"Which *Gamorah?*" said my father.

At this point Ephraim Klotz laughed his shrill laugh and my father could stand it no more. He rose from his seat and leaning over, gave me two resounding, fiery slaps in the face. My mother heard the commotion from the next room and came running in . . .

"Nochem," she cried, "God be with you! What are you doing? The boy is engaged to be married. Suppose his father-in-law hears of this?"

My mother was right. My future father-in-law heard the whole story. Ephraim repeated it to him himself. It was too good to keep.

The next day the engagement was broken and I was a privileged person no more. My father was so upset that he became ill and stayed in bed for days. He would not let me come near him, no matter how much my mother pleaded for me.

"The shame of it," he said. "The disgrace. That is worst of all."

"Forget about it," my mother begged. "God will send us another match. Our lives won't be ruined by this. Perhaps it was not his lot."

Among those who came to visit my father while he was ill was the bandmaster. When my father saw him, he took off his skullcap, sat up in bed, and extending an emaciated hand, said to him:

"Ah, Colonel, Colonel . . ."

More he could not say because his voice became choked with tears and he was seized with a fit of coughing. This was the first time in my life that I had seen my father cry. My heart ached and my soul went out to him. I stood staring out of the window, swallowing tears. How I regretted the trouble I had caused!

Silently I swore to myself never, never to disobey my father again, never to cause him such grief, never in this world.

No more fiddles.

The Lottery Ticket

"BENYOMCHIK—that boy of mine—is a regular lottery ticket."

That is the way Yisroel, the *shammes* at the old synagogue, described his young son, Benjamin, who was known in our town as a promising lad when he was still a pupil in Yarachmiel-Moishe's *cheder*. Yarachmiel-Moishe could not praise him highly enough.

"Your youngster," he said to Yisroel the *shammes* one morning in the synagogue, "is one of the best boys I have. He is a hard worker—a very hard worker. And the understanding he has! The memory! Oh-ho!"

The "Oh-ho" Yarachmiel-Moishe sang out with such enthusiasm that Yisroel the *shammes* glowed with pride.

"May God grant you health and fortune for these words," Yisroel said to the teacher and helped him put away his *tallis* and *tfillin*. This he did out of gratitude for the teacher's praise of his son. For the lessons the boy received Yisroel paid the same amount that all the other parents did—two *rubles* a quarter besides the usual presents at *Hannukah* and *Purim*, although Yisroel supported his own family on little more than the *Hannukah* and *Purim* gifts that others gave him.

Afterwards, when Benyomchik had gone through all of Yarachmiel-Moishe's classes, Yisroel the *shammes* wanted very much to send him to Eli-Maier, the *Gamorah* teacher, but Eli-Maier would not take him. In the first place, his school was already full. In the second place, Yisroel could not begin to pay what the well-to-do householders did. So Benyomchik did what many other boys do. If they have nothing to pay with, they study by themselves. That's what we have a large synagogue for, with a lot of bookstands, and candle-ends salvaged from memorials for the dead, and books—all the books one needs: Bibles, the tracts and commentaries, and whatnot. If a person only wants to, he can study anywhere, even in an attic. Do you know how many great people, scholars of renown, grew up among us that way, bent over tiny candle-ends in the synagogue? And how many more we might have had by now—holy men of genius, *Talmudists* and *Kabalists*—we cannot even guess.

But something happened: in the last forty or fifty years a ray of worldly light has stolen into our corner of the earth and has reached even into our very synagogues, even there where the impoverished lads sat with their tomes. There you found them secretly snatching their first taste of secular food, some rhetoric as an appetizer, then swallowing—or choking over—a Russian grammar, with maybe a few chapters of a novel for dessert. From studies like these, naturally, no *Talmudic* scholars or famous rabbis emerged. Instead, Jewish youths wandered off into the world and were ruined, became doctors, lawyers, writers of prose and verse, teachers—and plain non-believers. Not a single rabbi who was worth anything. That is, there were a number of rabbis. But what kind? Crown rabbis wished onto us by the Czar, whether we wanted them or not. As if he had said, "Here is a loaded bomb; hold on to it." But let us proceed . . .

Benyomchik did not study in the synagogue all alone. He had two companions, penniless boys like himself, and that was how the trouble started. One man by himself cannot do wrong as easily as he can with others. It was always that way. Look at Adam. So long as he walked in the Garden alone, all was still and heavenly. But as soon as Mother Eve appeared, all was changed. She talked him into eating of the fruit of the Tree of Knowledge, and who knows what more she would not have done if they had not been driven out in time?

It was the same with Benjamin. If Benjamin had sat alone in the synagogue, all would have been well. But he studied together with these comrades, boys as naked and barefoot, as hungry and thirsty as himself; and together they longed for the large, bright world, the world of wisdom and knowledge. They sat at the table, bent over the yellowed pages, but their thoughts were far away, among the great of the earth, among the learned ones, the fortunate ones. It pulled and dragged at them like a magnet—this outside world. So was it strange that one Saturday night three boys left their study table in the synagogue—Itzik, Yossil and Benyomchik—and disappeared? They were hunted everywhere, all over town, in every corner and hole, but they were gone without a trace. Well, the other two lads, Itzik and Yossil, were waifs, orphans without father or mother. Whom did they run away from? But Benyomchik! Yisroel the *shammes* turned the town upside down, searched everywhere, and calmed down only on the following day, when a letter came from the three boys, asking everybody not to worry; they were, bless the Lord, safe and sound. They had become aware (that is how they wrote) that here in the synagogue there was no future for them, and therefore they had gone off to attend a seminary, a *yeshiva,* in Vilna or Volozhin or Mir. They had cleverly listed all three seminaries so that no one should know where to go and look for them.

But all that was unnecessary. No one ran after them. The town itself was in fact happy about it. In the first place, it meant that there would be two or three fewer people to keep alive—you could not let them starve to death. And in the second place, it was such a fine thing to see poor boys who wanted to become educated. If all the others in the town could only have done it, they would have gone off somewhere too, rather than stay here and struggle for a living.

Whatever happened to the two other lads—Itzik and Yossil—no one knows, but after about six months Yisroel the *shammes* got a letter from Benyomchik—not from Volozhin, not from Vilna and not from Mir, but from another large city. He told them not to worry because at last he was on the right path, some day he would amount to something—if only, with the help of God, he succeeded in passing his examinations to enter the *gymnasium.* He wanted to prepare himself for the study of medicine and when he became a doctor he would be able to make a good living and could then support his father and mother in their old age. His father would not have to work so hard any more, being a *shammes,* and his mother a *shammeste.*

"And there is one thing, my dear and loyal parents," he wrote, "that you must never worry about. A person can have all the education there is and still remember his debt to God. I want you to know that I pray every day, that I use the *tfillin,* and wash before meals and say grace before and after I eat—that is, when there is something to eat. Usually we eat every other day, sometimes a piece of dry bread alone and sometimes dry bread with salt water. And when there is nothing at all, we suck a piece of sugar. Sugar is a remedy for hunger, it drives away the appetite. But there is something besides food, and that we have in plenty! Don't forget: we have four grammar texts to go through, and geography and history, and how many other things! Mathematics we won't even talk about. That is too simple. When we were still home we used to study algebra in the synagogue, and the rhetoric books we devoured in those days help us now when we have compositions to write. There is only one thing wrong: we have so far not been able to correct our accent altogether. But that will be done in time. So don't worry; everything will turn out all right. The important thing is not to become discouraged. We must have faith in the Eternal."

When Yisroel the *shammes* received this letter he went at once to Yarachmiel-Moishe the *melamed*, an old colleague, an honest man and a confidant.

"Do me a favor," he said. "Read this letter through and answer it. I could have written to him myself, but I am sure you can do it better."

Yarachmiel-Moishe the *melamed* knew very well that the *shammes* was telling a big lie, but you can't make it appear that you know. So he took out his glasses and put them on his nose—a strange pair of glasses, held together by a piece of wire and two pieces of string; lenses there were none—one frame was covered with a circular piece of tin and the other was empty, just a hole.

Yisroel could not resist asking, "What good are these glasses, Rabbi? Can you see anything with them?"

"They're better than nothing, and besides, I'm used to them," Yarachmiel-Moishe answered, and held the letter off at a distance, one eye (the one behind the tin) closed; and with the other he read like water going over a dam, in a loud clear voice, stopping every so often to look at Yisroel as if to say, "How is that for reading?" And Yisroel stood by, his head a little to one side, beaming with joy, as if to say, "And the letter itself—how is that for writing?"

And when Yarachmiel-Moishe took off his glasses and gave him the letter back again, Yisroel asked, "Well, Rabbi, what do you think of it?"

"What can I tell you? It's good. It's very good. He says that he prays every day, with his *tfillin* too. May it be no worse in the future."

"What I meant was that he is growing up. My Benyomchik

is becoming something," said Yisroel. At the tip of his tongue were other words but he was afraid to use them—words like "*gymnasium*," "examinations," and finally "doctor" itself. So he said, "I'm wondering what to think about it. You said that he was studying to be a—doctor? What do you think of that? What is your opinion, Rabbi? You're a man of experience."

Yarachmiel-Moishe knows that he is a man of experience, but what can he say? Naturally, if it were up to him, he would not have let him study in the *gymnasium*. What does a man like Yisroel want to have a son in the *gymnasium* for? And studying to be a doctor! But he wants advice . . .

Yarachmiel-Moishe looks with glazed eyes at the wall and sighs. The *shammes* understands what the sigh means; he feels a little like that himself, he is not too well pleased with the *gymnasium*. If it were only a *yeshiva* . . . And yet, there was the other side too: his son, Benyomchik—a doctor!

"But, Rabbi, he says he is not forgetting. He prays every day. He is still one of us."

And then, after another pause: "Rabbi, I asked you to do me a favor. Won't you answer the letter? And another thing, Rabbi. You know our town. People love to talk. So I want to ask you: keep it to yourself. You understand?"

"I understand. Of course I understand," said Yarachmiel-Moishe, and once more saddling his nose with the strange glasses, he took a piece of paper, pen and ink, dipped the pen into the ink, and waited for the *shammes* to tell him what to write.

"Tell him this," says the *shammes*, and dictates:

"To my beloved son, Benjamin. To begin with I want to tell you that we are all, bless the Lord, in the best of health, and may we hear no worse from you now or in the future, Amen. And secondly, tell him that Simma, my wife, and I send our friendliest greetings and ask him to write to us frequently, let us know how he is getting along, and tell him that we wish him all the luck in the world and that he should succeed in his work, and tell him not to worry. God is our father. The main thing is that he should take care of himself, in his health and in his habits and in his prayers: he should remember that he is a Jew. That is the main thing, and tell him that I am sending him a *ruble*, a *ruble* I'm sending him" (here the *shammes* feels through all his pockets) "and tell him that I would have sent more if I had it, but right now conditions are very bad. I am not earning a thing; no one is dying and no one is getting married and no one is having children. And what else do I make a penny from? I don't remember when there has been a wedding, not one since Reb Hersh married off his youngest daughter. That is, a few weddings there have been, but I am speaking of *real* weddings, weddings worth mentioning . . ."

"Sh-h . . . don't rush like that," says the teacher. "You're pounding away like a post horse. I can't catch up to you . . . Mmmmmm. Well. What next?"

"And tell him further . . . that there is nothing to say. And tell him that I send him my friendliest regards, and Simma, his mother, sends her friendliest regards, and all his sisters too, Pessil and Sossil and Brochele. And remind him to be sure to remember that he is a Jew, not to forget the synagogue. That is the main thing. And when you're through, I'll sign my name to it."

When the teacher had written all this down, Yisroel the *shammes* rolled up his sleeve, took the pen carefully with two fingers and prepared himself for the delicate operation. He spelled out his own name carefully—Y-i-s-r-o-e-l—and the name of his father—N-a-f-t-o-l-i—and the family name—R-i-t-e-l-m-a-n. And while he wrote, his tongue moved from side to side, following his fingers from right to left and from left to right.

It is to be understood that it did not take long for people all over town to learn the secret, that Yisroel the *shammes'* young son was studying, for getting ready to study, to be a doctor. And this did not hurt Yisroel in the least, though there were some people who teased him:

"So you're going to have a doctor in the family—going around bareheaded? With brass buttons, maybe, like a state official? How will that look, Yisroel? I mean for you—like a hen that hatches ducklings . . ."

Yisroel the *shammes* let them talk, and himself said nothing. But deep in his heart he thought: "Laugh, laugh at my Benyomchik! He's still my lottery ticket!"

One day—it was Passover eve—Simma the *shammeste* and her three daughters, Pessil, Sossil and Brochele, were cleaning up for the holiday, when the door opened, and in came a striking young man in a coat with white buttons and an odd-looking cap on his head. He fell on Simma's neck and then on the three girls, hugging and kissing and squeezing them.

The young man was Benjamin.

Simma was so happy she burst out crying. And Yisroel hurried in, frightened and out of breath. He shouted at his wife, "Stop crying, will you! Look how upset she is! Do you know what you're crying about?"

But when he himself had looked the boy over and seen how much he had grown and changed, he almost began to cry too. But a man does not do such things.

"When did you get here?" he asked his son. "Turn around, let me see what you look like from the back. What kind of suit is that? Take off your coat—why don't you take off your coat?"

And when Benjamin took off his coat and stood there in his blue uniform with silver buttons—his cheeks rosy and his eyes shining—he charmed not only the rest of the family but everyone who saw him. "What do you think of Yisroel-the-*shammes*' son?" they said. "How he has grown! What a fine looking boy he is!" And Mintzi, the neighbor's daughter, a girl of nineteen with black eyes and a heavy black braid tied with a red ribbon that suited her so well, came in to see if Simma had an extra pot that she could borrow, although she knew very well that in all her life Simma had never had an extra pot. But it gave her a chance to see Benjamin close up, to glance at him with her lively black eyes and to toss her head with the thick black braid and the bright red ribbon—it gave her a chance to turn around and run off, and a little later to come back again under another pretext, until Benjamin's three sisters looked at each other as if to say. "How do you like the way she runs in and out?"

In the meantime Benjamin called his mother aside. "Here is something for *Pesach*," he said, and pushed some money into her hand. Poor Simma! She had never held so much money before in all her life! And for the girls he had presents and presents—ribbons and combs and mirrors and trinkets without number! And for his mother a silk shawl, a yellow one with red and blue flowers. And once more Simma the *shammeste* burst out crying.

And Yisroel asked with a laugh, "What's all this? How did you ever get so much money, my boy?"

"Why shouldn't I have money?" asks Benjamin, proudly. "I'm earning money now, bless the Lord. Eight *rubles* a month. I'm a tutor. I have a few children to teach and I get paid for it. I'm in the fifth class at the *gymnasium*. There are eight classes altogether, so in three more years I'll be through. And then—the university, to study medicine."

Benjamin talks and talks, and they all stand around him. They can't take their eyes off him, and they think, "Can that really be Benjamin? That barefoot Benyomchik who used to spend all his time in the synagogue, studying? Eight *rubles* a month . . . eight classes . . . a silk shawl . . . the university . . . doctor . . .

The Lord alone knows if anyone else had such a happy Passover, such a cheerful *seder*, that year. And I am not talking about the wine, or the brandy, or the fish, or the dumplings, or the pudding. I am speaking now of the *Hagadah*, the Passover ceremonial, that Yisroel and Benjamin both chanted, one louder than the other. It was wonderful to listen to! When they came to *"Rabbi Eleazer omer, minayin shekol mako umako,"* and the men both began to sway with a new vigor and struck up a louder tone, Simma, who had been sitting all the time with her eyes on Benjamin, suddenly began to pucker up her lips as if to cry, and the three sisters, Pessil and Sossil and Brochele, seeing her, could control themselves no longer and began to laugh; and seeing them, the others began to laugh too, even Simma herself . . . Ah, what a Passover that was! You can well imagine!

The next morning, the first day of Passover, when Benjamin came to the synagogue, everybody gaped at the boy in the student's uniform with the silver buttons as if he were a strange animal from the jungle. The smallest boys, full of mischief, crowded around him and pointed at him with their fingers and laughed right in his face. But Benjamin stood all the time with his small prayerbook in his hand and prayed. And when he was called up to the *Torah* (Reb Monish, the *gabai*, arranged it in order to please Yisroel) and Benjamin recited the benediction in a loud clear tone with an accent and an emphasis that one saved for the holidays, the whole synagogue was agog with wonder: "What do you think about Yisroel's young scholar?"

And when they were all ready to leave the synagogue, the rich man of the village, Reb Hersh, turned to the *shammes*.

"Yisroel," Reb Hersh said broadly, as a rich man does when he speaks to one of the lesser creatures, looking a little to one side and clearing his throat and nose in a double cough, "Yisroel, ah-h, come here, hm-m, with that young man of yours. Let me—hm-m—take a look at him."

Hearing that Reb Hersh wanted to talk to Yisroel-the-*shammes*' "young scholar" the crowd gathered around to hear what the rich man would say and what the other would answer. Benjamin approached Reb Hersh as if he were an equal, not at all self-consciously, greeted him like an acquaintance of old, and Reb Hersh looked him over from head to foot, not quite knowing how to start. Should he address him in the respectful plural—a child like that? That would be showing too much respect for the son of the *shammes*. And yet, to use the singular, to say *du*, as you might say, "Hey, there . . ."—maybe that would not be right either. After all, he was a *gymnasium* student with silver buttons, he looked almost like a young prince . . . So at last he spoke to him neither one way nor the other, but vaguely and impersonally: "How are things? When did the visitor come? When is he going back?"

Benjamin put his right foot forward. With one hand he toyed with a button at his chest, with the other he stroked his upper lip. And he answered every question—confidently, without any shame or hesitation. Reb Hersh liked it—and yet he did not like it. "Not a foolish lad at all, but he doesn't know his place." And he became involved in a broad discussion about his school: "How many classes are there? What is the significance of eight classes? Why not nine? And what is the difference between one class and another?"

And Benjamin thought: "He looks so important, and yet he is such an ox!" And he gave him to understand what the difference was between one class and another. Reb Hersh did not like this at all, having a child explaining things to him, and making it sound so simple that it needed no explanation. He said, "Why, everybody knows that. But what is the sense of having eight classes instead of nine?"

"Simply because if there were nine classes, you would say: Why should there be nine and not ten?"

At this the crowd begins to laugh, that is, everybody laughs except Reb Hersh. He thinks: "A tramp—that's all he is."

And with his double cough he says, "Hm-m. It's time to go home. Hm-m . . ."

If you did not see Yisroel the *shammes* then, standing a little to one side, looking from one to the other and swallowing each word of Benjamin's, you have never seen a happy and fortunate man. He was waiting for Reb Hersh to stop questioning his son so he could take him home, where the women were waiting anxiously. On the table, the fresh crisp *matzos* were also waiting, and in the oven a delicious Passover *borsht* was simmering, and hot *kneidlach* with chicken fat, and maybe even a potato pudding! And at last when Reb Hersh had coughed his double cough again and gone off with a few of his close friends, Yisroel the *shammes* invited his one and only good friend and confidant, Yarachmiel-Moishe the Teacher, to come along with them, as the others had gone with Reb Hersh, for a glass of wine. And when they arrived he poured out for the old teacher a glass of genuine raisin wine, and Simma brought in such wonderful *chremzlach* that it would have been hard even for an epicure to tell if there was more honey in them or more chicken fat, because they were so sugary and so rich that they stuck to the gums and ran down his beard. Yarachmiel-Moishe, a quiet man, who rarely said a word, now at the first glass of genuine raisin wine found his head whirling round and his tongue running loose and wild. He called Benjamin over to him, and put him through a quick but thorough examination of the Scriptures and commentaries that he had once studied in his *cheder*.

Benjamin remembered not only the Scriptures, but the commentaries as well, so thoroughly that Yisroel the *shammes*' heart almost burst with pleasure. He followed the teacher out through the door. "What do you think of him?" he asked.

"A perfect vessel—a saint!" answered Yarachmiel-Moishe, puckering his lips and shaking his head.

"But a Jew all the same? He hasn't forgotten that?" said the *shammes*, and watched the teacher's eyes for the answer.

"With God's help," said the teacher.

"A lottery ticket! A lottery ticket! Do you agree with me?"

At this Yarachmiel-Moishe tossed his head—it was hard to tell if it was a nod or a shake—blinked his eyes and made a gesture with his hands that meant that he thought the boy either was, or was not, a lottery ticket.

"A good day!" he cried, and once more kissed the *mazuza*.

"May God keep us alive and well another year, and may we come to each other in joy—for your daughters' weddings and then your son's—and may the Jews have some relief from all their troubles, may there be good news for all of us, it's time that God had mercy on us, improved our lot, lightened our load . . . And may all things be good everywhere, and cheer in every heart. And—ah . . ."

Yarachmiel-Moishe himself did not know what more he wanted. It seemed as if he had already poured out everything that was on his mind. He stood with his tongue out, unable to say one thing or another . . . Yet how can a man go away like this, without a word of farewell of any kind? Fortunately he remembered one more thing:

"And may—may the Messiah come soon!"

"Amen!" answers Yisroel the *shammes*, and in his heart he thinks: First let my Benjamin graduate as a doctor. And *then* let the Messiah come.

As cheerful and bright as everything was at Yisroel the *shammes'* when Benjamin arrived, so was it dark and gloomy when he went away again.

And the three years passed, the three years before Benjamin could enter the university. It was not an easy time. Yisroel the *shammes* experienced one trouble after another at home, and his son Benjamin over there in the city. Many a night Yisroel could not fall asleep here, and Benjamin his son there. Yisroel could not sleep because he kept thinking of the difficult time Benjamin had, of all the hard work he had to do. And Benjamin could not sleep because he was getting ready for his examinations.

"If God helps me and I pass my examinations," Benjamin wrote home, "I'll come to see you again, my dear and faithful ones, and be with you all summer to rest my bones."

And Yisroel the *shammes* waited for the good news of the examination as a pious Jew waits for the Messiah.

At last summer came, but Benjamin did not. His letters began to come less and less often, and as time went on they became shorter and more gloomy. All he ever said was that on such and such a day he would have to take this or that examination.

"The next examination," wrote Benjamin in his last letter, "is my Day of Judgment, because if I get less than a ninety-four I shall not be able to get in, and if I can't get in now I shall have to stay over another year. And who knows what will happen next year? Maybe next year it will be even worse. What will I do then? What will happen to me? Why did I ever have to work so hard, wear myself out like this? Study so hard, starve day after day, freeze in unheated rooms and spend so many sleepless nights? I am not the only one to ask these questions. There are many others like me—Jewish boys—who stayed over from last year and can't get in because their average is not quite high enough. I don't know what I shall do . . ."

Yisroel the *shammes* went around in a daze. He could not understand why Benjamin's letters suddenly should have become so melancholy. He asked Yarachmiel-Moishe to write to Benjamin and ask him what he meant by "average" and "ninety-four." In short, he asked Benjamin to write and explain everything, and not to worry, but rely on the Eternal One who could do everything. And the main thing still was that he should remember he was a Jew, and if the Lord willed, all would be well . . .

But this letter was never answered, and neither were all the others that Yisroel sent later. But he kept writing and writing, until at last, ashamed to come again to Yarachmiel-Moishe, he gave up writing.

"What can be the matter?" Simma asked her husband. "There has been no letter for such a long time."

And she got an answer: "What do you expect? Is that all he has to do? Write letters? Wait a little. Let him finish his examinations, whatever they are, and then he'll write!"

But Yisroel himself went around with a heavy heart and low spirits. He could not find a place to turn. What went through his head during those days, may no other father ever know. And his dreams every night were frightful and horrible, with black canopies, black candles, everything black . . .

Have you ever heard of Lemel the *starosta*? Or is this the first time you have heard his name? In addition to being the *starosta*, the mayor, a man of substance and influence, what in plain Yiddish we refer to as a soup-ladle, right here in town, he was also a power of some sort in the provincial capital, knew all the important people, dealt with them, was intimate with them. Whenever he comes to the capital, he says, he never knows where to go first. Everybody wants to drag him off to himself. "*Pan* Lemel!" shout the Poles. "*Gospodin* Lemel!" plead the Russians. "*Reb* Lemel, you're ours!" say the Jews. He simply does not know what to do! And every time that he comes back from the capital he has news to bring, something startling to talk about for the next three months. A sensational bankruptcy, a terrible fire, a murder to make your hair stand on end. And although Lemel's bankruptcies took place too often, his fires and murders almost every week, it never occurred to anyone to contradict him. They knew he could not help it—he liked to talk, to tell stories, and if necessary, to make them up himself.

So you can imagine what a time our *starosta* had when an envelope came to his office from the provincial capital with a document instructing him to remove from the rolls of the Jewish community the name of Benjamin, son of Yisroel Ritelman, because of the fact that he had assumed another faith.

As soon as Lemel the *starosta* finished reading the message he forgot all his work and ran out into the street with the paper, stopped everyone he saw, whispered the secret into each one's ear, and soon had the story spread all over town.

No doubt you have heard of the halcyon days. The skies are clear, there is no breeze, not a drop of rain, everything is quiet, serene. The people are asleep, the town itself looks dead. Suddenly, no one knows how or where, something explodes, like a bomb from the sky, like an earthquake. The people awaken, start to run. They run this way and that. "What is it? Where? What happened?"

The story of Yisroel-the-*shammes*' son was like that bomb. It tore the town to pieces and woke up everybody. They were all as upset and excited as if this had to do with their own health or livelihood, as if this were the only thing they had to worry about. Some dropped their work, others left the table with their food untouched and went off to the marketplace to see what was going on. Around Reb Hersh's house there stood a whole ring of people, and Reb Hersh himself stood by the porch in a gabardine and skullcap, surrounded by his kinsmen, intimate friends, acquaintances, total strangers—men who catered to him, scraped and bowed and showed their respect for the man who might be able to do them a favor some time. Reb Hersh held forth and his followers echoed:

"Of course! Naturally! That's right, Reb Hersh!"

And Reb Hersh went on:

"A *shammes,* a ne'er-do-well, a pauper—and he wants to be better than anyone else! He has a son, so what does he have to become? A doctor. Nothing less. And if he became a *shammes* like his father, or, heaven spare us, a teacher, what would happen then? I'd like to hear what our *shammes* has to say now. Or maybe he doesn't know yet. I don't see him anywhere around? Where can he be?"

Where was he? There were some in the crowd who did not hesitate to hurry off to the synagogue to look for him. And some even went to his home, but they could not find him anywhere.

And the truth is that Yisroel knew nothing about it. At that moment, when all the town was in an uproar, Yisroel was sitting with his one and only good friend and confidant, Yarachmiel-Moishe the teacher. In the same mail that brought the document to the town hall there was a large envelope for Yisroel himself, and it was from his son. It was the longest letter that had come from Benjamin. With great difficulty he had read through a couple of pages, but had understood little more than a word here and there. So he took it to Yarachmiel-Moishe.

"It's here!" he shouted from the doorway, with joy.

"A letter from your son?"

"And what a letter! It's like a cushion!"

When he heard these words, Yarachmiel-Moishe told his pupils to take a rest, and he himself put on the glasses we had seen before, and began to read the letter in a loud, clear voice, almost a chant. At the start all was well, but soon he began to halt and stutter, as if he were walking over pointed rocks. He came upon hard, strange words he had never seen before. He had to set his glasses straight, he held the letter up to the window, shrugged his shoulders, chewed his words, muttered, "Hm-m . . . What language is this? Nation . . . emancipation . . . quota . . . he's beginning to use strange words, that son of yours . . ."

Yisroel sat at the end of the table, holding his head in his hands, and looked only at Yarachmiel-Moishe, listened to every word, tried to catch the meaning—and made nothing of it. He could not begin to understand why suddenly Benjamin should have to defend himself, try to justify himself, insist with so many oaths that he was the same person as before, that what he had done was out of greater love and greater loyalty . . . Yisroel could not understand why he should be any different now, and why he should ask his forgiveness. What was there to forgive? "But it could not have been otherwise," he wrote. "I have struggled so long with myself. I know the pain I am giving you, but the fight I have carried on since childhood for an education, my need, my desire for learning has become so great, so strong, that I *finally yielded.*"

"What? What was that? Read it again, read it once more. What did he say?"

Yarachmiel-Moishe adjusted his glasses to read it again, but just then the door was pushed open and in came Bassya-Hinda, the teacher's wife, a tall gaunt woman with a sallow face, carrying a large market basket. In the basket were all sorts of good things—potatoes and onions, two black radishes, a small piece of beef-lung that she had barely managed to coax from the butcher, because there are always customers by the hundred who want beef-lung. Women fight over it as men do over the greatest honors at the synagogue, and the reason is this: it costs so little and there are no bones in it, and if you cook it with potatoes and onions and a lot of pepper and it simmers long enough, it tastes quite well . . .

Coming in and seeing the *shammes* sitting with her husband and reading something, Bassya-Hinda took a quick glance to see if the poor *shammes* knew already. But she could not tell from their faces, so she put the basket down, and while she wiped her face with her hand, winked at her husband.

"'Chmiel-Moishe, come here," she said, and he, seeing that she wanted to say something to him, took off his glasses and excused himself for a minute. And there on the other side of the doorway, this conversation took place between husband and wife:

She: Does he know?
He: Who?
She: The *shlimazl.*
He: Which *shlimazl?*
She: The *shammes.*
He: Know what?
She: About his son.

He: Which son?

She: Benjamin.

He: What about him?

She: The whole town is full of it.

He: Full of what?

She: His son.

He: But what about?

She: Oh, you make me tired!

The Lord knows how long this conversation would have dragged on, if at this point the *shammes* himself had not forced his way into the room and in a frightened voice, asked, "What—what are you saying? What did you say Benjamin did? What?"

Bassya-Hinda did not know what to do now. Why should she be the one to tell him? Better send him straight to Lemel the *starosta*, let him take care of it himself.

"Nothing," she said, wiping her face again. "What do I know? They say a paper came in. I don't know—something about your son."

"What kind of paper?"

"Something. In the town hall."

"Who has it—the paper?"

"The *starosta*."

"What is it about?"

"Your Benjamin. Something."

"What's the matter with Benjamin?" he asked, this time angrily. "What happened to him?"

"I should know? Ask me! Go over there, go to Lemel. He's somewhere in the marketplace. He has the paper."

Paper . . . Lemel . . . the town hall . . . Benjamin . . . what did all this mean? Yisroel felt his cheeks grow hot and he heard a whistling in his ears. He pulled down his cap, bent over double, and stumbled out . . .

There are people who love to watch a person in agony, who stare at him when he weeps, look after him when he follows a corpse at a funeral, stand by when he wrings his hands. I do not care for such scenes. Say what you will, I don't like mournful pictures. My muse does not wear a black veil on her face. My muse is a poor—but cheerful one . . .

Where did Yisroel run? Whom did he see? What did he hear? What did he say? Do not ask, it will give you no joy to know. What will you have gained, for instance, when you have learned that there were people who finally lived to have revenge on Yisroel the *shammes,* who had gone around so long showing off his lottery ticket?

"He had it coming," said Reb Hersh, with his peculiar double-cough, and stroked his paunch comfortably. "It should be a lesson for people. A pauper should be careful how he jumps in your face. A doctor he had to have . . ."

Others, it is true, had pity on the *shammes,* "poor fellow"—and you know what that means. My grandfather Minda had a saying, "Look out for people who pity you, and God protect you from those who call you 'poor fellow.' "

So I won't tell you what Yisroel did or whom he saw, but it was dusk when he turned in at his cottage, looking like a ghost. Entering without a word, he sat down on the ground, took off his boots, tore his shirt at the heart as one does for the dead, and prepared to sit in mourning for an hour, as one does at a time like that. Simma did the same, and so did the three sisters. Together they sat on the ground, moaning and weeping for the one they had lost.

Later, when Yarachmiel-Moishe the teacher came to offer condolence, this is what he found: Yisroel sitting with his head thrown forward between his knees, Simma with her hands covering her face and Pessil, Sossil and Brochele sitting with red swollen eyes, each one looking with expressionless face into a separate corner, as if in their shame and pain they could not face each other openly.

He came into the house quietly without a greeting of any kind, as one does in a house of mourning, and slowly lowering himself to the edge of a bench at one side of the room, sighed. That was all. He didn't say a word. A little later, another sigh, and again silence; and later still a sigh again. It was only after a while that he looked around and decided that it was not right to sit there and not say a word, he ought to say something to comfort them. But what was there to say? When a family is in mourning because a person has died, you can come to sit with them for a while, and say, "The Lord giveth and the Lord taketh away." Or, "Man is, after all, like a fly." Or, "Death—that is something none of us can escape." Or, "Vanity of vanities, all of us will die." Or other such sayings that cannot make one especially happy, but are still a comfort. If a person says something, gets it off his chest, he feels a trifle better. But what can one say at a time like this, when it is a living person they are mourning for? Yarachmiel-Moishe turned a little on his bench with a shy cough, wanted to say something, but the words would not come. He tried a few different times, till finally he started again and it worked. And now he was unable to stop, he did not know where or how to end it.

"Ah, well, it's the same story as always. What can you call it—a trial from heaven, from the Lord. For everything is from Him; without Him nothing is done, nothing occurs, not a finger here on earth is lifted. He is a real Master, let us agree on that. Oh, what a Master! And we obey Him—how we obey Him! . . . So it was decreed that this had to happen, exactly as it happened. And here is the proof: that if it did not have to happen this way, it would not have happened. But it did happen, so it must have been ordained. If He had wanted something else to happen, it would have happened the other way. It would have . . ."

Yarachmiel-Moishe began to feel that he did not know what he was saying, so he paused, took a pinch of snuff, lowered his head to one side, and heaved a deep sigh. He told himself that it was time to go, but talking about going is an easy matter. How are you going to do it, though, if you are glued to the bench? There is no visit that is worse than one to a house of mourning. You are supposed to leave without a word of parting, without a sign or a look. But how can you do it? Yarachmiel-Moishe sat waiting for a miracle to happen. If only they would doze off a little so he could leave while they slept. Or if something happened outside, a riot, a fire—anything—so he could escape in the excitement. He sat looking around at the ceiling, at the four walls, and then he said to himself: "It is time to think about going. The children will turn the *cheder* upside down . . ."

When the hour was up, Yisroel and his family rose from the floor, quietly, without talking, put on their shoes and crawled off each to his own corner, to his own work. Yisroel rushed through his late-afternoon prayers and hurried off to the synagogue to be in time for evening services. After all, he was the *shammes*, his time was not his own. He had to be where he was needed. Work—that was the only remedy, the means of chasing all worries away, of forgetting all troubles . . .

In the synagogue a few busybodies came up to him.

"What do you hear from your lottery ticket? How is your son getting along?"

"A son? Have I got a son?" answered Yisroel with a bitter little smile.

And seeing the bitterness and the ache in the smile, the meddlers retreated. All they had to do was look at his face and they did not want to talk to him any more about his son.

What happened afterward? What became of Benjamin? Did he write any more letters? And what did he write? And did his father answer him? And if he answered, what did he say? Don't press me with questions. I shall not say a word. I'll tell you only that as far as Yisroel was concerned, there was no Benjamin any more anywhere. Benjamin was dead. In the lottery, Yisroel had drawn a blank.

The Miracle of Hashono Rabo

THE miracle of *Hashono Rabo*—that was what we called the train wreck that almost took place on *Hashono Rabo,* the day when our judgment is sealed in Heaven, and our fate decided. And it happened right in my home town of Heissin. That is, not in the town itself, but a few stations away, at a place called Sobolivka.

You who have ridden on the train in our region know what the service on the Straggler Special is like. When it reaches a station and stops, it forgets when to start again. According to the timetable, it has a definite schedule. For instance, at Zatkovitz it says that the train is supposed to stop exactly an hour and fifty-eight minutes; and at Sobolivka, the place I am now telling you about, not a second more than an hour and thirty-two minutes. But take my word for it, no matter where it stops—whether at Zatkovitz or at Sobolivka, it stands at least two, and sometimes more than three hours. It depends on how long the switching and fueling take, and what switching and fueling mean to a train like the Straggler Special, I don't have to tell you.

First of all the locomotive has to be uncoupled, and then the train crew—the conductor, the engineer and the fireman—sit down together with the stationmaster, the guard and the telegraph operator, and drink beer—one bottle after another.

And while these important operations, or maneuvers, are going on, what do the passengers do? You have seen what they do. They go crazy with boredom. Some yawn; some find themselves a corner and take a nap; and some walk back and forth on the patform, their hands clasped behind their backs, idly humming a tune.

On the day that I am telling you about, while the Straggler was waiting in the station of Sobolivka, a man was seen standing nearby, his hands clasped behind his back, watching. He was not a passenger, simply an inquisitive onlooker, a resident of Sobolivka. And what was a Sobolivka householder doing there? Nothing! It was *Hashono Rabo*—a half holiday; the man had been at the synagogue already, had eaten already, and as it was a half holiday and there was nothing for him to do at home, he took his walking stick and went out for a walk to the station, to meet the train.

Meeting the train, as you know, is an old custom in our part of the country. When the train is due, everyone who is not otherwise occupied, rushes off to the station. Maybe they'll see somebody there. See whom? See what? A man from Teplik? An old woman from Obodivka? A priest from Golovonievska? In Sobolivka that's great excitement—and you go. And especially since in those days the train was still a novelty, there was always something new to see, something strange to hear. Anyway, on that special *Hashono Rabo*, when the fate of all of us had been sealed already, as I told you before, there stood the train at the station, uncoupled and waiting; and watching it with a mild curiosity, in a half-holiday mood, stood a householder of Sobolivka with a stick under his arm.

Well, you may say, what of that? What if a resident of Sobolivka stands and looks at an uncoupled locomotive? Let him stand and look! But no. It had to happen that on this day, among the waiting passengers, was a priest from Golovonievska, a village not far from Heissin. Having nothing to do, the priest walked back and forth on the same platform, his hands also clasped behind his back, and he also stopped to look at the locomotive. Seeing nothing unusual, he turned to the Sobolivker and said, "Tell me, Yudko, what is there to stare at?"

The man answered crossly, "What do you mean—Yudko? My name is not Yudko. My name is Berko."

So the priest said, "Let it be Berko. Well, tell me then, Berko, what are you looking at so seriously?"

Without taking his eyes from the locomotive, the man answered, "I am standing here beholding the wonders of God. Think—a simple thing like that. You turn one screw this way, another screw that way, and this strange and terrifying machine moves off."

"How do you know that?" the priest asks him. "How do you know that if you turn one screw this way, another the other way, the machine will start?"

Answers the man from Sobolivka, "If I didn't know, would I have said so?"

Says the priest, "What do you know? How to eat potato pudding? But this is not a pudding."

At this the man becomes angry (the people of Sobolivka are famous for their tempers), and he says, "Well, then, my Father, maybe you'd care to climb up into the locomotive with me and have me show you what makes these things move and what makes them stop?"

This did not sound so good to the priest. What was this little man trying to say? Was he going to tell *him* the principle whereby a locomotive moved or stood still? So he answered him sharply, "Go, Hershko. Climb up then."

As sharply the other corrected him, "My name is not Hershko. My name is Berko."

"All right," said the priest. "Let it be Berko, so climb up, Berko."

"What do you mean—climb up? Why should I climb up? You can go first, Father."

"You're the teacher this time—not I," says the priest, with some bitterness. "So lead the way."

They argued, they bickered; the debate became heated, but in the end they both climbed up, and the Sobolivka householder began to instruct the priest in the workings of modern machinery. Slowly he turned one handle, slowly, he turned another, and before they could say a single word, they were horrified to find that the locomotive had begun to move. And away it went!

Now this is the best time, I think, to leave the two good men to themselves in the roaring locomotive, while we pause and consider who is this man of Sobolivka who was so bold and so brave that he dared to climb together with the priest into the locomotive . . .

Berel Essigmacher—that was the name of the man I'm telling you about. And why did they call him Essigmacher? Because his business was that of making vinegar—*essig* in Yiddish—the very best vinegar in our corner of the world. The business he had inherited from his father, but he himself had invented a machine—so he says—that gave the vinegar its distinctive and superior quality. If he only had the time, he could make enough vinegar to provide for the needs of three whole provinces. But why should he? He didn't have to. He wasn't that greedy. That's the kind of man this Essigmacher was.

He had studied nowhere, and yet he could do the most delicate work you could imagine, and he understood the workings of all kinds of engines. How did this happen? Well, all you had to remember, he explained, was that manufacture of vinegar had much in common with that of whiskey. Both were made in a distillery; and a still had almost the same machinery as a locomotive. A still whistled, and so did a locomotive. What difference was there? The important thing—so said Berel himself and showed you what he meant with his hands—the important thing was the power that came from the heat. You started, he explained, by heating the boiler, and the boiler heated the water. The water turned to steam, the steam pushed a rod, and the rod turned the wheels. If you wanted to turn it right, you twisted the lever right, if you wanted to turn it left, you twisted it left. It was as plain as the nose on your face.

And now, having introduced you to this man of Sobolivka, I have at the same time no doubt answered many of the questions you had in mind. So we might as well go back to the wreck of the Straggler Special.

You can imagine the horror and dismay of the passengers when they saw the locomotive go off by itself, no one knew by what strange power. And besides that, the confusion that overwhelmed the crew itself. The first thing they did was to jump up and chase after the engine as if they thought they could catch up with it. But it did not take them long to realize that they were wasting their strength; and as if to tease them, the locomotive suddenly proved that it could develop speed. In fact it flew like mad. It was the first time that anyone had ever seen it move so fast. There was nothing to do but turn back, and this they did. And then, together with the guard and stationmaster, they sat down and drew up a complete and detailed report; after which they sent off telegrams to every station along the line: BEWARE RUNAWAY LOCOMOTIVE. TAKE ACTION. WIRE REPLY.

What a panic this telegram created you can well imagine. What does this mean: Beware runaway locomotive? How does a locomotive run away? And what was this: Take action? What action could they take—besides sending telegrams? And so once more telegrams began to fly back and forth, forth and back, from one end of the line to the other. The instruments clicked and clattered as if they were possessed. Every station wired every other station, and the frightful news spread fast, till every town and every hamlet knew all the tragic details. In our town, for instance, in Heissin, we knew the exact number of people killed and injured. So violent a death! Such innocent victims! And when did it happen? On what day? Exactly on *Hashono Rabo,* when the tickets of our fate are made out, inscribed and sealed high up in Heaven! Apparently Heaven wanted it thus . . .

That is what people said in Heissin and all the nearby towns, and it is impossible to describe the agony and the suffering that we all endured. But how did that compare with the suffering of the poor passengers themselves, who were stranded in the station at Sobolivka without a locomotive, like sheep without a shepherd? What could they do? It was *Hashono Rabo*. Where could they go? Celebrate the holiday in a strange town? And they all huddled together in a corner and began to discuss their plight and to speculate about what had happened to the Fugitive, as they had now named the vanished locomotive. Who knew what might happen to a *shlimazl* like that? Just think of it—a monster like that careening down the track! How could it keep from colliding somewhere along the way with its sister train creeping from Heissin through Zatkovitz on its way to Sobolivka? What would happen to the passengers in the other train? In their imagination they saw the collision—a frightful catastrophe with all its gory details. They saw it before their eyes—overturned carriages, shattered wheels, severed heads, broken legs and arms, battered satchels and suitcases spattered with blood! And suddenly—another telegram! A telegram from Zatkovitz. And what did it say? Here it is:

THIS INSTANT LOCOMOTIVE FLEW PAST ZATKOVITZ WITH BLINDING SPEED CARRYING TWO PASSENGERS ONE A PRIEST. BOTH WAVED THEIR HANDS POINTED. CAN'T SAY WHAT THEY MEANT. NOW ON WAY TO HEISSIN.

What do you think of that? Two men in a runaway locomotive—and one of them a priest? Where were they going—and why—and who could the other man be? Asking here and there they finally found out that it was a resident of Sobolivka. But who? Did anyone know? What a question! Of course they knew! Berel Essigmacher of Sobolivka! How did they know? How does anyone ever know? They knew! Some neighbors of his swore they had seen him and the priest from a distance standing together near the unhitched locomotive, gesturing with their hands. What did that mean? Why should a vinegar maker be standing with a priest near a locomotive, gesturing with his hands?

The talking and the shouting went on so long that soon the story reached Sobolivka, and though the town is only a short distance from the tracks, still by the time the story was relayed from one person to another it had been altered so much, assumed so many different forms, that by the time it reached Berel's home the story was so fantastic that Berel's wife fainted at least ten times and they had to bring a doctor. And all Sobolivka came pouring into the station. The place became so crowded, the noise so deafening, that the stationmaster instructed the guard to clear the platform.

If so, what are we doing there? Let's be off and see what happened to our friend the vinegar maker and the priest on the Fugitive, the runaway locomotive.

It is very easy to talk about seeing what happened in the runaway locomotive, but we'll have to take Mr. Essigmacher's word for it. The stories he tells about his adventure are so remarkable that if only half of them were true, it would be enough! And from what I know of him he doesn't seem to be the sort of person who makes up stories.

At first—this is Essigmacher's version—when the locomotive began to move, he scarcely knew what was happening. Not that he was alarmed; he was simply upset by the fact that the locomotive would not behave as it should. According to logic, he said, it should have stopped dead at the second turn of the lever. Instead, it went faster than ever, as if ten thousand evil spirits were pushing it down the tracks. It flew with such speed that the telegraph poles shimmered and flickered in front of his eyes like the spots you see when you're dizzy. A little later, when he came back to his senses, he remembered that a locomotive had brakes that could slow it down or stop it altogether. There should be brakes somewhere—hand brakes—air brakes—a wheel that you gave a good turn and it came pressing down on the rims of the wheels and they stopped turning . . . How could he ever have forgotten a simple thing like that! And he made a leap for the wheel, was going to give it a turn, when suddenly someone grabbed him by the arm and yelled, "Stop!"

Who was it? The priest, pale as a sheet. "What are you trying to do?" he asked. "Nothing," said Berel, "I'm just trying to stop the engine." "May God help you," cries the priest, "if you ever touch anything on that machine again! If you do, I'll pick you up by the collar and throw you out of here so fast that you'll forget your name was ever Moshko!" "Not Moshko," Berel corrects him. "My name is Berko." And he tries to explain what is meant by a wheel that's called a brake. But the priest won't let him. He was a stubborn man!

"You've turned enough things here already, and look where your turning got us! If you touch that wheel, I'll touch *you!* You'll wish you'd broken your neck before you ever saw me!"

"But, Father!" pleaded Berel. "Don't you think that my life means as much to me as yours does to you?"

"Your life!" snorted the priest bitterly. "What good is your life? A dog like you . . ."

At this Berel became angry and he turned upon the priest with a fury that will not soon be forgotten. "In the first place," he pointed out, "even if I were a dog you ought to feel sorry for me. According to our law even a dog mustn't be harmed. It's a living thing. And in the second place, in the eyes of the Almighty, in what way is my life any less important than any other life? Are we not alike? Do we not all have the same pedigree? Are we not all descended from the same man—Adam? And are all of us not going to the same identical place—the rich, black earth? And thirdly, Father, look at the difference between you and me. I am doing everything I can to make the locomotive stop, that is, I have the welfare of both of us in mind; while you are ready to throw me out of here, that is, to murder a human being!"

That and many other fine things he told him. There in the flying locomotive he delivered a sermon complete with quotations and examples, until the poor, helpless priest was ready to collapse. And in the midst of the lofty discourse the station of Zatkovitz suddenly came into view, with the stationmaster and the guard straining themselves at the edge of the platform. Berel and the priest tried to signal to them; they yelled and waved their arms, but nobody knew what they were trying to say. The station flew past, and the locomotive was on its way to the next town—Heissin. As they went farther on, the priest became more friendly, but one thing he still insisted. Berel must not touch the machine. But he did say this much:

"Tell me, Leibko . . ."

"My name," corrected Berel, "is not Leibko. It's Berko."

"All right," said the priest, "let it be Berko. Tell me, Berko, would you be willing to jump off this locomotive together with me?"

"What for?" asked Berel. "Just to get ourselves killed?

To this the priest answered, "We're going to get killed anyway."

Said Berel, "Where was that decided? What proof do you have? If God wants to—Oh, Father, what He can do!"

Says the priest, "What do you think He'll do?"

Says Berel, "That depends on Him. Listen, Father, I'll tell you something. Today we Jews have a sort of holiday—*Hashono Rabo*. Today up in Heaven, every human being, every living thing, gets a certificate that's signed and sealed, a certificate of life or death. So, Father, if God marked me down for death, there's nothing I can do. What difference does it make to me if I'm killed jumping off the locomotive or standing *in* the locomotive? As a matter of fact, I can be walking along the street, and can't I slip and get killed? But on the other hand, if it was inscribed that I should go on living, then why should I jump?"

This is the way the vinegar maker of Sobolivka tells the story, and he swears that every word is true. He does not remember how it happened or when he first became aware that something had happened. It was somewhere close to Heissin; they could see the chimney on the station. Berel looked at the priest and the priest looked at Berel. What was this? The locomotive was slowing down. Little by little its speed decreased. Soon it was barely crawling. Now it paused, then moved a few feet farther, then thought it over and stopped completely.

What had happened? He suddenly remembered: the fire must have gone out. And when the fire in a locomotive goes out, the water stops boiling, and when the water stops boiling —well, you don't have to be a vinegar maker in Sobolivka to know that the wheels stop turning. And that's all there is to it.

And naturally, being Berel, he turned to the priest right then and there. "Well, Father, what did I tell you?" he said.

"If God Almighty had not decided this morning in Heaven that I should go on living here on earth, who knows how much longer the fire might have continued to burn, and how much farther we might have gone by now?"

The priest said nothing. He stood where he was, with his head down, silent. What was there to say? But later, when it came time to part, he came up to Berel and held out his hand. "Good bye, Itzko," he said. And Berel answered, "My name is not Itzko. It's Berko."

"Let it be Berko," said the priest. "I never knew you were such a . . ." And that was the last he heard. For rolling up the skirts of his cassock, the priest had started off with long strides back to his home in Golovonievska.

Berel himself went on to Heissin and there he had a real holiday. Like the good Jew that he was, he offered up thanks for his deliverance, and then he told his story from start to finish to everyone he saw, each time with new incidents and new miracles.

And everybody wanted the vinegar maker of Sobolivka to come home with him, spend the night with him, and tell him in person the story of the Miracle of *Hashono Rabo.*

And what a celebration we had that night! What a *Simchas Torah* that was! What a *Simchas Torah!*

GLOSSARY*

beigel (bagel): Hard circular roll with hole in the center like a doughnut.

blintzes: Cheese or *kasha* rolled in thin dough and fried.

borsht: A beet or cabbage soup, of Russian origin.

bris: Circumcision ceremony.

Bubi-Kama (Baba Kama): "First Gate," a Talmudic treatise on compensation for damages.

cheder: Old-style orthodox Hebrew school.

chremzlach: Fried *matzo* pancakes, usually served with jelly or sprinkled with powdered sugar.

datcha: Summer cottage in the country.

dybbuk (same as *gilgul*): A soul condemned to wander for a time in this world. To escape the perpetual torments from evil spirits it seeks refuge in the body of a pious man or woman over whom the demons have no power.

gabai: Synagogue treasurer.

Gamorah (Gemara): The Aramaic name for the *Talmud,* i.e. to learn. (See *Talmud*).

Gehenna: Hell.

gilgul (see *dybbuk*).

groschen: Small German silver coin whose old value was about two cents.

gulden: An Austrian silver florin worth about forty-eight cents.

Hagadah: The book containing the Passover home service, consisting in large part of the narrative of the Jewish exodus from Egypt.

Hannukah (Channukah): Described variously as "The Festival of Lights," "The Feast of Dedication," and "The Feast of the Maccabees." It is celebrated for eight days from the 25th day of *Kislev* (December). It was instituted by Judas Maccabeus and the elders of Israel in 165 B.C. to commemorate the rout of the invader Antiochus Ephinanes, and the purification of the Temple sanctuary.

*Many of the spellings of Hebrew words used in these stories are rendered phonetically as they occurred in popular usage. In such cases, throughout the glossary, the correct transliterated spelling is given in parentheses.

Hashono Rabo (Hoshana Rabbah): The seventh day of *Succoth* (Feast of Booths).

kaddish: The mourner's prayer recited in synagogue twice daily for one year by the immediate male relatives, above thirteen years, of the deceased.

kasha: Groats.

kneidlach: Balls of boiled matzo meal cooked in chicken soup.

knishes: Potato or *kasha* dumpling, fried or baked.

kopek: A small copper coin; there are 100 *kopeks* in a *ruble.*

kosher: Food that is permitted to be eaten and prepared according to the Jewish dietary laws.

kreplach: Small pockets of dough filled with chopped meat, usually boiled and eaten with chicken soup.

matzos: unleavened bread eaten exclusively during Passover to recall the Jewish *exodus* from Egypt.

mazl-tov: Good luck!

mazuza (mezuzah): Small rectangular piece of parchment inscribed with the passages Deut. VI. 4-9 and XI. 13-21, and written in 22 lines. The parchment is rolled up and inserted in a wooden or metal case and nailed in a slanting position to the right-hand doorpost of every orthodox Jewish residence as a talisman against evil.

Megila (Megillah): Literally, "a roll," referring to the *Book of Esther* which is read aloud in the synagogue on *Purim.*

Medresh (Midrash): A body of exegetical literature, devotional and ethical in character, which attempts to illuminate the literal text of the Bible with its inner meanings. The *Midrash* is constantly cited by pious and learned Jews in Scriptural and Talmudic disputation.

melamed: Old style orthodox Hebrew teacher.

nogid: A rich man, the leading secular citizen of a community.

nu: Exclamatory question, i.e. "Well? So what?"

Pesach: Passover, the festival commemorating the liberation of the Jews from their bondage in Egypt. It lasts seven days, beginning with the 15th of *Nisan* (March-April).

Perek: A chapter of the *Talmud.*

Purim: Festival of Lots, celebrating the deliverance of the Jews from Haman's plot to exterminate them, as recounted in the *Book of Esther.* It is celebrated on the 14th and 15th of *Adar,* the 12th Jewish lunar month (March).

Rambam: Popular name for Rabbi Moses ben Maimon (Maimonides) eminent, Spanish-Jewish philosopher and physician (1135-1204).

Rov: Rabbi.

seder: The home service performed on the first two nights of Passover (see *Hagadah*).

shadchan: Marriage-broker.

shammes (pl. *shamosim*): Sexton.

sheitel: A wig worn by ultra-orthodox married women.

Shevuos (Shabuot): Variously known as "The Festival of Weeks" and "Pentecost." It originally was a harvest festival and is celebrated seven weeks after Passover.

shlimazl: An incompetent person, one who has perpetual bad luck. Everything happens to him.

Shma Koleinu (Shema Koleinu): "Hear our voices!" The first words of a Day of Atonement hymn; a popular idiom meaning: "idiot."

Shma Yisroel (Shema Yisroel): The first words in the confession of the Jewish faith: "Hear, O Israel: the Lord our God the Lord is One!"

Shmin-esra (Shemoneh 'Esreh): Eighteen (actually nineteen) benedictions, forming the most important part of the daily prayers, recited silently, standing up, by the worshipper.

shochet (pl. *shochtim*): Ritual slaughterer.

shofar: Ram's horn blown in the synagogue at services on *Rosh Hashanah* and *Yom Kippur*.

Sholom Aleichem: Peace be unto you.

shul: Synagogue.

Simchas Torah: "Rejoicing over the Torah," the last day of *Succoth* (Feast of Tabernacles), celebrating the completion of the reading of the Torah.

starosta: Village elder or "mayor" in Czarist Russia.

succah: A booth made of fresh green branches in which pious Jews celebrate the Feast of Tabernacles. This is done symbolically to recall the forty years wandering—"that your generations may know that I made the children of Israel to dwell in booths, when I brought them out of the land of Egypt."

Succos (Succoth): The Feast of Tabernacles, survival of the ancient festival on which male Jews were required to go on a pilgrimage to the Temple in Jerusalem. Lasts nine days and begins on the 15th day of the seventh lunar month of *Tishri* (September-October).

tallis (tallith): Prayer-shawl.

tallis-kot'n (tallith katon): "Small *tallis*," a four-cornered fringed under-garment worn by male orthodox Jews in pursuance of the Biblical commandment to wear a garment with fringes.

Talmud: The Corpus Juris of the Jews, a compilation of the religious, ethical and legal teachings and decisions interpreting the Bible; finished c. A.D. 500.

tfillin: Phylacteries.

Torah: "Doctrine" or "law"; the name is applied to the five books of Moses, i.e. the Pentateuch.

vareniki: Fried dough filled with cheese or jelly.

verst: A Russian measure of distance, equal to about ⅔ of an English mile.

vertutin: Cheese or cooked cherries rolled in dough.

yeshiva: Talmudic college.

Yom Kippur: Day of Atonement; the most important Jewish religious holiday; a fast day, spent in solemn prayer, self-searching of heart and confession of sins by the individual in direct communion with God. It takes place on the tenth day of *Tishri*, eight days after Rosh Hashanah (New Year).

THE MARTYRED

A NOVEL BY

RICHARD E. KIM

"Mr. Kim's book stands out in the great tradition of Job, Dostoevsky and Albert Camus...."

—THE NEW YORK TIMES

"A major achievement, in my opinion."

—PEARL S. BUCK

75035/75c

PUBLISHED BY POCKET BOOKS, INC.

The brilliant best-selling novel of RODIN and the tempestuous world of the French Impressionists DAVID WEISS

95006—95c

PUBLISHED BY POCKET BOOKS, INC.